Whisper Falls

ELIZABETH LANGSTON

SPENCER
HILL
PRESS

Spencer Hill Press

Contact: Spencer Hill Press, PO Box 247, Contoocook, NH 03229, USA

Please visit our website at www.spencerhillpress.com

First Edition: November 2013.
Elizabeth Langston
Whisper Falls : a novel / by Elizabeth Langston – 1st ed.
p. cm.
Summary:
A teen boy in modern-day North Carolina, and an indentured servant girl from 1796 in the same area, meet through a waterfall that allows them to talk, and then to travel across the centuries.

The author acknowledges the copyrighted or trademarked status and trademark owners of the following wordmarks mentioned in this fiction: Colonial Williamsburg, Ford, Lexus, Mini Cooper, Propel, Spiderman, Volvo, The Weather Channel, Whole Foods, Wikipedia, YouTube

Cover design by Coelynn McIninch

Interior layout by Marie Romero

ISBN 978-1-937053-42-0 (paperback)
ISBN 978-1-937053-44-4 (e-book)

Printed in the United States of America

For Norah and Charlie…
We have not forgotten.

CHAPTER ONE

A DEN OF VICE

I perched on a stool in the dining room's corner, the mending basket at my feet, a torn pair of breeches draped across my lap. It was good that I had to sit with my back to the family. If my master couldn't see my hands, he couldn't tell they were idle.

Knuckles rapped for attention on the table. "Come, Jedidiah," my master said, "it's time for your lessons. Deborah and Dorcas, you may join us. Bring your stitching." Chairs, benches, and shoes thumped as the Pratts adjourned to the parlor.

I tossed the breeches into the basket and hurried to clear the table, anxious to complete my evening chores. Amidst the clatter of dishes, Mr. Pratt's voice rose and fell with his reading from the Holy Bible. As I tiptoed past the parlor door, my master paused, his gaze going from me to his elder son, a silent message passing between them.

Tonight, I would be followed.

The sun had already begun its descent when I crossed the yard to the kitchen building. In no time, I had the dishes scrubbed, the floor swept, and the fire banked. Tomorrow's meals cooked in pots nestled among the coals on the hearth.

Was it possible I had finished my work before my master's son finished his? I cast a glance toward the main house.

"Susanna?" a voice rasped from the rear door of the kitchen.

I whipped around, my heart sinking. In my rush to leave, I had forgotten the slave. How thoughtless. "Hector, have you come for your supper?"

He nodded and gave me a shy smile.

"I'm sorry, it isn't ready. I'll prepare your meal now." As I cut the cornbread, I pondered what else to serve him. The Pratts had eaten all of the stew.

"What's cooking?" he asked. "It smells mighty good."

"Chicken." It had been many days since Hector had had meat. I should have liked to give him some tonight, but had the chicken simmered long enough? I lifted the heavy lid of the pot, pinched a sample, and tasted. Yes, it would do nicely. I added a chicken wing and a boiled sweet potato to the wooden trencher and handed it to Hector. "Here you are."

He smiled again, backed down the steps, and ran to the barn.

I could finally take my evening break, but no longer held out hope I would go alone. Jedidiah had certainly completed his Latin lesson by now and lurked somewhere in the shadows.

With only an hour of daylight left to guide me, I raced along the faint trail through the woods and made straight for Whisper Falls. Behind me, twigs snapped and leaves rustled with an unnatural rhythm.

After arriving at the top of the bluff, I dropped to my knees, crawled behind a boulder, and then swung over the ledge, my hands and feet scrabbling at the rock wall. It took only a moment to reach the bottom. I slipped into the cave behind the waterfall, my heart pounding so wildly it shook my frame.

Above me, Jedidiah crept through the tall grasses, the shushing of his shoes faint, the pace stealthy. I shrank into the cave's musty depths, pressed myself against the damp wall, and strained to track his progress.

The shushing stopped.

There were no sounds besides the murmur of forest creatures and the whisper of the falls. What was he doing?

Perhaps he'd seen me disappear over the edge of the bluff. It would be my first mistake in the many weeks we'd been playing this terrible cat-and-mouse game. Was he waiting even now for my next move?

I would wait longer.

Pebbles showered down, cracking like gunshot against the granite cliff before plopping into the creek near my toes. I clapped a hand over my mouth to stifle a gasp.

"*Susanna!*" His frustrated groan floated past me on the warm May breeze.

He didn't know where I was.

Relief threatened to loosen my limbs, but I fought the feeling. It was too early to celebrate, although the wait would be over soon. Jedidiah feared the woods after dark.

I held my breath. Truly, for his own good, he should go home.

His shoes shuffled on the rocky ledge.

We listened for each other, neither admitting defeat.

An owl hooted.

Jedidiah made a panicked squawk. Footsteps thundered down the trail leading to the village. I released my breath on a hiss, inched closer to the mouth of the cave, and peered out. His blond head bobbed in the distance, merging into the trees.

My legs gave way, and I sank onto a moss-covered boulder. That had been too close. I could finally relax and enjoy my break—blissfully alone. My master had never understood why I should want an hour of silence, an hour with no demands or duties. He believed I must have a secret beau, and nothing I said could convince him otherwise. Indeed,

Mr. Pratt would be furious if he discovered how easily I evaded my chaperone. Not that his son or I would ever tell. By unspoken agreement, Jedidiah never mentioned my talent for hiding, and I never mentioned his incompetence as a spy.

Enough, then. With my hard-earned hour of freedom ticking away, I would not waste another precious second. I emerged from the protection of the cave, knelt on a flat rock, and lifted my face to the cool mist of the waterfall. There was nothing left to do but allow the cares of the day to fade. This evening, I would indulge in my most longed-for dream—the moment when I would leave my master's household forever. On my eighteenth birthday, my indenture would be ended. I would rise at dawn, pack my meager possessions, and walk the half-day's journey to Raleigh.

My master knew of my plans, and they enraged him. Mr. Pratt hated Raleigh. He believed our capital city to be a den of vice.

How deliciously enticing. It made me all the more eager to go.

Ta-thonk.

An unfamiliar noise invaded my reverie. I straightened and peered through the clear veil of Whisper Falls. On the bank opposite me, the woods rattled and hummed. The shadows wavered and shifted. A young man burst from the trees, wearing outlandish clothes and riding a strange mechanical beast.

I leapt to my feet, pulse racing. Common sense demanded I leave. Curiosity begged me to stay.

The young man rolled down the hill at a fearsome pace astride a two-wheeled cart built of thin metal bars. Legs cranking, he sped along the bottom of the trail, slammed into the bluff, and toppled to the ground.

With a dazed shake of his head, he sat up, arms resting on bent knees, and drank in a few hard breaths. Then in one smooth movement he rose, picked up the machine, and slung his leg over its peculiar saddle.

Curiosity won. I would stay.

CHAPTER TWO

OTHER FREAKS

Memorial Day had gone nothing like I planned. It really should've been simpler to launch my summer yard service.

My goal was to find enough customers to cover my mountain bike racing expenses. Since I was already out on summer vacation—and the public schools didn't let out for another two weeks—I had a competitive advantage that I intended to use. All six of my customers from last year had signed up again, and several had passed along referrals. I was on track to have as much business as I wanted this year.

I'd headed out this morning, expecting to be gone for two or three hours. Right. I'd forgotten how much people cared about their yards. The grass had to be so thick. So green. All this talk about grass made me glaze over.

One referral customer, Mrs. Joffrey, was especially intense about her lawn. I'd listened for five minutes about the height alone. The grass had to be exactly three and a half inches tall—not four and not three.

"Do you understand, Mark?"

"Yes, ma'am. Three and a half inches."

"Good, then. You'll start tomorrow morning? Eight o'clock sharp?"

I gave her the confident nod of an experienced entrepreneur. "I'll be here."

With an impatient glance at her watch, she hurried inside.

I checked my watch, too. Damn. My original plan for the holiday had included an extra-long afternoon training ride. Instead, I'd wasted most of today talking about grass.

I rode home and tore upstairs to my room. A stack of clean bike shorts and jerseys lay neatly on my bed. I threw on my gear and ran back downstairs.

A gorgeous smell halted me at the garage door. I looked in the kitchen.

Mom stood at the stove, throwing shredded cheese into a pan of steaming broccoli. A slow-cooker bubbled nearby.

"Pot roast?" I asked her.

She nodded. "With roasted potatoes."

My second favorite home-cooked meal. What a decision—to eat it fresh or go on the bike ride. "When will it be ready?"

"Now," she said with an apologetic smile. "I thought you'd already be done with training."

I'd thought so, too. Since I couldn't afford to miss a day, the meal would have to wait. "Can you leave my share in the slow-cooker for later? I'll get a protein bar to tide me over."

Her face fell. "That's fine."

I stared at her a moment. She was more upset than I would've expected. "Is something wrong?"

"Not really." She turned her back on me. "Maybe you could sit with me while you eat your bar."

I didn't want to, but didn't see how I could say no. "Sure, Mom."

By the time she joined me at the table, I'd finished the bar and was staring obviously at the clock.

"Mark?"

"Uh-huh?"

"Have you heard from your sister?"

Ah. Finally getting to the point. My mother wanted to discuss Marissa. "We talk most days."

"By phone or email?"

"Both."

"She won't pick up the phone when I call." Mom's voice wobbled.

Even though my sister had moved to Denver three weeks ago, she was still the main topic of conversation around here, just as I'd expected. Before she left, Marissa bet me twenty bucks that Mom would be smothering *me* by Memorial Day. I knew I'd win. Obsessing over my sister had become a way of life for Mom. She wasn't going to lose a bad habit that quickly.

Mom bent her head over her pot roast, pushing it around with a fork. "Has she made any friends?"

"A few."

"Has she registered for summer classes yet?"

"No."

Mom looked up from her plate, frowning. "Why not?"

Damn. Marissa had lied to my folks about why she'd moved to Colorado. She should be the one to tell them the truth. "You'll have to ask her."

"Why can't you tell me?"

"Mom, please."

She stabbed a chunk of beef. "Can I use your cell phone?"

"No, Mom." Did she really just ask me that? "It might work once, but then Marissa would never speak to *me* again either."

"You're right." Mom's eyes were wet.

It was horrible to see her cry, especially on days when she wore mascara. I needed help. "When will Dad be home from San Francisco?"

She wiped her nose on a napkin. "In two weeks."

That sucked. If Dad the engineer had been here, *he* would've listened to Mom whine about Marissa and then explained in logical detail how to get over it. Since Dad's solution wasn't available to me, I was stuck until he returned.

Maybe I should steer the conversation to a safer subject. "How's your new job?"

"Are you trying to distract me?"

"Yes."

"It's working." She added a glob of butter to her broccoli. "The job is tough. There's a lot to learn."

My mother had switched from trauma nursing to hospice care the same week Marissa moved. The timing wasn't so great.

"Like what?"

"We don't try to save people. Our goal is to keep them comfortable. It's a different mindset. I didn't expect it to be as difficult as it is…"

She talked for a while. When she paused to chew, I asked questions. And I actually paid attention to some of what she said, although I watched the clock, too.

Dad rescued us both by calling. While she paced around with the phone, I headed for the garage.

The delay meant I'd have to change my route. I couldn't train far from home this close to nightfall. Conveniently for me, there was a greenway that edged our neighborhood, connecting Umstead State Park to the other pedestrian/ biking paths leading into Raleigh. I would take the greenway toward Umstead.

Helmet on, I wheeled my bike across the backyard, through the wooden gate, and onto the wide pavement. No one else was out during the dinner hour. I loved the greenway like this. Quiet. Deserted. No people or dogs to dodge. It was as if I owned a dim, cool tunnel of trees.

A quarter mile away, a dirt track forked away from the greenway's pavement and into a dense pine forest. Ready to go off-road, I turned onto the rutted track, hopped over a pair of tree roots, and maneuvered down a slope toward the banks of Rocky Creek. Up ahead, I could hear Whisper Falls murmuring as it plunged from a low bluff into the shallow creek below. The bluff had a steady incline. Steep, but not crazy steep.

I didn't slow as I swooped along the bottom of the hill. I'd studied another cyclist—a guy with a lot of first-place finishes—who attacked inclines like this head-on, as if he would knock the hill down. I was going to give the technique a try.

I slammed into the approach, caught a tire on a rock, and lost my balance.

Okay, that didn't work. Fortunately, there was plenty of natural compost to break the fall.

I tried again and got a little farther this time.

"How foolish."

The words whispered past me, so faint it could've been my imagination. I looked around. Was somebody watching me? Did they assume I was being an idiot? Not that I cared. To train thoroughly, I had to practice skills like this, which meant I had to fall and bust my ass on occasion. All part of the process.

It was just irritating that anyone might've witnessed it.

I walked my bike down the hill and stopped at the bottom. Rocky Creek babbled a few feet away, boulders dotting it at irregular intervals. When I was little, I loved trying to hop across the creek without getting wet. I'd rarely succeeded.

The falls were the best thing about the greenway, and it wasn't only the eight-foot curtain of water that was cool. There was also the cave. Not very tall or deep, but eerie. Full of moss-covered rocks. A great place to hide and chill and be totally alone in the middle of the city.

Something hovered near the mouth of the cave, behind the falls. A rectangle of cloth seemed to glow in the fading light.

A shadow wavered and shifted. It was a girl about my age. She wore dorky clothes—a long-sleeved brown shirt, an ankle-length skirt, and a ghostly white apron. Silent and unmoving, she stared at me through a liquid sheet of glass.

I guessed it was my turn to speak.

"Did you say something?"

She waited before responding. When she finally spoke, her voice was low and husky. "You're being foolish. If you wish to reach the top, perhaps you'll arrive more quickly by carrying your odd machine."

And there it was, a completely wrong interpretation of a perfectly reasonable technique. The need to explain was irresistible. "I don't want to arrive at the top quickly. I want to get there by riding the bike."

She had no reaction—just watched with big, dark eyes in a pale, oval face.

This was stupid. Why couldn't I drop it? The daylight was disappearing while I wasted it on a stare-down with an Amish girl.

After securing the bike to a tree, I hopped from boulder to boulder along the creek's edge, stopping on a rock that would get me as close to the falls as possible without being sprayed.

"Do not take another step, or I shall scream."

I halted and gave her a closer look. The girl stood on a flat rock behind the falls, only a few meters away, her face expressionless and fists clenched against her sides. She was a head shorter than me, thin but not to the eating disorder level, with dark hair hidden under a cap. Her bare toes were visible below the hem of her brown skirt.

I couldn't stop a smile. She had nothing to fear from me. "Don't scream. You're safe."

"Indeed? Why should I believe you?"

"For starters, that's an incredibly expensive bike back there. I'm not leaving it alone."

"A bike? Is that what you call your odd machine?"

As if she didn't know what a bike was. "Right."

The girl was so still. Her face. Her body. Nothing on her moved except her lips and her eyes. "May I ask an impertinent question?"

"Sure."

"You wear most unusual clothes. Where are you from?"

Damn, she was frickin' strange. Did her keepers know where she was? They really shouldn't have let her roam around on her own. "I was going to ask you the same thing."

"You're the stranger in our village, not me."

"Right." Village? With a half million people? "I was born and raised in Raleigh."

Her chin jerked up. It was the first real reaction I'd seen from her.

"You cannot be speaking the truth. Raleigh is miles away, nor did it exist when you were born."

"What are you talking about?" I shifted onto the balls of my feet and scanned the bluff above her, looking for signs of other freaks in dorky costumes. But I saw no one.

A chill wind swirled around me. This was getting creepy, like I'd stepped onto the set of a bad reality TV show, only there were no cameras rolling anywhere that I could see. "We're in Raleigh right now. And the city's been here since the 1700s."

"Indeed, it has. Since 1794, to be precise. Two years ago."

CHAPTER THREE

UNCERTAINTY IN ITS WAKE

Who might this handsome stranger be? And why would he tell such an outrageous lie?

He had the smooth, supple hands of a gentleman but the lean body of a laborer. He spoke like one of the upper class, yet his manner was too familiar. No true gentleman would ever talk so directly with a servant.

His apparel added to the mystery. He wore a shirt made of silky green cloth, tailored close to his chest. His hat resembled a cracked bowl. Lustrous black trousers stopped above his knees, and he wore no stockings. I had never seen a man with bare legs. It was too interesting to embarrass me properly.

"This is psycho." His eyes narrowed to slits. "Who are you?"

I could see no reason to hide my name. "Susanna Marsh."

"What year do you think it is?"

Think? Did he expect me to make up an answer? "It's 1796."

He looked down at the water, his face tight. "Who's the president?"

"Mr. Washington." His questions insulted me. I might live in a village, but that didn't mean I was unaware of the outside world. "And you, sir? What is your name?"

"Mark Lewis."

"Why have you come to Worthville?"

"Worthville?" His gaze snapped back to mine. "Is this some kind of joke?"

"A joke?"

Truly, this was an extraordinary conversation. Was he unstable? A whisper of unease rippled through me. I was alone and far from my master's house. No one would hear me call. Glancing over my shoulder, I gauged my distance to the cliff behind me. If the young man were mad—if he were to leap into the cave with me—how quickly could I climb to the bluff above?

"I have answered your questions honestly. What part do you take for a joke?"

"It is *not* 1796," he said through gritted teeth, as if I were the one mocking him.

"Which year do you believe it is?"

"Nowhere near 1796."

He eyed the bridge of rocks that connected the two sides of the creek by passing behind the falls. He hopped onto the first boulder, then a second and a third. He disappeared. I braced to flee, expecting him to emerge on my side of the curtain of water, but he didn't come.

He stepped back into view, his eyes wide. "Where did you go so fast?"

"I have not moved."

"This is seriously weird." With a step sideways, he vanished again and then instantly reappeared. "You promise you're not moving?"

I nodded. "I promise."

"Okay, that's it." Removing his odd bowl of a hat, he set it on a dry ledge and turned to face me. "I'm coming over there." He crouched, ready to spring.

I shrank backwards, stumbling over my petticoat to land with a hard thump. Fear whipped through me, flooding my limbs with urgency. I rolled to my knees, scrambled to my feet, and clawed at the cliff, my toes fumbling for a hold.

Seconds passed, yet no hand wrenched me down to the cave floor. I paused long enough to glance over my shoulder and then stopped, arrested by the scene behind me.

The young man had not pierced the falls. Instead, the water bent, enfolding him in a crystal cape, and was gently delivering him back to his boulder. It was impossible, yet lovely to behold.

"Damn."

I blinked at the strong language. He'd forgotten me for the moment, his gaze tracing the falls from top to bottom. With a grunt of exertion, he sprang again, only to reap the same miraculous result.

He scowled at the water, an angry jut to his chin. When he punched at it with his fist, it bowed but didn't break.

"What is happening?" Even though he muttered, the words came through clearly.

Fear forgotten, I returned to my favorite rock and stood a respectful distance from the force of the water. The falls were different, somehow. Dazzling.

Fascination drove me one step closer, then another. When at last my toes gripped the edge of the rock, I glanced down and wavered. The falls pounded the stones below, the creek a boiling cauldron of foam.

Dare I take the risk?

The young man watched me, a challenge in the arch of his eyebrow. Did he find my caution childish? I didn't like that possibility. No, indeed. I squared my shoulders and stretched forward until my hand breached the flow. Water sparkled over my fingertips, yet they remained dry. When I withdrew my hand, the glittering glove disappeared.

It was so delightful I ignored the young man and the stones and the boiling foam. I played in the flow, marveling as it wound about my splayed fingers like fine silk ribbons.

Mr. Lewis raised his hand slowly and flattened it against mine, palm to palm, fingers to fingers.

I shivered with pleasure. It was most improper for us to touch this way, yet I didn't break the contact. People never touched me by choice. No, truly, that wasn't correct. I was grabbed, prodded, or shoved. But a caress? Never. It was alluring.

He offered his other hand, and I met it, too, pressing tentatively at first and then with greater curiosity, enthralled by his warmth. We touched through a shimmering barrier—a silken screen of water that did not wet.

"Where are you from?" I asked.

"I'm from the twenty-first century."

The words echoed hollowly in my ears. The twenty-first century? Why, no indeed. He had misspoken, or I had misheard, or...

I snatched my hands away. "What do you mean?"

"If you really live in 1796, I won't be born for over two hundred years."

Two hundred years?

I backed up until the rock wall stopped my progress. It was all a bad joke, a bit of foolishness at my expense, for what he claimed was impossible, and I didn't want Mr. Lewis to be a liar. "You're teasing me."

"No, I'm not." He gestured behind him. "You see that odd machine? Bikes were invented around 1820."

"It cannot be." I shook my head emphatically.

"I agree. It makes no sense."

Mr. Worth had thundered similar words from the pulpit on Sunday. *That which makes no sense must surely come from Satan.*

Could Mr. Worth's claim explain this young man? I didn't wish to believe it. Mr. Mark Lewis was too polite, too kind, too bewildered to be a demon.

But what other explanation could there be?

Perhaps I had eaten spoiled chicken. Yes, that must be the cause of this incredible dream. I was ill and overtired. I needed rest.

"It's time for me to leave." I felt along the cliff for the crevices which served as rungs on my rocky ladder. With a mighty pull, I lifted myself over the lip of land that hid the entrance to my refuge.

"Wait."

I persisted, ignoring the velvet voice of my dream demon. Swiftly, I pushed through the tall grasses, then plunged into the darkening woods toward the home of my master.

Behind me, the falls whispered: *come back*.

The Pratts always retired at dusk. Candles were a luxury my master didn't care to waste.

The house had settled into silence, save for the occasional scratching of squirrels across the gables. I climbed the narrow steps to the attic, stripped to my linen shift, and crawled onto a pallet of straw in my little corner under the eaves.

Yet sleep eluded me. Memories of the stranger haunted my thoughts. Merciful heavens, he'd been handsome, his hair the deepest of browns and eyes the rich amber of honey. How could evil have such a charming face or such a warm demeanor?

The image of his smile faded into the attic's darkness and left uncertainty in its wake. Of course, evil could be attractive. What better way to deceive?

I rolled to my back and wiggled for comfort.

Above me, the roof sloped sharply. I reached up and pushed aside a loose board. Fresh air trickled in, teasing me with its honeysuckle scent. Starlight pricked tiny white holes in the dark fabric of the night sky.

Come back.

Had the falls called after me? Or had he?

Could someone truly speak across the centuries?

If so, why should I be the one to hear?

Perhaps our meeting had been a hoax. Solomon Worth might have plotted such a deed. When I rejected his offer of marriage last year, he had blazed with outrage and proclaimed that my ingratitude at the honor of his proposal must surely be a sign of madness. Did he seek to have me doubt my senses? Had Solomon hired the stranger to extract revenge?

I hoped not. Mark Lewis intrigued me. He spoke of things yet to come. I wanted him to be real.

A yawn interrupted my musings. Sunrise was drawing steadily nearer. I needed to awaken before the family to serve their breakfast, but there would be no porridge or toast awaiting them if I didn't sleep soon.

The loose board fell into place, blocking the night sky and the honeysuckle breeze. I smiled into the echoing void of my space under the eaves and prayed for sweet dreams.

CHAPTER FOUR

GIRLS AND CYCLING

I hadn't completed the training I intended to tonight, but it didn't matter anymore. This ride was over. The scene with the girl had blown my concentration.

There were only two walkers left on the greenway, their shadows slipping like headless silhouettes from tree to tree. I headed home at a slow, steady pace. But there was nothing slow or steady about my thoughts. They raced out of control, replaying what had just happened.

And something *had* happened. I wasn't crazy. But what? When I banged my head after the first crash, had I blacked out?

Probably not. I hadn't hit hard enough.

How could I explain the water? It had taken control of me, swinging me around like a toy. That hadn't been my imagination.

Or had it?

What about the girl? If I dreamed up the water, I dreamed her up, too. But where would the dream have come from?

I'd seen *The Crucible* in American Lit this past semester. Had images of colonial costumes been hibernating in my brain all this time, waiting to take over?

Maybe. It was hard to know.

When I reached the garage, I checked my bike, determined to blot out the past hour. It was better to focus on important things. Bike maintenance. *Me* maintenance. I could use some calories.

I went inside, fixed a plate of pot roast and potatoes, and then leaned against the counter to eat it. But thoughts of Susanna wouldn't shut up.

Was it possible that she was real even if the water wasn't?

That wasn't such a bad idea. Susanna had been real, the water had been my imagination, and the two were merging in my memory.

Yeah. I'd go with that theory for the moment.

I'd met a strange girl. We'd had an interesting conversation. And I wouldn't mind talking to her again, if we could get past the time warp stuff.

Of course, I would have to apologize first. Fear had flashed in her eyes when I tried to jump through Whisper Falls, and I felt really bad about that. I'd been too confused by the glittering water to consider whether she'd feel threatened.

I would've apologized immediately, except I was distracted. When she stumbled, the dorky cap came off, and gorgeous brown hair fell to her waist. I didn't know many girls who wore their hair that way, which was too bad because it was really hot.

Damn. I needed someone to tell me I wasn't crazy.

After hunting down my phone, I texted Carlton to arrange an IM session. I hadn't heard from him since he left for his dad's beach house a few days ago. If he had some free time tonight, we were going to talk.

With a cookie in one hand and a bottle of water in the other, I ran up two flights of stairs to the rec room. Carlton wasn't online yet.

While I waited, I typed "Worthville" into a search engine. It pulled up a few hits. Our county had a village called Worthville in the eighteenth century. It had a wheat mill, meetinghouse, general store, and some farms. Pretty dull. The family names coming up were Worth, Pratt, and Foster. There was nobody with the name Marsh.

I wasn't sure what to try next. This was where my sister would be useful. Marissa had a bachelor's degree in history. She could tell me how to find out more.

Cool, she was online. I had another subject I wanted to cover with her, anyway.

> ME: *you owe me twenty bucks*
> MARISSA: *memorial day isn't over yet*
> ME: *yeah, those last 3 hrs could be crucial*
> MARISSA: *hehe*
> ME: *could you call mom?*
> MARISSA: *what does she want to talk about?*
> ME: *grad school*
> MARISSA: *no thanks. don't want to be bitched at*
> ME: *she'll figure out that you're not actually going*
> MARISSA: *if i get a job first, she can't complain*
> ME: *yes she can*
> MARISSA: *shut up*
> ME: *why can't you and mom leave me out of this? it's not my problem*
> MARISSA: *sometimes things become your problem just because you're there*
> ME: *i don't believe you just said that*
> MARISSA: *change the subject*

Since asking politely hadn't worked, I'd have to come up with another plan—as soon as I figured out what that was. Until then, I was going to put her history degree to use.

> ME: *how do i find out about wake county villages from the 1790s?*
> MARISSA: *did not see that coming. anything good on the web?*
> ME: *nope*

MARISSA: *try state archives or historical society. visit in person. they're careful with artifacts*

Carlton pinged me—which was a convenient excuse for saying goodbye to my sister. Plus, I needed more time to figure out another way to get Mom and Marissa talking.

ME: *thanks. gotta talk to carlton. later*
MARISSA: *ok*

I finished the last bite of cookie, washed it down, and wiped my hands. The session with Carlton might take a while.

ME: *how's the beach?*
CARLTON: *awesome*
ME: *any shark sightings?*
CARLTON: *no but I saw a film crew*
ME: *for what movie?*
CARLTON: *something with gabrielle stone. i hear she might be joining our senior class*
ME: *to be normal?*
CARLTON: *if you can call neuse academy normal. they rejected senator stanton's son*
ME: *where do you hear this stuff?*
CARLTON: *around. have you talked to alexis?*

Alexis? Why was he asking about her? He had to know she was the last person I wanted to think about.

ME: *drop it*
CARLTON: *just curious*
ME: *don't be*
CARLTON: *ok. how'd training go today?*
ME: *fine, but something strange happened on the greenway*

CARLTON: *?*
ME: *a girl in colonial costume talked to me*
CARLTON: *there's got to be more to this story*
ME: *she says it's 1796 where she lives*
CARLTON: *and?*
ME: *what do you think?*
CARLTON: *you're taking steroids and it's screwed with your head*
ME: *besides that*
CARLTON: *she's a ghost*
ME: *could be*
CARLTON: *probably not. even a ghost would know it isn't 1796*
ME: *so why would she say it?*
CARLTON: *she's crazy*
ME: *possibly. what else?*
CARLTON: *she's messing with you*
ME: *why?*
CARLTON: *maybe halligan's paying her to throw off your training*

Did Keefe Halligan want to win the Carolina Cross-Country Challenge so badly that he'd try to throw me off with a prank?

Well, sure, although this one seemed pretty weird.

ME: *what's the point of the colonial costume?*
CARLTON: *ask him. seems stupid to me*
ME: *why now? we don't race til july 30*
CARLTON: *better expect this kind of shit for two more months*
ME: *maybe*
CARLTON: *damn, lewis. figure it out for yourself. gotta go*
ME: *later*

Carlton hadn't helped. Even though I had no trouble believing Keefe might try something psycho, I didn't see how he could've talked Susanna into the plan. It was easier to believe she'd escaped from some brain-washing cult than that she worked for Keefe.

Okay, it was more than that. I didn't want Susanna to be a fake.

Morning bike rides were the best. I left the house around dawn and sped through Umstead Park on a bike trail. Totally alone. Totally quiet.

Okay, maybe it wasn't *totally* quiet. There were some sounds, like gears shifting. Wind whooshing. My own breathing. They were good sounds, the kind that drove me to train even harder.

Three miles later, I left the park to head for the trails around Lake Crabtree. As I crossed the bike bridge over I-40, the noise of the highway intruded on my solitude. Below me, a few white headlights traveled east. In the opposite direction, hundreds of red taillights flashed on and off as westbound traffic thickened even at this early hour.

The trail dipped down an incline, briefly hugged a ridge, and then swooped into a grassy bowl of land. The sounds of the interstate faded.

The trails along the northeastern corner of Lake Crabtree were relatively easy. I rode through that part first. It'd be good to test my body against the tougher sections when I was no longer fresh.

When I reached the south side of the lake, there were other cyclists ahead of me, racing through its hills and past its wetlands. Crabtree trails were usually a fun, fast ride, but the crowd forced me to take this section slowly. I circled back north, completing my intended distance but without the speed I wanted. Tonight's ride would need to be harder.

When I got home, my mother sat at the table, her eyes tracking me across the kitchen. Even when she was quiet, she was noisy.

Her nose wrinkled at my sweaty clothes. I nodded but didn't stop, just continued with my summer morning routine. Shower. Work clothes. Back downstairs. She sat in the same spot, cradling a coffee mug and watching me through narrowed eyes. I couldn't tell if she was mad, so I made my breakfast and wondered how long the silent treatment would last.

"Mark?"

Not long. "Yeah?" I bit into a toasted bagel.

"Did you talk with Marissa last night?"

Every muscle in my body tensed. "We IM-ed."

"Why didn't you tell me?"

Because I didn't know I was supposed to. I shrugged and hoped she would drop the subject. I didn't want to be late for Mrs. Joffrey.

"Does she know I want her to call me?"

"Yes."

"I see." Mom went into auto-pilot cleanup mode. She slipped off her chair, rummaged in a drawer for a rag, and mopped up bagel crumbs. With an exaggerated sigh, she threw the rag in the sink. "Does she ever complain about me?"

I reflected on the wisdom of being honest. "Possibly."

"Like what?"

"Really, Mom." I edged closer to the garage door. No way was I repeating what Marissa had said. "She's my sister. Our conversations are private."

Mom's nostrils flared. "I deserve to know what she says."

"You'll have to ask her." What had gotten into my mother? She acted like she was about to explode. "Why don't the two of you work this out—and leave me alone?"

"I can't if she won't speak to me."

Mom stormed from the room. I grabbed a ball cap and shades, and ran out the door before she could return with more questions I didn't want to answer.

After hitching the equipment trailer to my mountain bike, I rode two blocks over to my first yard of the day, arriving a couple of minutes behind schedule. Mrs. Joffrey stood on her veranda in an orange dress and heels, swinging a ring of keys around her finger.

"Morning, ma'am," I said, pushing the mower up the circular driveway.

She glared, her mouth a red slash across her face, her keys going round and round like a hula hoop.

I stopped at the top of the driveway and considered my next move. This was the second woman today who was pissed in my general direction. And, for the second time, I hadn't earned it. But nothing was happening and I had five yards to mow, which meant I'd be the one to move things along. "Sorry."

"Fine, Mark. Don't be late again." She caught the keys in her palm and gestured toward a wicker table. "Your check's over there."

Cool. Back on safe ground. "Thanks."

She clopped down the wooden stairs and crooked her finger. "I have some instructions we didn't cover yesterday. Follow me."

She headed into the garage and pointed at a grungy broom. "I don't want you using a leaf blower. Sweep the driveway before bagging the waste."

"Okay." Holy shit. Why?

"Also, when you trim the holly bushes…"

Trimming bushes wasn't part of the deal.

"...use those hand clippers."

Hand clippers?

She tapped her watch. "I'll be back in an hour."

"I'll still be here." And I'd be ready to explain how to make special requests.

She walked around me and slid into her Volvo.

Once I had the backyard mowed and edged, I focused on the front yard and tried not to think about how badly the extra chores screwed up my schedule. Fortunately, my other Tuesday clients had jobs, so they wouldn't care when I arrived.

I was nearly done with the mowing when I noticed a car roaring down the street, a familiar—and unwelcome—green Mini-Cooper. It squealed to a stop behind my trailer.

Not cool. Alexis knew better than to track me down at work.

The car door slammed. "Mark?"

I shut off the mower, rolled my shoulders, and ignored the tightness in my chest.

She studied the fresh grass clippings, not so good for her white, sequined sneakers. Too bad. I wasn't going any closer.

She stayed at the curb. "Did you get my texts?"

I took off my shades, wiped my dripping face on the tail of my T-shirt, then put the shades back on. Yes, I had seen her eight texts come in. No, I hadn't read them. "What did you need?"

"I miss you. I thought maybe you could come over tonight." She smiled slowly. "My parents won't be home."

Damn.

I had the odd sensation I got whenever I hit an obstacle on a trail. The bike was going down. It would hurt when I landed. There would be bruises and scratches for days. But for just a moment, I was suspended in midair, dreading the inevitable impact, feeling only detachment.

"*You* broke up with *me*, Alexis. What's the point?"

"I want us to talk."

Right. Talk wasn't all she wanted. "I don't think that's a good idea."

Her tongue flicked over her lips, shiny and pink with strawberry gloss. I remembered exactly how they tasted.

"I made a mistake, Mark. I want us back together."

Really? She dumped me in the middle of the dance floor at prom, and it was a *mistake*? Watching her stalk away from me had to rank among the worst moments of my life. I'd stood there, dying inside, in front of a frickin' ballroom full of classmates.

"We're not getting back together."

"Mark, could you please come over here? It'd be easier to discuss this if I didn't have to yell."

I shook my head. No way was I getting within reach of her.

"Fine. I'll tell you from here."

She bent down to brush a speck of nothing from her leg. I had a clear view of what her cami was barely covering. It was embarrassing to think that might've worked on me a couple of weeks ago.

She straightened and crossed her arms. "I've thought it over, and it's okay about the vacation in July. You don't have to go with us for a whole week."

"Thanks, since I already said no."

"It'll be enough if you fly down to Florida for the weekend." She nodded as if everything were all set.

"No."

This conversation was so weird. Didn't she get that we were over? It wasn't as if she would be alone for long. She was hot and popular. All the guys at Neuse Academy wanted her. She'd find someone else before our senior year started in the fall.

In the two weeks since prom, I'd dealt with the breakup. I'd refocused my energy on mountain biking. Placing well in my age division wasn't a sure thing. I had to train hard every single day. It had been a relief to take off whenever I wanted without feeling guilty about neglecting her. If dating meant I had to choose between girls and cycling, maybe I shouldn't date.

"Please, Mark. I'm okay with your training schedule. Don't worry about the rest of the summer. If you share your calendar with me, I'll work around your races." Her smile was wide and determined and strawberry-pink.

"Stop, Alexis."

Between my training and my job, I didn't have a lot of free time. Maybe she thought it would get better later on in the summer. But my schedule wouldn't lighten up until after the Carolina Challenge. If I placed high enough in that race, I'd advance a category. Then training for fall competitions would start.

Why wouldn't she just let it go? She would never be happy unless she was number one in my life, and that wasn't going to happen. "We can't get back together."

Her perky expression finally slipped. "Why not?"

I shook my head. She knew why not. She'd given me an ultimatum in front of everyone. We'd made our choices on the dance floor. Repeating the argument was just painful.

She wilted, her butt landing on the hood of the car. Shaky hands went for her hair, ruffling it into golden spikes. "I can't believe you're picking your bike over me."

My breathing grew even and disciplined, as if I were riding up the last, long incline at the end of a race. As awkward as this scene had been, it was almost over. "We can't fix this, Alexis. I'm sorry."

"Yeah, me, too." She whipped off her shades. Her eyes were wet. She dabbed at them with her fingertips. "I'll make sure the next guy doesn't play year-round sports."

"Nice." Just when I was starting to feel bad for her, she said something bitchy. I should be grateful, though. Being angry was a much easier way to end the drama. I wrapped my fingers around the mower's handle, gripping it so hard it should've bent.

"Bye, Alexis."

"Wait, if we could just—"

I checked my watch and swore. Mrs. Joffrey would be home any minute. The last thing I needed was for her to find me talking instead of working. I flipped the power switch. The mower drowned out the rest of what Alexis said.

When I turned the corner on the next row, she was still standing at the curb, hands over her mouth, sneakers sparkling. When I turned the corner on the last row, her Mini Cooper had disappeared.

CHAPTER FIVE

FEIGNED HUMILITY

I tossed and turned on my straw pallet until well past midnight. But when sleep finally claimed me, my dreams were particularly sweet—filled with crystal capes, fresh breezes, and the gentle touch of a handsome stranger. Even now, he smiled warmly at me.

You must wake up.

I smiled back. "But I don't wish to."

He laughed, extended his hand, and squeezed my toe—

Squeezed my toe?

My eyes popped open. It wasn't his voice I'd heard, but that of a girl.

"Susanna, please wake up."

I snapped to a sitting position and banged my head against the roof of the eaves. Merciful heavens, how could I have overslept?

"What time is it, Dorcas?" I asked as I rolled from my bed.

"Time for breakfast," she said. "Papa is angry."

"I shall be there shortly." I tied a homespun petticoat over my shift, laced up my stays, and pinned on a calico bodice. With shaking hands, I secured my hair to the top of my head, grabbed a cap, and hurried down the stairs.

My master sat in the tall chair at the head of the table. Discontent shadowed the hard planes of his face.

"Where is my porridge?"

I dropped my gaze to the ground. Perhaps if I feigned humility, my punishment might be less severe. "I'm sorry, sir. It will only take me a few minutes to fetch."

"Be quick. We are waiting."

His control alarmed me more than anger would have. "Yes, sir."

I ran to the kitchen and halted in its front doorway, dismayed to find the building occupied. My mistress bent over the stone hearth, poking at a kettle. The tea wouldn't be ready in time for breakfast, but I left this unsaid. I put on a fresh apron, grabbed a rag to wrap about the kettle's hot handle, and nudged her aside.

"Allow me, Mrs. Pratt."

She backed away, her fashionable leather shoes squeaking across the rough lumber of the floor. "Where is the milk?"

The Pratts's slave boy had left the milk in the same spot every day since they bought him four years ago. How could she not know? I waved toward the rear door of the kitchen. "Hector leaves it in a jar on the cellar steps."

"Mr. Pratt will want milk with his porridge."

"Of course." It wasn't something I would likely forget.

She sniffed, but didn't move. "My husband is greatly displeased with you."

"I did notice his mood when we spoke."

After settling the tea kettle, I hoisted the pot of oats from the coals and set it on the worktable. Crossing to the cupboard, I found a tray and six bowls. Mrs. Pratt plopped onto a bench and watched me, humming under her breath.

The porridge was soon divided among the bowls. I added a wedge of cheese to the tray and fetched a pitcher for the cider.

"Will it be much longer?"

My jaw tightened with irritation. Much as I preferred to work alone, an offer of help from her or her daughters would have been welcome this day. Perhaps the wives in other fine households also lifted no finger, but they kept more than two servants for a family of eight.

"No, ma'am. Only a few minutes."

"I don't like to spend time in this kitchen. It is too small and smells of burnt meat." She yawned noisily. "I shall never be anything more than an adequate cook. Whatever shall we do when you leave?"

"You will find new servants, ma'am." When I smacked the pitcher onto the tray, cider sloshed. I'd have to wipe the dishes now. Yet another delay, and one of my own causing. "Mrs. Pratt, breakfast is nearly ready. Perhaps you would like to wait in the dining room?"

"I suppose I shall." In a swirl of muslin skirts, she rustled through the door.

Breakfast was soon served. My master and mistress, along with their four oldest children, gathered around the dining table and ate without speaking. The only sounds were the click of spoons against bowls and the thud of cups against the tabletop.

I played in the corner with the two littlest ones. Dinah stood at my side, clutching my knee, while Baby John bounced in my arms and chortled at the tendrils slipping from my hastily pinned cap. I tugged Dinah's thumb from her mouth and laughed when she put it back in.

A chair scraped. "Susanna, come," Mr. Pratt said.

The others froze. After pressing a kiss to Dinah's brow, I tucked her hand into mine and rose, John heavy on my hip. I sucked in a steadying breath as I took the babies to their eldest sister. When my master and I left the main house, John whimpered after me, chubby arms waving.

Mr. Pratt paused at a tree to select a branch. I walked behind the kitchen, having learned long ago it was best not to see the switch. Facing the vegetable garden, I waited.

"Lift your skirt."

The branch sang through the air and flicked my calf. As always, nothing could prepare me for the first hideous slice. My throat ached with the effort to contain a moan.

Whop.

My fingers twisted convulsively in my petticoat. Yet I did not sway. I did not scream. I remained still and studied the garden.

Whop.

The corn had ripened.

Whop.

Peppers dotted their vines in fat globes of red.

Whop.

There was a hot stillness when he was done lashing me. Blood seeped from a cut and dripped in a thin trail to my ankle.

He leaned close to my ear, his voice soft and raspy. "I often told your father that he was a fool to teach you so much, but Josiah Marsh would not heed my warnings. I pity you. Girls gain nothing from education but dissatisfaction. It deceives you into believing you're better than you are. And you, Susanna, are not nearly as clever as you think. Even after seven years, you cannot last a month without errors. You are fortunate to have a master who corrects you so tirelessly."

The switch landed on the ground at my toes.

I held my head high, mute with contempt. If Mr. Pratt was seeking a reaction, he would be sorely disappointed.

"Work is the best cure for laziness. After you finish your chores, find the Negro. Tell him you are there to help with mucking out the barn." The crunch of Mr. Pratt's boots disappeared around the corner and blended with the sounds of the day.

I waited until I was sure I was alone and then lowered myself onto a stump. With gaze forward and back straight, I focused on the woods, pretending myself away from here, perhaps within my cave. I should have liked to be there now, hidden from view, sitting in the dim, musty depths, watching the water pour down. The very thought of Whisper Falls soothed me. My time there was special. Sacred. Safe from prying eyes or cruel intentions.

Sweat trickled down my legs, stinging the wounds, mixing with the blood. The present intruded. I stood, ignored the ache, and moved stiffly into the kitchen. The thrashing had not been so severe that I would be unable to perform my duties, although they would be completed more slowly. Coupled with the extra work in the barn, I would forfeit my evening break—a loss I felt more keenly than the switch. If Mr. Pratt offered to trade another beating for my hour of solitude, I would gladly accept.

Even more, I regretted losing the chance to see Mr. Mark Lewis again. And I didn't care if he was a demon. He couldn't torment me as much as the devil in whose home I lived.

Chapter Six

A Little Edgy

The meteorologist said the heat index would rise to one hundred by early afternoon. The more training I finished in the morning, the better. I got up early and was on the bike by six AM, heading down back roads to get in some variety.

Today's goal was to improve endurance.

After a couple of moderate hills and a straight stretch through some open fields, I was past the point where the muscles protested. Plenty hydrated. No cramps in sight. I was in the zone.

My thoughts drifted to the scene at Whisper Falls. After a couple of days of thinking it over, I had a pretty solid theory. The whole thing had been some kind of elaborate illusion. A good one, too. The girl, the costume, the disappearing act—all had to be a new type of remote-controlled computer technology, like seriously realistic animation projected on the back side of the waterfall.

But who was the mastermind?

There was no way it would've been Alexis. If she'd plotted revenge, it would've been cleaner, meaner, and more obvious. And she would've never involved Susanna. Alexis didn't like to share the spotlight with other girls.

Keefe? He was as determined as I was to place first in our age division at the race in July. He was capable of trying to weight the odds in his favor. Carlton might've been right. Maybe Keefe hired Susanna. Not that something like this would gain the advantage he hoped for. It would just piss me off enough I'd try even harder to beat him.

However, there were three major problems with Keefe as mastermind that I couldn't overlook.

First, the timing. Two months in advance was insane. It gave me plenty of opportunity to shake off the prank.

Secondly, the girl. Susanna was an odd choice for an actress. She'd been a statue with hardly any change in emotion.

Lastly, no way was Keefe smart enough to figure out the water. That was a great trick—the way it felt pouring over my skin. Slick. Warm. Much warmer than creek water should be. And it had lifted me twice and returned me to the rock wrapped in a tingling cocoon.

The water was *not* faked.

A car whizzed past me, so close its side mirror almost brushed my hand. While I'd been lost in my thoughts, traffic had picked up on the back roads. There were some aggressive drivers today. Without bike lanes, I couldn't afford to be distracted. I had to focus.

Today's goals were endurance *and* avoiding jerk drivers.

Two dangerous close calls later, I circled back toward home. But instead of taking the most direct route, I headed for the greenway and Whisper Falls. Might as well check to see if there were any signs of a prank.

It was quiet this early. A light rain had fallen overnight. I slipped down the muddy trail and locked my bike against a tree. The waterfall looked postcard perfect.

Heart pounding, I edged along the rock bridge behind the falls from my side to hers. Standing in the same spot where my mind imagined she'd stood, I saw nothing unusual. The rocks within the cave were undisturbed, the moss heavy and green. No one had walked here recently, not even a crazy girl with dorky clothes and a rare-but-beautiful smile.

On impulse, I yanked off my gloves, stuffed them into my pocket, and slowly poked a hand through the water. No sparks. No glittery coating. It was wet, transparent, and normal.

I withdrew my hand, feeling stupid. This was Whisper Falls. I'd been here hundreds of times. It was water pouring down. Plain, old, boring water. Not some bizarre portal to the past.

Why had I come here again?

I climbed on my bike and headed home, done with the falls and the girl. The scene hadn't been a prank. And it couldn't have been real.

So what had it been?

This was the first time I could remember wishing a bang to the head had caused hallucinations.

After showering and changing, I pounded down the stairs to the kitchen. My mother stood at the island, dishing up a plate. She handed it to me. "I made you breakfast."

"Thanks, Mom." Two scrambled eggs. Whole wheat toast. Peach jam. Fresh blueberries. It was the perfect balance of protein, carbs, and delicious.

Honestly, this surprised me. I talked about my ideal training breakfast occasionally. I just hadn't realized she listened. Maybe she was emerging from the empty-nest thing, and it was my turn to be adored.

I shoveled it down. She watched from the island.

"Mark?"

Her voice had a hesitant tone, as if she were about to ask me something I wouldn't like. Which meant this breakfast came with strings attached. The question was, how big?

"Yeah?"

"Your grandparents could use some help with their yard."

That seemed simple enough. Was there more of a catch? I finished a mouthful before answering. "I talked to Granddad yesterday. He didn't mention anything about needing help."

"He didn't ask. Your grandmother did."

Maybe Mom wanted me to spy on her parents. She worried they were too old to live at the lake house on their own. It sure didn't seem like it to me. "When should I go over?"

"Soon."

Vague was good. If she left it up to me, she couldn't get mad if it took me a few days. I definitely couldn't do it today. My schedule included an afternoon training ride. And if there was any daylight left, I might take another look around the falls.

The Granddad Rescue could be Friday, which would give me plenty of time to warn Gran I was coming. Which would give her plenty of time to fix my favorite cake. Yeah.

"Sure, Mom. Mowing and everything else?"

"Just everything else. You'll insult your grandfather if you mow…"

Granddad would be insulted no matter what I did.

"…and don't take any pay."

I looked up from my plate. She had to be kidding, right? Did she honestly believe her parents wouldn't force cash into my hand? Or that I would refuse to take it? Really, one of the best parts of having grandparents was how much it pissed off my mom when they spoiled me.

I smiled. "I promise not to *ask* for money."

"Good. If you see anything—" She cut off in mid-sentence when her cell phone rang. She snatched it up, read the caller ID, smiled, and answered. "Hi," she said in the low, happy tone she used with my dad. She hurried out of the kitchen into the dining room.

While I finished my breakfast, I could hear her going through a pattern of speaking and silence. By the time I put my plate in the dishwasher, she had returned to the kitchen.

"Here," she said, handing me the phone. "Your father wants to talk to you."

"Hey," I said, "what's up?"

Dad's voice was quiet. "Can your mother hear you?"

"Uh-huh."

"Go somewhere else."

I took the stairs two at a time and went to my bedroom. "Okay, I'm alone."

"How has your mother seemed recently?"

"A little edgy. Quiet." Exactly as I would expect without Dad or Marissa around.

"One of her favorite patients died."

"Wow. She didn't mention that to me." When my mom took the hospice nursing job, she'd said she was a good fit because she was so calm and objective. Maybe it was turning out to be harder than she anticipated.

"Your mom is pretty upset. Can you take her out to eat somewhere tonight and just hang out?"

"Sure, Dad."

"Thanks. I'll pay you back."

"Not necessary." I hung up and walked back downstairs to hand the phone to my mom. But I didn't ask about dinner right away. Too obvious. I could call her later.

Time to change my plans. Tonight, instead of visiting the falls, I'd investigate the girl online. If she ever showed up again, I'd be ready.

Chapter Seven

Meaning of the Phrase

I had not liked losing my break Tuesday evening. Over the next two days, I strived to be the most pleasing servant possible, lest my master find some excuse to deny me more hours of peace.

I made it to supper of yet another day with no corrections.

The Pratts lingered over their meal. Sitting in my corner, I stitched buttons to my master's green waistcoat and swallowed my sighs of impatience. When my master finally retired to the parlor with his family, I collected the dishes and hurried to the kitchen.

It took little time to complete my chores. After scraping the excess stew onto two trenchers, I washed the dishes and swept the floor. Once I gave Hector his half of the supper, I would be free to go. I peered from the back door in the direction of the barn, but there was no sign of him.

I carried the trencher to the slave's shack. It was empty. After setting the wooden dish on a stump inside the door, I strode to the barn.

"Hector?" I called.

"Yes?" He backed out of the horse's stall and latched it behind him.

"I left food in your room."

He nodded. "Going for a walk in the woods?"

"Yes."

"Alone?" He smiled, one eyebrow arched.

"Yes. Jedidiah is too busy to follow this evening."

"Tomorrow, then." Hector didn't get an evening break, although I had never heard him complain. Perhaps he didn't share my need for solitude. Hector spent most of his time alone already.

I slipped unseen among the trees at the rear of the property and strolled along the banks of Rocky Creek. Would the stranger appear tonight? Would such a gentleman want the company of a girl in the laborers's class?

Spurred on by a mixture of curiosity and excitement, I stopped at the falls and climbed down the cliff. When I reached the cave, I looked across the creek to the other side. Mr. Lewis's side. The woods were dark and dense.

Crouching, I ventured into the cool, shadowy depths of the cave. My heart settled into a gentler pace as I perched on a mossy boulder and waited.

There was much to love about my hideaway. In front of me, the waterfall murmured, lulling me with its song. For a brief while, I could sit without moving, without talking, without doing anything for anyone.

Time passed. He didn't come.

As the light faded, my disappointment grew. I hadn't realized how much I hoped he would come until he did not. It robbed the evening of its pleasure.

It had been the same yesterday. For two evenings now, I had sat alone. I must accept what this meant. His reason for coming the first time had passed, and there was no further purpose to bring him here. Mr. Lewis would not return.

Upon reflection, I had to conclude this to be a fortunate circumstance. Truly, the young man and his odd machine didn't exist. My imagination had taken flight. Or perhaps it had been spoiled chicken.

I rose to leave.

A flicker of movement appeared at the top of the slope. I hesitated, hope blooming.

Mr. Lewis rolled down the path, tied the machine he called a "bike" to a tree, and picked his way across the boulders. As he drew nearer, he peered through the falls.

Today he wore different clothes. Trousers of a heavy, blue fabric. A yellow shirt with a row of buttons and sleeves stopping high about the elbows. He looked fine.

"Susanna?"

I stepped forward, schooling my face into calm welcome. "I am here."

He smiled. "Hey."

A simple word. *Hey.* I was unaccustomed to it. Might it be a shorter version of *hello*? Perhaps it was a new greeting they used in our state capital. "Hey."

He extended his fingers to the waterfall, but couldn't pierce it. Withdrawing his hand, he met my gaze. "Are you real?"

"I believe so."

"Will your hand go through the water?"

"I shall try."

Creeping as close as I dared to the rock's edge, I held my fingers under the flow. It was the same as Monday. A warm glove bubbled around my hand. For yet another meeting, the falls would serve as a barrier between us, as surely as if they were made of liquid glass. It was a reassuring prospect, for now.

"Okay, I have some questions for you." From his pocket, he drew out a flat piece of black slate, no bigger than a folded letter. He stared at it with a frown. "Who is the current governor of North Carolina?"

"Mr. Ashe."

"When was North Carolina admitted to the Union?"

"I was eleven. 1789, perhaps."

He nodded. "How many states are there?"

"Fifteen."

"Sixteen." His gaze flicked up to meet mine. "Tennessee was admitted in 1796."

"I have not heard this news."

He touched the slate. "Yeah, it was admitted on…June first."

"And today is June third."

"Right." His lips twitched. "News travels much faster in my world." He slipped the slate into his pocket. "I'm glad you showed up."

His statement filled me with a pleasant glow, even as I marveled at its honesty. In my village, people rarely spoke so openly. I never did. A frank opinion could become a weapon in the wrong hands.

It must be quite lovely to say whatever he wished without caution. I wanted to try. "Do you truly accept that we are separated by over two hundred years?"

"It's either that, or someone slipped me some really good drugs." He studied the falls, starting at its top, along its arching path to the creek below. "Nobody I know could've passed that quiz. It was too random. I don't think we have the technology to fake the water—not yet, anyway. And I'm pretty sure I'm not crazy. So I'll just have to go with 'Whisper Falls is a portal to the past.' For now."

His words made no sense. This undoubtedly strengthened his case. I gave him a nod. "I want you to be real. Therefore, I shall question no more."

"I like your logic." He laughed. "Do you come here every night?"

"As often as my master permits."

"Your master?" His eyes narrowed. "Are you a slave?"

"Indeed not." How curious. He knew little about our laborers if he could mistake me for a slave. "I am bound."

"What does bound mean?"

Even more curious. Perhaps they no longer bound children when he lived. "I'm an indentured servant."

He looked down, as if to ponder the tips of his odd black shoes. "Indentured? I thought that was only for criminals."

Did he think me a criminal? The comment prickled. I couldn't let it pass. "No, indeed. Indentures are for anyone who..." I paused. Indentures were a common way for parents to reduce the number of children in their household. My stepfather had had no interest in the expense of feeding me. Five months after their wedding, my mother's husband bound me to the Pratts. It was one of the last things he ever did, for shortly thereafter my stepfather died. It would embarrass me to admit to this gentleman that my mother had married someone who gave me away. "An indenture may be signed for anyone who wishes to learn a trade."

"Like an apprentice?"

"Indeed."

"What trade are you in?"

"Housewifery."

His brow creased. "Why did you choose that?"

"Mr. Crawford, my stepfather, chose for me."

"Did he ask your opinion?"

"My opinion didn't interest him in the slightest." I made no effort to keep the disgusted edge from my tone.

"How long do you have to stay in your trade?"

"Until my eighteenth birthday."

"Which is when?"

"October first."

One corner of his mouth twitched into a half-smile. "You're two months older than me."

"Or two centuries."

"True."

We watched each other warily. I wondered if our discovery would prove to be a blessing or a curse.

He gestured at my rock. "Want to sit?"

"Yes, thank you, Mr. Lewis."

"Call me Mark."

His request made us equals. The sin of pride swelled within me, but I tamped it back, not ready to reflect on the emotion or its consequences. Instead, I merely nodded and lowered myself to the boulder with an inelegant plop.

He sat, too, his movements quick and graceful. "I came out here the other day to look for evidence of someone playing a joke on me, but I couldn't find anything."

"Who would play this joke?"

He shrugged. "My girlfriend. Ex, actually."

Girlfriend? I wanted to be clear about this word. "You have friendships with girls?"

"Yes. Well…" His lips puckered as he thought. "Guys and girls *can* be friends in my century. But when I say girlfriend, I mean the person I'm dating."

"Dating?"

"Sorry. Dating means a guy and a girl are interested in each other."

"Like courting?"

"Yeah." He shook his head. "Or maybe not. I'm not sure."

"Do you plan to marry this girlfriend?"

"Marry Alexis? *No.*" His eyes widened with horror. "Besides, she ended the 'courtship,' I guess you'd call it."

"Are you distressed?"

"I was, but it's okay now. Dating isn't about getting married any more. We have fun. Break up. Do it all over again with someone else."

"In my century, courtship has too many rules to be fun."

"Like what?"

"The gentleman must approach the woman first. Most unfair." Mark nodded, as if in agreement. "Do you have this rule, too?"

"Sort of. Girls can do the asking, if they want. But usually the guy asks."

"I see." In two hundred years, girls would have freedoms they didn't use. How extraordinary. Perhaps this freedom wasn't as enjoyable as it seemed. "The couple may not touch or be alone."

"We don't have those rules. We can be alone. And as far as touching goes..." He stopped and looked at his shoes.

"What about touching?"

"There's plenty of that." His face reddened. "Have you ever been courted?"

I nodded while noting his blush. I would like to know more about the touching. "Two gentlemen courted me. I rejected one. My master rejected the other."

"Your master did?"

"Until I'm eighteen, I can marry only with his permission."

Solomon Worth and Reuben Elliott had each offered for me. Mr. Pratt had refused to release me early from my indenture to marry Reuben. My master had, however, made an exception in Solomon's case. Truly, Mr. Pratt had had no choice. Solomon's father was my master's uncle. Mr. Pratt would never do anything to offend the Worth family. I was the one who refused Solomon. I had known him from childhood. My father had been his tutor. Marriage to Solomon Worth would seem like indentured servanthood— except there would be no end.

"How many girlfriends have you had?"

"Alexis was my first."

"How many more girlfriends will you be dating before marriage?"

"I don't know. Ten. Twenty."

"Do you pick unwisely so very often?"

He laughed. "I guess so."

The lightness of his tone bewildered me. Choosing one's husband or wife should be treated with gravity and respect. "Why did you choose this girlfriend?"

"Alexis picked me."

"Why did you agree?"

His brow creased in concentration. "At our school, everyone thinks she's amazing. When she asked me out, I was seriously flattered."

"I do understand. It is indeed flattering for someone to want you, even if you don't want them back." There had been a moment—a brief moment—when Solomon's attentions had filled me with pride. "What makes her amazing?"

"She's smart. And she's hot."

I frowned. "Does hot mean feverish?"

"No, it means pretty."

"Why does hot mean pretty?"

"I'm not sure." His face flushed crimson. He brushed at the laces of his shoes. "Can we talk about something else?"

"Certainly."

"Cool."

It was most perplexing, the number of words he used that made no sense. "If hot means pretty, does cool mean ugly?"

He laughed. "No, sorry. Cool means very good." He peered at me through the dark brown hair hanging over his brow. "I looked up your town. It really did exist."

"What a comfort, since it is where I live."

"The web didn't have too much information, though."

"The web?"

"Yeah. I don't know how to explain that. It's…" He shrugged. "The web's like a huge library, full of books, maps, and pictures. Sometimes lies."

"Where is this library?"

He paused, as if my question were hard to answer. "We have special machines to see inside the library. I have one of the machines at my house."

"What kind of books are in the library?"

"All kinds." He looked thoughtful. "Do you go to school?"

"I cannot. I have too many chores."

"Do you know how to read and write?"

I snorted. "Of course. It has fallen to me to teach Dorcas."

"What kinds of things do you read?"

"The Holy Bible."

"Anything else?"

"No." Perhaps that wasn't precisely true for me. My father had taught me to read when I was a little girl. As the town's tutor, he'd owned many volumes. Papa had encouraged me to study geography, history, and natural philosophy. He often claimed I was his best pupil. Even now, hidden in my corner of the attic, I had two of his books—my much-loved legacy from Papa. "The only book my master owns is the Holy Bible. He will not allow novels in his home. He calls them the devil's missives."

"You never read fiction?"

"I do not." I frowned, taken aback by Mark's tone, as if he couldn't imagine anything more barbaric. "How many books are in your web?"

"Billions."

I shook my head in confusion. "Billions?"

"It's a huge number, like..." He paused, rubbing his temple. "It's like counting the stars."

Stars? I glanced up at a sky of blue-black velvet, decorated with a sprinkling of stars and a tiny sliver of moon. How had night fallen without my notice? Startled, I rose. It wouldn't go well for me if my master saw me return after dark.

"I have enjoyed our conversation, but I must leave."

"I've enjoyed it, too." He stood as well and extended one hand through the falls. This time his arm slid through, all the way to his elbow. "Hey, look. It let me through a little farther."

"Indeed, it has."

"The waterfall thinks I'm safe. And it should."

Dare I rely on its judgment, too? Of course, it only deemed him safe to his elbow, a simple enough part to trust. "It has proven to be an excellent chaperone."

"More like a bodyguard." He smiled. "Will I see you tomorrow?"

"Perhaps." I took his hand in mine and squeezed it lightly. It was most improper of me, but Mark Lewis was used to plenty of touching.

"It would be easier if you lived in my world. I'd just friend you."

I dropped his hand as if it were a live coal, the simple word reminding me of my real life in Worthville—a world where there were rules and a rule maker I had to obey for another four months. "Do not call me a friend. It's forbidden."

"You're forbidden to have friends?"

"Yes." I fumbled for the granite ladder. "Mr. Pratt says I shall become careless if I focus on anything besides his family and my chores."

"Mr. Pratt sounds like a major control-freak asshole."

I didn't know the meaning of the phrase, but I suspected I would agree if I did.

After crawling over the rocky ledge guarding my cave, I turned. He stood where I had left him, visible through a veil of water. "Good night…Mark."

"Your master doesn't have to know about us, Susanna. I can be your secret."

I lifted a hand in farewell and turned to run home—
except this time, I ran with a smile on my lips, for I had a
secret friend. Mark could be someone with whom I talked
and laughed. Someone with whom I could be equals—if
only for an hour at a time. Someone Mr. Pratt could not
take away.

CHAPTER EIGHT

INNER RADAR

Even though I had no customers scheduled for Fridays, I would be working today. After loading my lawn care equipment in the back of the truck, I drove southwest out of the city. Forty-five minutes later, I pulled onto the half-mile driveway leading to my grandparents's log cabin on the banks of Jordan Lake.

Granddad sat on the front deck, doing a crossword puzzle and drinking coffee. He waved me over. I approached carefully, unsure whether he'd been warned about me and, if he had, how mad he was about it.

"Why are you here?" he asked, giving me a hard stare from under bristling eyebrows.

"Yard work."

"Don't remember asking you to do that."

"You didn't."

"Your mother did?"

"Yes, sir."

His scowl deepened. "Did she cook up this plot by herself?"

"I think she talked it over with Gran."

"Better go in and ask your grandmother what she wants you to do." He tapped the puzzle book. "You can tell her I'm pissed as hell."

"I don't believe I'll do that."

"Smart boy."

I walked through the front door. It was quiet in the house except for the hum of the air conditioner. I glanced up at the loft overlooking the two-story great room. Gran wasn't there.

But I could tell where she had been—the kitchen. Gran had been baking this morning. A tray of cinnamon rolls lay on the counter top, oozing with gooey, buttery frosting. Yeast rolls browned in the oven. My grandmother had been expecting me.

I tore a corner from a cinnamon roll at the back of the tray and went looking for Gran. I found her in the bathroom, frowning at the toilet. I didn't want to know why.

"Hey, Gran, I'm here."

"Mark." With a happy sigh, she gave me a hug, her head hitting me mid-chest. "Did your grandfather see you?"

"He did."

"Did he harass you any?"

"No."

"Liar." She smiled. "Want something to eat before you get started?"

"Have I ever turned down one of your cinnamon rolls?"

Gran laughed and pushed me into the hallway.

There was a huge photo of my mother and her sister hanging on the wall across from the bathroom door. In it, Mom was ten, Aunt Pamela five. My mother stood behind her sister, arms curved protectively, while Pamela clung to one of her hands.

It always made me smile to see Aunt Pamela holding my mother's hand like that, an unconscious indication of how much she'd depended on her big sister. Their relationship had totally turned around when they grew up. Mom became the kind nurse, and Pamela became the kick-butt Army officer with the soft but *do-not-mess-with-me* voice.

My aunt was the person who had helped me the most when I was bullied over my weight in middle school. Any time she called or emailed, she reminded me to be strong and not give in.

"Bullies are stupid, Mark," she would say. "It won't take them long to make a mistake. Wait and be ready."

That became my motto. I ate a healthier diet and looked for a sport I could get into. It was my dad who bought me a mountain bike. I loved hitting the trails with him—and I turned out to be good. As my muscles grew, so did my confidence. And just like my aunt said, when the bullies got stupid, I was ready. The bullies earned their "reward" without my landing a single blow.

If there was anything I'd learned from my warrior aunt, it was that "small" didn't have to mean "defenseless."

After Aunt Pamela died in Afghanistan, Gran moved the photograph of her two daughters to this spot, where she'd see it each time she left the bathroom. Why? Didn't the memories kill her? It hurt me to see it, and I was just a nephew.

I stopped in the kitchen for a couple of cinnamon rolls. After my second breakfast of the day, I gave Gran a sugary kiss on her cheek and headed outside.

Granddad waited for me on the deck, work gloves on. "What'll you do first, Mark?"

"Edge the flower beds."

"Good choice."

I eyed his gloves. "What are you doing?"

"Supervising."

"Why do you need work gloves?"

"Self-respect." He winked.

I went to the back of my truck, donned my gloves and goggles, and grabbed the weed whacker. Soon I was edging the beds while my grandfather raked mulch and pointed out my every mistake, his supervisory skills in full force.

When I reached the end of that project, I took a wipe-the-sweat break. "Okay, Granddad," I said in between chugs from a bottle of water, "what's next?"

"I want to know what happened to the girl."

I stiffened. "Alexis?"

He grunted.

"We broke up a couple of weeks ago."

He leaned on his rake. "Do you miss her?"

My ex-girlfriend was a topic I would not discuss. I mopped my face with a towel, glad for the cover. "Not sure yet."

Granddad grunted again. "Get the grass blower. We'll clear off the deck and the walkways."

I finished off my bottle and grabbed the blower from the back of my truck, glad my grandfather hadn't spent much time on the Alexis thing. I liked efficiency in conversations.

After completing every task Granddad could dream up and polishing off an awesome lunch of my favorite dishes, I drove home, eager to squeeze in a training session before a visit to the falls. The sight of a black Ford SUV waiting at the curb in front of my house put a hold on the plan.

I parked the truck, exhaled a hard breath, and slid from the cab. Keefe met me halfway up the driveway.

He looked past me instead of at me. With a ball cap pulled low over his eyes, he seemed kind of fidgety.

"What do you want, Halligan?" I asked. He didn't act any happier to see me than I was to see him.

"How's training?"

As if I would tell him. "Fine."

"Alexis dumped you."

My inner radar went on full alert. Why did Keefe care? "I'm not dating anyone right now."

He shuffled his feet. "Are you trying to get her back?"

"None of your damn business."

He knew better than to fish for information from me. Every time I looked at him, my brain flashed back to middle school and memories of lying on the ground in a ring of bullies, being methodically and viciously kicked. In the bathroom. On the ball field. Behind the cafeteria. The helpless, hopeless fat kid at the mercy of thirteen-year-olds. Keefe's face had always appeared on the fringe. Had he been a bystander—or was he the ringleader, watching while the others did his dirty work?

"You still want her." Keefe jingled his keys, his lips thinned into a superior smile. "I'm going to win."

"We'll see." I kept my face neutral. What were we talking about? Alexis or the race?

He shrugged and walked backwards down the driveway. "She won't be by herself very long. Guys are getting in line to have a shot at her."

My hackles rose. That was the point of this visit. Keefe was letting me know he intended to get in that line. The urge to curse his ass slammed me, but I fought it back. Aunt Pamela had always said that being nice to the enemy was the best possible revenge. "Good luck with Alexis."

"Yeah, I'm sure you mean that."

The thought of them together made me smile. Her demands would completely screw up his training schedule. "Actually, I do."

His eyes narrowed suspiciously. "Uh-huh. See you at the race." He jumped into his truck and screeched down the street.

The conversation left me in a pissy mood, which a dozen miles of biking at top speed did nothing to fix. Back home, I cleaned up, made a fast PB&J, and jogged straight to the falls. Susanna stood in the tallest part of the cave, waiting calmly.

I had to figure out how to get her to branch out on facial expressions. "Hey."

"Hey." She studied me for a long moment. "You've had a peculiar day."

"I have." I flopped onto the rock and gestured at the one across from me. "How could you tell?"

"Your face speaks." She sat in the middle of her rock, well away from the edge, her legs tucked beneath her skirt. "What did you do?"

"I hung out with my grandparents." Did her face speak? If body language was seventy percent of communication, I'd be practically deaf where Susanna was concerned. "My grandmother cooked a special lunch."

"What made your meal special?"

"The quiche."

She frowned and shook her head.

At least I understood that gesture. I'd have to define terms again, which should've been annoying, but wasn't. Actually, it was fun, like unraveling a mystery for another person, someone who really wanted to know. "It's a pie with eggs, cheese, and ham."

"Is this a treat?"

"Big time." I smiled with remembered pleasure. When my grandmother pulled the pan out of the oven, I had nearly collapsed with joy. The only problem was that I couldn't eat the whole quiche by myself. Granddad wanted some, too. "What's a treat for you?"

"Eating my fill."

Holy. Shit.

Talk about a depressing answer. And she said it matter-of-factly, like it was a normal part of her life.

I lost the smile and looked at her. Really looked at her. She didn't look hungry, but then again, she didn't look anything other than calm. How did it feel on the inside—to want and not get? Did the mind learn to ignore the stomach? I'd never had to worry about having enough food to eat. There was always plenty on the table and plenty in the fridge.

Well, I knew one thing for damn sure. She wouldn't go hungry while I was around.

"Let's try that again. If I were to bring you any treat, what would you want?"

Her gaze flicked to mine, then down. She stared into the water foaming past her rock. "You would bring me anything?"

"Yes."

"Ice cream." Her lashes lay like dark smudges against her cheeks. "My mistress has had it before. It sounds lovely."

"I could bring you ice cream next time I come."

There was a faint curve to her lips. "Whisper Falls allowed your arm to pass through, but will it permit your arm *and* a dish?"

"Yeah, there is that one little glitch." I'd give it a try, anyway. Ice cream, probably vanilla to start with, as much as she wanted.

She shifted her legs. Grimy feet and ankles emerged from her skirt.

"Are you barefoot all the time?"

Her eyes rose warily to my face. "Yes."

I waited, but she added nothing. If my grandfather liked how I used an economy of words, he'd love Susanna.

"Do you have shoes?"

"One pair, for the winter." Her fingers picked at some dried mud on the curves of her calves.

Wait a minute. I focused harder.

It wasn't mud she picked at. It was dried blood. There were several thin lines of scabs criss-crossing her calves, relatively fresh, with numerous scars hinting at older wounds.

I knew the amount of force it took to cause that kind of injury. My throat burned with something sour and angry. "How did you get those marks on your legs?"

She went completely still except for her eyes. Even though she wasn't looking at me, I could see her eyes tracking down her calves. Then, slowly, she drew her legs back to her body and covered them with her skirt. "My master thrashed me."

I swallowed hard and said, in as controlled a voice as I could, "Why did he thrash you?"

"I made a mistake."

All voice control left. "He beat you until you bled for making a mistake?" She had so many marks. There was a hollow ringing in my ears. I'd been beaten up plenty of times, but not like that. "What kind of mistake?"

She wrapped her arms about her legs, rested her chin on her knees, and closed her eyes. When she spoke, her voice was light, almost dreamy. "I overslept. Breakfast was late."

My jaw clenched so tightly, it was a wonder my teeth didn't crack. "How often does he beat you?"

"Perhaps once each month."

I jumped to my feet, too outraged to sit still any longer. Her master was a complete asshole. A prick. A bully. How could he hit her? "What can you do about it?"

She straightened, knees down, chin high, hands folded in her lap. "There's nothing I can do. It's Mr. Pratt's right to punish me as he sees fit."

Her response put my outrage on pause. Beating her was his *right*?

Hell no.

Why wasn't she pissed? This couldn't be legal in any century. I faced away from her to fume at the trees. After sucking in a couple of deep breaths, I spun around. "I can't believe he can just whip you, and it's okay."

"To whom shall I turn?"

"Don't you have policemen or mayors or somebody in charge?"

"Indeed we do, and it does me little good. The town magistrate is Mr. Pratt's *uncle*."

Damn. That did make things tougher, but maybe she'd given in too soon. "Have you asked the uncle for help?"

"Mr. Worth has seen my wounds, yet he does nothing. I shall not humiliate myself further by begging." She stood, cheeks flushed, face grim, hands on hips. "You can't tell me masters in your world don't thrash their servants."

"Americans don't have masters anymore. We have employers. And if the government finds out they hit their workers, they're thrown in jail."

She snorted. "I don't believe people have changed so much. The strong will always hurt the weak, and there will never be enough justice to stop them."

We glared at each other across the divide, breathing hard. Breathing in rhythm.

She looked away first, arms dropping. Her face slipped into its familiar, neutral expression. "In my world, I have no recourse. I have learned to accept it. Since my failure to act offends you, I shall go."

Her weary, softly spoken words doused me like ice water. What was wrong with me? Had I really just argued with the victim? Like I didn't know how it felt to be one?

"No, Susanna. Wait." I threw myself at the waterfall, but it stopped me at my wrists. "I'm sorry."

She hesitated, then held her hands next to mine. Hers were rough and red, the nails dirty and broken.

"Our worlds are very different," she said, her voice flat.

The falls pushed me upright on my rock, away from Susanna, as if protecting her from my stupidity. What an idiot I was. Even the falls were disappointed in me. "I shouldn't have yelled. I just hate to think of him hurting you."

"I don't like to think about it, either. Therefore, I don't." She turned away from me and walked to the cliff.

Watching her climb the rock wall was amazing. She had such grace and strength. I wanted her to come back, tomorrow and the next day and every day after that. Had I completely screwed things up with my mouth?

"Don't leave pissed."

"If pissed means angry, have no concern." She smiled from high above me. A slow, sad smile. "I had *pissed* beaten out of me long ago."

CHAPTER NINE

A WORRISOME TENDENCY

The argument with Mark wove through my thoughts, leaving me unsettled and confused. I rose well before dawn and crept on quiet feet to the kitchen.

With the porridge and tea warming on the hearth, I had begun to add pork to a pot of beans when the clatter of wheels and a horse's hooves caught my attention. I straightened and turned. Mr. Pratt loomed in the door. His slave waited in the yard, standing quietly beside the wagon.

Mr. Pratt tossed a wide square of coarse cloth onto the worktable. "Pack bread and cheese for the Negro."

It was too early for Hector's breakfast. Indeed, it was too early for our master to be stirring. "Is Hector visiting somewhere?"

"I sold him."

Sold him? I pressed my lips together to stifle my surprise, my gaze darting to Hector. He stared at the ground, shoulders hunched.

"Be quick, Susanna." My master spun around and stalked from the building. As he passed the black boy, he said, "Mind the horse until I get back."

Once Mr. Pratt had disappeared into the main house, I hurried to the door and studied Hector. There was a new, blood-crusted gash curling along the side of his neck.

I couldn't imagine what he'd done to earn this punishment. "Do you know where you're going?"

Hector bobbed his head once. "Mr. Jasper Bell."

I knew the family well enough. The Bells lived a half hour's walk west of town, on the road to Hillsborough. There were two other slaves already on the farm. "Mr. Bell is a kind man."

The boy raised his solemn gaze to mine. "Yes."

"He raises horses. You may like it there."

"Yes."

I smiled. "Let me prepare your food."

After setting a round loaf of bread and a slab of cheese in the center of the cloth, I frowned in dismay. The meal seemed so forlorn, a sad farewell to our Hector. I glanced through the front kitchen door. Mr. Pratt remained within the main house. I slipped into the pantry and grabbed some dried apples and a hunk of ham. Slicing a hole in the bottom of the loaf, I stuffed the extra items inside where my master wouldn't see.

After wrapping the package, I carried it out to the boy. He gave me a conspiratorial smile.

Mr. Pratt erupted from the house and strode swiftly toward us. "Get in."

Hector nodded and climbed into the back of the wagon.

"Hold breakfast until I return," Mr. Pratt said and snapped the reins.

I waited as the two of them disappeared into the shadows, my surprise being replaced with alarm. Why had our master sold his slave? Hector was strong and able. He had tended both the garden and the animals and had often helped in the mill. Who would do the work now?

The normal mealtime came and went. It wouldn't take long for my mistress to send a messenger to discover what was wrong.

A girl's skipping steps approached the building.

"Susanna," Dorcas said, as if she were singing.

"Good morning to you, too." I gestured her nearer. "Why have you come?"

"Mama wants her tea. Is it ready?"

"It is, indeed, but your papa hasn't returned from his errand. So we must wait."

"Oh, very curious." She brightened. "Where did he go?"

"I'm sure he'd want to tell you himself."

The wagon heaved past the kitchen. Dorcas ran to the doorway and watched it stop at the barn. "Papa took the horse out?"

"He did."

"I shall warn Mama." She ran at full speed to the main house, the door slamming behind her.

By the time Mr. Pratt reached the yard, I had the tray ready. He preceded me into the house and went straight to the dining room. Conversation around the table stopped instantly.

Dorcas managed to remain silent until the food was served and blessed. But then she couldn't contain herself any longer.

"Papa, I want to know where you've been." With a squeak, she turned to scowl at her older sister. "Don't pinch me, Deborah."

Mr. Pratt cleared his throat. "I sold the Negro. I delivered him to the Bells this morning."

My mistress set her teacup into its dainty saucer and gave her husband a false smile. "Whyever did you do that?"

"It was time," he said. "We shall all have new chores until I can make other arrangements."

Dorcas wiggled on her chair with excitement. "May I gather the eggs? I should enjoy that chore."

"Yes, Dorcas, you may." Mr. Pratt stared at his elder son. "Jedidiah, you and I shall tend the animals. You will also be expected to help out in the mill."

"But, Papa…" the boy sputtered.

His mother patted her son's arm until he lapsed into silence. She frowned down the table, eyebrows arched. "Jedidiah goes to the tutor in the morning."

"He can awaken earlier." My master leveled his gaze on me next. "You must take over the garden. Dinah and Delilah are old enough to help."

I nodded and cuddled Baby John so tightly he made a grunt of protest. I relaxed my hold even while trying to relax my thoughts. I had a full day. How would I fit such a huge chore into my schedule?

Mrs. Pratt's lips thinned primly. "How long will these new assignments be in effect?"

"Until other arrangements can be made," her husband repeated.

"Perhaps you should tell me why you sold the boy."

Mr. Pratt looked at his wife with a long, blank stare. The rest of us held our breath. Several seconds passed before she looked away.

He picked up his spoon.

"Papa, what will Deborah do?" Dorcas asked. "She doesn't have a new chore."

He transferred his gaze to his eldest daughter. "She'll learn to spin."

"Spin? I should like that very much." Deborah's lips curved into a tremulous smile. "Who will teach me?"

"The best spinner in the county. Your mother."

All eyes turned to my mistress. She looked about her, first surprised, then deeply pleased. "Well, perhaps not the best."

"You are too humble," Mr. Pratt said. "I shall fetch the spinning wheel from the attic today."

My mistress dropped her gaze to her bowl. Mr. Pratt nodded with satisfaction and became engrossed in his meal. The children followed suit.

Was I the only one who had noticed my master never gave a reason for selling Hector?

Of all the chores my master could have assigned to me, tending the garden was the one I minded least. I loved to be outdoors, and the garden was one of my favorite places. I could walk among the cornstalks and think my private thoughts. There were colors here, and shapes. Peppers and squash. Melons and peas. Each different. Each perfect. A feast for the eyes and the tongue.

"Here, little ones," I called to my two helpers. I handed each girl a cob and pointed to the half-filled bag of corn. The yield was poor today. I squinted at the horizon, hoping for a thunderstorm, but the sky remained its same splendid, cloudless blue.

"Susie?" a familiar voice called. "Where are you? I have peaches."

I waded through the rows of corn until I reached the garden's edge. My sister Phoebe searched for me, one hand shielding her eyes from the sun's glare, the other clasping a bucket of ripe, velvety fruit to her chest.

I checked her from head to toe. Her complexion was clear, although too brown, and her hair hung in golden ringlets against her bodice of pale blue. With a smile of pride, I joined her.

"Your peaches look delicious. Did you pick them?"

"Mama did." She blinked vaguely in the bright haze, then moved into the shadow of the stalks. "She wants me to trade them at Mr. Foster's store, but I don't wish to go into the village. People stare."

"They find your beauty astounding." My sister had inherited the prettiness common among the women in my mother's family. The ladies of the village couldn't help but notice and envy. "Their attention is kindly meant," I added, hoping I was right.

"I don't care why they stare. I don't like it." Her pout only lasted a moment. "Might the Pratts take the peaches?"

Tugging my little helpers closer, I asked in a falsely puzzled voice, "What do you think, Delilah? Would we like peaches, Dinah?"

Two tiny blonde heads nodded in unison.

"I agree." I turned to Phoebe. "We shall be glad to take them. Fresh peaches would make a delightful treat to end the week." I had coins hidden in a jar in the kitchen cellar. Unbeknownst to Mr. Pratt, my mistress gave me her spare cents, trusting me to make special purchases when the need arose. It had been a while since she'd given me any, yet I had been frugal. There was sufficient to pay Phoebe. "Will you want to be paid in coins?"

"Mama said she would rather trade for vegetables and bread."

"Very well." I hoisted the bag of corn. Dinah and Delilah grabbed handfuls of my petticoat and tramped along behind me.

My sister fell into step beside us. "Susie, what's your favorite chore?"

"Caring for the babies. They are so sweet." I smiled indulgently at my two little helpers before frowning at my sister. At twelve, she still demonstrated a worrisome tendency toward absentmindedness. "Phoebe, please be careful with the peaches. You have dropped one."

She stopped to remedy her mistake and then hurried to catch up. "Would I like caring for babies?"

"You stayed with our brother Caleb after his wife had our nephews. Did you like that?"

"No." Phoebe shuddered. "Perhaps it was worse because they were twins."

It was worse because of my sister. She had fallen asleep when she was supposed to watch them. And she had scarred one of the babies by dripping candlewax on his leg. Neither of our brothers would ever again leave Phoebe alone with their children.

"You wouldn't like minding babies. Why do you ask?"

"I may soon tend five. Is that a lot?"

The question sent my heart racing. I stepped into her path, bringing her to a halt. "Indeed, it is many children. Who told you such foolishness?"

She stared at me silently, lips trembling.

"Tell me quickly. Has Mama found you a job caring for children?"

Phoebe shook her head.

I released a shaky breath and continued up the slope toward the kitchen.

"Susie, don't be angry. Mama doesn't like the idea, but Mr. Shaw insists."

"Mr. Anthony Shaw?" I stopped again and frowned at my sister. "Whyever should he comment on the subject?"

"He's courting Mama."

The news stunned me. "Truly? Mama wishes to marry again?"

My sister nodded.

Why would my mother consider another husband? Were two not enough? Although our father had been a good man, Mama hadn't chosen well the second time. My stepfather had eaten often and worked little. When he had grown weary of having so many children around, he had bound me out.

"I cannot believe you heard right. Mr. Shaw's wife was buried but two months ago."

"He says they will wait a respectable period for mourning."

He had not waited a respectable period to seek a replacement. Did he have no shame?

"His five children are all under the age of six."

"That is true."

"One is an infant." The first Mrs. Shaw had died in childbirth.

"Yes."

"Has Mama agreed to his proposal?"

"Not yet."

Surely our mother would not be so foolish.

"If there are no wedding plans, why have they discussed you?"

"Mr. Shaw's sister lives at his house, but she'll go home soon. He needs someone to tend the children. If Mama keeps laundering clothes for hire, she won't have time. He says the task will fall to me." Phoebe's face crumpled with anxiety. "It frightens me to tend children."

My sister was wise to be concerned. With tasks she disliked, she was clumsy and easily distracted, terrible qualities in a girl with babies under her charge. Phoebe was simply too happy to be useful in a normal household. I walked steadily toward the kitchen, more worried than I wanted her to realize.

"If you were Mama, what would you have me do?"

"Work with fabric." I heaved my bag of corn through the rear entrance to the kitchen and wiped my brow with the sleeve of my bodice. "You have a talent for coaxing beauty out of cloth and thread."

"I do enjoy needlework." Her brow puckered. "I might be good at spinning. What do you think?"

"An excellent skill. Your fingers are so clever."

I hauled the bag into the pantry while Phoebe sat on the back steps with my two helpers, talking brightly about her future in spinning. I listened with part of my mind, the rest consumed with my sister's news.

A marriage to Mr. Shaw, while practical for him, would be nonsense for my mother. As a widow, she controlled her own property and children. If Mr. Shaw were her husband, he would control them, instead. Since he was younger than she and healthy, land she'd inherited from my father would likely pass into Mr. Shaw's hands. She owed it to my brothers—and Papa's memory—to save the farm for a Marsh.

My mother wasn't thinking clearly. She had little to gain and much to lose. It should be easy enough to present this logic to her. I would find Mama at church tomorrow and persuade her to abandon this path.

A dozen peaches remained after the noon-time meal. I loaded some into my apron and walked to the village, eager to restock our dwindling pantry supplies.

The store was empty when I entered. Mr. Foster emerged from the back, his footsteps slowing as he caught sight of me.

"Good afternoon, Susanna. How may I help you?"

I set the fruit on his counter and nodded briskly. "I would like to trade for ginger and sugar."

He took the peaches, added them to a basket sitting on a shelf behind the counter, pulled out a journal, and made a notation. "I won't be trading today. I cannot extend the Pratts any more credit."

I mulled over the statement, unsure of a response. "I am sorry to hear it." Without spices, our meals would be tasteless.

"You tell Jethro Pratt he needs to bring his account current. These peaches will help only a little."

Behind me, heels clopped into the store. I glanced over my shoulder to see the Widow Hinton walk in. I couldn't pursue this subject before a witness. Giving a final nod toward the storeowner, I said, "I shall deliver the message, Mr. Foster."

The exchange surprised me. My master was particular about his business. Something must have happened to make it difficult to manage his bills. But what? The mill thrived, did it not?

Of course, there was a new mill at Ward's Crossroads, a solid half-hour wagon ride away. It was too far to affect the Pratts's mill, surely. Yet something was clearly amiss. My master had said nothing to me. Nor had he said anything to my mistress. She wasn't one to hide her feelings.

Although I dreaded a discussion with him, I had no choice.

My master didn't return from the mill until suppertime. I waited until he had adjourned alone to the parlor before approaching.

He sprawled at his desk, jacket off. His white shirt and green waistcoat clung to his frame, soaked with sweat. Heavy stubble darkened his chin. His appearance surprised me. He had always been particular about his clothes.

"Mr. Pratt, may I have a word?" I stayed at the threshold.

He jabbed his quill into an inkpot, then scratched in his journal. "What is it?"

"We're running low on staples." His hand stilled, but he didn't respond. Perhaps I should be more explicit. "Flour, cornmeal, —"

"Yes, yes. I know what staples are." He rubbed the tip of his nose. "Are you certain?"

"I have enough to last a week or two."

"When I come home from the mill Monday, I shall bring more." He sighed noisily, dropped his quill, and glanced over his shoulder with an impatient scowl. "Anything else?"

Mrs. Pratt prided herself on what a fine catch she had made for a husband. *Tall, handsome, witty—the ingredients for greatness,* she would say. In my opinion, she overestimated his destiny. His perpetual scowl did nothing for his appearance. And his manners, for all that his early days had been spent as the youngest son of a planter, weren't pleasing or refined.

I bowed my head and forged on. "Sir, we need sugar and —"

"Yes, yes," he interrupted, "I shall visit the store Monday."

This message would make my master angry. But how angry? And what portion of the blame would he heap on me? I squared my shoulders. "I am sorry, sir, but Mr. Foster bids me to tell you that our account must be paid before we may purchase any more."

Mr. Pratt erupted from his chair. Crossing the room in two bounds, his fingers clamped around my wrist to yank me closer. "Have you gossiped about me?" Spittle foamed between his clenched teeth.

"I do not gossip." I held my breath against the rank odor of his body.

"Then why have you been talking with Mr. Foster?"

"I went to fetch the supplies."

"That's my wife's duty."

Mrs. Pratt hadn't performed that particular duty in many months, but he wouldn't hear it from me. I remained silent and fixed my gaze on his neckcloth, frayed, limp, and clumsily tied.

"Your voice has an insolent tone. Are you showing me your temper?"

"No, sir."

"Good. You know how much I dislike temper in a servant." He flung my arm away, smacking it into the wall. I swallowed a moan and backed up into the dining room, hoping to lengthen the distance between us.

"Susanna?"

I paused. "Yes, sir?"

"If you are wise, you will keep my secrets."

CHAPTER TEN

THE FIRST LANDMINE

Susanna hadn't shown up tonight.

Maybe she was avoiding me, which would be understandable since I'd been such a jerk to her. Or maybe her master had detained her.

Or maybe the falls had stopped working.

I needed to chill before worry made me crazy. She would show up again. I just had to be patient.

To get my mind off the *why*s, I climbed to the rec room and looked for something to do. There were plenty of distractions: a pool table, an old-fashioned pinball machine, a monster TV, and a laptop attached to every peripheral known to humanity.

I stared for two minutes, realized I didn't feel like playing games, and sat down in front of the computer.

My customers needed bills. I ran a professional operation here. After logging in, I updated my accounting system and emailed the invoices.

Cool. Another ten minutes burned.

The restlessness returned.

It might've been different if my best friend were around. But since Carlton had to spend part of his summer vacation with his dad, I'd be on my own for the rest of June.

Bored, bored, bored.

The computer pinged at me. It was an incoming video call from my sister. I clicked ACCEPT.

Marissa had a determined thrust to her chin. "So, tell me about the girl."

"Hello to you, too."

"Oh, please. Such a stupid diversionary tactic won't work."

I made a sour face at the webcam.

My sister stuck her tongue out in response. Very mature.

"Fine, Marissa. Which girl do you mean?"

Her eyes widened. "How many do you have?"

"None." I was reluctant to mention Susanna. Talking about her would be a conversational minefield. And there was the whole *does the portal still work?* problem.

Damn. I wouldn't consider that possibility again. Done. Erased.

"I understand Alexis is history."

I'd be glad when *talking* about Alexis was history. "You called Granddad."

Marissa tossed her head. "Why haven't you mentioned the breakup to me?"

My cursor hovered over the KILL CALL button. *Oops, how did that happen?* "I haven't told you about Alexis because it's not important."

"Yes, it is." She leaned closer to the camera, staring at me like a fixated cat. "She was your first love. Granddad and I are worried about how you're handling it."

"Alexis wasn't my first *love*. And I'm handling it just fine."

"Good. So tell me about the other girl. I promise I won't say anything to Mom."

"You aren't speaking to Mom."

"Minor detail."

I considered Marissa's request. It might help to discuss Susanna with someone, and my sister was far, far away. Plus, there was the KILL CALL button for emergencies, and I had the absolute best shit on Marissa that ever existed. Blackmail was a beautiful thing.

"If you say anything, I'll tell Mom and Dad about Fletcher."

Her mouth pinched. "They know about Fletcher."

"Yeah, but they don't *know* about Fletcher." And my folks would be interested to find out that Marissa was living with her boyfriend while *he* attended grad school and *she* supported him.

"They'd better not find out." Her eyes had a nasty squint to them.

"If I hear anything about Susanna come out of Mom's mouth, the next word out of mine is *Fletcher*."

"Deal." She pounced. "So, her name's Susanna?"

"Yeah." It was nice to discuss Susanna. It made her more real.

"How serious are you?"

"She's my friend."

Marissa settled back in her chair. "Ah. That serious."

"No, really. We're friends. Serious is the wrong word."

"What's the right word?"

"She's important."

"What's your important friend like?"

Images of Susanna flashed through my brain. Climbing the rock wall. Sitting statue-still on a boulder. Wiggling her fingers in the falls with a little kid's delight.

"She's like no one you've ever met."

"I've heard that one before."

If only my sister knew. "Susanna is quiet."

"Is that good?"

"Yeah." Quiet was great. It was one of the best things about being around her. Everything she said was interesting. One hundred percent. No stupid stuff.

"Is she hot?"

I frowned. "Yeah, I guess."

"You guess?"

I thought about the way Susanna looked. So many things contributed to hotness. Her hair was hot, but her body had to count, too. And under all those layers of clothes, it was hard to say.

Then there were her smiles, which were amazing to the point of surreal. "Susanna is pretty. It's just not a good enough way to describe her."

"Oh, man. You have it bad." Marissa laughed. "How old is she?"

Should I remind my sister we were just friends or would it be a wasted effort? "She's seventeen."

"Same age as you. Where does she go to school?"

Damn, I'd stepped on the first landmine. "She doesn't."

"Graduated early?"

"Dropped out." An involuntary dropout, which would remain unsaid.

Marissa wrinkled her nose. "How long have you been dating?"

"I met her a few days ago. And we're not dating."

"All right. How often have you hung out?"

"Maybe a couple times."

"That's all?"

Could I change topics without making Marissa more suspicious? Probably not. I'd do my best to explain Susanna's master, even though it wouldn't be easy to do in twenty-first century terms.

"Her employer is an asshole."

There was a pause. "How do you mean?"

Could I trust my sister? Maybe it would help to talk it over with someone. I just couldn't accept that there was nothing Susanna could do about Mr. Pratt.

"Her employer knocks her around."

Another pause, longer this time. When she spoke, her voice was soft and incredulous. "Does he abuse her?"

"Yeah." What a horrible word. But my sister was right. Hitting? Knocking around? Why had I used terms like those? Susanna was *abused*.

"What kind of job does she have?"

I should've thought this through before I said anything, although it was better talking to Marissa than Mom. Marissa was far, far away.

"I think she takes care of kids."

"Mark," she said, leaning so close to the camera I could only see her from the nose up, "do something about this. Turn him in."

Her statement twisted like a dull knife in my gut. "I can't. She won't go along with it."

"Have you seen the...?" She waved her hand, at a loss for the correct phrase.

"Scars or scabs?" I looked down at my balled-up fists. "Yeah. Both."

There was a huge, sucking gasp. "You have to do something."

Me? Like what? If the citizens of Worthville lived with it, what could I do from two hundred years away?

"It's complicated. There are extenuating circumstances."

"I can't believe I hear you saying that."

"Please, Marissa. Trust me." How had Susanna's acceptance of her abuse seeped into me? If Fletcher were treating my sister that way, I'd beat his ass before drop-kicking him over to the cops. With Susanna, I'd strutted around like a pissy little kid, told her she wasn't doing enough, and walked away. Why had I given up so easily?

All this emotion made me ache. "I want to do the right thing, but I don't know what that is. I have to research the law, and afterwards...it's complicated."

"What's complicated?" She frowned, her eyes big and round. "Is Susanna an illegal immigrant? You can't tell the police because you could get her deported?"

"Something like that." I gave Marissa a tight smile and grabbed the mouse. The cursor hovered over KILL CALL. "Sorry, Big Sis. Gotta go now. Later."

Click.

The conversation with my sister guilted me into action. I brought up a browser. Time for a little investigation. But where did I begin? How did I explain to a search engine what I wanted? There were so many keywords to choose from. Post-Revolutionary labor laws. Colonial abuse. Eighteenth century Wake County. Indentured servants in the late 1700s.

Probably I should try the last one.

There were hundreds of links, and nearly all dealt with the *convicts-from-England* type of indentured servants. Not the *hey-honey-let's-get-rid-of-a-kid* type.

Did all indentured servants get contracts with the same terms? The same length of service?

It was another thing to investigate.

Okay, I'd try *Wake County 18th century* next.

Five hits later, I discovered something that captured my attention. Something I hadn't been looking for. Something none of the research I'd done so far had turned up.

The 1800 census documents for Wake County listed Worthville and its residents.

The 1810 census did not.

In the first decade of the nineteenth century, Worthville vanished from the records.

CHAPTER ELEVEN

ACHING SIN

Sunday morning teased us with a light, sweet breeze, but we were soon to learn it was a cruel joke. As the day wore on, the sun blazed ferociously through the treetops, its heat stifling even in the shade.

I followed the Pratts down the trail to the village, my stomach twisting with each step. The meetinghouse, never pleasant for servants, would be miserable long before the worship service ended.

We emerged from the woods and joined the townsfolk streaming to church. In the distance, the slight forms of my mother and sister, arrayed in their finest gowns, trudged along the Raleigh Road, little puffs of dust in their wake.

I hurried to my mistress's side. "Mrs. Pratt, may I speak with my family?"

"Certainly. But don't delay."

"Yes, ma'am."

I ran toward my mother and sister, anxious to say my piece. "Mama?"

Her gaze met mine briefly and skittered away. It was always so. My presence seemed to embarrass her, although I couldn't be certain of the source. Perhaps it was because she was ashamed that a Marsh was indentured. Perhaps it was because her actions were to blame. She would never share the reason for her discomfort. I would never ask.

I fell into step beside her. "I would like to have a word with you."

"Of course."

My sister danced ahead.

"Phoebe says you are to marry Mr. Shaw."

"He has asked. I have not decided."

"She believes the Shaws plan to move into your house. She expects to tend his children."

"That is Mr. Shaw's wish."

"Do you believe Phoebe will mind children well?"

My mother wrung her hands nervously. "She can learn."

The sheer foolishness of the response stunned me. "Are you willing to risk the health and safety of the Shaw children while Phoebe learns?"

My mother didn't answer, her pace slowing as we approached the meetinghouse yard.

I spoke quickly, before my time ran out. "You know as well as I that Phoebe's true talent lies in needlework. She has a delicate touch with stitches and a good eye for color and pattern."

"She is indeed clever with her hands."

"Might we find someone to apprentice her in spinning and weaving?"

"Mrs. Drake is the only lady in Worthville who will teach lessons in making cloth, and she cannot take Phoebe."

"Have you asked?"

"I have."

We halted in unison and watched my sister. She talked nearby with the Foster daughters, her hands gesturing rapidly. With a cry of delight, she returned to us.

"Mama, the Fosters have invited us to dine with them after church. May we go?"

"Yes, that would be lovely." Her smile faded as my sister ran off. "You are right, Susanna. Phoebe is still too much of a child herself, but I don't know how to convince Mr. Shaw. He expects her to be useful."

I swallowed the anger threatening to clog my throat. "He cannot choose her future if he's not her stepfather. You haven't given him your decision. Perhaps your answer should be no."

Her gaze strayed to where my sister held hands in a circle with her friends, chattering all at the same time. Mama's face softened. "Perhaps you are right."

My mother strode past me to join the Fosters and Phoebe. I watched her go, hopeful my logic had made an effect.

The Pratts had already stamped up the steps in two pious columns and marched down the aisle to the front pew—their pew, as no one else dared to take it. In my mind, positioned as it was before the pulpit, no one else wanted it. Mr. Worth spat when he preached.

I took up my position in the back, where the indentured servants stood throughout the entire worship service. While our Heavenly Father might love us equally, it was apparently not a belief of His congregation.

In preparation for the service stretching before me, I leaned against the wall and stretched my legs as my gaze wandered among the heads of the worshippers. I easily found the Fosters on the same pew as my mother's gold-and-silver coronet of braids and Phoebe's bouncy curls.

Someone slipped into the spot next to me.

"Good morning, Polly," I said.

"Morning, Susanna." She gave me a tired smile, her plump face wan.

"Are you unwell? Shall I find Mrs. Butler?"

Hot fingers gripped my wrist. "No, please. Say nothing to my mistress." Polly stared at me with wide, despairing eyes.

"All right." I squeezed her hand briefly. Too much contact would draw the attention of others, which neither Polly nor I wanted. I would, however, be certain we spoke in more detail after the service.

There was a commotion at the meetinghouse door. The Widow Drake swept in, tall and straight, dressed from neck to toe in rustling black. A girl of about my age trailed after her, neatly clad in a moss-green gown with white linen apron and cap.

Did Mrs. Drake have a new apprentice? Was that why she had no time to teach Phoebe?

Mrs. Drake murmured into the girl's ear and then continued alone to her pew near the front. The girl moved to Polly's other side and looked about her with interest.

I caught the new servant's glance and exchanged nods of greeting. No one would call her a beauty, but the sweetness of her smile and the black silk of her hair were pleasing.

The service had just reached the sermon when the stillness was shattered by a low moan, quickly muffled, from Polly. I looked at her and bit back an exclamation. Her lips glowed gray against a pasty complexion. A red stain spread down her petticoat.

"Polly," I said in a whisper, even as she slumped against me, "we shall leave."

The congregation rippled and shifted, but no one turned to see what had caused the disturbance. I clamped my arm about her waist. The new girl did the same from the other side. We ushered her from the building.

The privy was our first stop, but the stench in the noon-time heat overwhelmed Polly. We encouraged her closer to Rocky Creek. She doubled over and retched into the reeds at the stream's edge. With stumbling steps, she plunged into the water and squatted in the shallows, splashing her sweating face.

I spoke in a soft undertone to Mrs. Drake's companion. "I am Susanna Marsh, and she is Polly Young."

"Mary Whitfield." The girl frowned. "I fear she is…"

"Indeed." I had witnessed enough miscarriages with my mistress to recognize the signs. "Mrs. Drake's home is not far. Can you fetch a clean petticoat and some cloths?"

Mary retraced her steps and quickly disappeared from sight. I knelt on a rock near the distraught girl and pondered what to do.

The water about her knees swirled in crimson waves. She cried out and clutched at her belly, her shoulders heaving.

"Polly, did Mr. Butler force this on you?"

She nodded.

"How far along?"

"I missed two monthlies." She panted in pain. "I am ruined."

"You are fifteen," I said, smoothing damp wisps of hair from her brow. "You had no choice. He's your master."

She closed her eyes. Tears made dirty trails down each cheek.

I soothed with a patter of sympathetic words, even as outrage roared through me like a white-hot flash of lightning. There had been rumors, quickly hushed, of a similar outcome with the Butlers's previous servant. Did Mr. Butler have no honor? Did Mrs. Butler have no sight?

The new girl soon returned. We washed Polly's face and legs. While Mary changed her into a fresh petticoat, I scrubbed the soiled one.

Footsteps drew near. "What's going on?" Mrs. Butler had arrived.

"Polly has taken ill," I said, meeting her gaze boldly.

She eyed me, then Polly, then me again. Her lips pinched. "Is it over?"

No need to explain. Mrs. Butler knew.

"Yes, ma'am," I said.

Her expression gentled as she approached her servant. "How do you feel?"

"Poorly," Polly whispered on a sob.

I moved closer to my friend, chin lifted. She linked her hot, shaking fingers with mine.

"I am..." Mrs. Butler's voice trailed away.

What had she been about to say? Sorry? Perhaps she was, but not sorry enough to protect the girls who worked in her household.

The older woman extended her hand. "Will you be able to walk to the wagon?"

Polly drew in a shuddering breath and released my hand to take her mistress's. "Yes, ma'am."

"Very well." The two joined hands and trudged up the slight incline of the creek bank. When they reached the top, Mrs. Butler turned to me briskly. "Please find my son Martin and send him to me. Tell my husband to hitch the wagon. We shall be leaving shortly."

Church had let out for the day. Townsfolk clustered in small groups in the shade of the trees. They grew silent when I approached.

The townsfolk knew, too.

After completing Mrs. Butler's bidding, I scanned the crowd and found the Pratts standing by themselves in the shade of an old oak.

"Mrs. Pratt—" I said.

My master interrupted. "Where have you been?"

I looked his way with reluctance. "Mrs. Butler's servant fell ill. I helped the girl until the Butlers were able to depart."

"It's a pity. We continued our education on the seven deadly sins. The sermon was most enlightening." He made a ticking sound with his tongue. "You will wish to skip your meals today and learn the true meaning of hunger. Only then can you understand the aching sin of gluttony."

No food for the rest of the day? My mind reeled at the thought. Did he truly believe I didn't understand how it felt to be hungry?

Perhaps I could sneak a quick bite in the pantry, although I knew from experience that, if I were caught, the punishment could be worse than a few missed meals.

I glanced at Mrs. Pratt in the bleak hope she would intervene, but she merely looked away.

I couldn't go to the cave on Sunday. The lack of food and the list of chores once handled by Hector overwhelmed my efforts.

On Monday evening I was ready in time, yet Mark didn't come. I had an hour of solitude to sit in the cave and watch night fall on the forest.

Although my body rested, my mind did not. So many thoughts demanded attention.

What would happen to Polly Young?

What difficulties prevented my master from paying his bills in a timely manner?

Why had Mrs. Drake chosen Mary Whitfield?

I wanted to share my questions. I wanted to talk with Mark. My secret friend. He had a lovely voice, deep and expressive. He didn't mind explaining things to me. I, who was more accustomed to impatience, enjoyed being the student of an eager teacher.

Friend. Before Mark, I'd known its definition. Now I knew its meaning.

As I clambered down the rock wall on Tuesday, he waited on his side of the falls. I smiled, my gaze drawn to an object he cradled in his hands.

He extended it toward me. "Let's see if Whisper Falls will let this through."

The object emerged on my side. It proved to be a red bowl, covered by waxy paper, and a silver spoon, its handle decorated with vines and roses. I accepted the gift and gasped, startled by its feel. The bowl was snow-cold and heavy. Within it lay a pool of soupy white pudding. Excitement beat inside me like a trapped bird.

"Have you brought ice cream?"

He nodded. "Go ahead and eat. It'll melt more if you don't."

I lifted a spoonful to my lips, oddly hesitant. What if I didn't like it? Or worse, what if I liked it too much?

Cautiously, I sampled the treat and couldn't stifle the groan of pleasure at the taste of sweetened cream. Yet it was the texture against my tongue that was most remarkable. Thick, silky, and deliciously cold.

I closed my eyes, wavering on my feet, entirely focusing my senses on this delight. It was more heavenly than I could have imagined. When Mark chuckled, I opened my eyes.

My cheeks blushed at my own greed. I held the bowl out to him. "Shall we share?"

He shook his head. "I can have all I want anytime. This is yours."

I needed no further prompting. Swiftly, the ice cream disappeared. Until the last bite I savored it, committing the treat to memory.

With a guilty laugh I stared into the empty dish. "Thank you. It was…" I felt the unexpected prick of tears.

"Susanna? About what I said Friday?"

I shook my head vigorously, not wishing to discuss my punishments again. "You have apologized once. It is enough." I thrust the bowl through the falls to emphasize my point, and my feet slipped on the mossy rock. I clawed frantically at the air before plunging into the creek.

CHAPTER TWELVE

SERIOUS ATTITUDE

It was like a scene from a bad movie—the heroine, in her long gown, teetering on the side of the pool before falling in, all in slow motion.

Except Susanna didn't stand up. She thrashed on all fours in the stream below my rock, screaming like a terrified animal caught in a trap.

"Help me!" she shrieked.

I knelt and grabbed her shoulders. "I'm here."

Her flailing fists knocked my hands away.

"Susanna, stop fighting me."

She didn't appear to hear. As she struggled to her feet, she tripped on her skirt and went under again. I lay on the boulder and fished in the water for something to grasp. Cupping her face, I held it above the water.

She sputtered. "Help me, Mark." Her thin fingers clutched my wrists.

"Calm down. I'll get you out." It killed me to see her like this. I locked an arm around her waist and hauled her onto the boulder. "You're fine now. I have you."

Her cries morphed into hiccups. She hunched over and buried her face in her hands.

I cradled her. "You're fine," I said. "Susanna, you're fine."

Her trembling faded, bit by bit. When it had stopped, I asked, "Do you think you can stand?"

She nodded.

"Slowly." I stood and drew her up with me, my arms still securely around her. She was rigid, fists balled against her cheeks.

Beneath my hands, her body was warm and wet. Her tunic gaped open to reveal a transparent shirt clinging to the tops of her breasts. I hugged her tightly against me, blocking the view.

She sucked in a sobbing breath.

"Better?" I asked.

She nodded.

"Okay. I don't know where that came from, but you really don't need to fear the creek. It's shallow enough to stand in."

"My father drowned in Rocky Creek."

Damn. No wonder. "I'm sorry, Susanna. How did it happen?"

A shudder racked her body. "There was a terrible storm one afternoon. It was raining hard. The creek was rising, threatening to spill over its banks. He came to see if it threatened our farm and fell in. The current bore him away." Her voice was soft and childlike.

"How old were you?"

"Eight." I could feel her smile against my chest. "My papa was a good man. Everyone admired him. He was the town tutor. He taught me everything he taught the boys."

I could hardly believe what she'd told me. Her father had died in this creek, yet Susanna came down to the falls every free moment she could spare.

"Why do you spend so much time near the water if you fear it?"

"It's the last place Mr. Pratt would think to look for me."

Damn. She hid in a place that reminded her of a huge tragedy, just to have some time alone.

"You're safe now. The creek barely comes up to your knees."

"I know, but the falls are so strong." Her voice squeaked.

"All you have to do is stand up and walk away." I brushed wet hair from her face.

"Mark?"

"Yeah?"

Her brow creased anxiously. "The bowl smashed."

"Not a problem."

Her head tilted up. "Mark?"

"Yeah?"

"Am I in your world?"

"Yeah."

The curtain of water flowed behind us, glittery and crystal clear. The falls were about as hard to understand as she was. Why had they picked now to let one of us through? Not that I was complaining or anything. I was really glad that we could be this close. I just didn't understand what the gain was for the falls. We were already friends. What else did it want for us?

"You're in twenty-first century Raleigh."

She released a deep sigh. "I want to go home."

I wasn't going to encourage this decision. Holding her made me feel all sexy and heroic.

She wiggled free and turned her back to me.

I looked down at my empty arms. She'd needed me and I'd responded without thinking. It felt good. No, it felt great. Too bad it had ended so soon.

"Do you want me to see if the falls will let me jump over there and help you across?"

"Yes, thank you." She stared at her toes.

I leapt to her rock and paused. It was quiet. No airplanes, traffic, or chainsaws. Just birds and insects and the rushing of water. It smelled weird. Earthy, like insane compost. And her world seemed absurdly bright for this late in the evening.

How could they stand the daytime sunlight without wearing shades?

Damn, I was standing in 1796. The frickin' eighteenth century. I looked over my shoulder and gave her a smile. "Whisper Falls has some serious attitude. It finally gave in about us."

She watched me silently. Susanna had withdrawn into statue mode.

I offered my hand. "Come on. I won't let you fall."

She landed beside me on her rock and then shrank away—soaked, stiff, face averted.

What had I done?

Susanna confused me. How could a girl go from fine to ballistic to catatonic all in the space of five minutes?

"What just happened here?"

She started to walk past me. When I touched her arm, she hesitated.

"Susanna, say something. How did we go from friends to strangers so fast? I don't understand what went wrong."

"Nobody ever sees me upset. I do not permit it." As soon as she spoke, she clapped a hand over her mouth and met my gaze, wide-eyed.

"Then it's a good thing it happened in front of me." How must it feel to never show emotions or voice opinions? To want peace so badly she fought her worst fear each day? It left me in awe.

She searched my face. I could almost hear her thinking, her brain clicking through all the angles. Then she smiled, slowly and sweetly.

Damn, her smiles were like crack.

"You are right. I am fortunate you were the one to witness that. Thank you." She picked her way over to the cliff.

It was still light out. I wasn't ready to let her go. I had to do something to hold her attention.

"Hey," I called after her, "I learned something interesting about your town."

"Yes?" She looked over her shoulder, a foot already poised on a ledge.

I knew how a cat felt when it had a dead mouse to present to its owner. Or maybe, on second thought, that wasn't such a good analogy.

"Worthville disappeared from the census between 1800 and 1810."

She blinked as if she thought I was joking. "Worthville disappears?"

Shit. Where was my brain? I couldn't have eased that in a little nicer? "Yeah."

She shook her head in denial, watching me with big, round eyes. A few seconds passed. She slumped to a boulder and laid shaking fingertips to her lips. "Merciful heavens," she said in a horrified whisper.

Why did I constantly screw up with her?

History had never been my favorite subject, nothing more than dry facts to memorize. Distant tragedies were something my brain acknowledged as sad without penetrating any further. But this was her world.

"Sorry, Susanna. I shouldn't have blurted it out like that."

Her gaze flicked from place to place, as if seeking answers among the shadows. "When does my village vanish?" Her voice cracked on the last word.

"I don't know, exactly."

"How does it happen?"

Great show-off I was. Hadn't even bothered to look up the details. What was wrong with me? Like some kind of selfish jerk, I'd told her horrible news just to keep her near me a minute longer.

"I don't know how it happened, either."

With a choked moan, she rocketed to her feet, climbed to the top of the bluff and paused, a dark silhouette against the night sky. "So you have learned nothing else?"

"Not yet."

"Then look no more. I don't wish to know."

Chapter Thirteen

Unworthy Retort

With Hector gone, chores consumed me. There were no spare moments to dwell on Mark's news. It was the first time I had ever been thankful for too much work.

"Susanna, we have eggs."

I turned from the worktable. Dorcas and Delilah stood framed in the doorway, each grasping the handle of the egg basket.

"Excellent work, young ladies," I said. "Please bring it here."

Delilah scrambled onto the bench while her elder sister approached me.

"Is it baking day?"

I wrestled a lump of bread dough into a pan before covering it with a cloth. "Indeed, as Wednesdays always are," I said, mopping my face with the hem of my apron.

Dorcas twisted to and fro, her little girl skirts swishing below her knees. "I should like a tart. Could you make one?"

"I suppose I could." My lips fought a smile. "If you were to have a tart, what kind would it be?"

There was a hopeful huff. "What kind of fruit do we have?"

"Berries and peaches."

"Oh." She perched on a stool by the worktable and clapped her hands, golden curls quivering. "A berry tart would be lovely. What do you think, Delilah?"

Her little sister nodded eagerly.

"Let me see what I can find."

I crossed to the pantry and reviewed the supplies stacked on ceiling-to-floor shelves. We were still low on all our staples. Most vexing. Mr. Pratt had not fetched more as he'd promised. Until he restocked, I would have to prepare recipes with less flour and spices.

"Would a cobbler do?" I called.

"Merciful heavens, yes," Dorcas answered.

I laughed to hear her repeating my favorite phrase. She noticed too much.

After measuring the flour, I reached for the sugar cone and judged it with my eye. It would last us through the month. I must be thrifty with the sugar, as well.

An idea stirred, a happy memory of my grandmother's favorite sweet. Much better than a cobbler, in my opinion.

I grabbed a pitcher of milk.

Dorcas sighed with pleasure as she watched me carry ingredients to the table. "May I help?"

"No, little one," I said with a smile. Dorcas would likely place more fruit in her mouth than in the recipe, "but I would enjoy conversation."

A shadow darkened the door. "Conversation about what?" Deborah watched us with suspicious eyes.

I clamped my lips together, reluctant to answer the unwelcome visitor.

"Susanna is making a cobbler." Dorcas leaned her elbows on the table and propped her face in her hands.

Deborah sniffed. "Is Jedidiah's dinner pail ready?"

I added a double portion of berries to the baking dish. "On the bench."

Deborah snatched up the pail in one hand and held the other out to Delilah. "I'm taking our brother's meal to the tutor's house. Would you like to walk with me?"

The little girl slid off the bench and grasped her eldest sister's hand. They disappeared through the doorway, Deborah's strident voice talking as they went.

I relaxed again.

"Susanna, do you want to hear the news?"

"If you like." I found a wooden bowl and spoon, only listening with part of my attention. Dorcas needed little encouragement.

"All right, then. Did you notice that Deborah seems upset today?"

Deborah Pratt was unpleasant far too often for it to be news. "What's the reason for her unpleasant mood?"

"Jacob Worth ignored her at the tutor's yesterday." Dorcas sighed. "I can't wait until she's old enough to marry and leave our house. Then I shall be the eldest daughter."

"She's only thirteen. I fear you have a long wait."

"Mama says fifteen is an excellent age to marry for a clever girl. But you are right; two years is quite a long time," Dorcas said, her lips puckering into a tiny rosebud of despair. She watched as I added flour and sugar. "Do you like cobbler?"

"Very much," I said, reaching for the milk.

"Do you ever get to eat any?"

I glanced at her face, but it was guileless. She hadn't learned the rules yet. Servants ate only what the family left behind. "Not often. The Pratt children like to eat the entire sweet."

"Yes, we do, and there are so many of us." She bobbed her head, her cap slipping. "Three after me. Since you joined our family, you've had many babies to raise."

I didn't know whether to laugh or ignore her. Dorcas dearly loved stories from her infancy, and she never grew weary of hearing them. I went along—as she knew I would.

"Indeed, I have. You were still toddling when I arrived. You were far too busy to mind if you fell over and bumped your head."

"I was a sweet baby."

"The best. Always cooing and beaming."

"I was no trouble."

My eyebrow shot up in mock surprise. "I don't remember it the same way."

She giggled. "I was an easier baby than your sister."

"That is true." Phoebe had been delicate at birth. Although not quite six years old myself when she was born, I tended to her and my mother while my father and brothers handled the chores. That period had given me the knowledge to care for babies, a skill which the Pratts had used often. "My sister didn't begin life with your robust health."

"Susanna," Dorcas gasped and surged onto the worktable to frown at the bowl, "you are adding too much milk."

I smiled at the top of her head. "I thought I would make a sonker."

"What is that?"

"It's a cobbler with too much milk. Sonkers were a specialty in the town where my grandmother grew up. She taught my mother how to make it, and my mother taught me. I cannot share the recipe with anyone."

"It's a secret?" Dorcas asked in a reverent tone.

"Indeed. My mother and I are the only two in the county who know how to make sonkers."

"I shall look forward to this treat." She slipped off her stool and circled around to my side. With lightning speed, she stuck her finger in the bowl, skillfully avoided the tap of my spoon, and tasted the batter. "Mmmm. This will do nicely."

"I am happy it pleases you." To conserve the sugar, I had used a small portion. It was gratifying that Dorcas hadn't complained.

"Phoebe is such a fortunate girl. I should like very much to have you for my sister." She leaned against me, one arm hooked about my waist. "Will you truly leave on your birthday?"

I nodded gravely. "I must."

"I shall miss you fiercely. Will you write me letters? Will you come back to see me?"

Her questions caught me unawares. Averting my face, I set down the spoon and wiped my hands on my apron. For seven years, my master and mistress had treated me with less care than one of their livestock. I was expected to do my chores with consistency. Accept my punishments with humility. Eat the dregs at the bottom of the kettle with gratitude. Confine myself at night to a leaky, drafty space no bigger than a coffin.

Since they wanted only work from me, work was all they received. I gave them no opinions. No thoughts. No feelings. I saved the best of me for my haven at the falls.

With my time short here, it would be far easier if I could leave without regrets. Yet Dorcas was such a delight, it was impossible to steel my heart against her. Picking up my spoon, I gave her a smile. "I shall only be as far away as Raleigh. We shall visit. And you have three lovely sisters to keep you company."

"I don't think Deborah is lovely at all. She tattles on me all the time." An indignant Dorcas continued at length, recounting another event where Deborah's excellence at snooping had earned Dorcas extra hours stitching samplers. Relieved at the change in topic, I nodded at intervals while I finished preparing the treat.

As I lifted the dish of sonker, she poked me in the side. "Can you keep a secret?"

"I suspect I can." Hiding a smile, I crossed to the stone hearth. Her secrets were rarely interesting enough to remember.

"I think Papa sold Hector because he's a thief."

"A thief?" I shook my head. "You must be mistaken. Hector would not steal."

"I heard Papa tell Mama he found a jar of stolen coins hidden in the cellar."

Her words sent a chill skittering down my spine. A jar of coins? I closed the Dutch oven lid, picked up the pitcher of milk, and walked outside to the cellar. My jar rested on a rickety shelf near the entrance. I lifted it and gave a little shake. It was empty.

Had Mr. Pratt found my missing coins? My mistress had given them to me. Hector hadn't stolen them. Had Mrs. Pratt said nothing in his defense?

It was wicked to press Dorcas for details, but I would do so anyway. I had to know. When I reentered the kitchen, I asked, "What, precisely, did your father say about Hector? Do you recall?"

She pursed her lips. "Let's see. It was something like… 'Anyone who takes what is mine will find the punishment severe.'"

My master liked his cobblers to have a crisp crust. Berry sonker would not please him.

I prepared a tray with six bowls, spooned a small portion of sonker into each, and carried the treat to the dining room.

A hiss whistled through his teeth. "Is this a pudding?"

"No, Papa," Dorcas said. "It's a cobbler with too much milk."

I nodded in confirmation, gaze lowered, biting my lip against an unruly bubble of laughter.

"Look at me." His upper lip curled.

I met his gaze and felt an odd sense of power. He wasn't nearly so intimidating perched on his mahogany chair. From this angle, I noted thinning hair and sagging skin. He was simply a man in his thirties, aging without grace.

But the eyes—they remained sharp. At this moment, they flared with irritation and something more. Suspicion?

"Why did you make this particular dessert?"

The children and Mrs. Pratt watched, still as stumps.

"Milk is plentiful," I said, "and the recipe permitted me to be frugal with the flour and sugar."

Anger stiffened his jaw. He wouldn't wish to comment on the state of our pantry. It was a rare show of defiance from me, one for which I was likely to pay.

He tapped his lips with a long, bony finger. "A decision both bold and economical." His glance took in his family. "Who would like to try this pudding?"

The rest of the family ate with relish until each bowl was scraped clean. Anticipating that my master wouldn't be interested, I'd reserved a small amount of the treat from the baking dish. I would take the last bit to Mark.

When I left the kitchen after supper, Jedidiah followed me at a discreet distance. Unfortunately for him, he was too discreet, for I dodged behind a bush, waited for the boy to pass, and followed *him*. He rounded the next curve, scanned the clearing, and peered into the growing shadows. With a snort of dismay, he ran down the path toward the village.

I made my way to the falls and climbed down while hugging a dish to my breast. Pausing at the bottom, I strained to see through to the other side. Neither Mark nor his bike was there.

Perhaps it was too early.

Perhaps he wouldn't come.

It was only when I turned toward the cave that I saw him, waiting in its deepest recesses.

Smiling with delight, I joined him. "You have been brave to venture into the wilds of Worthville."

"If you don't want me here…" He rose in a show of leaving.

"No, no," I said with a laugh. "Please, stay."

He laughed with me and sat.

I sat, too, a proper distance away. "Where is your bike?"

"I walked today." He gestured vaguely at the trail in his world. "I don't live far. If you turn left at the top of the incline, we're about a five-minute walk up the greenway."

"What is a greenway?"

"It's a trail that the government takes care of. No one is allowed to cut down the trees along greenways or build anything on their edges. That way, they stay perfect for walking and biking."

"Why can you not use roads?"

He gave me a half-smile. "People can't walk on roads. It would be too dangerous. The wagons we have now are very powerful and can cause a lot of damage."

"What about horses?"

He shook his head. "We don't ride horses much."

I loved to hear him speak about his century. The effort he took to explain things charmed me. "How else do you use them?"

"We don't use them at all. People in the city don't keep farm animals anymore."

"You have no animals?"

"None except a cat—although, strangely enough, at my house we have a barn."

I wouldn't like to live in a place without farm animals. "A barn for one cat?"

"Actually, my dad stores his toys in the barn."

A barn for the toys of a man? "I see."

"No, you don't."

"You are correct." I held out the dish and smiled, happy to be here. "I brought you something."

"What is it?"

"Berry sonker."

He sniffed. "Did you make it?"

"I did."

He dipped the spoon into the dish and scooped up a small bite. "Oh, man. That's amazing." A second spoonful disappeared much more quickly than the first.

I relaxed at his reaction. "So, you like it?"

"Yeah. It tastes like my grandmother's bread pudding." He finished his portion. "Now I feel bad that you tried harder with your treat than I did. I got your ice cream from the store."

At a store? Mr. Foster had ready-made items to buy on occasion. Pickles. Meat pies. Candies. But nothing so fragile as ice cream. "They make it at a store?"

"They make it in Vermont."

I knew enough geography to know the distance from Vermont. It would take weeks of travel. "The state of Vermont? Are you sure?"

He nodded.

"How can it come so far and not melt?"

"We have vehicles that can keep things frozen, even during the summer."

My mind struggled to keep up with such ideas. "You must have many interesting inventions in your time."

"You don't know the half of it. A lot of the things you would think of as magical, we've figured out."

"Like what?"

"Those vehicles that keep the ice cream cold move by themselves."

"How?"

"They burn oil, which pushes them along."

I liked the tone of his voice—the way he spoke to me. Not as if I were stupid, but with the ease of two equals.

"What else is different?"

It was a pleasure to watch him when he concentrated. His eyes brightened. His brow scrunched. His whole face revealed his every emotion.

"There are more girls in college than guys."

"Truly?"

"Totally true.

"How long do you go to school?"

"Probably twenty years."

Twenty years of school. How lovely that sounded. "Can you think of other changes?"

"We've had a black president. Elected twice."

I gasped. "A black man? For president of the United States?"

"Yeah." He laughed at my shock. "And we have vehicles that fly through the sky."

"Like birds?" Might he be joking?

"Huge birds. We call them airplanes." He reached into his pocket and drew out the small piece of black slate. "We can talk into a machine and people can hear us far away." He slipped it into my palm. "It's called a phone."

This object was a machine? How could that be? It was smaller than a slice of bread, as light as a serving spoon, and had no handles or moving parts. This "phone" looked rather fragile and useless to me.

"How far away can you hear?"

"Thousands of miles. Maybe even on the moon. I'm not sure."

"The moon?" I handed it back to him.

"Yeah. We've been there, too."

I checked his expression carefully to see if he was teasing me. He appeared ready to burst into laughter at any moment. So perhaps he was. Certainly I didn't believe him, though I wouldn't admit it. Yet I loved being here with him, secluded, listening to his impossible, magical tales.

"Do you talk to your friends on your phone?"

"Not much. I mostly use my phone to play games or listen to music."

"How do you get musicians in that small box?"

He shook his head. "You wouldn't understand."

I jerked as if his comment was a slap. He was correct, of course. I couldn't understand his world. Couldn't even know the difference between truth and joking. But it hurt all the same. I shifted away. "Indeed."

"Hey, I didn't mean that the way it sounded."

I had no response.

He moved until our knees nearly touched. "Tell me what you do for fun."

You wouldn't understand. I swallowed the unworthy retort and pondered what else to say. There was little time for fun in my life. "I stroll in the garden."

"Still sounds like work to me."

"I suppose it is. But there are so many interesting things to see outside. I like to be in nature. I like to study plants. That makes the garden fun."

"What else?"

I met his gaze. He had beautiful eyes. I couldn't remain cross while they smiled at me so warmly.

"Independence Day comes in three weeks. We take the entire day off and celebrate."

"Doing what?"

"The highlight of the day is a village-wide dinner. After spending the afternoon feasting, we spend the evening dancing." Anticipation rippled through me. "Of course, we hold the races in the morning before the heat makes it unbearable."

"What kind of races?" He hunched over, his elbows resting on his knees.

"Horse races and foot races. I especially enjoy watching the gentlemen run. Do you race?"

"On my bike." His face grew thoughtful.

"Are you good?"

"Pretty good. I have a big race coming up at the end of July." He picked up a stray branch lying nearby and stripped the bark, one section at a time. With a sharp fling, he tossed each strip into the stream. "I have to train extra hard. Most of my competitors started biking at an early age. I didn't start until I was thirteen."

His voice had rarely held such a tense edge when speaking with me. This topic had created a curious change in him.

"If you like biking so much, why did you wait until thirteen to compete?"

He flung another strip of bark. "I was fat."

The years since had altered him profoundly, then, for he had a strong, lean body. "You are not fat now."

"I had a lot of help." His head swiveled toward me. "My aunt pushed me into trying all kinds of sports until I found something I really liked. Since my father loves mountain biking, he talked me into giving it a shot—and got me hooked. We'd go on rides together and I pedaled off the weight. Solved a bunch of my issues."

I nodded with empathy, recognizing the hardened look of remembered suffering. "How peculiar. In my world, only the upper class can afford to be fat. It's a reason to be envied, not despised."

"Yeah, well, it sucks to be a fat kid in my century. You're treated like total shit."

I flinched at the harsh language but held my tongue. Here was something that had not changed across the centuries. People still found ways to keep others in their places.

The mixing of classes was what I loved about Independence Day. Villagers filled the lane, each eager to celebrate. For one day, a man's speed or a woman's baking received more praise than the size of their purse.

"Do you know what I like best about Independence Day?"

"What?"

"Country dances." I stood. "Would you like to try?"

He stood, too. "No."

"You don't like them?"

"No. I mean..." He shook his head. "I've never tried one. But I have tried square dancing, and I don't like it."

"You will like country dances if I am your partner."

"I don't think that'll make a difference."

He had the look of a petulant boy. I gave him an amused smile. "It is understandable to fear doing poorly at new skills."

"Excuse me? I'm not afraid."

I patted my hand over my mouth, hiding a pretend yawn. "Merciful heavens, I am tired. I believe I shall go."

"Wait." He caught me by the elbow. "Maybe—"

"Please, Mark." With a reproving look, I gently disengaged my arm from his grasp. "Do not concern yourself. I withdraw the request."

CHAPTER FOURTEEN

EVERY GUY'S DREAM

Unbelievable. Susanna was using reverse psychology on me, and it hadn't even been invented yet.

Even worse, it was working. "Stay, Susanna. I'll do the damn dance."

She brightened immediately. "Excellent." She looked around our surroundings. "Where shall we try?"

The cave was too rocky and uneven. "Out here?" I took a step onto the narrow ledge at the base of the bluff.

She caught my arm, yanked me back into the shadows, and clamped a hand to my lips. "Do not speak," she whispered, her body wedged between mine and the damp wall.

I didn't know why we were here, but I wasn't complaining. I braced my hands on either side of her head and leaned into her warmth.

A few seconds passed before I heard anything. Someone was running on the path above us. The footsteps stopped on the bluff.

Susanna was as still as a statue. The pounding of her heart was the only sign she was tense.

Boots crunched, stamped, and then took off, their thuds fading fast.

She relaxed.

I didn't move except my hands, which dropped to her upper arms to steady her. Damn, Susanna had seriously toned biceps. No wonder rock-climbing was so easy for her.

"Mark," she said in a disapproving voice, "you may release me."

"Sorry." The whole *no touching* thing was a pain to remember. I backed up and watched as she stepped into the open. "How did you know someone was coming?"

"The night creatures." She gazed down the creek. "Birds and insects may alter their tunes when a person approaches."

I'd never noticed. "Do you know who it was?"

"My master's son, Jedidiah Pratt."

I'd forgotten about the Pratt kids. "How old is he?"

"Fourteen." She studied the bluff as if measuring its height.

"What's he like?"

"He would be kind if he were another man's son."

When she said stuff like that, I didn't know how to react. I wanted to be pissed on her behalf, but she didn't seem like someone who'd accept sympathy.

"What was he doing up there?"

"Jedidiah spies on me. Not well, as you can see. His father wants to ensure I do not meet young men on my walks."

"Except you do."

"They mustn't find that out." She glanced over her shoulder and smiled sadly. "Perhaps I should go now."

"No, you shouldn't. You asked me to dance, and that's what we're going to do."

"The ledge is too narrow."

I pointed. "The path on the other side has a flat section."

"Your side?" She nibbled on a knuckle, eying the pouring water with suspicion.

"Now who's afraid?"

She sniffed primly. "Let's go, then."

I passed through the falls first and offered a hand to help a wary Susanna to cross. While I halted on the widest part of the dirt trail, she lingered behind, half-turned toward the falls, sneaking a peek at her side.

However long it took, I could wait.

"What's that odor?" she asked.

"Like what?"

"It smells of smoldering refuse." She rubbed her arms. "The scent clings to my skin."

Her world smelled like compost to me. Mine smelled like garbage to her. "That's just the way it is here."

"You have many marvels in your century, but none to sweeten the air? I shall do my best to tolerate it." She strode forward and planted herself squarely before me. "All right. Imagine there are other couples."

Okay, I'd agreed to do this, but I hadn't agreed to enjoy it. "I don't want to imagine that."

"Hush. I shall not permit you to spoil my fun." She gave me a hopeful smile. "Please, Mark. I love to dance."

I felt like a total jerk. "Okay. I'm yours. Let's do it."

"Thank you. Now, you stand over there."

I backed up a few feet and crossed my arms.

"Good. We're ready." She curtsied and remained low. "First, you must honor me."

"What does that mean?"

"Bow."

That was stupid. "You can get up now."

"Not until you honor me."

I waited. So did she.

"Damn." I bowed.

"Excellent." She rose. "Now, take both my hands. Circle left."

Clop, clop, clop.

"Circle right."

Clop, clop, clop.

"You have all the delicacy of a cow. Might you try a bit harder?"

"I'll try when we get to the fun part."

She gave the 1796 version of eye-rolling. "Clasp opposite hands. Circle for four paces. Change direction."

We repeated the steps several times. With each circuit, she upped the speed until we were practically running.

"What do you think?" she asked when we stopped, looking happy and tired and ready for another round.

Country dances were too much effort. I liked dancing in my world better. "There isn't enough contact."

"That isn't true. Our hands were clasped for the whole of the dance."

"In my century, the guy and the girl touch everywhere."

"Everywhere?" She blushed.

"Yeah." This would be my second chance to hold her—only this time, she wasn't upset. I stepped closer and held out my hands, not smiling anymore, ready for some serious contact. "Let me show you how we dance."

She looked up at me, her face half-shadowed, her hands slipping into mine. "That is fair."

"We'll be hugging, sort of," I said, wording the instructions as gently as possible, controlling the urge to grab her. I didn't want to scare her off.

"All right."

"Why don't you start by putting your hands on my shoulders?" When I felt the light touch of her fingers through the fabric of my shirt, I dropped mine to her waist.

We merged together and swayed, our feet barely moving. I could feel the stiff ridges in her corset. Curious now, I let my fingers roam her back and sides. The damn thing was unending, like a fence guarding some of the girl's best parts. I'd bet corsets drove colonial guys crazy.

She whispered, "It seems to me this is merely a way to engage in a most improper embrace."

"Oh, yeah." I slid my hands to her hips. Much better. Nothing but thin cloth between my hands and her skin.

"Mark?"

"Uh-huh?"

"I shouldn't permit such liberties."

"But you will anyway?"

"Indeed. I find it quite intriguing."

"Good." I smiled. "Lay your head against me and relax."

Long minutes passed and still we danced, holding each other. It was weird. And nice. And I wasn't ready for it to end.

"Hello?" a familiar voice called from the top of the trail. "Mark?"

Susanna and I sprang apart and glanced up the hill where a figure stood, outlined against the sky.

"Holy shit." I stepped in front of Susanna.

"Who is it?" she said, her fists against my back. "Is this your girlfriend?"

"*Ex*-girlfriend. And yeah, it's Alexis."

"You won't want her to see me. I shall go."

Before I could respond, Susanna hopped across the rocks and jumped through the falls. But instead of making straight for the rock wall, she turned and stared, unsmiling.

Did she think I was ashamed of her? I wasn't. I didn't want the two of them to meet, but that wasn't because of Susanna.

"Mark?" Alexis was directly behind me now.

"What?"

She linked her arm through mine. "Who was that girl with you?"

"A friend."

"A friend you dance with?"

I drew my arm away from hers. "Okay, then, a really good friend."

Alexis wrinkled her nose. "Where did she go?"

Even though I was pissed that Alexis had tracked me down, her arrival had revealed something interesting. "You can't see her?"

"No. Can you?"

Susanna stood on the other side of the falls, her image clear to me. "She moves fast."

"Whatever." Alexis caught my arm again, turning her back on the falls. "How do you know her?"

Great. I'd have to come up with a half-truth I might need to remember. "She lives around here."

"Where does she get her clothes? The Pentecostal Thrift Store?"

"Not cool, Alexis." I glanced toward the cave. It was empty now. I started up the trail, Alexis hanging on beside me.

"You're not training tonight." She sounded like she was accusing me of a crime.

"I finished earlier." When we reached the greenway, I hesitated, not sure what would be the polite thing to do. I knew what I wanted—to go home alone. "Where's your car?"

"Parked at the entrance to Umstead." She gestured vaguely in the direction of my house. "Can I walk home with you? I'd like to talk."

At some level, this was surreal. Alexis McChord didn't need to beg. Ever. She was hot, rich, and had parents who didn't check up on her. She was every guy's dream. "About what?"

"Us."

"There is no 'us' anymore."

She stalked away a few paces, flung out her arms, and let them drop against her thighs with a smack. Then she spun around to face me, lips thinned to a slash of bright pink. "I went out on a date last night."

That was fast, so fast it pissed me off. It had barely been a week since she had asked me to try again. What was up with her? Was I really so easy to get over? Of course, whoever the guy was, she wasn't hooked on him yet, because she was here with me.

"I doubt he'd be real happy to know where you are right now."

"He won't find out."

"I'm sure." Okay, done with this conversation. I glanced at my watch, hoping she would get the message.

"Don't you want to know who?"

Of course I did, but no way would I ask. "No."

"Keefe Halligan."

I couldn't think of anyone I'd hate more to see her dating. "Good luck with that."

"He's a jerk. We won't go out again."

I clenched my jaw and fought off the desire to smile. It was none of my business who she dated, but I was real glad it wouldn't be Keefe.

Her fingers combed through her hair, messing it up, a sign she was near tears and didn't want me to see them. "Have you changed your training schedule?"

No need to ask why Alexis wanted to know. I stared down the dirt trail, even though Susanna was long gone. "For my friend?"

"Yes. Have you changed for her?"

"A little." Until Alexis asked the question, I hadn't thought about it, but she was right. I used to train in the evenings, and now I rode in the afternoons. The heat didn't matter because I'd do whatever it took to fit my schedule around Susanna.

Alexis pressed her fists to her eyes, but tears seeped out anyway. "Why did you change for her and not me?"

I didn't know how to answer. Instead, I took her lightly in my arms and let her cry, right there in the middle of the greenway, with dozens of people strolling past, talking on their cells and walking their dogs.

And I felt bad for Alexis, but nothing more.

Another Friday, another day off. No yard work for paying customers or grandparents. I could do whatever I wanted.

Today's goal was information.

Marissa had suggested the North Carolina State Archives or the Raleigh Historical Society as good places to look for information on eighteenth century Wake County. I hopped on my bike and headed downtown. It took longer than I planned, but—with parking spaces impossible to find and a bike rack directly out front—taking the bike paid off overall.

When the historical society opened at ten, I was waiting.

A guy about Marissa's age unlocked the door, three minutes late. "Can I help you?"

"Sure." I had to look up at him—not something I was used to. But this guy was big. Football tackle big. "I'm looking for information on Worthville, North Carolina."

"Not familiar with that, dude." He shrugged his shoulders and lumbered through a warped doorframe into a gift shop.

I followed. "It was a town in Wake County around 1800. While George Washington was president."

He puffed his lips out and shook his head. "That's a new one on me. Just a second." He walked to a narrow stairwell. "Mamie, ever heard of a place called Worthville?"

A woman shouted back, "Who wants to know?"

"Some kid."

Kid. Right.

"Be there in a sec, Randall."

The guy turned around, shrugged, and resumed his guardian post at a desk by the front windows.

I wandered around the gift shop, looking at the items. There were thick books, crocheted doilies, and Christmas ornaments. Not sure why anyone would want the Raleigh Trolley hanging from their tree, but this gift shop had them, just in case.

An elderly woman exploded into the room, presumably Mamie. She was as small as Randall was big. She had on a red spandex skirt and a sheer white top and wore her hair in a weird style, like someone had pinned a bird's nest to the top of her head.

"Hi," she said through bright red lips. "You're the one who wants to know about Worthville?"

"Yeah." I couldn't look away from her hair. "Can you help?"

"Sure can. Follow me."

We crossed into an exhibit hall. She headed straight for a blown-up reproduction of an old map. "This shows Wake County at the end of the eighteenth century."

I studied it, trying to orient myself. The Neuse River made a diagonal slice across the county. Raleigh was a little square near the center. I tracked north along the river to a tiny squiggly line where Rocky Creek should be.

And there it was. I shivered.

"The dark blotch northwest of the capital is Worthville." Her brown eyes peered sharply at me. "We don't receive too many requests for information about that town. What do you want to know?"

The position on the map was perfect. Of course. No more than a mile or so from where I lived, and where Whisper Falls was located.

"Why did it vanish?"

"A tornado." She traced the area around the falls with her finger. "It struck the county in 1805. Wave after wave of thunderstorms. Most communities did fine. Not Worthville. The town was flattened. A few townsfolk died the same day and many more over the next few weeks from their injuries. Very sad." Her face wrinkled with detached grief.

1805. Nine years after 1796. I let out a noisy, relieved breath. "How many survived?"

"I don't think any family was left fully intact." She removed her purple-rimmed glasses, cleaned them on the tail of her gauzy white shirt, and pushed them back on. "The newspaper reported a couple of eyewitness accounts. Most homes along the main street and the meetinghouse were destroyed. So was the mill. I think it must've broken their spirits, because no one stayed to rebuild. The villagers scattered to other places."

It was eerie to stand there and stare up at that map. Of Susanna's friends and family, how many would be gone in nine more years?

"I couldn't find the cause of the disappearance online."

"The *Raleigh Register* from that decade hasn't been completely digitized yet." She walked over to a glass display case and pointed. "We have some editions here, though nothing as late as 1805. They have it on microfilm in the State Archives if you're interested."

I was interested, way more than I would've predicted. "I'll be heading over there soon."

She looked at me with open curiosity. "How did you hear about Worthville?"

I'd anticipated the question and had a vague answer prepared. "I ride my mountain bike out around Umstead Park, so I've done a little research on the area and stumbled across info about Worthville."

"It's fascinating, I know. In 1805, they called the storm a hurricane because they didn't have a better word for it. But we're reasonably certain it was a tornado. It must've been terrifying. No warning. A sudden, horrific noise—and their lives changed forever." She moved to another glass case filled with various bars of twisted iron. "Have you seen the mill ruins or the graveyard?"

"No."

"They're deep in the woods of Umstead. I know it's a huge park, but you can always ask one of the rangers for directions." She gestured in invitation. "Anything else you would like to know?"

I nodded. "What was life like for indentured servant girls back then?"

"In the Carolinas or farther north?"

"Does it make a difference?"

"Immensely. Women in this state were generally more advanced than their northern sisters. Carolina women would've had better lives at all levels of society. It's a source of great pride to us." Mamie smiled with satisfaction.

If sixteen-hour workdays and regular beatings were better, I hated to think what life would've been like in the North.

"I'm talking about here."

"Well, naturally, the lives of indentured servants would've been harsh by our standards. Brutal, even. But it was a system that met its purpose. The servants received an education, and their masters received cheap labor."

"How were the servants treated?"

"It varied by master. As well as could be expected for those who survived."

I frowned at her, chilled at the implication. "What do you mean?"

"An inexcusable percentage lost their lives before reaching the end of their contracts. They were literally worked to death. In most cases, though, the local townsfolk were motivated to keep the treatment tolerable. The system would've fallen apart if the majority of servants had died.

There are plenty of documents available on the State Archives website if you want more details."

"Thanks." I turned to go, then hesitated. "Did anyone record indentures?"

"Certainly. The Wake County Register of Deeds has a few images available online, and the State Archives will have originals."

"Thanks." I'd hit the county website first to see what I could find.

"My pleasure." She walked with me to the front door. "This is one of the more obscure set of questions I've had in a while. Are you planning to present this in a class project?"

"No, you wouldn't believe me if I told you why."

The first thing I did when I got home was check out the county website, and I totally won the lottery. There was a document listing the families who had lived in Worthville at the time of its final census. I hit the PRINT key. Definitely had to show this to Susanna if she'd let me.

A quick glance at the clock put me into action. She could be there any time now. I ran down the stairs and skidded to a stop in the kitchen. There was an odor that was vaguely familiar but out of place in our house. Grease—the kind that fried things and made them more delicious than steam. In the three years since I'd lost the last of the weight, my mom had avoided grease for months on end, even though my race training made it unlikely I'd ever be fat again. So I was surprised and happy to smell it now.

I walked up behind my mother and looked over her shoulder. "Is it almost time to eat?"

"A few more minutes." Mom stirred something in a pot. "Why? Going out?"

"Uh-huh." The pot held potatoes, and there was a stick of butter nearby, a promising sign. I opened a cabinet and grabbed a couple of plates.

"With Alexis?"

I shuddered. She was the last person I wanted to spend time with. "*No.*"

My mother twisted from the stove and stared, a curious squint to her eye. Must've answered more loudly than I meant to.

"She called last night asking for you."

"And you told her where I was." Mystery solved.

"Is that a problem?"

"Not really." I shrugged. Might as well get the subject over with. It could prevent more surprise visits on the greenway. "Alexis dumped me on May twenty-third."

"Prom night?"

"Yeah." I half-sat on the edge of the table, faced my mom, and tried to ignore how hard my stomach clenched at the memory. "During the first dance, we started arguing about whether I'd go on vacation with her. And when she finally got it that I really meant no, she broke up with me and left."

"She left the dance floor?"

"And the ballroom."

"Ouch. Were you in the middle of the floor by yourself?"

"No. Forty other couples were out there with me." That had been an awful moment. Not that I remembered precisely everything about it, or anything.

Mom muttered a single, vicious word under her breath.

I laughed. "Did you just say 'bitch'?"

"You weren't supposed to hear that." She swung back to her pot, spoon banging wildly.

I crossed to where she stood, wrapped her in a hug, and gave her a noisy, smacking kiss on the cheek. "Go, Mom!"

She laughed as she threw the stick of butter into the potatoes. "Are you upset about the break-up?"

"No." Too loud again. "I'm fine with it," I said with greater control.

"How come?"

Mom and I rarely had a conversation this long about my social life, so it was a little strange talking about it with her now. "I need to stay focused on the Carolina Challenge."

"Good. I wish you'd told me earlier. We've been ready for you to move on. Alexis wasn't right for you."

"Why not?"

A little laugh. "She's pretty self-centered."

"I thought that was fairly standard among kids my age."

"It is, but Alexis takes it to an extreme." Mom sighed. "The endless texts are over."

"To me?"

"No, to me."

I grabbed some silverware and slapped it on the table beside the plates, then frowned in the general direction of my mother's back. I hadn't known that Alexis texted my mother, and I didn't much like knowing it now.

"Why did she text you?"

"To find out where you were."

Liking it even less. "Did you tell her?"

"If I was ticked at you, sure."

Last Tuesday at work—that was how Alexis had found me. Well, fine. The whole thing worked out in the end. Alexis had her pick of guys, I had no one harassing me about my schedule, and Mom had fewer texts.

"Why didn't you say something?"

"If you'd known, would you have made an issue of it with her?"

"Probably not." I sniffed, more interested in food than ex-girlfriends. "What are we having?"

"Fried chicken. Fried okra. Mashed potatoes. Apple pie with ice cream."

My *first* favorite home-cooked meal.

"What's the occasion?" I picked up a wooden spoon and sampled the potatoes. Oh, yeah.

"Your dad comes home tomorrow from his business trip. We need to take care of our junk food fix before he returns." She spun around with surprising speed and grabbed the neck of my T-shirt. "We'll keep this meal a secret between the two of us."

Tell my health freak father? Not a chance.

"I won't say a word." I wanted this meal to be repeated as often as possible.

We ate in silence. It was too good for talking.

By the time dessert was ready, the light was fading fast.

"Hey, Mom, I'm about to head out. Can I take the last drumstick with me?"

"Sure. Where are you going?" She stacked the dirty dishes and carried them to the sink.

"On the greenway."

I tucked a flashlight and the stapled print-outs under my arm, then wrapped the drumstick in a paper towel. So Susanna could eat her fill.

"It's a little late." Her narrowed gaze took in all the stuff I carried.

"I'll be careful."

A quick check of my watch made me groan. I ran the entire distance, crossing my fingers Susanna was still there.

I saw her outlined through the falls long before I arrived. She returned my wave. Her figure seemed less like a trick of the light the closer I went.

"Hey." I took a flying leap and sailed through the falls.

She smiled, her gaze going to the items in my hands. "What did you bring?"

"Leftover chicken." I held up the sheets and braced. The second item might be less welcome. "And some information about what happens to Worthville."

CHAPTER FIFTEEN

THE DANGER OF KNOWLEDGE

Mark's betrayal tore at my gut. I never asked anyone for anything. Yet I'd expected Mark, of all people, to honor my wishes. I should not like to have friends if this was how it felt when they wounded me.

"I asked you not to find out. Was I not clear? Did you misunderstand?"

His lips thinned into a straight line. "I didn't misunderstand."

"Then why did you persist?"

"I figured you would change your mind."

"You were wrong," I said, enunciating each word through gritted teeth.

"Sorry. I won't make that mistake again." He shuffled the papers, slid them into his pocket, and nodded toward a boulder. "Want to sit?"

Did he truly believe we could go on as before while his actions lay between us?

"No, I do not want to sit."

"Okay." He gazed out at the creek.

I didn't know what to do next. I couldn't bear to be with him. And I couldn't bear to leave.

"Do you think me too simple-minded to make good choices?"

"There's nothing simple about you." His hands clenched and released. "In my world, girls say stuff all the time they don't mean."

"Perhaps that is protection against gentlemen who do not respect their judgment."

"Come on. You know better than that." His voice sounded weary. "I respect your judgment. I just wanted to be prepared."

"For what, precisely?"

"When I was dating Alexis, she would say 'no' one minute and 'yes' the next. I never knew what to expect, so I always arrived ready for anything." He took a step closer.

I flinched away. "How does this apply to me?"

"I figured if you didn't want to see the data, I could keep it in my pocket. If you changed your mind, I'd have it with me."

"But you know what happened to my village. I can see the truth of it in your eyes."

"You're right." He stared at me, stony-faced.

"The fate of my village separates us. As long as you know something that I do not, we cannot be equals. You have forced me to decide between receiving knowledge I do not want or being the lesser friend."

"Okay, you're pissed at me. Got it. Can we move on?"

"Indeed, we can. What will our next topic be?"

He muttered a word. It sounded suspiciously like "shit."

A gust of wind brushed past our granite hideaway, heavy with the scent of wood smoke. In the gathering dusk, the creek and forest had faded to silvery shapes and shadows. It held a different kind of beauty.

I leaned against the rock wall and closed my eyes. The minutes ticked by slowly while we waited in a painful silence. As the sense of betrayal ebbed, disappointment flowed into its void. A better emotion—disappointment. I knew it well. I had practice in moving past it.

"Let us speak next of your friend Alexis."

"That wouldn't be my choice of topic."

"I can ignore preferences, too." I pushed away from the wall, chin high. "Did your friend Alexis seek you out because she had changed her mind about something?"

He tensed. "She wants us to date again."

"How did you answer?" I waited, oddly anxious.

"I told her no. We had too many problems to fix. Alexis is part of my past."

Relief rippled through me. When the girl had taken Mark's arm, a wicked envy had sliced through me like a sharp blade. She was a beautiful creature with her wispy golden hair and smooth, golden skin. Perhaps all the girls in his world were as lovely and confident. Would I ever touch him so casually?

"Do we have too many problems to fix?"

He shook his head immediately. "No, Susanna. I didn't mean to upset you so badly, but I had to know what might happen."

"I shall move to Raleigh soon."

"You could come back to visit."

The statement lingered in the air, hinting at the disaster to come. He knew the when and the how. What else had he learned? What stories did his information tell? I frowned at him as temptation built. Was this what he'd expected—that my resolve would waver?

He crossed his arms. "Are there really thirty indentured servants and slaves in Worthville?"

Irritation flared and then quickly died away. In spite of my protests otherwise, I was intrigued. "Thirty is possible. There are not so many at present, but no doubt the number will grow with the years."

"How long have you been indentured?"

"Since I was ten."

"That sucks."

"Sucks?" He had used this word before, almost as if it were a curse.

"Sucks is slang in my world."

"Slang?"

"Yeah. Slang is where you take a word that means one thing and use it to mean something else. Sometimes the opposite."

"A word can mean something different than what it means?"

"Sure." A corner of his mouth twitched. "Like when we say something is fine, it probably isn't fine at all."

"Can a slang word retain its original meaning?"

"Yes."

"So if I say 'fine,' it can mean 'fine' or 'not fine.'"

"Exactly."

I shuddered. How difficult that must be—never to trust the meaning of words. "I should think your conversations become quite treacherous."

"Most of the time, you can tell the difference by looking at the person."

"What if you cannot see the person as they are speaking?"

"Then you're screwed."

"Screwed?"

"It's slang for *you have problems*." He averted his eyes. "It has another meaning, too, which I'm not saying."

I would remember *screwed* and ask again later. "Explain *sucks*."

"If something is terrible, it sucks."

"Do you think it is terrible for parents to bind out their children?"

Mark looked at me, sympathy sobering his face. "At the age of ten? Yeah."

We agreed. It had sucked. It sucked at ten and, with a master such as Mr. Pratt, it had sucked every day since.

Mark's compassion invited me closer. We had been apart long enough. I offered my hand.

He linked our fingers firmly. "I'm not apologizing any more for finding stuff out. I'll do what's necessary to keep you safe." His voice rang with intensity. "Even if I piss you off."

I swallowed back the whisper within me, a desire that wouldn't stay quiet. Perhaps I did wish to know what he'd discovered. The information was here, within reach. All I had to do was ask and I would know the town's fate, whether it had been abandoned or destroyed.

The temptation was too strong to be denied. Perhaps just one question. "When does Worthville end?"

"1805."

I would be gone, but so many others would not. I had to know more. "How?"

"A storm."

It would have to be a fierce and terrifying storm to destroy a town. If I read his document, I would learn more about the villagers. How they had fared. Their marriages and babies. Had my mother remained a widow? Had my sister moved away or stayed here to marry?

Tension gripped me like a vise, until I could hardly breathe. Would I be able to face the people involved later, knowing their fates?

"What type of information do you have on those sheets?"

"Records from the 1800 census."

Four years hence. "Does my name appear?"

"It contains heads of household with the number of family members, slaves, and servants. There are mostly men's names."

I dropped his hand and backed up a few paces away, preparing myself. To learn the future was frightening, but I wouldn't stop now—not when I was so close.

"I am ready. Please tell me what you found."

He drew in a deep breath. Papers rustled briefly. "There are twelve families listed. First is Betsy Drake with one servant."

It would be someone new. Mary Whitfield would likely be gone and married in four years.

I nodded for more.

"Next on the list is…Reuben Elliott and wife. No children."

"Ah." Whom would he marry? Someone from Worthville? Or would he find his bride farther away, perhaps in Hillsborough? I was glad for him.

"The third is Robert Foster, wife, two servants, and nine children."

They had eight at present. Most of the Foster children were younger than Phoebe. And soon there would be another.

I nodded.

"Jethro Pratt…"

I clenched my fists, nerves quivering under my skin.

"…wife, four children, an indentured servant, and a slave."

An icy shiver rolled down my spine. Had I heard wrong? "Did you say four children?"

He looked again. "Yes. Four."

"Look for Jedidiah Pratt's name. Is he a head of a household in 1800?"

Mark shook his head.

"What about Jacob Worth? Is he listed with a wife?"

"Not on this sheet."

I grabbed it out of Mark's hands and searched the names. Jethro was the only Pratt, and he had four children.

"What's wrong, Susanna?"

"I expected six." I could barely choke out the words.

"Damn."

Were two of my babies gone? Which ones?

Already the danger of knowledge had struck, but I would hesitate no more about learning the future, not where the children were concerned. "Can you find the names?"

"Maybe."

"Please try." I reached for the wall. I wanted to see my little ones without delay. To ensure they were safe in their beds. "I shall not return again until after the Sabbath. Might that be enough time to learn more?"

"I don't know. I can't make any promises." His voice softened. "Hey. Do you have favorites?"

I paused, one foot planted on the bottom rung of my rocky ladder. Could I name the two I loved most? Did something become more true once it was said aloud?

"Dorcas and John."

"Will you want me to tell you, even if it's bad?"

"You won't need to say a word. Your face will shout the tale."

Chapter Sixteen

Upper Body Strength

The garage was ablaze with light on Saturday at seven AM, and it couldn't have been because of my mother. She wasn't awake this early.

"Dad?" I called. He hadn't been here when I went to bed, so he must've taken a red-eye back from California.

My father poked his head out the door of the storage room. "Morning, Mark. How've things been?"

"Great." I nodded calmly, but inside I was smiling big. Everything flowed better when Dad was home.

"What about business?"

"It's great, too," I said, crossing to his side. "I have ten clients."

We shook hands before he pulled me into a manly, back-slapping hug. He was decked out in biking gear.

"Is it okay if I ride with you?"

It was more than okay. "Sure."

He carried his mountain bike out of the storage room. "What's the plan?"

I lifted mine down from its rack and checked it over. "How about the American Tobacco Trail?" I hadn't ridden on the ATT in a while, but the weather would be perfect for it today.

"Sounds good."

"Aren't you tired?"

"I slept on the plane."

That couldn't have been enough, but he still wanted to ride with me.

"Won't Mom wonder where you are when she gets out of bed?"

His lips twitched into a half-smile. "Your mother knows where I am." He smacked a switch on the wall, and the garage door rolled up. "Will we take the truck to one of the ATT parking lots?"

"Yeah, the one off I-40."

Soon we were cruising along the interstate. Dad slumped in the passenger seat, eyes shut.

"Are you sure about this?" I asked, hoping he was.

"Yeah. It's just better for my health if I don't watch you drive."

"Thanks."

He laughed.

I let him relax for a couple of minutes while I drummed up the guts to bring up the next subject. "Dad, I need to talk to you about Mom and Marissa."

"Might as well stop right there." He straightened in his seat, eyes open, arms crossed. "I'm staying out of that."

"I want to, but I can't, they won't let me."

"Yes, you can. You've got shoulders. Shrug them."

"Maybe you can shrug off Mom, but I can't."

"You're smart. You can figure out a way to not engage."

Right. "Dad, you haven't been here for the last couple of weeks. It's been pretty bad."

"What do you want me to do?"

"Tell her I hate being in the middle."

"She knows that."

"Yeah, but she might do something about it if you reminded her."

His only response was to grunt impatiently.

I pulled off I-40 and parked in the lot. Ten minutes later, we were riding south at an easy pace.

"What's the goal today, Mark?"

"Speed. Especially downhill. There are a few decent inclines a couple of miles ahead."

"Are they on the trail?"

"No."

"Good." He took a swig from his water bottle. "You might not know this, but when Marissa first opened her bank account, she gave me the password."

Interesting change of subject. I was curious where this was headed. "And…?"

"I can access all of her transactions. She hasn't written any checks to the University of Colorado."

"I see."

"I suspect you do."

"Have you told this to Mom?"

"Not yet."

"Look, Dad…"

"That's enough." He pedaled in concentration until we passed some pedestrians. "Your sister needs to tell us what's going on. It's her story, not yours. So don't say a word. Not to me. Not to your mom."

After my dad and I got home and cleaned up, my mother claimed him for the rest of the day. "Couple time," she called it. She had a to-do list a mile long, which seemed to make him happier than it would've made me. It involved a lot of driving on his part and shopping on hers.

I wouldn't be heading down to the falls tonight with Susanna busy until Monday. So I downloaded a movie and flopped on the couch to watch. But I had a hard time paying attention. My mind kept drifting to Susanna. While

I was slumped over being lazy, was she working? Avoiding punches?

Halfway through, I flicked the movie off. I needed to *do* something.

Unable to contain my restlessness, I jumped up and looked around until my attention landed on the computer. Might as well get on and check email. Carlton pinged me immediately.

Good, a distraction.

CARLTON: *what's up?*
ME: *nothing much*
CARLTON: *how's training?*
ME: *dad's home. he timed me today*
CARLTON: *and?*
ME: *not where I want it to be yet. how's your dad?*
CARLTON: *great. focused on his boat*
ME: *been skiing?*
CARLTON: *some. heard from alexis?*

Why did he keep asking about her? To piss me off? I had nothing else to say about Alexis. He knew that.

ME: *i saw her thursday*
CARLTON: *really?*
ME: *not something i would joke about*

There was a long pause—not the kind that meant he was typing a lot, but the kind that meant he didn't know how to respond. Carlton could come up with something funny faster than anyone I knew. So he was thinking something serious, which was strange and interesting.

CARLTON: *you saw alexis on thursday?*
ME: *i just said so*

CARLTON: *did you track her down?*
ME: *other way around. why?*
CARLTON: *doesn't sound like her*

I fell back against my seat and stared hard at the screen. What was going on here? Carlton was the only friend who'd stuck with me when everyone else sided with Alexis. How did he know whether something sounded like her? And why did he even care? The whole time I dated Alexis, he had complained that she was some kind of high-maintenance toddler we were babysitting, and avoided us whenever he could. He'd been happy when she dumped me.

ME: *since when do you know so much about alexis?*
CARLTON: *since I got to the beach. she's been texting me*
ME: *how often?*
CARLTON: *every day*

She had to be pumping Carlton for information about me, but it couldn't be doing her any good. I wasn't telling him anything she'd want to know.

ME: *what does she ask about?*
CARLTON: *the colonial girl. alexis claims halligan isn't involved*
ME: *alexis went on a date with him*
CARLTON: *she told you that?*
ME: *apparently so, since i know*
CARLTON: *she won't go out with him again*
ME: *don't care*
CARLTON: *alexis saw the colonial girl*
ME: *and?*
CARLTON: *now we know the girl isn't a ghost*
ME: *i already knew that*
CARLTON: *does colonial girl have a name?*
ME: *she does*

CARLTON: *and?*

I didn't want to tell him. It wasn't as if I was ashamed of her. Exactly the opposite. And I wasn't worried about trying to explain the falls or Worthville. There was no need to explain circumstances I never planned to bring up.

It was mostly about the friendship between me and Susanna. The wrong person could mess it up—and I wasn't sure who the wrong people were.

Why did I hesitate with Carlton? He was my best friend. If he were here, he would already know everything.

Of course, if he were here, I wouldn't be hanging out with Susanna.

CARLTON: *still there?*
ME: *yes*
CARLTON: *her name?*
ME: *marsh*
CARLTON: *her name is marsh?*
ME: *that's what i said*
CARLTON: *is she hot?*
ME: *yes*
CARLTON: *alexis doesn't think so*
ME: *alexis wouldn't*
CARLTON: *got some bad news*
ME: *don't care*
CARLTON: *yes you do. alexis says halligan's racing on grandfather mountain in 4 weeks*

So Keefe had decided to go through with it. As much as that race would be great training, it was still too close to the Carolina Challenge for me. I'd be afraid I couldn't recover fast enough.

This conversation was all screwed up. Carlton was supposed to be getting info out of me. Instead, I was getting a lot out of him—and I wished I wasn't.

ME: *can we stop talking about alexis and halligan?*
CARLTON: *i gotta go anyway*
ME: *later*

The chat left me pissed off. I'd lost interest in the computer, in the movie, in everything I could think of. I needed to work off the irritation, but it was too late to ride. I left the rec room, stood in the hall, and tried to figure out how to settle down. The garage door whined open, signaling the return of my parents. I didn't want to face them, either. My mom would be bubbling-over happy, and I wasn't in the mood for that.

I crossed into the weight room and stared at the equipment. Yeah, this was what I needed—to work out. I reset the weights on one of the machines and sat down.

Tonight's goal—upper body strength.

Wrong. Tonight's real goal was sweating off Carlton's preoccupation with my ex.

CHAPTER SEVENTEEN

A BROODING DARKNESS

Mark's news weighed heavily on my heart.

All weekend, I watched the Pratt children with anxious eyes, bereft at the thought of losing any of my little ones. The knowledge made me indulgent. I found it difficult to refuse any request.

Dorcas burst into the kitchen on Monday morning dragging Delilah behind her. "May we walk with you to the village?"

"Indeed, yes. I should like the company."

I packed the last few items in a pail and covered it with a cloth. Jedidiah had lessons at the tutor's house this morning, and it fell to me to deliver his meal. Deborah coveted this chore—and a glimpse of the much-admired Jacob Worth— but she would forfeit the errand today. Her mother had displayed an uncharacteristic passion for teaching her the art of spinning.

Dorcas and Delilah ran ahead, skipping and holding hands. Had we been walking at a normal pace on the most direct route, we would reach the village in a few minutes. But we weren't interested in a quick trip. It was a beautiful day, worth enjoying, and we did everything in our power to lengthen the journey. First, there was a detour through the woods to pick blackberries amid a vicious array of thorns. Next we stood on the sturdy bridge over Rocky Creek to watch the water bubbling past. Then we managed a stop by the well to cool our scratches before wandering through the shade at the side of the lane.

As we passed the Widow Drake's house, a figure appeared in the open doorway.

"Hello," Mary Whitfield called with a wave. "What brings you to town?"

"I'm taking a meal to my master's son."

"May we talk a moment?"

"I'd like that." I turned to the little girls. "Shall we play here?"

"Oh, yes," Dorcas said. Delilah agreed with a nod. The two ran to a tree and promptly stomped around it in circles, Dorcas in the lead.

I joined Mary in the shade of the porch. "How do you like working with Mrs. Drake?"

"She's very kind. She teaches me to spin at present. Once I have it mastered, I shall try weaving." Mary held up reddened, calloused hands with a laugh. "They do look a sight."

"Indeed." I slid my fists into the pockets under my petticoat. My scarred hands looked far worse. "Have you seen much of the village?"

"The people are very kind." She rocked on her heels, the tips of her boots peeking in and out from under her petticoat. "Have you met the cooper's apprentice?"

"Reuben Elliott?" I eyed her speculatively. Was Mary interested in him? "Indeed, I have. A nice man."

"Is he promised to anyone?"

"Not that I've heard."

She nodded. "I find this village charming."

"Indeed." How many years did she have left on her contract? Would Reuben wait? Perhaps Mrs. Drake would release her early. I hoped it went well for them. "I shall see you at church on Sunday, Mary."

"No doubt."

I tramped down the steps and into the lane, calling Dorcas and Delilah to come with me.

The tutor had four students. From the window, we could see the boys bent over their papers, quills scratching. I circled to the rear of the property and knocked on the kitchen's door. The tutor's wife scowled as she took Jedidiah's pail.

The girls scampered ahead of me, down the dusty lane winding past the half-dozen buildings at the center of town. When they came to the place where the lane forked, they stopped.

"How long does it take to get to your mother's property?" Dorcas said, pointing down the road heading east from town.

"If you stay on the Raleigh Road for a twenty minute walk, you will come to my mother's farm."

"Who else lives with them?"

"No one."

"What do they grow?"

"They have a small garden, a horse, a cow, and chickens. The rest of the land is rented by another farmer." I shooed the girls forward. "It's nearly time for our meal, little ones."

"Shall we visit Papa first?" Dorcas asked.

Not waiting for my reply, the sisters ran through the narrow stand of trees hiding the mill from the rest of town. I followed at a distance.

When I arrived, I stuck my head in the door of the mill. It was quiet—an empty kind of quiet. Both millstones, the old one for grinding corn and the new one for grinding wheat, were extraordinarily clean. There had been no business here today.

The girls rushed past me, peeking around corners and down the stairs. As the emptiness penetrated their enthusiasm, their giddiness faded.

"He's not here." Dorcas huffed a mournful sigh. Delilah mourned, too.

"Perhaps he's running an errand."

"We can play hide and seek while we wait."

I shook my head vigorously. "This is a poor place to play a game."

Dorcas cupped a hand around her mouth and whispered in her little sister's ear. Both girls giggled as they darted through the door we had just entered.

"Girls, come back."

Their laughter ended abruptly.

I stood in the threshold, scanning the mill yard. "Girls, I am not amused. Come at once."

Silence greeted my calls.

Irritation didn't improve my seeking skills. I took a calming breath as I circled around the yard carefully, glancing behind the obvious hiding places. They weren't here. Had they run to the back?

I walked around to the opposite side of the mill and stood, hands on hips, surveying the area. Where might two little girls be?

Could they have reached the forest so quickly? I didn't think it likely.

That left the millpond and Rocky Creek. Tension showered over me like a cold rain. Did their silence have a more ominous source?

They could be hiding near the wall beside the sluice. I never approached it willingly, so strong was my fear of the water roaring down its chute. But if the girls had strayed too close, I had to check. Nerves prickled along my arms as I took hesitant steps nearer.

Something thumped near the sluice. I crept closer, gripped the wall, and peered behind.

My master glanced up with surprise. "Susanna?"

"Sir." I bobbed my head.

He picked up a shovel, stamped a bald spot of earth with his boot, and walked around the wall. "Have you come to visit with me?"

It was such an absurd question, I would've laughed if fear had not had me in its grasp.

"No, sir. We took Jedidiah's pail to the tutor's house. Dorcas and Delilah insisted we visit here on the return journey."

"Where are they?"

I had to choose an answer carefully. If he knew they hid from me, they would be punished and so would I. Even now, I could only hope they were wise enough to remain out of sight.

"They are hungry and have run ahead."

"Why are you not with them? And why have you come near the water?"

"I am not so very close to it." I clamped my lips shut.

He studied my face at length, until the scrutiny made me uncomfortable. "You haven't lost your fear of the water, have you? Not in all the years since your father passed."

"I am fine." I dropped my gaze to the ground, thinking hard. Were the girls safe? Did I risk their lives to avoid a few lashes of the switch?

No, truly, Dorcas was too clever. She must be hidden nearby, muffling Delilah's giggles, watching me and her father. I wished to spare her punishment for her disobedience.

But what if I was wrong?

My master moved closer to me and grasped my chin in his hard fingers, forcing me to look at him. "Do you often allow Delilah and Dorcas to run about Worthville without you?"

My mouth went dry as my mind sought a plausible reason. "They are nearby. I thought to catch my breath in the shade before following them home."

The intense stare continued, but his fingers released me. I gave a perfunctory curtsy and turned to leave.

"Susanna?"

"Yes, sir?"

"I want you to stay."

I hesitated. "Right now?"

"In October. I'm accustomed to you. Don't leave at the end of your indenture."

Not leave? Was he mad? I shook my head, too stunned to respond.

"We'll pay you a fair wage once your contract ends."

I shuddered. Could he not discern how deeply I longed to flee his house?

"I must decline your offer. I shall leave on my birthday as planned."

"You won't find a better position."

I bit back a laugh at his foolish claim. Despite being nephew to our town's magistrate, no sane villager or farmer in the area would apprentice their children to the Pratts. A *worse* job was not possible.

"I do not worry about my chances."

A brooding darkness settled over his features. "Is that so?"

His expression made me nervous. Backing away from him, I said loud enough for two little listening girls to hear, "I am heading to the house."

"Your plan to move to Raleigh is sheer madness. No one will want a girl of your age with no references."

Was he right? I didn't think so, but I couldn't be sure. "It is a risk I am willing to take."

"You won't find a welcome at your mother's home, either."

I frowned. "How can you know such a thing?"

"Mr. Shaw will marry your mother this fall. Once he moves into her farmhouse, there will be no room for you or Phoebe."

"When did he tell you this?"

"Yesterday after church. Your mother has convinced him that Phoebe shouldn't tend children. He will bind Phoebe out." Mr. Pratt smiled—a mean smile, like a snake about to strike at its prey. "If Susanna Marsh must leave our house, perhaps Phoebe Marsh will take her place."

A shrieking giggle pierced the air. Delilah erupted from the shadows behind the wood pile and ran toward us. "Papa, I should like for Phoebe to live at our house." She stopped at his side and looked up, beaming. "I was hiding from Susanna."

Dorcas plodded into the sunshine, her face flushed crimson. With wide, panicked eyes, she stared at me. There was no way to comfort her.

"You hid, did you, Delilah?" His fingers tousled her curls while his furious glare latched onto Dorcas. "I suppose you proposed the game to your little sister."

Dorcas nodded slowly, her lower lip trembling.

"After supper, you will await me behind the kitchen for your punishment."

Delilah looked from her father to her sister, let out a wail, and rushed to me, slamming into my legs, rubbing her face against my petticoat. I patted her shoulder absently. Her cries couldn't change the outcome that her ill-timed words had started, but it did hurt me that she recognized what lay ahead.

"And you, Susanna," my master said, in a conversational tone, "do you often lie about the disobedience of my children?"

"Yes, sir."

"You, too, may join me after supper." He smiled tightly. "Perhaps you should deliver Dorcas's punishment."

"I shall not." I lifted my chin, firmness in my response. He could threaten to beat me unconscious, but I wouldn't thrash Dorcas.

"Very well. It will be enough to have you watch."

CHAPTER EIGHTEEN

NEW OR BEAT-UP

Between mowing yards and training, there hadn't been time to hunt for the names of the Pratt children, especially since I didn't know where to start. But I wouldn't go to the falls empty-handed. Susanna was getting protein bars.

The Whole Foods store was crazy on Monday, as if everyone on this side of Raleigh had stopped in for heat-and-serve vegan meals. I walked past the deli and headed to the section devoted to energy bars. I liked to keep a stash on hand for those times when my parents forgot to get food I liked while grocery shopping. After today, Susanna would have a stash, too.

It was hard to know what she would like. Not peanut butter or chocolate. They might be too intense. Fruit might be good. Strawberry, apricot, or fig?

I got all three. She could toss them if she didn't like them.

After checking out, I walked out to the bike rack and stowed the stuff in my pack. As I was preparing to unlock the bike, I noticed a SALE sign on my mom's favorite store, Meredith Ridge Books.

A bookstore—where people bought novels.

The devil's missives.

Oh, yeah. Tonight, Susanna would have food *and* fiction.

It took about a millisecond for me to become obsessed with picking the perfect novel. I headed into the bookstore. The sci-fi section I could rule out. But what about the YA bestseller section?

I skimmed the titles, hoping for inspiration. It was a bust. Susanna wasn't likely to appreciate demons, cheerleaders, or zombies.

"May I help you?"

A clerk hovered at the end of aisle, which was convenient, for a change.

"Sure. I'm looking for a gift."

"For whom?"

"A girl."

"What age?"

"She's seventeen."

"Do you know what she likes?"

Here was the tricky part. I didn't, because Susanna didn't, either.

"She's been living in this strange outpost kind of place, where there aren't libraries. So she's probably open to almost anything."

"Fantasy? Dystopian?"

Okay, not specific enough. "I'm thinking late eighteenth-century novels. Maybe 1790s to 1810s."

"Ah, I see. *That* open." She wove her way to the back of the store and stopped. "Jane Austen? We have new copies, plus a few antique volumes."

I felt like smacking my head. "Perfect. Thanks." I waited to survey my options until the woman wandered away.

The bookcase had six shelves, one for each Austen title. There were dozens of copies of each book, organized from newest to most beat-up.

I read the blurbs. *Persuasion* won. Ships won out over creepy castles and afternoon teas every time.

So, new or beat-up? I picked up the oldest copy. Would this one feel the least strange to her? It had a torn-up leather binding. I checked the price and coughed. It wasn't cheap.

I carried my selection to the counter and slapped it down. The clerk smiled her approval.

After my afternoon training ride and cleanup routine, I went to the kitchen to make a sandwich. Mom walked in from the garage. Or maybe I should say, trudged in. Her face looked as gray as her scrubs. I now recognized the look. Someone at the hospice center had died. Someone she really cared about.

"Bad day, Mom?"

"Yes."

I caught her in a hug as she tried to walk by. "Want to talk about it?" I said into her hair.

"Uh-uh." She kissed my cheek and leaned back. "Did you just shave?"

"Yes." I sampled the results of my sandwich-fixing skills, which were exceptional.

She dropped her purse on the island and leaned a hip against the counter. "You're also wearing jeans."

I nodded. It was true.

"So, you're not training tonight?"

"Already done."

"Are you dating someone?"

"No. Will Dad be home soon?"

"In about an hour."

That was good. She wouldn't be home alone this evening.

I opened the fridge and snagged a bottle of water. Before I could close the door, she caught it and picked up the mayo and the roast beef from the counter. Really, she shouldn't do that. It wasn't responsible parenting to straighten my mess. Not that I was complaining, or anything.

"Are you hanging out with Carlton?"

"He's still with his dad."

"Oh, right. Then where do you go every evening?"

Concentrate on the sandwich and don't meet her eyes. "The greenway."

"I'm your mother. I've watched you lie for seventeen years. I know when you're avoiding the truth."

I gave her my best innocent puppy look. "I sit by the creek."

"Why?"

"To think. Or not think."

She snorted. "What are you not thinking about?"

Here, at least, was a safe topic. I didn't think about a lot of things. "Mostly Alexis."

"I thought you were over her."

"I am. Which is why I'm not thinking about her."

"Ah." She looked at her watch. "The greenway officially closes at dusk."

"Which is why this interruption is a problem for me."

She rolled her eyes and disappeared up the back stairs.

I slipped from the rear of the house, pushed through our gate, and emerged on the greenway. I was rarely out this early, so the number of people around at this hour surprised me a little. Couples pushed strollers. Joggers raced by, headphones on, oblivious to the rest of us. I strolled along the pavement with the Jane Austen book and tried to act like I didn't know how it found its way into my hand.

When I reached Whisper Falls, Susanna wasn't waiting on the other side. She had to come. I wanted to give her a real gift tonight.

But where was she? It couldn't be more than thirty minutes to sundown.

I stayed on my side and flopped on my favorite rock. Gross. Wet. The falls were kicking up some serious spray. I got up and wandered around the trail until I found a fallen log to sit on with a clear view of the falls.

Two minutes passed—two minutes of nothing occupying my attention except kamikaze mosquitoes and decaying leaves. Okay, I was bored. I flipped open *Persuasion* and turned to the first page.

The first sentence was incredibly long, one hundred words or more, with commas and semi-colons all over the place. English teachers today had to be upset over that sentence.

I read on.

Jane Austen might've put a lot of words in the first sentence, but those words were doing their job. The dad was a total jerk.

When I was halfway through the third page, I felt the wind stir and looked up. Whisper Falls shimmered, its spray dissipating. Were the falls letting me know she was on the way?

Through the window of water, I watched the cliff until the sound of approaching footsteps distracted me. From far down the creek, Susanna walked stiffly along the bank until she reached the falls. I rose.

She peered at me, her hands clenched against her waist. "Have you any news about the children?"

Chapter Nineteen

Written In Bruises

He hopped through the falls, packages cradled in his arms. "No news yet."

"When might we know something?" I had counted on an answer and fretted at the thought of another anxious night.

"I'll try to have something tomorrow." He nodded toward the wall. "Why didn't you climb down the cliff tonight?"

I wouldn't mention tonight's thrashing. Indeed, I couldn't talk about the past hour at all. It would change our time together, and I wouldn't allow Mr. Pratt to ruin my visit with Mark.

"I had no fear of being followed, so I walked downstream until the land flattened and doubled back here."

"I've never seen you do it before." He held out his hand, palm up. "I brought you some food."

He offered me what felt like three small logs wrapped in bright, thin, crinkled fabric. "How can this be food?"

"The food's inside. You rip off the wrapper." He tapped one. "Each bar is like an entire meal."

Truly? If the bar contained an entire meal, how did it taste? I shuddered to think. It must be one of their inventions, but I couldn't imagine a good reason for this change. Food ought to be a pleasure.

I had no wish to offend him, so I slipped the bars into my pockets. "Thank you."

He laughed. "You're not going to eat them, are you?"

"I might."

"They taste pretty good."

"I trust your opinion," I said with a smile.

"No, you don't, but it's okay." He held out the second object. "You'll like this better. I bought you a book."

I balanced it on my palm. The volume was light and slim, bound in worn, black leather. Adorning its cover were the remnants of a painting. A young woman in a yellow bonnet and green gown stood poised on a cliff, gazing pensively into the sea.

"What kind of book is this?"

"It's a novel from your time." He paused. "Well, almost from your time."

A novel? I shivered. How I should love to read of interesting places and peoples. Did not such a lovely painting promise lovely words? Yet, if Mr. Pratt ever learned of this forbidden treat, the consequences would be dire. It would be unwise to give him more reasons to punish me. I returned the book with reluctance.

"I cannot accept. I am not permitted to read novels."

"Read it in your free time."

"He decides whether I receive free time. If he knew I read novels, I would lose my break."

Mark put his hands behind his back like a stubborn little boy. "Do you let your master control your thoughts when he's not around?"

Control my thoughts? I didn't like that phrase. "Mr. Pratt controls my actions. My thoughts belong to me alone." I snapped open the book.

At the top of the first page was a pen and ink drawing of a large house with a sweeping drive and tall trees. A horse and carriage approached from the lane.

My fingertips caressed the text with something akin to reverence. Papa had once told me that a book was mere paper splattered with ink until a reader's mind gave it life. I had forgotten the thrill of embarking on such a journey.

"Come on, Susanna. What are you afraid of?"

Discovery. If Mr. Pratt found the book, he would beat the devil out of me.

Excitement won over trepidation. He must never find out. I read the first sentence aloud. "Sir Walter Elliott..." I blinked in surprise. "Where does the story take place?"

"England. We're friends with them now."

"We are not friends with England in my century."

He laughed. "Pretend it takes place in New England."

I sniffed and looked down at the book. "Sir Walter Elliott, of..." I stopped. A strange word.

"Kellynch."

I nodded. "...of Kellynch Hall, in..." I stopped and closed the book. Reading an English writer's novel required too much effort. "There are too many unpronounceable names."

"Skip over what you don't know. You'll get it eventually."

"Quite the word of encouragement. No doubt I shall succeed any moment." I opened the book again. This time I read silently, skipping over the unpronounceable names.

It was an intriguing story. Three sisters, and only the youngest was married? How very unfortunate.

When the first chapter ended, I slipped the volume into my pocket and gazed along the creek, clearing my mind of fears. I would keep *Persuasion.* There were plenty of hiding places in the kitchen or in my corner of the attic. None of the Pratts would ever know I'd read a novel.

"What do you think?" he asked.

I'd forgotten how it felt to receive a real gift, not a castoff or an impulse. He'd carefully planned, selected, and given me a present. Emotions welled inside, painful in their intensity.

"I don't know what to say. It is lovely."

"*Thank you* works."

"Thank you." I laughed and held my hand out to him. Even though I had nothing in return for Mark, the need to give was strong. "Come with me."

"Where?"

"I want to introduce you to Worthville."

He didn't move. "I'm fine where I am."

"You can only see the creek from here."

"That's plenty."

"What are you afraid of?" I smiled to ease the sting of my teasing.

"All right." He crossed his arms. "Are we climbing the wall or walking downstream?"

My legs wouldn't be able to tolerate climbing this evening. "We shall go down the creek."

He gestured for me to lead. As I walked along the bank, he hovered beside me protectively. When we reached the point where the land flattened, we stopped on the path through the tall grasses.

He stood tensely beside me. I remained quiet, allowing him to adapt. Everything about my century was gentler to the senses: crisper sights, softer sounds, lighter scents.

His body was still, but his eyes were restless.

I pointed east. "If you continue on this path, you'll meet the road from Worthville to Raleigh."

"What about the other way?" He nodded toward the trail fading into the woods one hundred feet or more away.

"It stops at the Pratts's property."

"The Pratts?" He dropped my hand and turned his back on my world. "What if one of them shows up? Maybe I should go."

"If I am not worried, neither should you be."

"Really, it's getting late."

I bounced on my toes, eager for him to understand. "Before you leave, I want you to look up."

"Why?" He looked to the sky, his eyes widening. "Wow."

Stars dotted the night, tiny white lights pulsing in the blue-black heavens.

"Is it not wondrous?"

"Yeah. There are millions of them."

"Indeed. You do not seem to have so many on your side." I watched his profile and hoped he shared my awe.

"No, we don't." A slight smile played on his lips. "What day is it here?"

The huskiness in his voice puzzled me. "Monday, the thirteenth of June."

"It's the same day in my century. And we have the same moon." His gaze met mine. "Susanna…"

I knew a sudden shyness. There was a look on his face, a stillness to his body that had never been there before. Though I couldn't give the emotion a name, I felt it, too. We had something special. Something hard to define. Something past friendship.

"I must go now," I said and rose up on tiptoe to kiss his cheek, marveling at its velvet skin. "Thank you for the book."

He drew me into his embrace and sighed. "Thank you for the stars."

If novels were sinful, I should spend many nights in prayer, for this story was a delight. I could hardly bear to put *Persuasion* down long enough to retire.

It was still dark when I awakened and dressed. After setting the tray for breakfast and putting water on to boil, I entered the pantry and strained to read, hidden from view.

"Susanna?" Jedidiah called as he tramped up the back steps of the kitchen.

I pressed the book into a crack in the wall and joined my master's son. "Please put the milk on the worktable."

He did as I requested and then faced me. "Are Papa's suspicions correct? Do you have a young man that you meet in the woods?"

Jedidiah never spoke to me on personal matters. Indeed, he rarely spoke to me at all.

"I do not have a beau."

"I didn't think so." His voice cracked on the final word. He stomped to the front door. But instead of proceeding into the yard, he turned and gave me a hard stare, reminiscent of his father. "I don't mind the hunt."

In all the weeks Mr. Pratt had been sending his son to trail me, Jedidiah and I had not alluded to our evening game. Without any sign I understood him, I crossed to the hearth.

"I haven't figured out how you disappear so completely. But one day, I shall." He stalked away.

I finished the preparations for breakfast, his words lingering in the air. His comments concerned me, although perhaps I should be glad. With this warning, I could ponder new ways to elude him.

Morning chores proceeded at an agonizing pace. I served the meal, tickled the babies, washed the dishes, and stirred the stew. Once I had a moment to spare, I took a heel of bread and slipped into the pantry. Within seconds, I was eating my breakfast and reading my book. Before I'd finished the chapter, children's voices filled the kitchen.

After hiding the book, I emerged from my new reading corner to find Mrs. Pratt standing in the room with her four youngest children. I nodded briskly and busied myself with the stew. It would be a bit thin today. The lack of rain had slowed the garden.

No sooner had my mistress set Baby John on his feet than he toddled straight to me.

"Hello, big boy," I said and lifted him to my hip with one arm. He patted my mouth with a chubby hand. I obliged with kisses.

"May we help you with anything?" Dorcas asked.

"No, indeed, not this morning. Perhaps you would like to play."

Dorcas nodded eagerly and darted through the rear door, Delilah at her heels. I held Dinah's hand while she made careful progress down the back stairs.

Behind me, Mrs. Pratt groaned. I glanced at her over my shoulder. She sprawled on the bench, her face pale.

"Do you feel unwell, ma'am?"

She nodded, fanning herself. "I'd like some fresh cucumber. With salt."

I stopped bouncing John to gape at her. Cucumber with salt? She only asked for cucumber when she was with child.

Realization rattled through me. Another baby.

Seven children. Yet, in 1800, there would be only four.

Three gone. Not two.

I leaned against the worktable as anguish washed over me. Which three? I had to learn the truth. When Mark returned with his news, I would hear it out, all of it. I had to know—and I would have to hide the knowing.

A sobering thought struck. The months before my mistress's confinements were never pleasant, nor would I be here for the birth. The Pratts would be desperate to find a replacement. Although my mistress would never entrust my sister with the care of a newborn, might she consider Phoebe for a housemaid?

Here was yet another possibility I must ponder how to thwart.

"Mrs. Pratt, will you have the cucumber with your meal?"

"I'd like it now," she said with a peevish snarl, mopping at her neck with a cloth.

"Very well." I hitched John higher and crossed to the rear door.

Dorcas beamed at me from the bottom of the stairs. "May we come with you and John?"

"Certainly."

"Susanna," Mrs. Pratt said, "put the baby down and do my bidding at once."

When I lowered him to the floor near the bench, he whined and clawed at my petticoat. "No, dearest," I said, pressing a quick kiss to his brow, "I shall return soon."

I paused in the rear doorway and noted with concern that Mrs. Pratt rested her head against the wall, eyes closed.

"I don't mind taking him with me," I said, foreboding quivering in my belly.

She groped along the bench until her fingers touched John's arm. "He'll only slow you down. I shall tend to my son."

I hurried to the garden and wove frantically through the rows of faded green vines. Few cucumbers looked fat enough for picking.

"Susanna?" Dorcas called. "Wait for us. We can't keep up."

"Not right now." I grabbed the nearest cucumber and yanked with haste, anxious to return to the kitchen and the baby.

"Please, Susanna. Delilah and Dinah are too slow—"

Her statement was interrupted by a scream.

John.

I raced up the steps and in through the door. Mrs. Pratt stood frozen beside the bench, hands clamped over her mouth. He lay wailing on the hearth, blood pouring from a gash on his forehead.

My heart thumped. Even minor head wounds bled prodigiously, but might this one be truly severe?

"John, don't cry. I'm here," I said with more calm than I felt and hoisted him into my arms. He rubbed his face against my shoulder and hiccupped.

Mrs. Pratt bustled over. "Mama's here, baby." She held out her hands.

He shook his head and clung to me. Her lips thinned angrily.

Running footsteps pounded in the yard and stopped in the open threshold.

"What has happened?" Mr. Pratt roared. He stood there, eyes bulging, taking in the scene.

Mrs. Pratt shrank in terror, staggering backwards until the worktable blocked her.

Teeth grinding with rage, he snatched the baby from my arms, shoved him at his mother, and rounded on me. "Did you neglect my son?"

"No, sir, I —"

His hand whipped out before I could raise a defense. Crack.

Pain exploded in my cheek. I fell to my knees, my eyelids fluttering against the blackness blurring my vision. I braced shaking hands against the floor and tried to push upright.

There were gasps from the front door where Jedidiah and Deborah stood watching. Beside her mother, an open-mouthed Dorcas dashed tears from her cheeks.

"Stupid, ungrateful wench. You injured my son."

His voice boomed within my aching head. I waited for Mrs. Pratt to correct the misunderstanding.

She said nothing.

"Mama?" Dorcas prompted.

"Hush. This is not your business," her mother hissed.

"But Susanna was in the—"

"Silence," Mr. Pratt shouted.

My mistress wouldn't accept the blame. Of course she wouldn't. She feared him, as we all did.

I flexed my jaw, to see if it worked. It moved well enough to speak. I must address his false impression. Truly, the undeserved punishment wasn't what bothered me most. It was the very idea that I would have allowed an accident to befall my beloved John.

"I did nothing wrong, sir."

"My son's blood is staining the hearth and you call that nothing?" His boot flew forward. I closed my eyes as the blow slammed into my hip and knocked me backwards.

What little fight there had been left me. I ached too much to move.

Seconds passed with no sound but Baby John's hiccups and Dinah's sniffles.

Someone knelt beside me. A little hand stroked my hair.

"Children, return to the house." The click of boot heels crossed the room and disappeared into the yard.

Jedidiah took his two youngest sisters by the hand. Deborah fetched John from her mother's arms, and the children left together—all except Dorcas.

"Susanna," she said, her voice urgent with fear. Her small fingers stroked my face insistently.

I reached up and laid a hand over hers, halting the motion. The comfort had been kindly offered but did no good. My tongue flicked dust from my swollen lips and tasted blood.

"I think I can stand now."

Little fingers gripped my shoulders and guided me up. I remained still and waited for the dizziness to pass.

"Dorcas," her mother said, "run along."

"But, Mama—"

"Now."

Footsteps dragged dramatically across the floor, thumped down the back stairs, and blended into the outdoors.

A board creaked as soft slippers crept closer. "Susanna?"

"Yes, Mrs. Pratt?"

"I didn't intend for that to happen, but I couldn't risk having his anger unleashed on me."

"I have noted your delicate condition."

There was a catch in her throat. "Then you understand why I didn't share the truth."

"You are wrong. I do not." I seized the worktable's edge and struggled to my feet. My side throbbed. My thigh burned. It might be hours before I could resume my chores. My master had never hurt me so severely.

"You are a clever girl. Of course you understand." She sighed. "Perhaps you should rest for the remainder of the day."

"I accept the offer."

A rest was more than I had expected. Perhaps my mistress felt a bit of guilt. It could not be a bribe for silence. I wasn't permitted to tell their secrets, anyway, although this particular secret had been written in bruises that were easy to see.

"Very well." She cocked her head expectantly. "Are dinner and supper ready? Can you instruct Deborah and Dorcas in how to prepare the tray?"

A spark of anger briefly flared. Why offer me rest and take it away in the next breath? And why pose it as a question? She knew I couldn't refuse.

"I shall wait over there." I limped to the corner and perched on the bench.

"Excellent. I shall fetch them." Her slippers shuffled as she walked to the door.

"Mrs. Pratt?"

"Yes?"

"You will need assistance with the new baby in a few months. Have you considered how difficult it will be to replace me from the girls of this town?"

She glanced over her shoulder. "I don't intend to replace you, Susanna. I shall persuade you to change your mind."

CHAPTER TWENTY

GENETIC MATERIAL

I'd kept Susanna waiting long enough. She wanted to know about the Pratt children, and I was going to find out.

Search engines could only show me so much. Since I'd exhausted what the Internet had available, it was time to do research the old-fashioned way. I rode downtown to the government district.

After locking my bike next to the concrete building housing the State Archives, I pulled open a tall glass door and stepped into the narrow lobby. A security guy greeted me, checked out my driver's license, and directed me to the second floor.

Security was even tighter upstairs. I received a visitor's badge, a stern lecture on the privilege I was about to receive, and a locker key. After stowing my backpack, I entered the Search Room.

The space had serious AC, a nice contrast to the heat and humidity outside. It smelled like musty old stuff and was quiet—much quieter than a library. A handful of people dotted the room. I went to the desk.

"May I help you?" The research assistant was a tall, thin, college-age girl with black braids and not-so-invisible braces.

"I need Wake County census records from 1800."

"Fine." She pointed to a door behind me. "Microfilm. It's self-service. Do you know how to use the machines?"

"Sure." I'd never tried, but I was reasonably confident I'd manage.

My confidence was misplaced.

After a couple of screw-ups and whispered directions from the old lady sitting next to me, I fed the 1800 census film into the machine and skimmed along until I found Worthville. I squinted at every page. Every note. Every appendix.

Major problem.

I went to the desk. "I need the names of the children."

The research assistant shook her head. "You won't find those from the census. They didn't collect names from the whole family until 1850."

Great. I had expected the hard part to be biking down here. "What do I do?"

"Wills. Guys put a lot of information in their wills." She slid a call slip across the counter.

I filled in county, document type, decade, and signature and then slid the call slip back.

"Fine. Give me a moment." She disappeared through a metal door behind the desk.

I waited, tapping my fingers, and looked about the room. I was the youngest person in there, which was no surprise. There were a few old people bent over folders, holding magnifying glasses or snapping digital photos.

"Here you go," the girl said and handed me a box across the counter. "The rules for handling documents are printed on the top of the box. Read them before starting. If you need something copied, let me know."

I crossed to a table and flopped onto a heavy upholstered chair. After skimming the instructions, I opened the box. It contained all wills registered in Wake County during the 1790s. There was a folder marked Pratt. I laid it on the table but hesitated to open it. Even though I didn't know these people, Susanna did. She cared about them, and two of those kids were going to die.

I opened the folder and froze as my fingertips brushed a document. I'd known I'd have access to originals, but this was a little freaky. These sheets were more than two hundred years old, and I was holding them. It seemed weirdly trusting for the state government to give the general public this kind of access.

The first page in the folder showed the will for a Mr. George Pratt. He had significant acreage in southeastern Wake County, plus a lot of slaves, horses, and other livestock.

I set aside George's document. The next will belonged to Jethro.

It was a good thing the research assistant could make copies, because I hadn't thought to bring a camera. I'd take her up on her offer. For now, I was consumed by my first real exposure to Susanna's master.

The will had been written in a strong, looping script, faded but still legible. There wasn't much property to pass down. He divvied up the contents of his estate among his wife and children. Even his indentured servant was left her *customary freedom dues*, whatever that meant.

If a researcher had been looking at the document, it would've seemed like the perfectly ordinary will of a perfectly ordinary guy. Jethro had done the right thing by his family—which was good for them, but pissed me off. His one connection to history was positive.

Okay, time to find out the information that brought me down here. I read the names of the four children.

Susanna would be half happy.

I loaded my backpack with water, snacks, and copies of Jethro's will. By the time I left the house, it was late enough that the greenway was already deserted.

Susanna huddled in the depths of the cave, more like a lightening of the shadows than an actual visible person. Motionless as a statue.

The curtain of water had narrowed. Lack of rain slowed everything. Even the creek was sluggish. I swung my backpack through, to make sure it could pass. It did.

I stepped through the falls sideways and ducked under the lip of the cave. She sat on her rock, watching me from the shadows. Sorrow surrounded her like a mist. I was about to make things worse.

"Hey," I said, sitting beside her.

She stirred slightly. "Hello."

The whole mood was unsettling. The moist, eerie cave. The gray of twilight. Susanna's distress—as if she'd become one with the gloom.

I reached inside my backpack and tried to keep my voice steady. I was the bearer of bad news—not a role I was used to. "Here's something you'll be interested in."

"What is it?"

I held it out. "Jethro's will."

She stood stiffly and limped toward the mouth of the cave.

Limped? Something was wrong. I must've learned to read her body language because, although she was often quiet, today it went beyond her normal attitude in a way I couldn't identify.

She tilted the paper, frowning. "Where should I look?"

I walked up behind her and pointed to a name in the middle. "Dorcas."

Her hands seemed to spasm, crumpling the document. "Dorcas lives."

"Yes, she does."

Susanna swayed. I shifted, feet planted, ready to catch her. She made a sobbing sound and mopped her eyes on the sleeve of her shirt. "That is good."

Now for the sad stuff. I took the sheet from her and smoothed it out. "Jethro Pratt mentions bequests to four children: Jedidiah, Deborah, Dorcas, and Drusilla."

"Dinah and Delilah are not there." Her voice thickened. "Nor John."

"I'm sorry."

"Merciful heavens." Her arms dropped and her mouth opened as she panted. "My babies." The last word was drawn out in a low, wavering moan.

Her babies. Did she really think of them that way? Not surprising, actually. I could easily believe those two parents had done little more than contribute genetic material.

I waited in silence, watching her shoulders heave, not knowing what to say or do. I lifted my hands a couple of times. To hold her. To steady her. Would she accept my touch? I had no clue how she felt. Did she need to grieve without my clumsy efforts getting in the way?

I let my hands fall again.

She took a deep breath and held up the document again. "Is an indentured servant included?"

I frowned at the loops and swirls. "Yeah. Lydia Hinton."

"That is excellent news." She stared at the faded handwriting, rolled up the document, and clutched it to her chest. "Thank you, Lord."

Not sure why the name Lydia made her happy, but I wouldn't pursue it for now—something else distracted me. There were muddy-looking stains on the shoulder of her shirt. Splotches and dribbles. I circled around to her side, fighting off a growing tension at what the stains suggested. It had to be blood, lots of blood, all over the front of her shirt.

I glanced up to say something and gaped in shock at the sight of her face, revealed by the faint light. "Oh my God. What happened?"

She pursed her lips. Her puffy, split lips. "It's Baby John's blood you see on my shoulder. He was injured this morning."

John—one of her favorites. "And whose fault was that?"

"My mistress." Her eyes shimmered in a bright pool of tears. But they didn't fall, as if held there by the sheer force of her will. "I received the punishment."

"Clearly." Anger left a metallic taste in my mouth. "Where was your mistress when your master was throwing punches?"

"Watching."

Bitch. I shook with the urge for violence, something I'd never experienced before, not in all the time the bullies had beaten me up around school. There were plenty of kids who had watched and done nothing.

It had taken some well-placed video cameras and a YouTube account before the bullies got the justice they'd earned. The memories still left me enraged.

"What did you do?"

"What could I do?"

"Susanna—"

"I did nothing." She spun around to face me, eyes blazing. "Are you disgusted? I lay on the floor with the entire family present while my master kicked me. Do you wish I had fought back? Are you disappointed I accepted my punishment meekly?"

Where had that come from? "No, I don't think—"

"I tried to share the truth. I promise to you, I did. But the truth is of no consequence when there's blame to be laid."

"Susanna, stop—"

"In your century, it must be easier for you to seek justice, so do not presume to judge me. You don't know how it feels to be trapped with no recourse. The law is on his side. The townsfolk may disapprove, but they must look the other way. It's the Golden Rule, you see. If they wish to treat their servants as they see fit, they must let Jethro Pratt do the same."

"I don't judge you—"

"It's a harsh thing to live as I do, loathing my job, treated like the livestock." Her face hardened. "Papa wanted so much more for me than this. He taught me with the boys. He encouraged my questions. Then he died and everything changed. He would be so ashamed to see what I have become—a house servant who cooks and cleans all day. Yet I cannot yield to anger, because if I do, I shall never stop. And what good would that do? I shall have to wake up the next morning and start all over again. Until October, the Pratts *own* me."

She clutched my shirt between both hands and yanked me closer. Her eyes were wet and blank, her voice soft and flat. "When he thrashes me, he asks me to lift my skirt. Then there's a long pause, while he looks at my bare legs, picking the spot he'll hit first and thinking about how he'll scar me this time. It's a game, you see. He tries to hurt me so badly I'll weep. But I don't cry. I don't make a sound. It's my only way to win."

If Jethro Pratt had been within reach, I would've beaten the crap out of him and never had a moment's regret. But he was out of reach—by two hundred years.

Susanna collapsed against me, shoulders shaking and tears soaking my shirt. I rested my hands lightly on her back and racked my brain for some way to help. But what could I say? What had happened to her was evil. She was in an impossible situation, and there was no way out until her birthday.

ELIZABETH LANGSTON

"I'm here. I'm on your side."

She coughed. "I'm sorry, Mark. I didn't mean to yell at you."

"You don't ever have to apologize. I'm different from the Pratts. You can get pissed around me. You can yell and scream and call me names all you want. I'm not going anywhere."

"Thank you."

Damn. How long had she had that all bottled up? I eased an arm around her waist. When my hand brushed her hip, she flinched.

"Sorry. Does it still hurt?"

"Yes."

"I can help if you'll let me."

She nodded.

I knelt beside my backpack and rummaged around until I found my emergency pack of ibuprofen. "This medicine will take away the pain."

There was a flicker of interest on her face. "Herbs?"

"Nah, we have better stuff now. Pretty much guaranteed to work."

She looked down at the two orange pills in my hand. "How do they do that?"

"I don't know for sure." I handed over my bottle. "Hold them on your tongue. I'll give you a swallow of water."

She took a sip and gagged down the pills.

"Come on." I took her hand and led her to the deepest part of the cave. "Sit on my lap and let me hold you."

I could almost feel her blush through the darkness. "I don't know…"

"It'll be okay. No one can see us." I waited until she sat, then wrapped her in my arms. "The medicine'll take a few minutes to kick in, but the pain'll ease up soon."

"All right."

She calmed down in stages.

At first, it was just a wiggling of her head as she relaxed against my chest.

Then her hands stopped fidgeting.

Finally, her body lost its tension.

"Better now?" I asked.

"Better in my body. But my heart grieves at the news you brought. What can I do about my little ones?"

"You're already the best thing in their lives. Just take care of them." I hugged her more securely. Night had fallen. She ought to leave, but for one sweet moment longer, I intended to enjoy our closeness.

"My mistress expects a child, and now I know it will be a girl." There was a hint of a smile in Susanna's voice. "Baby Drusilla. Named for her mother."

"Her mother?" Something tickled at the corners of my brain. "The Mrs. Pratt in the will is not Drusilla."

Susanna stiffened. "Do you remember her name?"

I nodded. "Phoebe."

CHAPTER TWENTY-ONE

REPROACHFUL SIGHS

I was living a nightmare. If only I were asleep, so I could awaken and make it end.

After the household settled and drifted into silence, I retired to the attic, stripped to my shift, and lay on my pallet. But rest did not come. Had I truly thought it would? I curled into a tight ball, facing a horror too large to absorb.

I took tiny breaths, stared wide-eyed into the darkness, and refused to think.

The night crept toward midnight. Creatures howled, the roof creaked, and I stirred painfully, as numb things do when they awaken.

Thoughts flooded in despite my efforts to hold them at bay.

Phoebe—my sweet, innocent sister—the wife of Jethro Pratt.

I pieced together the strands of a story that had yet to happen.

At my urging, Mama convinces Mr. Shaw that Phoebe should not care for his children. He seeks another situation for her.

Mr. Shaw binds Phoebe over to the Pratts. She becomes their housemaid.

Mrs. Pratt dies, leaving behind Baby Drusilla. Phoebe, committed to stay until her eighteenth birthday, is forced to take care of the children.

Three of the Pratt children don't survive.

Phoebe marries Mr. Pratt.

Why would my sister agree to become his wife? She was only twelve now. In 1800, she would be sixteen. Why would she marry a much older man—especially one so cruel?

Phoebe would struggle as the Pratts's servant. She would be clumsy and forgetful. Discipline would come at regular intervals. How would she react to the thrashings? To the whispery voice spewing venom?

Grief stung my eyes, my nose, my throat. I wept into my pallet and mourned my sister's bright future. Living with this family would rob her of her finest qualities. I had barely survived, and I was strong.

Was that why Phoebe would agree to the marriage? Would she be beaten so low she believed there was only one path left?

Or worse, would he ruin her, leaving her with no choice but marriage to him?

Where would I be while all of this was happening? Why would I not stop them?

The question lingered in my mind. Crisp. Clear. Bristling with potential. Here was the power of knowing the future. I could change it. I would find a way to keep that beast from putting his filthy hands on my sister.

The tears dried. My throat stung, awash with the sour taste of bile. Driven by a fierce need for movement, I rose from my bed and paced down the length of the attic, weaving among the cluttered items stored there by the Pratts. With each step, the wisps of grief faded, replaced by raw resolve.

In my pacing, I made an odd discovery. Fury wasn't hot at all. No, indeed. It was as cold and hard as ice.

He would not have Phoebe.

I weighed my options.

Naturally, I couldn't count on my brothers. Their wives were reluctant to have Phoebe around.

I wouldn't ask my mother to plead Phoebe's case with Mr. Shaw. A woman blinded by the need for a husband wouldn't risk her betrothed's wrath.

Nor could I approach Mr. Shaw himself. I only had honor on my side, and he had already proven himself lacking that virtue.

Fleeing was a frightening possibility, but one I must consider. Phoebe and I could run away, to Boston or New York or Charleston, any large city where we could blend in. But that would require Phoebe to keep our secret. It was, perhaps, too much to expect. Nowhere would be secure. Nor did I relish a life of hiding for me or my sister. I would be hunted. Capture brought a fearsome punishment— flogging, chains, and a tenfold repayment of the weeks absent from my master. Running away would be a last resort.

What else could I do to save her?

Unless she had a useful skill, no one else would want her.

If only she knew how to spin and make cloth. But for even the most talented of students, it took months to learn.

If only we had more time…

Time. We needed more time.

I knew what must be done. Phoebe would have to learn to spin, and I would have to stay here as long as that took.

In the stillness of the nursery, I tended napping infants, immersed in my book. It drew me in so deeply I lost my sense of time and place.

Running feet pounded toward the door. "Susanna, look what I brought you," Dorcas said.

"Shh." I tapped a shushing finger to my lips. "Don't wake John or Dinah from their naps."

"All right," she said in a loud whisper.

With regret, I closed the book quickly and returned it to my pocket before she could glimpse its cover. Dorcas walked in and solemnly handed me a fistful of wildflowers.

"I picked them for you," she said.

"Thank you most kindly. Would you like me to plait some into your hair?"

"Would you?" Her eyes shone.

"Indeed, yes." I patted my lap.

She climbed on, wiggled her hips to and fro, and sighed with anticipation. "Will everyone be able to see?"

"Yes."

"I shall be the fairest of all."

I laughed. "Be still, silly. I cannot plait your hair if I must chase it about your head."

She twisted on my lap and kissed me on the chin. Her breath smelled of blackberries.

Her kiss gave me a pang. The older members of the family rarely showed affection—certainly not to each other and never to me. At nine, Dorcas should have learned this rule, yet seemed oblivious to it. Would her affectionate nature land her in trouble one day?

With the plaiting done, I slid her from my lap and picked up a broom. While I swept, Dorcas admired her reflection in the window, twisting her head from side to side to inspect her hair from every angle.

A squeaking sound drew my attention. Dinah rolled off her pallet onto the floor and blinked up at me sleepily. "Nana," she said.

"Your nap is over too soon, little one." I put away the broom, lifted her to my hip, and brushed the damp curls clinging to her face.

A wail from the other end of the pallet revealed that the second of my tiny charges had awakened. I lifted John, as well.

Dorcas tugged my petticoat. "Papa says Dinah is too old to be carried. He says a girl of two should be doing chores."

"Perhaps we should find one for her," I said. My sweet and unspoiled Dinah wouldn't live to her sixth birthday. I had no interest in making her perform chores. "Your mother might wish Dinah's help with the spinning."

Dorcas giggled. "You are teasing. My mother would never let a baby near her wheel." She planted herself in my path, beaming. "Mama has shared some excellent news. She says she'll teach Phoebe how to spin."

"Your mother's skill is extraordinary. We are most grateful."

"And you will stay with us even after the tutoring ends."

"I shall, indeed."

Mrs. Pratt had driven a hard-fought bargain, a skill learned, no doubt, from her husband. Phoebe would receive lessons four days each week. Mrs. Pratt would keep any thread Phoebe spun or cloth Phoebe wove. And I would work an extra day—without pay—for each lesson my sister received.

"So you won't leave on your birthday."

"I shall remain here throughout the winter."

"I am so happy you will stay."

I knelt on the floor and included all three children in a hug. Even though it had been crushing to delay my freedom, more time with the children eased the disappointment.

The sun bore down on the village, relentlessly bright. I visited the drooping garden in the afternoon. Heat rose in waves and, with it, the scent of baking manure and rotting vines. I gathered yellow squash and tender peas. None of it would entice the appetites of the family.

Supper would consist of stewed squash with bacon and cornbread. There would be reproachful sighs, but I could not change the lack of variety. We were, to put it simply, running out of food.

Perhaps it was time to unveil the apple butter. I had been saving it for a special occasion, but it might be wise to share some at supper. It would be an unusual accompaniment to cornbread, but no one would complain.

I entered the pantry to retrieve the hidden jar.

Someone rapped on the threshold behind me. I turned to see who it was and stiffened with dismay.

My master filled the doorway, a heavy sack slung over his shoulder.

The sight of the flour relieved me. The sight of him did not.

"Thank you, sir. I shall bake wheat bread tomorrow."

He lowered the bag to the floor and nudged it to the side. "I have heard good news. You will stay with us."

"Yes, sir." I turned away from him and straightened the other supplies, the very picture of efficiency.

"Your decision pleases me."

My hands stilled. "I hope to be of service to Mrs. Pratt as she approaches her confinement."

He chuckled low in his chest. "You are lying."

A flush rose from my neck to cheeks. He was right, but until Phoebe was no longer in danger, I had to ensure the conversation never mentioned her.

"I don't understand what you mean."

"You have realized you cannot bear to be separated from us."

A bubble of laughter at the absurdity of his claim rolled from my belly to lodge in my throat. I coughed into my hand and strained to resist the smile tugging at my lips. Could he truly be so deluded?

"While there is much to recommend steady employment," I choked out, "I do expect to leave this household by next spring."

There was a brief silence, then he came farther into the tiny space and braced his arms on the shelves on either side of the pantry, blocking me in. I sobered instantly.

"Are you laughing at me?"

"No, sir."

I backed up a step. He followed until his neckcloth brushed my sleeve. He was a tall man and strong after years of lifting large bags of milled grain. Leaning closer, his chest trapped me against the wall, his labored breaths disturbing the tendrils escaping my cap.

"In recent weeks, you have developed a most unpleasant insolence." His voice was soft and venomous. "How do you account for that, Susanna?"

Mark. I had indeed changed. Our conversations had loosened my restraint, the banter sharpening my mind and tongue. Strange that being a better person made me less desirable as a servant. But I could say none of these things to my master. It would be wisest to play innocent.

"I work as hard as ever."

"It is not your work I fault. You do not respond to discipline as I had hoped. Indeed, your behavior worsens. Perhaps I shall have to find new ways to teach you a lesson." He tugged a loose strand of my hair and then trailed the back of his fingers down my neck.

I stood my ground. If he was trying to frighten me, he would see no evidence of it in my demeanor.

He eyed me grimly. "Do not challenge me, Susanna. In any battle between us, we both know who will win."

Chapter Twenty-Two

Advanced Search

Susanna wanted to see Phoebe's marriage license and indenture. No matter how hard I tried, I couldn't find either on the web.

I didn't want to ride down to the Archives again, but it looked like I'd have to. Another eight-mile bike ride, weaving in and out of state capital traffic, over potholed, torn-up, orange-barreled roads might be great training, though.

It was too late to go down there today; it would have to wait until tomorrow.

All right, enough about Worthville.

The Internet turned out to be useless for young adult fiction. I wanted to buy Susanna another novel, but a simple query brought up thousands to choose from.

I even tried Wikipedia. Eighteenth-century American literature. Not helpful.

"Hi, Mark."

My mother's voice made me jump. She'd never managed to sneak into the rec room without me noticing before. I glanced at her reflection in the mirror. She wore an oversized T-shirt and carried a beat-up suitcase. A light smile curved her lips, something I hadn't seen in a while. It was nice.

"Hey. What are you doing?"

She set the suitcase down. "Packing up some winter clothes for Marissa. She wants me to send them out there."

"Marissa contacted you?" Good news. I needed to check in with my sister.

"She texted me, which is close enough. What are you doing?"

"Checking out book titles on the web."

"Why?"

"Actually, you could help. You were a girl once."

"Still am, last time I checked."

I gave her a look over my shoulder. "You know what I mean. A teen girl."

"That's true. It was one of the many stages I passed through on my way to fifty." She looked past me to the computer screen, then dragged over a chair and plopped down.

"Okay, then. I need some advice on buying books."

She laughed. "For teen *girl* literature?"

"It's not for me." I'd have to explain now. I'd held off telling my folks about Susanna. It had to be obvious I was spending time with someone and equally obvious that I wasn't bringing her by the house. Once I raised the topic, there were bound to be questions which I could never answer. But still, it would be nice to get it out there.

"I want to pick out a book for a friend."

"Which one?"

"You haven't met her yet." It was hard to know how to describe our relationship. Friend seemed too little. We had something more special than that, but girlfriend wasn't right, either. And how could I explain why they never saw her? The two-hundred-year separation gave new meaning to the term *long-distance*. "We're just friends."

"What's her name?"

"Susanna."

"That's pretty. Where did you meet?"

If I reminded my mother of who was in charge of this conversation, I'd hear one of those boring lectures about who owned the house. "We met on the greenway."

"How old is she?"

"Seventeen."

"Where does she go to school?"

"She's done already." Not stepping on that landmine again. I'd learned my lesson with Marissa.

My mom's mouth opened to ask some more, so I held up my hand and hoped she would stop. She did. "Susanna likes to read and can't afford it. So, I thought I'd buy her a few books."

My mom had that *on-hold-for-now-but-I-won't-forget* look. "What are Susanna's interests?"

"Colonial history. With themes about injustice." That last part was my addition.

Mom nodded approvingly. "*The Witch of Blackbird Pond.*"

"Go, Mom. You just popped that right out there." I checked the inventory at Meredith Ridge and put the most ancient copy on hold.

"Flatter me all you want, but we need to find out more about this girl. When are you inviting her over?"

I frowned. So not going there. Time for a diversionary tactic. "Did you come in here for a reason?"

"I did." She crossed her legs, uncrossed them, stood up again, and walked away a few steps.

It shouldn't have been so easy to divert her. Something about this conversation made her nervous. Very interesting.

"Carla is getting married again."

That wasn't anything new for Mom's best friend. "Which husband is this? Third?"

"It's her fourth marriage. The wedding is on Mackinac Island."

That could be cool. "Are you going?"

"Yeah." Mom stopped pacing and looked at me uneasily. "I want your dad to go with me."

My mom hated to fly. She had to want to go to this wedding pretty badly to get on an airplane. "He'll go if you ask him. When is it?"

"July thirtieth."

"Wow, Mom. That's a decent amount of warning this time…"

Wait a minute.

July thirtieth was the day of my big race.

The day my folks were supposed to be my cheering section at *the most important race of my life.*

"Mom, did you forget the Carolina Challenge?"

"No, I didn't forget. I'm really sorry we have to miss your race."

I popped out of my chair. "You can't miss it."

"It's terrible timing, I know, but what else can I do?"

"You can skip Carla's wedding."

My mother scowled. "Don't take that tone of voice with me, young man."

"What tone of voice is that? The one reminding you that this race has been on the schedule for months?"

"I have to be there. I'm the matron of honor."

"Yeah, for the fourth time. The way Carla goes through husbands, there'll be other chances."

"That's enough, Mark. We aren't missing her wedding."

I stalked all the way to the door and then stopped to frown at her over my shoulder. "I can't believe you're going to leave me here alone with no one to support me."

She shook her head. "You're not staying at the house alone. You'll have to sleep somewhere else."

"What?"

"You're not old enough to stay home by yourself for that long."

How could this get any worse?

"Where exactly did you have in mind?"

"Watch your mouth, Mark, or you'll find yourself grounded." Her eyes narrowed into her infamous, pissed-off slits.

Was this my mother's lame attempt at bluffing? Probably. But it wasn't worth the risk. I counted backwards from ten before continuing. "Do you have a suggestion for where I should stay?"

"With Gran and Granddad."

Could we stop this day and start it over again? "The lake house is too far away. It'll mess with my training schedule." It would also mess with seeing Susanna.

"Ask Carlton."

"I hate staying over there." His mother threw a lot of loud parties, and I needed good sleep—especially the night before a race.

"Then maybe you should plan to go with us to the wedding."

"Like hell." I stormed out before I said something even more punishable.

Dad was the only person alive who could get my mother to change her mind. I would have to get to him and convince him that I was right. It shouldn't be too hard, since I *was*.

I texted him that I wanted to talk when he got home. But it was late when his Lexus pulled into the garage, and he went straight to bed. Our conversation would have to wait another night.

I finished my Thursday lawns pretty quickly and then headed out early for a short training ride. There wasn't much time left in the afternoon, and I really needed to check on some things for Susanna, so I took my truck downtown to the Archives. Fortunately, the parking gods were on my side for a change. It took hardly any time to run in, collect the data, and get home again.

After dinner, I ran along the greenway, skidded down the rutted trail, and charged across two hundred years. Susanna wasn't waiting for me in the cave, but voices floated down from the bluff. I paused to listen.

No, it was just one voice, and it belonged to Susanna.

I climbed the granite ladder and peered cautiously over the edge. Tall grass and a dusty shelf of rock blocked my view, but now I was sure. She was somewhere nearby, and she was singing. Weird.

Pulling myself onto the top of the bluff, I crawled on my belly to the nearest clump of grass. She was a few feet away, profile to me, hands on hips, singing a hymn or something. At the end, she spun slowly until she faced me. Our eyes locked.

She mouthed, "Mark, wait," and then strolled down the trail leading to Raleigh.

Moments later, a boy—medium-height, blond, wearing dorky pants and socks that met at the knee—emerged from the trees backing up to the Pratts's property. He hurried along the trail, crouching often, his gaze darting this way and that. Once past me, he broke into a flat run and disappeared around a bend, not far behind Susanna.

Weirder.

"Hello," she said, looming above me. She looked over her shoulder. "Don't stand."

"Okay." I craned to see the woods. Nothing moving there. "What was that all about?"

"I must devise new methods to confuse my spy. His hunting skills improve." She scowled. "I cannot let him discover my hiding place in the cave. We shall have to stay here tonight, in case Jedidiah returns." Her smile radiated victory. "Are you comfortable?"

"I'm great. Just wondering how easy it would be to look up your skirt from this angle."

She laughed. "Indeed? Is this a favorite pastime of a twenty-first century boy?"

"I'm sure it's been the favorite pastime of boys in every century." I shifted around to half-recline on a flat slab of granite, my body hidden by the grasses. "How was your day?"

The smile disappeared abruptly. Everything about her darkened. "It has been unbearable since I last saw you."

"Phoebe?"

She bit her lip and nodded.

I reached into my pocket and pulled out the copies I'd made this afternoon at the Archives. "I got more information. Maybe we'll come up with something."

"I have already solved the problem. Phoebe will be safe now. She will never be a servant for the Pratts." She stared at the creek, arms crossed, chin high.

"What?" I felt a twinge of fear. Anyone who'd ever read a time-travel book knew that we couldn't screw with history. Who knew where the repercussions would end?

Susanna hadn't read about time-travel.

"How did you solve it?"

"I have agreed to stay past my contract in exchange for lessons for Phoebe."

"Oh my God, are you insane?"

Forget repercussions to history. What about Susanna? I jumped to my feet. My parent's trip was trivial compared to this. That problem would be over in a few days, but this one could last for…I didn't want to guess for how long.

"Why did you do something so stupid?"

She flinched but didn't budge. "I shall do whatever it takes to keep Phoebe from falling under my master's control. If that is stupid, then I am proud to be a fool."

"I agree with your goal, but there has to be another way."

"It's the only option. If Phoebe is useful, Mr. Shaw will allow her to stay with our mother. Now, lie down or descend to the cave. I cannot have Jedidiah seeing you if he returns."

I flung myself back to the ground, banging my head in the process, which pissed me off even more. "How long will you stay past your contract?"

"Perhaps until next spring."

I suppressed a wild scream. Of all the dumbass things to do. Completely idiotic. Totally...

Damn, I'd run out of synonyms for stupid.

"Do you realize you've made it even easier for Mr. Pratt to see your sister?"

"She will take lessons while he is at the mill."

"What if he comes home early?"

"His wife will not permit him to enter her parlor while she is spinning. Phoebe is safer in a room with Mrs. Pratt than she would be anywhere in the county."

Susanna had thought through the Pratts's involvement, but I still had a bad feeling about it. There were so many other things that could blow up. "Have you signed any paperwork?"

"We didn't draw up papers. My mistress and I agreed."

"Good. It's not legally binding." I didn't really know what to do at this point. Was it possible to ignore the deal and hope history would return to the way it had been?

"My sister's future requires that I uphold my end of the promise."

I closed my eyes and counted to ten in French, because everything sounded better in French. She was not going to let this go. "Why didn't you wait to talk to me?"

"It's my problem. I shall handle it alone."

"We're friends. We're supposed to help each other."

She frowned down at me. "Do you have a better solution?"

"Not off the top of my head. But it hasn't been all that long since you got mad at me for ignoring your ideas. How come you didn't wait to hear mine?" I rattled the sheets. "I collected data. Maybe, somewhere in here, are other possibilities."

"This solution is acceptable. I am ensuring that Phoebe has a valuable skill. If she can make beautiful thread or cloth, Mr. Shaw will be able to sell it for a good price."

"Yeah, what if she's bad at it?"

"She will be good."

"I like your confidence in your sister. So, let's assume she is good. That's not the only thing that can go wrong. What if she breaks her finger? What if he can't sell what she makes and he binds her out anyway?"

"He wouldn't do that." Susanna scowled as the possibilities sank in.

"He might." As I'd suspected, she hadn't planned for everything. "Phoebe's learning something she might never use. Your sister doesn't need training. She needs a job away from Worthville before your mom gets married."

Susanna shook her head. "My mother won't let Phoebe leave." She stepped to the bluff's edge, then flopped down, her legs dangling over the side. "My mother will talk Mr. Shaw into keeping my sister." Her voice was dull.

"Uh-huh. I hope that works out for you." Why did I bother? She'd made up her mind. I had to not care that she'd just tied herself to Pratt for months. Her decision.

The end of her indenture had been in sight. I'd hoped to reach it with her, counting down to her release from prison, because that's what it was. Prison.

I was tempted to walk away, except what happened to her was important to me, even though there wasn't one frickin' thing I could do about it. I crumpled the sheets in my hand. It had been a wasted trip downtown to copy these. If I'd just come here last night and she'd told me her plans, I could've saved myself the effort.

Wait a minute. I smoothed the sheets and read them again. "When did you make the deal with your mistress?"

"Yesterday morning."

My head grew warm and full, like the one time when my dad had left a glass of whiskey within reach when I was little. After one swig, I'd puked for hours.

"I have your sister's indenture. She's bound over to Mr. Pratt in October."

Susanna gave a determined shake of her head. "It will be different now."

"I copied these documents this afternoon—a day after you agreed to stay." I crawled to her side and handed them over. "History didn't change."

She stared at the sheets like they were poison. "It cannot be. Mr. Pratt cannot afford to bind her if I am here. He wants to acquire an apprentice or a slave for the mill. He wouldn't have two servants in the house instead."

"You're looking at the indenture."

"I cannot believe my eyes. It has to be wrong. I have agreed to be here. The Pratts would never choose Phoebe over me." Her voice sounded panicked. "I wouldn't leave their household while repaying my debt for Phoebe's lessons. I gave my word."

There was no need to say anything. Susanna could read the indenture lying in her lap, binding Phoebe Marsh from October thirtieth until the event of her eighteenth birthday or matrimony. It was signed by Anthony Shaw, Jethro Pratt, and a county clerk.

"Will she know how to spin by the end of October?"

"It is not possible to learn enough by then, not even for the most apt pupil." With a groan, she dropped her head in her hands. "I delayed my freedom to rescue my sister," she said, her voice husky, "and now we are both trapped."

Okay, I didn't understand what was going on anymore—whether history had been affected some or none. But screw it. There were two centuries for things to straighten out again. Susanna was my concern now.

"I'm not going to let you do this alone. There's still time. We'll figure it out."

"How?"

"Find her a job somewhere else. Like Raleigh."

"Raleigh?" Her laugh held a hint of bitterness. "The state capital would be an excellent option if we lived there, but eight miles might as well be one thousand. I cannot go with her, and she will never go alone."

"I'll take her."

"You?" The corners of her lips twitched. "With your peculiar clothes and manners, the people of Raleigh will clap you in jail as a lunatic."

"I'll wear a costume." The offer had been impulsive, but the more I thought about it, the more I liked it. And the idea had a long-term benefit, one I hated to remind her of. "If Phoebe is living in Raleigh, she won't be here when Worthville is destroyed."

Susanna sucked in a quick, sharp breath. "Merciful heavens. You are correct." The silence lengthened as she thought hard. "We must do it. Raleigh is a good solution. If only my mother will release her."

"Your mother is releasing her. It's only a question of when."

"Mama can be stubborn."

"Then you'll have to be persuasive." I slipped over the bluff's edge, climbed down the granite ladder, and paused in front of the falls. "How long do I have?"

"They plan to marry in the fall." She hopped to her feet and brushed the dust from her skirt, a faint curve to her lips. "Mr. Shaw is only recently widowed. It's customary to wait several months. Any earlier than September would be scandalous."

"September gives me plenty of time. So, it's a deal?"

"A deal?"

"Yeah. You talk your mother into letting Phoebe go. I'll find her a job."

Even though I had months to find something for Phoebe, I began the search immediately. For one thing, I didn't know if they used the same process back then as we use now. Secondly, if a good job opened up in the summer, better to snag it than count on the good jobs showing up later on.

Researching the job opportunities in post-revolutionary Raleigh became the focus of my next free afternoon. Once I'd satisfied my paying customers, I cleaned up and climbed to the third floor rec room for a marathon of web surfing.

There were mixed results.

Our state government, in the days when they had more budget money than sense, had paid for a project to digitize all of the newspapers ever printed in our state (or colony or province or lord proprietorship or whatever it had been called across the centuries). A month ago, had I known, I would've thought, *damn, what a waste*. Today, I was thinking, *cool for me*.

I typed a narrow set of keywords into my Advanced Search. Summer 1796. Job advertisements. Raleigh newspaper.

Should be simple. Right?

Wrong. New Bern. Fayetteville. Hillsborough. All had newspapers.

But Raleigh? No.

Really? The frickin' state capital didn't have a paper until 1799? That was totally screwed up. It probably drove our early state politicians bonkers—which, come to think of it, was a bonus.

I printed the first page of the first edition of the Raleigh paper. If the upper-class families of 1799 had been living there for a few years, maybe they'd need servants in 1796. I skimmed the content. It read vaguely like an old-fashioned gossip page. An article near the top made fun of the legislature. The bottom had a detailed report of a supper party thrown by a state senator. The dessert had been a "delicious new sweet known as the sonker." Yeah, I could agree with that.

I kept looking through the online records until I found a 1796 edition of the *North-Carolina Minerva and Fayetteville Advertiser*. It had dense columns of text without pictures. There were long letters to the editors, a bizarre obsession with the cargo of ships, numerous missing horses, runaway wives (huh?), and runaway slaves. But no job advertisements.

Newspapers were a bust.

My next query targeted anything on household servants. The search engine returned hordes of indentures. Not the information I wanted, but astonishing enough to stop me. Hundreds of children had been apprenticed, some as young as two. Apparently, the town leaders could act like their own version of Child Protective Services. They got to decide what to do with orphaned kids.

And the town leaders weren't the only ones to blame. Back then, an orphan was someone without a *father*, which meant mothers were binding them out, too.

What must it have felt like to be one of those poor kids? They were handed over to strangers. Told to work their asses off for years. And the cold-hearted jerks forcing them into slavery? Their parents.

It had happened to Susanna, although the cold-hearted jerk in her case was her stepdad.

I clicked on one of the links. A copy of a yellowed document filled the screen. The text was faded but readable. If Susanna's indenture were typical, a lot was pledged on her behalf.

To faithfully serve.
To readily obey his lawful commands and those of his wife.
To reveal no secrets.
To comport herself with the dignity and humility of a good and faithful servant.
To never absent herself from his service without his leave.

In return, the master must provide room and board, instruction for reading and writing, and training in 'the trade and mystery of housewifery.'

Mystery? Didn't seem like much of one to me. More like endless drudgery.

I copied and pasted everything the jerk owed Susanna into a file. This web page also mentioned "freedom dues." I needed to remember to see if she knew what that meant.

Okay, time to refocus. Jobs in 1796 Raleigh.

No matter how hard I tried, I could find no useful information. This surprised me a lot. I was so used to being bombarded with data that it was just obnoxious I couldn't find the one bit I really wanted.

Come on, people. Wanting a job was universal. It couldn't have changed that much over time. There had to be positions that needed filling and people who wanted to fill them, especially in the state capital during the years it was under construction. Without a paper, how did the unemployed find work back then? Show up and hope for the best?

Wait. That had to be it.

If I wanted to know, I'd have to show up, too.

Dad's car was parked in the garage when I returned from my afternoon ride. I glanced at my watch. He was home seriously early.

I walked into the kitchen to find my father sitting on a stool at the island, still wearing his suit and tie. His laptop lay open before him.

"Hey, Dad." Puzzled, I closed the garage door behind me. "What're you doing here?"

"Checking airline fares to Michigan." His lips twitched into a resigned smile. "Have you figured out what you're going to do while we're at the wedding?"

Perfect. Mom wasn't here, and Dad was essentially inviting me to defend my position. Now if I could just manage not to screw this up...

"I want to stay at home *alone*."

"Convince me why you should."

I'd bet he agreed with me and couldn't come right out and say so because, hey, he wanted to stay on his wife's good side. So I had to do all the work on this one.

What might change Mom's mind?

"I run my business out of the garage. I can't provide as good a service to my clients if I'm staying somewhere else."

"Nice try, but you won't get behind over a long weekend."

"Someone has to take care of Mom's cat."

"Toby only likes your mom, anyway. He doesn't come around you unless you're feeding him. Just drop by the house once a day."

"I'm seventeen. I can handle a weekend by myself."

"If we were away at the beach, maybe. But we'll be in northern Michigan. We can't get back here quickly if you have an emergency."

No logic in the world could soothe that fear. "Okay, then. I'll find someone to stay here with me."

"It has to be someone we know."

I frowned at him. "You know my friends."

"Your mother thinks you have a new girlfriend."

"I've already told Mom I'm not dating." I pulled out a stool, sat on it, and decided it was the right time to tell Dad something about Susanna. "There is a girl, but we're just friends. Not even thinking about anything else."

"Were you thinking about having her stay over here or staying at her house?"

"You wouldn't let me do that."

"I'm glad you realize it." He loosened his tie. "So, who will you ask?"

"Probably Carlton. I'll talk to him about it when he gets back from the beach in a few days."

"Sounds good." Dad snapped down the lid of his laptop. "I support your plan. All you need to do now is to get a commitment from Carlton and his mother—then convince Mom."

CHAPTER TWENTY-THREE

A PERFECT CIRCLE OF HORROR

With a fire in the hearth and the oven heating for baking day, the temperature in the kitchen rose to an unbearable level. I left both the front door and rear door ajar and stood in the slight breeze flowing between them.

Even the dough seemed too miserable to rise. "Double, you little fools," I muttered at the bread pans. "Higher."

There was a spate of giggles behind me. I crossed to the back door and found three young ladies squirming on the stump, hands clapped over their mouths.

"Phoebe," I said, attempting to maintain a stern scowl, "what is the matter?"

She shook her head, smothering her laughter.

"And you, Delilah, did someone give you a dose of giggle medicine?"

"No, Susanna." She slid from the stump and thumped up the stairs to my side. I sat on the top stair and pulled her onto my lap.

"Very well, young ladies. Tell me why you laugh."

The two older girls exchanged glances, then giggled anew. Phoebe hopped to her feet. "You scolded the bread dough."

Dorcas stood, too. "You called them little fools."

My lips slid into a smile. "So I did. Do you think the loaves will obey me?"

Three heads wagged in unison.

"Nor do I. Now, I think the time has come for little girls to complete their chores." I tugged Delilah's braid. "You must return to your sampler."

"I don't like to sew." Her lower lip rolled.

"It is an important lesson for a little girl to learn." I rose, carried her down the stairs, and set her firmly on the ground. "You must go now. Dorcas will oversee."

Dorcas and Delilah clasped hands and broke into a run.

With the little girls gone, I turned to Phoebe. "Did you have a lesson with Mrs. Pratt today?"

"I did. She says I learn quickly. Deborah was much displeased by the praise."

I couldn't stop a smile. My sister's natural talent was gratifying. "If you're done, it's time to go home."

"First, let me tell you the news."

My heart skipped a beat. "Bad news?"

"Oh, no," she beamed, "it's good."

I gestured for her to follow me into the kitchen. "Come. We shall sit."

Crossing to the bench, I picked up a bowl of butter beans that needed to be shelled. Phoebe perched beside me, kicking her legs.

"So, tell me your tale. I have to check the dough soon."

She hopped off the bench and twirled, her arms outstretched. "There will be a wedding."

"For whom?"

"Mama."

This should not be news. We had known for several days that she had accepted Mr. Shaw's offer. Unless…

The news was the *date*. I sucked in a deep breath and said with more calm than I felt, "When is the wedding?"

She sighed with anticipation. "It's in three weeks. The Sunday after Independence Day. She says it will be small and quiet, but there will be a feast and cake."

I crushed the beans and pods under clenched fists. We needed more time. It was too soon, for propriety and for me. Why could they not wait a respectable six months from his first wife's passing?

I bowed my head and avoided Phoebe's gaze. "Have they given a reason for that date?"

"Mr. Shaw's sister must leave the day after the wedding to return to her home in Virginia. And Mr. Shaw is most anxious to have a Baptist preacher perform the service. The Baptists have their turn in the meetinghouse on July tenth."

July tenth. A disgracefully short period of mourning for the late Mrs. Shaw. I had hoped to have many more weeks before Mr. Shaw had control of my sister. But time had run out. Although I didn't like making decisions this quickly, they were giving me no choice.

"What does Mr. Shaw say about your spinning lessons?"

"If I don't learn well, he will find me an apprenticeship in some other trade." My sister's brow crinkled with concern.

After seeing the indenture Mark had found, I had known this was the outcome. But somewhere, deep in my heart, I had hoped the document was wrong. Mr. Shaw had always struck me as the meek, dull sort—not interesting enough to earn the animosity I felt toward him now.

"Did Mama hear him say that?"

"Yes, but she believes that I shall do well with spinning and he will let me stay home. What do you think?"

"He will bind you out." My mother was daft—willing to take on the care of another woman's children at the risk of losing her own. "I shall look for the perfect place for you. Would you like my help?"

"Oh, thank you, Susie." She snuggled against me. "I shall not worry if you are involved. Shall we be together?"

"I hope so."

"Shall we stay in Worthville?"

"We shall not." I spat out the response as if it tasted foul.

My sister jumped at my vehemence. "Do you not like it here?"

"I should as soon be a tavern wench as work in this house."

"A tavern wench?" she repeated, her mouth a perfect circle of horror. "Surely not."

"Indeed, I would leave tomorrow if it were possible." I sat on the bench and attacked the butter beans with vigor. They could not, fortunately, fight back. "It might be the very job I seek when I move to Raleigh."

Her eyes grew large and round. "Mr. Shaw won't approve."

For the first time since I had learned of their engagement, I tried to imagine my mother with her betrothed, but his image kept merging with my first stepfather. Both were short of body and long of face, with eternally disapproving expressions. Perhaps my mother had a fondness for sullen men.

"I am glad to remind you Mr. Shaw has no authority over me."

"Mama will try to persuade you otherwise."

"She won't succeed." My jaw flexed at the thread of anger which had never completely faded. Mama had stood by as her second husband bound me out according to his own whims. Even now, she would allow her last natural child to live the same terrible fate as I, turning Phoebe's future over to a man who had clearly shown himself to be undeserving of respect. My mother would receive no further consideration from me.

"What are we to do?" Phoebe said with a catch in her throat.

I brushed empty pods from my apron with brisk hands. "I shall take care of you." I held up a thoughtful finger.

"How are your stitches? Have you any pillowcases or napkins completed? There are plenty of jobs for a girl who is clever with a needle."

"I am quite skilled with insects. I have nearly finished a handkerchief with bees. Would you like to see?"

"Of course. I shall come to visit soon enough. Now, shoo. It's time for me to check the bread and prepare dinner."

She stumbled through the door and skipped from view, the tune she hummed floating in the air.

The rest of the day dragged. I had to talk to Mark. He must come.

Evening finally arrived. With the chores done, and Jedidiah at his lessons, I hurried to the cave without fear of detection. When Mark appeared at the top of his hill, I gestured for him to hurry.

"What's up?" he said, leaping through the narrow ribbon of the falls. "Is everything okay?"

I shook my head. "We must move my sister by Independence Day."

CHAPTER TWENTY-FOUR

TOTAL TRAIN WRECK

It would've made me really happy if Susanna was joking, but the look on her face made it clear that she was dead serious.

I said with exceptional restraint, "Independence Day is barely a week away."

She nodded grimly. "It is fast, I know."

"Fast?" Okay, I was beginning to lose my restraint. "How about insane?"

"Difficult, perhaps, but hardly insane."

"Why do we have to move her so quickly?"

"My mother plans to wed Mr. Shaw on July tenth."

Damn. "Okay, that's a good reason."

Her hands twisted in the folds of her apron, her only sign of agitation. "What have you learned so far?"

"Nothing much." I must be as crazy as she, because I was already sifting through ways to ramp up the speed. "I thought we had months."

"We must look for jobs in a dressmaker's shop, or we may find a large household which requires a skilled needlewoman."

"Right. What, exactly, can a skilled needlewoman do?"

"Embroidery, hemming, and mending."

I snorted. "How large does a household have to be to afford someone who does nothing but stitch all day?"

"Very large. And she would certainly be assigned other duties."

"How many large households will Raleigh have?"

Her face scrunched in thought. "Three or four."

I felt like one of those cartoon characters whose eyes were popping out of my head on threads. "Really? It ought to be easy when I have three to choose from."

"Or four." She ignored my sarcasm. "Phoebe's needlework is truly exquisite. A wealthy family will want her."

Here was the first weird side effect of being with Susanna: the things she needed me to do. Alexis had only asked for trivial stuff. I'd done some of it to keep the peace and blown off the things I really, really didn't want to do. But in Susanna's case, she asked for crazy-important, scary-as-hell, life-and-death things, which I couldn't blow off.

"Let me make sure I understand. First, I'll find your one-talent sister a job with a rich family living near the state capital. And second, we'll move her there, all within the next week."

"Precisely." She gave me the kind of smile a teacher gives to an idiot who has finally said something smart.

"Okay." Crazy or not, I felt engaged by the challenge. It would be a tough, non-stop push to succeed, but already I could feel the energy flowing. "What's the plan?"

"You should start by checking with your web for large households."

"My web? Great idea. I'll give that a try." I pulled out the print-out from the 1799 *Raleigh Register*. "As it happens, I did find a family like that. The Etons sound rich. Do you know who they are?"

"Mr. Nathaniel Eton was a great hero in the war. He fought most bravely and will soon serve the people of North Carolina in our new government."

"Sounds like they like to have fun. They throw parties and serve sonker."

Susanna blinked. "Sonker? Are you sure?" She snatched the document and scanned quickly. Her lips moved as she read the article. "How can this be?"

"What's the problem?"

"Nobody in the county knows the recipe but my mother and I," she said, the words so faint I leaned forward to hear.

"How can you know that?"

"The recipe is a secret." She looked up, a smile brightening her face into something amazingly beautiful. "Do you know what this means? I may be the cook for the Etons."

"So, this is good?"

"Indeed." She read the article again.

The news disturbed me. It reminded me that our time together might end. The falls would stop, or we would stop. The fracture in time would heal.

I had to put it from my mind. It would drive me insane if I focused on Susanna's future instead of the search for Phoebe's job.

"I have a logistical question. How long will it take to get to Raleigh from here?"

"An hour or more by horse," she murmured. "Hours by foot."

"What about your mother? Won't she have to agree to Phoebe's job?"

"Indeed. I shall assume that task." She folded the document and handed it back to me. "I am determined to persuade her. The larger problem is to keep the secret from Mr. Shaw. So I must wait until all of the details are worked out. The more time she has to consider my plan, the more likely she will talk with him. And that I cannot permit." As her smile faded, her eyes narrowed with fear.

"We must settle my sister's future by Independence Day. Please say you'll help us."

The odds were against us. There were no known jobs. We had an immature girl with a doormat for a mother and a jerk for a stepdad-to-be. Susanna couldn't leave Worthville to run any negotiations, and I—who had no experience with eighteenth century behavior—would be her sole set of eyes and ears.

Just when I thought I understood how big the problem was, it got even bigger. My gut told me it was a total train wreck. But we had to win.

How was I going to pull this off?

The obstacles didn't matter. I couldn't refuse.

"I'm in."

The hunt for a costume began as soon as my morning customers had been handled.

My first stop was the junk room— or guest bedroom, as my mother preferred to call it. I stared into the closet for so long, my eyes were starting to cross. Halloween costumes of all shapes and sizes were in there, but none that looked remotely colonial.

I was going to solve the costume problem today.

The stairs creaked. I hadn't really spoken to my mother since the wedding situation first exploded, but desperation was a great equalizer, especially since I needed information she was likely to have.

"Mom," I called, "if you were going to a costume party, where would you look for a costume?"

"The junk closet in the guest bedroom."

"Besides there?"

The brush of her bare feet on carpet came closer. Her head appeared in the doorway. "Are you going to a costume party?"

"Could be."

"When?"

"Independence Day." I faced the shelves. The back of my head had a way better poker face than the front.

"What are you going as?"

"George Washington."

Oddly, she kissed me on the cheek. "*Guess Me!* on Hillsborough Street. If anyone has the father of our country, it would be that store."

"Thanks."

It took me fifteen minutes to bike there. My mom was wrong. They didn't, but they called around and sent me to another shop downtown.

Sash and Dash was hidden between two chic boutiques. If I hadn't known exactly where to look, I wouldn't have found it. The shop smelled the way I would've expected— musty, sweaty, and thick—like the fabrics had released microscopic fibers into the air that I was breathing in. I would've brought a mask if I'd known.

"Can I help you, hon?"

I heard the voice but couldn't find its owner. It came from the corner, so I headed there. An elderly woman with long, curly gray hair and ten earrings in each ear looked up. She wore lots of eye makeup and her lips were black. Intentionally.

"Need something?" Her voice had a heavy-smoker huskiness.

"Yeah. I'm looking for a costume."

She made a sound that was somewhere between a laugh and a pig snort. "Well, it's either that or the bathroom. We don't have much else in here." She unrolled from the beanbag chair she had been sitting in and creaked to her feet. She was nearly as tall as I was. "Did you have something specific in mind?"

"George Washington."

"General or President?"

"President. Second term."

"That narrows it down." Her nose scrunched. "I had you pegged for Spiderman. Or Dr. Frank-N-Furter."

"What?"

She laughed/snorted again. "Georgie, huh? Let's see." She wandered through a long rack of clothes, made a hard right, stopped, pushed a few hangers aside, and grunted. "Here's something."

She took a pair of pants in ugly, dog-poop brown. They tied on, which was probably fine because they were too big. I swung them around. The back was split open.

"My ass will show through these."

"Then, obviously, you'll have to sew them."

"Is the store not responsible for that?"

"Do I look like a seamstress?" Her laugh morphed into a mucousy cough. "I'll sell them to you for ten bucks."

"Sure. Whatever." My mom had a sewing machine. She would take care of them for me. I just had to work out how I would answer all of the questions she would ask. "I need more than pants."

"They're called breeches. And yes, you do." She pulled out a white shirt. Huge sleeves with buttons at the wrists. It was open to mid-chest but had laces. "How about this?"

It stank. Like beer and BO. "I assume you're not a laundromat, either?"

"You catch on quickly. I'll sell this one for ten bucks."

"Do you ever rent?"

"If you want to rent, you try *Guess Me!* on Hillsborough Street."

"Yeah, they sent me here."

"So you're stuck. Twenty bucks."

"Okay." I'd expected to spend more on rentals. So far, so good.

"Shoes, my young Georgie?"

"Probably."

They were awful. Big, black, cracked leather things with thick heels and silverish buckles.

"What do you think, hon?"

"I think not."

"Wise choice. No one'll look at your feet."

Yeah. Black athletic shoes would have to do. "Anything else I should have?"

"Hat." She handed over a tricorn hat made of navy felt. "It's on the house."

The hat was the nastiest thing I'd ever tried on. "Sure."

"Jacket." She held up a blue wool coat with big buttons and gold trim and waggled her eyebrows.

"In the summer? No way."

She shrugged and tossed it on a dresser piled with similarly discarded items. "You must have stockings."

"Why?"

"Back then, bare legs were not smoking." With a jerk of her head, she wove her way through the maze of her shop toward the front.

I followed.

Fingers flying, she rang up my stuff on an antique cash register. "You can buy stockings at the drug store. Knee highs. Like your mom wears."

"My mom does not wear knee highs."

"Your grandma, then." She held out her hand, palm up, and wiggled her fingers. "Twenty bucks. Hand 'em over."

I stopped at Meredith Ridge Shopping Center on my way home, bought *The Witch of Blackbird Pond* at the bookstore, and then headed into the drug store for fake stockings.

Damn. If someone had told me a month ago that I'd be taking time away from my training and my business to hit the State Archives or to buy a costume with stockings, I would've said they were crazy.

But then, I hadn't met Susanna yet—and for her, I'd do whatever it took.

The hose aisle was easy enough to find. I hadn't expected so many kinds and colors, though. Not just black and brown. There were red, purple, blue, and *yellow*? Seriously?

The sizes weren't helpful. Small. Medium. Large. Queen.

Really? They had queen but not extra-large or gigantic or guy-with-big-calves?

"Hey, Mark."

Alexis's voice. Of course. Why did she keep popping up in places where I was and didn't want her to be?

"Hey," I said as I grabbed a package and flipped to the back. There was a size chart. Cool.

"So…" She stepped closer. "What are you looking for?"

I looked at the display and then at the package in my hand. How much more obvious could it be? "Knee highs."

She blinked. "Why?"

"My mom. Is queen the biggest?" I flipped to the front and rechecked the color. Dark brown was good.

"Uh-huh." She pointed at a different package. "Your mom is more this size."

"Nah, I'll take these." I lowered my voice, as if I were telling a secret. "She's allergic to bee stings. One got her in the leg." I made a muffled explosion sound. "Serious swelling."

"Uh-huh." She fell into step beside me as I walked to the front. "Tell her I hope she feels better."

"Sure thing."

Alexis detoured to another aisle while I waited my turn in the checkout line. I was proud of myself. That had gone well. Very polite. Civil. Mature.

I glanced back over my shoulder as I exited the store and froze.

She stood beside Carlton in front of the refrigerators, choosing cold drinks.

They were holding hands.

Carlton had been home since Sunday. We'd texted a couple of times but could never seem to work out anything. I'd been too busy with Susanna to even think about why.

Now I knew. *I* wasn't the problem.

My insides felt hollow and expanding—a great big void, waiting for the right emotion to fill it up.

I didn't feel jealousy. At a purely selfish level, I wanted Alexis to be focused on another guy. It meant I wouldn't run into her on the greenway anymore. It was great, too, that it wasn't Keefe. That would've pissed me off, because he'd been involved with the bully ring somehow and Alexis knew it.

So what emotions were left? Anger? Sadness?

Aunt Pamela had once said that the worst kind of betrayal could only come at the hands of a friend. I'd never really understood what she meant until this moment.

Carlton's head whipped around and our gazes locked. The muscles along his jaw tensed. He flushed a dark red and then looked back at the cold drinks.

Alexis finally had a boyfriend who didn't play competitive sports year-round, and she hadn't had to look any further than my best friend.

Chapter Twenty-Five

Defiant Spirit

My master signaled his son to stay with his lessons tonight, but their silent exchange held a sinister cast.

I set out on my break cautiously, but there were no signs of a spy. With the cave as my destination, I strolled quickly through the woods and emerged on the ribbon of grasses edging Rocky Creek.

Behind me, a twig snapped.

I hesitated. The murmurings of the night creatures had already suggested another presence. The twig provided confirmation. But it was only one twig. Whoever spied from the shadows possessed skill.

Even if Jedidiah had not stayed home for his lessons, I would know it could not be he. Jedidiah was not so quiet.

It must be my master who hunted me.

In another few steps, I might have given my secrets away. My intent to approach the creek was clear. Any change would alert the hunter that I was aware of him. I would go to the creek but not the cave.

I remained on the bluff, upstream from the falls. The water was slow-moving and shallow. Kneeling on the bank, I made a show of splashing water on my face and arms.

Night was falling fast. I resumed my walk on the trail to the village, looking straight ahead, hoping Mark would make no attempt to catch my attention. The forest enveloped me under its dense cover. The occasional brush of boots against bark warned me that Mr. Pratt still followed.

My mood diminished with each step that took me nearer the town and farther from Mark. Since I could not be with him this evening, I would indulge my thoughts instead. What had he learned? Would we be successful in finding Phoebe a good job?

How could I wait another day? I wanted my sister's life settled now. This minute. I could not permit Phoebe to suffer the same misery as I had.

My first year with the Pratts had been the worst. I had been young enough—and foolish enough—to believe I could prevail. I was Susanna the Undaunted. I would not be cowed. Josiah Marsh's daughter might've changed houses, but she wouldn't change herself.

Mr. Pratt had taught me quickly I could keep none of my former self and work for him. *Spare the rod and spoil the child* was his personal creed. He had determined to beat every trait out of me, except the ability to work. A sharp tongue drew slaps to my mouth. A cross look resulted in bed without supper. Rebellion brought a thrashing—in the evening, of course, so I had the full night to recover.

I grew quite skilled at removing blood from clothes and forcing my emotions into the hidden corners of my soul. I lived in resignation with my lot.

Since meeting Mark, however, contentment had turned to turmoil. Had he caused the turmoil or had he only illuminated it?

Perhaps he was responsible for the increase in my distress. Until I met Mark, the final months had not seemed so interminable. I could only have endured my servitude for eight years by ignoring my longing to leave. Had those feelings died, or had they merely lain dormant until Mark's presence coaxed them to stir?

Truly, the answers didn't matter. I couldn't imagine my life without a friend—without *him*—anymore.

I finished a slow circuit through the town and returned to the Pratt property. As I entered the kitchen to check tomorrow's porridge, the door to the main house made a soft snick. My master had spent his evening seeking to unmask my secrets. His efforts had been in vain.

Saturday was a rare, mild day. The children played outside, weeded the garden with me, or hunted berries in the thicket. They were all thoroughly grimy by evening, just in time for their monthly baths.

After supper, I set the large tub in the center of the kitchen and filled it with heated water. Once my master and mistress had bathed, the children took their turns. Deborah assisted me with the little ones. I would bathe last.

The family retired to the main house.

I removed the long, sharp thorns that pinned the edges of my bodice together and laid them carefully on the worktable. My cap and hairpins followed.

With reluctance, I gripped the side of the tub and stared at the murky water within. I dreaded the thought of another cold, dirty bath.

A defiant spirit possessed me. I yanked my hand away and gave the tub a hard kick. It tipped over, flooding the floorboards of the kitchen, the bath water seeping through the cracks.

I would bathe under the moon and the stars, in water I shared only with the rocks.

It was too late to be out, *and* it was the night before the Sabbath. But I didn't care. When I reached the bluff, I sought a view of the other bank, gleaming silvery-gray in the moonlight, knowing Mark would not be there but looking nonetheless. I climbed down the wall, undressed to my shift, and draped my garments over a boulder.

The falls streamed over the top of the ledge and fell in ropes of water that separated, intertwined, and danced apart. The creek was like a serene, shallow pool.

I sucked in a nervous breath. The falls would not pound my head. The creek's current would not pull me under. It was safe. Completely, utterly safe. I put one foot in, then another, and waited. The stream lapped about my ankles.

It was foolish to pause, wasting my precious time. I waded to the falls and stood under its gentle flow, the water deliciously cool in the warm evening.

I returned to the house a long time later, refreshed and happy to have conquered the creek. On tiptoe, I ascended the steps to the attic, meeting no one on the way, and prayed that my sleep would be as lovely as the final hour of my day.

The Pratts rose early the next morning, donned their Sunday best, and waited for their simple breakfast of porridge and cider. Once the meal was eaten, we marched— parents in the front, children lined up behind like little ducklings, me a respectful distance to the rear—on the path to town.

The Methodists had the meetinghouse this Sunday, but no preacher. Mr. Worth, as the most prominent Methodist in town, would lead the worship service. He would speak on his favorite topic, lust and its perverted partners, fornication and adultery.

The Pratts clattered up the steps into the meetinghouse. I lagged behind, preferring to remain in the shade of the building until the last possible moment. Mary Whitfield greeted me quietly, her eyes darting here and there, looking for someone. Reuben Elliott, no doubt.

A flutter of movement filtered through the trees, not the breeze or an animal, but a flash of white which contrasted starkly against the pine trunks. A traveler passed alongside the creek and stopped where the path reached the main road. I squinted. It was a young man in a white shirt and dark hat. He glanced furtively in our direction before turning toward Raleigh, pushing an odd machine.

Mark was here?

Lightheaded from joy, I nodded to Mary, hurried to the privy, and ducked behind it. No one had noticed. I darted into the woods, paralleling the road until I rounded the bend, out of sight of the churchgoers. From ahead came the soft crunch of shoes on pine cones.

"Mark?" I called as loudly as I dared.

He emerged from the trees opposite me.

"Hey." Pushing his bike, he met me in the center of the road.

I admired his costume. The breeches and shirt fit comfortably. "You look well in our clothes."

He glanced down with pride. "It was a lot of trouble to put together."

"I am glad you made the effort. We couldn't have explained you otherwise." I gestured at his shirt, glad of the casual relationship we had. "Perhaps it would be best to wear your shirt loose, as the tradesmen do."

"Tradesmen?" He smiled. "Why can't I be a gentleman?"

"If you wish to be a gentleman, you will need a waistcoat and jacket. No respectable man is without them."

He frowned. "The lady at the store didn't suggest a waistcoat."

"Perhaps she doesn't visit my century often." I laughed with the sheer delight of being in his presence. I had gone too many days without my friend.

He removed the blue hat, stuffed it into the back of his breeches, and strapped on the cracked bowl. "I need to go."

"Where?"

"I'm heading to your Raleigh to size things up."

"For what purpose?"

"A job for Phoebe."

"Today? It's the Sabbath." What did Mark and his family do on Sundays? "The likely households will all be attending church."

He slammed a fist against the open palm of his other hand. "I should've thought about that. Will there be anyone around to ask?"

I considered the possibilities. "The taverns will be open, and there will be servants about, tending to horses and children. They might know of families requiring more staff."

"Cool. That's what I'll do—ask anybody who smiles at me until I find some answers. Once I have a few names, I'll return to my world and check the web to see which families are the best bets."

My heart thumped with a fullness such as I had never known. No one had ever tried this hard to help me. "Will anyone from your world notice if you are absent?"

"It won't be long—and no, my parents won't notice. I left a note." He looped an arm about my waist and drew me into a hug. "We'll figure this out, Susanna. I promise."

"Thank you." I pressed a kiss to his cheek. "Be careful."

He released me, and then mounted the bike, his attention focused on the road. "Where will you be this morning?"

"At the meetinghouse."

"How long does your church service last?"

"Three hours or more."

"That's too bad."

"Your comment is especially apt when the speaker is Mr. Worth." I backed away, worried about the length of my absence yet reluctant to say good-bye first.

"I'd better be going. I'll let you know something as soon as I can." He pushed off. Within seconds, he disappeared over the hill.

I turned toward the meetinghouse, my delight fading to nerves. Why had I let Mark do this? He did not know our roads, our manners, or our speech. What if he said the wrong thing or approached the wrong person?

What if he were hurt?

I was the only person who knew he was here—the only person who could help him if things did not go well. The thought was terrifying.

Even if it had not been Sunday, I would still have spent the next three hours in prayer.

CHAPTER TWENTY-SIX

ANOTHER MOMENT OF STUPIDITY

Susanna had called the ground beneath me a road. What a joke. It was more of a rough track, cleared of trees but not roots. I could just imagine how it would feel to ride in the back of a horse-drawn wagon—like being a human-sized pinball batted around inside a colossal arcade game.

Not that I was complaining. For me, this miserable excuse for a road ended up being great training. It had plenty of hills, a couple with challenging grades. Today's project would double as a decent workout. Eight miles to the part of Raleigh that existed two hundred twenty-two years ago and then eight miles back.

The scenery was amazing. Trees lined the trail, miles and miles of them, so thick it was like being under a canopy of green, surrounded by the scent of pine straw and fallen leaves. Yellow and purple wildflowers clumped in wiry patches. I was in awe.

From the woods to my right, something crackled and thudded. Three deer loped across the road, zigzagging directly into my path. It happened so fast I had no time to react. Down I went into the hard-packed earth. No natural compost to soften the blow.

A thin cloud of dust puffed around me, clogging my throat and nose. Everything ached. Full mountain bike protective gear would've been hard to explain and had seemed like an unnecessary precaution this morning, so I'd only worn the costume. I cursed the deer and my lack of padding.

A couple of branches snapped nearby. I rocketed into a sitting position, whipped off my shades, and stared into the pines on the north side of the road. Nothing moved.

Snap.

The sound was closer this time, my signal to go. I sprang to my feet, righted the bike, leapt on, and pedaled with the speed born of a super rush of adrenaline.

Something—really, some *things*—ran in the woods, paralleling my track. It (or they) kept up with me for a few seconds and then swerved away. I didn't let up for several minutes.

As my heartbeat slowed, my thoughts electrified. The whole idea of coming here had seemed like some sort of virtual reality game—minus the virtual. The past spread around me, quiet, beautiful, but also wild. Not that I hadn't encountered wild animals in my century. I had. It just felt different here, as if modern-day animals were smarter and knew how to stay out of a human's way. The ones here might be purely aggressive.

This experience intimidated me in ways I hadn't expected. And it wasn't just the forest and the animals. How would people react to me? How would I react to them? What would they do if they figured out just how alien I was?

After a half hour or so, I climbed a low, steady incline and crested a ridge. I'd arrived at the edge of town. Braking, I slipped off my bike, arrested by my first glimpse of eighteenth century Raleigh. The capital city lay before me, a grid of dirt roads, wooden buildings, and sparse trees. At its center squatted a bald patch of land—Union Square, where the State Capitol building would show up in another fifty years. Right now, all I could see was the second story of a large-but-unfamiliar brick building, topped by a domed steeple.

My insides quaked. I'd lived in this place my entire life, yet it was as foreign to me as another planet. It was real. And it was freakish. I fought the urge to turn the bike around and race back to the world I knew.

Okay, take a breath. Refocus.

Susanna needed me. I had a mission to complete and the clock ticked on. After securing my bike, I sucked down a swig of water, switched out helmet for hat, and pulled out a copy of an ancient map.

The Internet reported that a tavern near Union Square served as the hub of the community. I walked on the road down the ridge, warily eying the thick undergrowth on either side.

Just past the brickyards, I managed to reach an actual city street without injuring myself or encountering any poisonous snakes.

At street level, the reality of this Raleigh was disappointing. I half-expected a replica of Colonial Williamsburg. Nice wide lanes with smooth surfaces. Whitewashed fences around lawns and big houses. Rows of shops.

Wrong.

The closer I walked to the center of town, the weirder things became.

The sun-baked streets had hardened into ruts clogged with debris and horseshit. There were definite signs of a building boom, yet it was eerily silent. Partially finished structures stretched before me across the jagged skyline. Inhabited buildings were littered with wood chips and sawdust, the gaps between boards promising a cold winter. One-story houses were wedged between taverns and shops, smoke wisping from their brick chimneys.

It was like walking into a cheesy theme area at an amusement park. Historyland.

The smell of human piss permeated the air. I cupped my hand over my nose and tried not to gag. There must not be enough outhouses, because people seemed to be doing their business wherever they wanted.

Traffic thickened. Carriages rolled by, carrying women in puffy-sleeved dresses. Beside them, men in dark jackets and hats clip-clopped along on horseback.

The unfamiliar sounds made me think about my world even more. I never paid attention to construction noises or mowers. I never noticed emergency vehicles or trains. But I missed them here. It was crazy.

And even though their clothes were new to me, no one stood out. The ladies looked alike. Their dresses might be in different pale shades, but there was only one style. Fashion had changed a lot by the twenty-first century. We could get away with just about anything. Long, short, full, tight, colorful, monotone, boring, slutty. So much variety. It took this place of sameness to make me notice.

"Son, watch out," someone yelled.

A carriage bumped straight towards me. A heavy hand landed on my shoulder and gave a rough jerk. I fell back a couple of steps. The carriage rolled by in the exact spot where I'd been standing.

"Thanks." I turned around, heart pumping. A man scowled behind me, as wide as he was tall.

"Just watch what you're doing." He scratched his scraggly beard. "Going to services?" He studied my outfit with a skeptical frown.

"No. Not today."

"What are you looking for?"

"Information."

He didn't show any surprise. "The best place would be the tavern." He jerked a blackened thumb ahead of me. "It'll be thataway."

"Thanks."

Susanna had been right about the vest. All men had on one of those and a lot of the guys wore jackets, which had to be horrible in this heat.

I found the tavern and ducked in. It was dark and reeked of burned meat and stale grease. Long tables crisscrossed the dirty floors. Two men sat at the far end by a big stone fireplace, hunched over, drinking from tankards.

An older woman approached me. She wore gray from neck to ankle with a really clean apron. She had tired eyes and a nice smile. "Can I be helping you?"

"Yes." Another moment of stupidity. I should've scripted what to say. "My..." I paused. What should I call Phoebe? A friend would be too suspicious. Not my sister, since I couldn't even describe her if they asked. Maybe cousin would be best. That was kind of vague. "My cousin Phoebe is looking for work. Have you heard about any jobs?"

"Indeed." She shuffled to the entrance to the tavern and pointed past the meetinghouse. "I've heard the Whitakers are looking for a kitchen maid. They live a block off the square."

"Any others?"

"New families move in daily. Many want servants." She cocked her head and peered at me through bleary eyes. "How old is your cousin?"

I didn't know, so I'd have to make something up. We could always fix the lie later. "Fourteen."

"Well, then, the Palmers and the Haywoods are looking for house maids." She lowered her voice and leaned closer. "The Bishops seek a laundry maid. I should not consider them unless I was desperate. I have my doubts as to the kind of household they maintain."

This was great. Three possibilities, with one more in the last-resort category. "Thanks for the information."

"You are welcome." She gave me a hopeful look. "Might you want a bite to eat?"

I was starving. "Not today."

"No money?"

I shook my head.

She held up a detaining hand and disappeared into the back. A moment later she came back, a thick slice of bread in her hand. "Here you are. Perhaps I shall see you again next time you come this way."

It was so incredibly nice of her. The bread was warm, yeasty, and coarse-grained. Mmmm. "Thanks. I'll remember." I didn't even know whether dollars had been invented yet or how I could repay the tavernkeeper. It was a question I'd save for Susanna.

The return trip was easy and fast. As I climbed the final hill before heading for the falls, I peered at the empty lane of Worthville. Everyone was in church, weren't they? Susanna had said it would be hours.

Maybe I could take a quick look around.

I rode onto the path that led to the falls and then maneuvered into the trees to hide my bike. Keeping to the edge of the forest, I crept closer to the village.

The lane was still quiet. Through the meetinghouse windows, I could see faint movements. Church hadn't ended.

Perspiration soaked my hair and itched under my clothes. I smelled like an entire locker room, nasty and sour. I stepped into the shade under an oak just as the meetinghouse burst into noise. Benches scraped against wooden floors. Children shouted. Heavy shoes stomped and squeaked.

It was too late to escape unseen. Maybe a confident stroll would work.

A family came out—husband, wife, two kids. They wore somber clothes in brown and gray. The adults talked until they noticed me.

I nodded politely and turned to leave.

"You, sir," the man called.

Caught. "Yes?"

"Are you lost?"

"No."

A tall man thumped down the stairs, a short, overweight woman on his arm. Behind them trailed several kids. The husband stopped on the opposite side of the lane, clasped his hands before him, and studied me. His wife stayed behind him, peeking around his shoulder. A serious teen guy and a bold teen girl eyed me from their father's shadow.

Susanna appeared in the meetinghouse door, her arms and skirt full of little kids. She crossed to where the tall man and heavy woman waited and then followed the direction of their gazes. When she saw me, she shuddered and looked away.

I'd made a horrible mistake.

CHAPTER TWENTY-SEVEN

CRIMSON HAZE

Had Mark gone mad?

My mouth went dry with dread. This day could not end well for me.

"You are a stranger in our town," Mr. Pratt said. "Who are you and what is your business?"

"My name is Mark Lewis."

The town cooper drew even with my master. "Mr. Lewis reports that he is not lost."

Mr. Pratt cleared his throat. "What is your reason to visit Worthville this Sunday?"

I raised my head. Mark met my gaze, apology in his expression.

My master flushed. "Sir? Your purpose?"

Mark gazed back calmly. "Just walking through."

Several of the menfolk formed a line on either side of Mr. Pratt.

"That is a peculiar activity on the Sabbath," Solomon Worth said in a menacing tone, rubbing his fist.

Merciful heavens, Mark did not realize his danger. I would have to soothe the tension before it ignited. "No doubt Mr. Lewis is returning to his home after a long journey."

Mark nodded. "Miss Marsh is correct."

His response sent a jolt rippling through the crowd.

Mr. Pratt turned to stare at me. "Do you know my servant, Mr. Lewis?"

"We've met. I'd like to talk with her again."

"No, indeed, Mr. Lewis. You may not speak with my servant."

The crowd had grown silent. Not even the babies fussed.

Mark shifted his gaze from me to Mr. Pratt. "Why not?"

"She's busy. She has chores."

Mark smiled, a tight, superior smile. "Chores on the Sabbath? In Raleigh, we allow our servants to honor their day of rest."

Pride swelled within me at Mark's answer. He displayed an air of confidence and disdain rather than the deference my master preferred in such exchanges. I shifted John to my other hip as I fought to keep my lips straight.

"Susanna," my master said with a frightening softness, "you may speak briefly with this visitor."

I laid Baby John in Deborah's outstretched arms, ensured that Dorcas held hands with Delilah and Dinah, and then moved to the center of the lane, leaving a proper distance between me and Mark.

"Do not tarry long," Mr. Pratt warned. "You wouldn't wish to miss your dinner." He stormed into the woods, the family trotting after him.

One by one, the townsfolk drifted to their homes. When nobody remained within earshot, I said, "Why have you come?"

"I'm sorry. I wanted a quick look, but my timing totally sucked." His lips twisted. "Did you just rescue me from something?"

"Indeed." I didn't wish to dwell on his error, but neither would I say it was all right. Even though Mark had meant no harm, I would pay the consequences. "We are here now and cannot talk for long. Tell me what you learned."

He pulled a sheet of paper from his pocket. "I talked with a lady in a tavern. She mentioned four families needing maids. One for the laundry, one for the kitchen, and two for the house."

A household employing laundry maids would be an important one. But a housemaid job would be the least likely to ruin Phoebe's hands.

"Which families?"

He handed over the list.

I read quickly. "Both Mr. Haywood and Mr. Whitaker are statesmen, but I prefer the position in Mr. Haywood's home. A job cleaning inside the house would be better than washing dishes in the scullery or laundering sheets. Is it time to take Phoebe to Raleigh?"

"Not yet. I want to check on these people and make sure they're all right. And now that I know what to look for, I might find one or two more names. I'll come back on Tuesday, and we can decide the best date then."

"I shall wait to talk to my mother until we speak again."

He walked backwards. "I'm sorry."

"It wasn't wise for you to come, but I'm glad you did."

He nodded, spun on his heel, and ran.

From the shade of an oak, I watched until Mark disappeared beyond a rise in the road. Around me, the townsfolk had dispersed, retreating to their homes for a cold dinner.

I trudged along the path to the Pratt house. Despite the heat, chills rolled down my limbs. I would be punished for Mark's visit. The only question was how severely.

The family was gathered at the table, eating bean soup and bread. All looked up when I entered. No one spoke.

Mr. Pratt reclined in his chair and steepled his fingers under his chin. I went about my chores, pouring cider. When I reached his side, he said, "Where did you meet Mr. Lewis?"

I filled my master's cup as I sorted through several lies. "I met him on the Raleigh Road."

"When?"

"Three weeks past."

"For what reason?"

I gave a deliberately casual shrug. "He asked directions."

"On such slim acquaintance, I wonder why he would speak with you today."

My mind fumbled for a reasonable response and came up with nothing. Why had I not anticipated these questions?

"Mr. Lewis," I said, drawing out each word slowly, "is on a journey from Ward's Crossroads. I pointed the way to Raleigh."

Mr. Pratt grunted skeptically. "Mr. Lewis seems remarkably willing to travel without knowing the route."

I nodded vaguely and turned away.

"He is most handsome," Deborah said. "Such beautiful teeth."

Her father rapped his knuckles on the table before her. She sniffed and lowered her gaze.

My master glared at me but said nothing more. I circled the table to serve my mistress.

She took a dainty sip. "I crave cake, Susanna. You must bake me a ginger cake tomorrow."

I glanced down the length of the table at my master. We had run out of ginger. There was also no sugar left, and my mistress did not care for honey.

Mr. Pratt dismissed her request with the wave of a hand. "Susanna doesn't need to fire up the oven. You may wait until baking day."

"I don't wish to wait until Wednesday for cake."

"But you will."

She sent me a resentful glare and then fumed over her dish.

After I finished serving the cider, I took Dinah and John to their room for naps. By the time I made it back to the first floor, the rest of the family had left the table.

I departed the house with arms full of dirty trenchers and an empty pitcher, glad to return to the kitchen and its solitude. Dropping my load of dishes into the washtub, I pondered the scene in the dining room. It had gone better than I expected.

Long, hard fingers grasped my upper arm and jerked me backwards until I stumbled into a solid body. My master's other hand splayed across my belly, pinning me to him. Shock crawled like tiny spiders up my neck.

"Is Mr. Lewis your secret beau?"

"I have no secret beau." The cloying scent of sweaty wool filled my nostrils. My master had never touched me with such intimacy.

"Has he made advances toward you?"

"Mr. Lewis has done nothing improper." Blood thrummed in my ears, muffling sound.

"Has he kissed you?" Mr. Pratt's breath rasped in my ear.

"No."

"He had better not come near you again. You belong to me."

Belong? Merciful heavens, I was indentured—not enslaved. My master had begun to sound like a crazed man. I must try to calm him.

"Mr. Pratt, please release me. I must go to the little ones. They may wake from their naps soon."

"Nothing else is completely mine," the whispery voice continued as if I hadn't spoken. "I own the farm and the mill. Yet Drusilla won't let me forget they came to me as her dowry. Fat, stupid cow."

I struggled, but his iron hold tightened.

"Please release me, sir. I don't wish to share these confidences."

"You will listen if I say so."

He was too strong to escape. Panic nearly squeezed the breath from my lungs. We were alone. If I screamed, no one would come.

Horror shuddered through me as I recognized his body's hardened response to our contact. My fear excited him.

He barked a laugh, low and wicked. "You may not associate with Mr. Lewis or any other man."

Not associate with Mark? That was one order I had no intention of obeying. Mr. Pratt would have to chain me to the kitchen to prevent my time with Mark.

With resolve came clarity. Pleading hadn't worked, nor had struggling. I would change tactics. I went limp.

He grunted in surprise as my body sagged. He held on a moment longer and dropped me. I lay where I landed. He nudged my back once with the toe of his boot and stepped over me. Heels clicking, he stalked to the door.

"I do not tolerate anyone stealing what is mine. If Mr. Lewis is caught near you again, he will regret it."

With the breakfast dishes washed and the beans cooking in a kettle, I slipped into the pantry with a wedge of cheese and reached beneath the shelves for my copy of *Persuasion*. The second reading of this novel was providing as much enjoyment as the first.

"Susanna, there you are," Mrs. Pratt said from just behind me.

How had I not heard her enter the kitchen?

There was no chance to hide the book below the shelves. I slid it into my pocket and hoped she hadn't noticed the furtive movement.

"Why are you skulking in the pantry? Come out here." My mistress bustled over to the bench, lowered herself, and smoothed the skirts of her new cream frock over her swelling belly.

"We must plan a second baking day for Friday."

Perhaps now I understood why my master could not pay his account at the store. My mistress spent large sums on fashion.

"A second baking day, ma'am?"

"My contributions to the Independence Day celebration are always the envy of the village ladies, and this year will be no different." She fanned herself, anticipation softening her face. "I want to bring unusual dishes. No one else will think to bring a sweet potato tart and a berry sonker."

I watched my mistress with foreboding. The time had come for her to learn of the family's dire circumstances, and I would have to be the one to tell her. I didn't relish the task or the consequences.

"I cannot bake treats this week."

"Whyever not?"

"We have run out of sugar and spices."

She paused in her fanning and gave me a hard stare. "You must be mistaken."

"No, ma'am."

With a groan, she rose and pushed past me to charge into the pantry. There was the clack of jars opening and closing. She emerged, a petulant curl to her lip.

"How very stupid to let the staples fall so low. Why have you not warned Mr. Pratt?"

I didn't allow the insult to alter my expression. "I warned him two weeks ago."

Her nostrils flared. "I shall speak with my husband. You had better be telling the truth. Now, go to Mr. Foster at once and fetch more." She waved me toward the door.

"Mr. Foster will not sell to us."

Her eyes narrowed in confusion. "For what reason?"

"Perhaps your husband can explain."

I could only imagine the scene. Mrs. Pratt would rage at my master. He would know the source of her information, and I would be lashed again for sharing his secrets. It might be wise to check the garden.

Mrs. Pratt's expression passed through a variety of emotions in rapid succession, ending with determination.

"Follow me." She disappeared into the yard.

I glanced around for a place to hide my book. In the large kettle?

"Susanna?" Mrs. Pratt huffed from the doorway. "Was I not clear?"

"Yes, ma'am."

I hurried to keep pace. Her lumbering walk was surprisingly swift. She headed to Mr. Foster's store and paused outside. "Wait here."

"Yes, ma'am."

She clomped up the wooden stairs and through the threshold. Voices raised and faded. After a time, my mistress returned.

"You may enter and collect a new portion of sugar. Mr. Foster will also provide cinnamon and ginger." She awaited me at the bottom of the stairs.

A thin-lipped Mr. Foster stacked the supplies in my arms. As I accompanied my mistress to the Pratts's property, I pondered what else to serve for dinner. A skillet of cornbread would go well with the pot of beans, and perhaps I should search the garden for more cucumber.

Deborah had the four youngest children in the yard. When Dorcas spied us, she ran over. "Mama?"

"Leave me be, Dorcas." She turned to her eldest daughter. "Is your Papa home?"

"Yes, ma'am." Deborah gulped. "He says he has returned for dinner."

Mrs. Pratt gave a sharp nod and entered the house. The door closed with a soft click.

Deborah scooped up John and followed me to the kitchen. "Where has Mama been?"

"The store."

Dorcas poked her head in the door. "What do you have?"

"Spices."

"Will you make a treat today?"

I shook my head regretfully while I fetched cornmeal and a bowl.

Shouts erupted from the house. Dorcas spun around and ran. Deborah and I rushed to the door.

"I do not know what to make of this," Deborah said, her arms tightening protectively around the baby.

"Nor do I."

She quivered with fright. "I do believe it is time to check on the chickens."

"A wise choice." Backing into the kitchen, I wondered how quickly I could disappear into the garden. If only I hadn't started the cornbread. I returned to the worktable and mixed the batter with vigor.

"Delilah, Dinah, come," Deborah called, urging her youngest sisters closer. No sooner had they thumped down the rear stairs than Dorcas slipped in through the front door.

"Susanna, I have never heard them so angry. Papa told Mama the mill is faring poorly at present..."

I had wondered about that, although it made little sense. After the excitement of adding a new grindstone for wheat—shipped all the way from France—I would have thought their business would increase. How could any of us have known that closing the mill for a few short weeks would have such a lingering effect?

"...and Mama told him to visit his brother and ask for supplies."

Mr. Pratt had not seen his older brother in the entire time I had worked here, which was nearly eight years. Mr. George Pratt lived but a day's drive away.

"Dorcas, perhaps you should join John and your sisters at the chicken coop."

"There is no need. Deborah can tend them without me." She ran to my side. "Why does Papa hate his brother so? He told Mama we would go hungry before he'd beg Uncle George."

"Dorcas, hush." My protest was half-hearted as conscience warred with interest. "You should not gossip."

"It's not gossip if it's the truth." Her face crumpled in dismay. "Mama said she would go to Uncle Worth for food. She said she wouldn't let her children starve because Papa was too proud to seek help."

"Truly, you must stop." As I looked about for the iron skillet, I marveled at Mrs. Pratt's boldness. My master valued his reputation too greatly to allow Mr. Worth to be approached. But would it be enough to conquer his estrangement from his brother?

"Are we going to starve, Susanna?"

I wanted to reassure her, but our supplies were still too low. With the garden suffering in the heat, we might have to try fishing or hunting if something didn't change soon.

"Your parents won't let it come to that. They will resolve the issue, I have no doubt."

"Papa told Mama that Uncle George stole his inheritance."

I held up my hand. "Not another word, Dorcas."

"Is Uncle George a thief?"

"Don't let your father hear you say such a thing," I said, pouring batter into the skillet. While I was placing it in the ashes of the fireplace, the shouting stopped.

Dorcas watched me from the doorway, eyes wide with worry. "Susanna, you must hide. Papa has been yelling your name."

"Thank you."

I grabbed a bucket and ran through the back door, not stopping until I reached the garden. As I peered through the cornstalks, I saw my master exit the house and march to the kitchen. Moments later, he came out the back and spoke to Dorcas. She shook her head. He scanned the yard and stomped to the house with his daughter following silently. I squatted and hugged my bucket, hoping he had given up his search for me.

Within easy reach were peppers and cucumbers. I picked the ripest ones, all the while reflecting on Dorcas's earlier gossip. Mr. Pratt had never spoken well of his brother in my hearing. But stealing? It was a strong accusation. Mr. George Pratt was the oldest brother. It was his due to receive the entirety of their father's property. He couldn't steal what was rightfully his.

I lugged the bucket to the kitchen and set it on the worktable. Mrs. Pratt would like the cucumber, so I retrieved a knife and a platter. As I bent over the scarred wooden tabletop, *Persuasion*, nestled in my pocket, thumped against the table's edge.

"What was that noise?" my master asked from the door.

Icy tendrils of fear curled down my neck.

"The platter," I said, my voice hoarse even to my own ears.

"What is in your pocket?" He trapped me between his body and the worktable. With one hotly exploring hand, he felt beneath my petticoat and drew out the book, his face purpling with fury. A shove sent me sprawling to the floor.

"How did you acquire this?"

I stared at him with obstinate eyes, lips pressed together in mute protest.

"Where did you find this…this…filth? From that young man?"

The sight of my adored leather book in his hand enraged me. I scrambled to my feet.

"I want it back."

He held it high above his head. "Not in my house."

"I won't keep it in your house." I lunged for my book.

He threw it into the fire.

"No!" The scream echoed, long and loud, in the small building. My gift from Mark. In horror, I watched as flames licked the cover and curled the pages. I ran to the hearth, knelt, and reached.

The next moment, my master was above me. He kicked the iron skillet from the embers, knocking it against my outstretched arm. Hot metal seared my skin.

I fell backwards, landing on my bottom, staring in shock at my arm.

"Susanna?" Dorcas asked from the doorway.

My master said, "She is fine, Dorcas. Run along."

"But, Papa—"

"Go."

I looked up, trying to focus, but unspeakable pain blinded me. The air about my master swarmed with a crimson haze that faded to black.

I awakened on the floor, peering through half-closed eyes at the ceiling beams, my forearm in an agony so profound I thought I might go mad.

It hurt too much to cry. Or breathe. Or think. I begged Almighty God for the pain to end.

Outside, little girls shrieked. In the kitchen, it was quiet except for the occasional pop of the fire. I rolled to my side and lay exhausted, cheek pressed to the rough floorboard, dust tickling my nose. My eyelids drooped.

Please don't let the children come in and see me like this.

Their terror would be harder to handle than my pain. I struggled to sit and then paused, head swimming, panting noisily. The room wobbled about me, then righted itself. Pain swirled around me like smoke. The smell of it filled my nose, the taste filled my mouth.

Cradling my burned forearm against my belly, I scanned the hearth with desperate eyes. Remnants of the book rested crookedly in the ashes. My heart shattered at the sight. A gift from Mark. My beautiful book.

Stumbling to my feet, I staggered into the pantry. With a quivering hand, I knocked the top from the jar of honey and dripped some on the wound.

The suffering didn't abate. Honey might encourage healing, but it did not alter the pain.

Mark had medicine. Little orange pills. I would go to him.

I plunged down the familiar path to the falls and hopped through to Mark's side.

The two previous times I had been in his century, he had been with me. This time, on my own, his world overwhelmed me.

There were too many noises. Muffled mechanical moans. Shrill laughter. The incessant yapping of dogs. The sweet sounds of birds and insects were drowned out.

Odors clung to the air, heavy but undistinguishable. I could see pine trees but not smell them. It was as if the scents of the earth had faded into one. A stew.

The colors had lost their intensity. Objects blended with their backgrounds.

This century lacked distinction.

But I had not come here to admire his world. I had come for Mark.

The incline rose before me. At its top waited the greenway. The hill seemed so high. Shadows flickered past, twenty-first century people chatting. Would they be friendly? Would they help?

I trudged up the trail until it changed from hard-packed earth to an unknown substance. I hesitated, frowning at the mottled black surface with its nasty smell. Lifting my foot, I nudged it cautiously and snatched my stinging toe away. The substance was exceptionally hot—too hot to walk on. And yet, had Mark not said that was its purpose?

Ring-ring.

A bell, outside? Whirling around, I sought its source.

"Watch out," someone screamed. A bike whined by.

I leapt backwards and landed in a bush. Tiny leaves and twigs scratched my injured arm. I gagged with pain.

The crimson haze returned.

Why had I come here? I gazed with longing down the trail to the falls. Should I return home before I hurt myself even more in this peculiar place?

"Hello, miss. Are you okay?"

I squinted toward the voice. An elderly gentleman peered at me from the black path.

"Yes, sir," I said and winced at the obvious lie. "Pardon me, but do you live nearby?"

"This is my neighborhood."

"Please tell me where Mark Lewis lives."

"I'm afraid I don't know him."

"I see." When he turned to leave, panic gripped me. This man was the only one who had stopped to offer assistance. I tried once more. "Sir, do you know a nearby house with a barn? It is the kind of barn that stores a man's toys."

"Certainly." He pointed in the direction from which he'd come. "Just up there. Around the bend. It's not far." He reached out to me. "Let me give you a hand."

I thanked him and then crept along the side of the path, head bowed, hope spurring me on. I could do this. I would keep going now because it wasn't far.

So many bare legs moved past me. And they all wore shoes in the summer. Shoes, bare legs, and breeches that stopped high on the thigh. I blushed at the sight of so much skin.

Where was Mark's house? How much farther? The ache in my arm grew by the moment until I could scarce take another step. I felt out of breath, too weary for much more.

I scanned the houses on the opposite side of the trail and spied a barn.

CHAPTER TWENTY-EIGHT

A GAZILLION QUESTIONS

When it came to grocery shopping, my mother and I had a good division of labor. She went to the store. When she got home, I put away the groceries. She hated the unloading part so much that it got me off chores for the rest of the day.

While I carried bags in from the garage, Mom made a cup of coffee and prepared to supervise me.

I targeted the refrigerator stuff first: eggs, milk, cheese.

Her attention wandered. "There's someone standing at our back gate," she said, spying through the window over the kitchen sink.

I hauled a cloth bag into the pantry. "Maybe he's lost."

"It's a girl."

"Uh-huh." Not interested. I stacked cans on the lowest shelf.

"She looks Amish or something."

"Amish?" Foreboding ripped through me. Could it be...? I charged to the window. "Holy shit."

"Watch your mouth."

I didn't even register my mother's remark because I was flying out the back door. "Susanna?" I shouted as I raced across the yard.

Her face crumpled when she saw me. Tears? From Susanna? This visit could not be good.

"Why are you here?"

She couldn't speak for crying. I vaulted over the gate and skidded to a stop next to her. "What's wrong?"

She extended her left arm. A massive, ugly blister bubbled on her skin. It had to hurt like hell. "Did your master do this?"

"Yes," she choked out between gulps.

The world around us went out of focus, leaving only me, Susanna, and this horrible wound. "Did he do it on purpose?"

She nodded.

My body pulsed with a rage so deep I could've killed him had he been within reach. But there wasn't time to plot revenge. For the present, my energies had to be directed toward her.

"What's going on?" Mom spoke from the fence.

Where had she come from? I hadn't heard her walk up. I hoped she hadn't overheard anything. But I wasn't sorry about her being here. We could use her skill.

"Susanna's been hurt."

"Let me see." Mom went into professional nurse mode. Peeling the sleeve away, she studied the damage and made tick-tock sounds with her tongue. "How did this happen?"

Susanna hesitated. "It was an accident. I…burned my arm on a pan."

Mom's face was stern. "How did the pan connect with your arm?"

Susanna shook her head.

"Okay, dear. I'll drop the interrogation for now." My mother continued her inspection. "Susanna, we must take you to the emergency department."

"We can't, Mom. Just—"

"Mark." She gave me her *don't-question-the-expert* frown.

"Wait here a moment," I said to Susanna, then pulled my mother to the side. There was no good way to explain

Susanna—at least nothing believable, even though she was standing there, in living color, looking every inch the eighteenth-century girl. With each second that passed, Susanna rasped with pain. She had come to me, and I wouldn't let her down. I had to come up with a story my mother would buy long enough to make her shut up and pitch in. If it was totally made up, well, too bad.

"We can't take her to the emergency department. We can't take her anywhere. My friend lives in one of those freaky communes that won't let her seek medical care. It's us or nobody. You have to do the best you can right here."

Mom's lips pinched together against a gazillion questions she was dying to ask.

Susanna gave a hiccupping gasp.

"Fine," Mom said and turned to her patient. "Let's take you inside where it's cool."

Susanna's gaze shifted to our house. She shook her head, her eyes wide and wary. "No, please."

"Okay. We'll take care of it outside. I'll figure something out," my mother said. She pushed through the back gate and hurried across the yard.

I sat on a strip of grass beside the greenway in the shade of the barn, drew Susanna onto my lap, and tried to imitate the soothing sounds my grandma used to make when I was little.

Pedestrians grew quiet as they passed us. Noisy—silent—noisy again. Not that I blamed them for their curiosity. We had to look pretty odd. Really, they should be grateful to us. We were giving them a story to tell later over a beer.

"The book," she whispered.

Where had that come from?

"What book?"

"The one you gave me. *Persuasion*," she said and laid her head on my shoulder. "He tossed it in the fire." Her voice cracked on the last word.

A wave of guilt rippled through me. This was my fault. She had known he would hurt her, and I taunted her into keeping the book.

"I'm sorry. You predicted this."

"No, please don't be sorry. Reading the book gave me so much pleasure."

She sounded a little bit calmer. "What did you like about it?"

Her face grew thoughtful. "Anne is the only person of value in a family of truly vile people, yet she doesn't permit them to taint her. It's such a hopeful story." She glanced up at me. "My master burned your gift."

Holy shit. He burned *her*. It didn't matter about the book. "I'll buy you another copy. A thousand copies. Whatever you want." I kissed her on the forehead.

"I loved that one."

My mother's sneakers rustled in the grass. She set down a large tray full of medical stuff and then knelt before Susanna. After making sure the patient had downed a couple of ibuprofen, Mom opened the first aid kit, snapped on a pair of gloves, picked up scissors, and cut Susanna's sleeve up to the elbow.

"I know this is against your religion, dear," my mother said as she worked, "but you ought to see a doctor. It's a second-degree burn."

"Mom."

"Okay. Just saying." She bent over the wound, her movements gentle.

At first, the pain must've been bad. Susanna kept shuddering. But the agonized hisses faded and the little wiggles stopped. As her comfort level improved, she laid her head on my chest as we both watched my mother dress the wound.

Mom was amazing. I'd never seen her in action. It was intense.

When the cleaning and bandaging were finally done, my mother leaned back on her heels and sighed. She scrutinized her patient from head to toe, her gaze sharpening when they reached Susanna's calves with their criss-crossing scars and scabs.

Susanna carefully adjusted her skirt so only her feet showed, and met Mom's gaze calmly.

My mother nodded curtly at the implied *don't ask* message, dropped her nursing stuff onto the tray, and ripped off the gloves. "All right, I think that's it."

"Thank you, Mrs. Lewis."

"You're welcome." Mom picked up a bottle of Propel and held it out. "Let's get some fluids in you."

Susanna took the bottle and looked at me uncertainly. "What is this?"

I unscrewed the top. It would save me the embarrassment of having to explain that our patient hadn't dealt with squeeze-tops before. "It'll taste a little like lemonade. You probably won't like it, but do what my mom says. Think of it as medicine."

She took a sip, snorted, coughed, and smiled. "It's quite tart. How much must I drink?"

"The whole thing," Mom and I said together.

We all laughed, although I wasn't sure why. It wasn't funny.

Susanna drank the rest of it, wincing the entire time. When she was done, she set the empty bottle on the tray. "You have been kind, Mrs. Lewis, but now I must go."

"I was glad to help." Mom frowned. "Are you sure it's okay for you to return to your...to wherever you live? You may stay here, if you want."

They exchanged glances. Susanna's was full of pain; my mother's, full of concern. Susanna shook her head. "Thank you. I shall be fine. Truly. But I am grateful for the offer."

I rose and pulled Susanna up with me. "Do you want me to walk you home?"

"No. It would be best to return alone." Susanna looked at me with her gorgeous brown eyes, bright with gratitude and shimmering with something more—something that caused a fierce protectiveness to roar through my veins. She was more than a friend. More than a girlfriend. She had become part of who I was. I loved her.

It all made sense now. The changed training schedule. The chick books and dorky costume. The journeys into the unknown. All because I loved Susanna.

I loved her in ways I understood, full of physical aches and the need to be near her whenever I could. But I also loved her in ways that were unfamiliar, with an intensity that made me willing to attempt the impossible.

"Hey," I said with a smile. My doubts about Phoebe were gone. We were going to save her, and Susanna would be next. "I'll see you tomorrow."

"I shall look forward to it." Susanna pulled her gaze away from mine reluctantly. She turned toward my mother and bobbed a quick curtsy. "Good-bye, ma'am."

Seconds later, she was running down the far side of the greenway.

Mom sent me a puzzled frown. "Why is she barefoot?"

"They only wear shoes in the winter." I watched until Susanna was out of sight.

"I don't think that burn was an accident."

"Yeah, I know."

"Damn," she muttered under her breath. "She's been hurt before. Why did you let her go back?"

"She has a sister to protect. She won't let us do anything for her until Phoebe is safe." I opened the gate and waited for her to pass through. "Really, Mom, I can't say anything else about Susanna right now, but I will someday."

"Can't the law do something to her commune?"

"The law's on their side at the moment." Mom and I had bonded over Susanna. It felt good. "I'm doing everything I can."

"Okay. I'll just have to trust you."

I wrapped her in a quick hug. "You were great today. Thanks."

I hadn't found anyone to stay with while my parents were gone. Clearly, Carlton was no longer an option. He wouldn't want me around, and I didn't want to be there.

It would've been so much easier to solve if Marissa were here, but she wasn't. So, time for the backup plan—my grandparents.

I called.

A gruff voice answered. "What?"

"Hey, Granddad." What should I do? Dive right in, or suck up first? "How are things?"

"No need to suck up. What do you want?"

A man of action. I could respect that. "While Mom and Dad are in Michigan—"

"You want to stay with us."

I needed to take control of this conversation. "Actually, I was hoping one of you could sleep over here."

"Not going to happen. We like our own beds."

Okay, the alternative to Plan B. On race morning, I'd have to wake up an extra hour early, but what other choice did I have?

"May I stay with you while Mom and Dad are gone?"

"Sure thing. It'll cost you, though."

Why hadn't Gran picked up? "How much?"

"A month of mowing, and I want the deck power-washed."

Wow. My mother must've inherited the Unreasonable Gene from her father. But at least this option didn't involve negative cash flow. "Fine."

"A fast answer. You must be desperate there, Mark. Must have put it off too long, waiting for a better gig." His laugh slid into a dry cough. "I hear you want to buy a leaf vacuum."

"Yes." I wanted to turn all of my mowing customers into leaf-collection customers. It would keep the revenue up during the winter months.

"Good. I have a proposition for you."

Did my grandfather sense blood in the water and was circling in for the attack? "What proposition is that, Granddad?"

"Promise to vacuum the leaves on my yard in November, and I won't check the guest bedroom at night to see if you're there."

Wow.

My grandparents went to bed by nine PM. I could be back in Raleigh by ten. This conversation was totally working in my favor. Almost too good to be true.

"What's the catch?"

"Your grandmother is never to know about our little bargain. So she has to see you at supper each night. And I get a text each morning by eight letting me know you're all right."

Oh, man. Did he really expect me to refuse? "Deal."

"Nice doing business with you."

Click.

Oh, yeah.

Less than an hour later, the front door banged. I tore down the stairs, taking them two at a time. My dad sprawled on the living room couch, laptop case at his feet, suit jacket tossed over a chair.

"Dad, I solved the problem."

He didn't open his eyes. "How?"

"I'm staying at the lake house."

"You sound too happy about that. Do I want to know?"

"You do not."

"Have you explained your plans to your mother yet?"

"No. But she'll be fine with everything." I smiled.

"How can you be so sure?" He rose to a sitting position and looked at me curiously.

"She met Susanna today. I think we're good."

CHAPTER TWENTY-NINE

GREATLY COVETED

I was slow serving breakfast on Tuesday morning. I couldn't balance a tray on my bad arm, so I had to carry the dishes in multiple trips.

Mrs. Pratt and the children waited at their places. On my second trip, Dorcas hopped to her feet. "Mama, may I help Susanna?"

"You may."

"Delilah, come with us."

Once we reached the kitchen, Dorcas pointed at the little bit of bandage that peeked out from beneath my sleeve. "I've never seen a bandage look like that."

"I only had one hand free to secure it." The more I lied, the easier it became.

"It looks better than a two-handed bandage."

Both sisters bent over my arm for a closer inspection. Delilah lost interest first. I assigned her the task of carrying spoons. She was delighted.

Dorcas placed bowls on the tray, lifted it, and followed me from the kitchen. She quickened her steps to draw even with me. "How did you hurt your arm?"

"I burned it in the hearth."

Her silence was heavy. She looked up at me, her eyes sad and wise.

When we entered the dining room, my master had not come to the table yet. I set a bowl at his place and looked inquiringly at my mistress.

She smiled primly. "Mr. Pratt won't dine with us today. Jedidiah, the blessing, please."

Questions hovered on my tongue, but I held them in. Dorcas was as curious as I. Surely I needed only be patient.

Once the porridge was served and the cider poured, I sat in the corner with John and Dinah. She stacked blocks, he knocked them over, and then they both looked to me for praise. Naturally, they received it profusely.

The family ate without speaking, although not in the usual absolute silence.

After a few moments passed, Dorcas sighed loudly, squirmed, and sighed again.

I smiled.

"Is there something you would like to say, Dorcas?" her mother asked.

"I would like to know where my papa is."

"He's visiting his brother George."

"Merciful heavens." Dorcas glanced over at me before turning back to her mother. "Do they like each other?"

Deborah kicked her.

"Ouch." Dorcas scowled. "I don't care what you do to me. I want to know."

"They are brothers. Of course they like each other." Mrs. Pratt preened, face glowing with satisfaction. "I expect Uncle George to send many gifts and treats. Your father will bring them when he returns later this week."

I tweaked Baby John's cheeks. Days without my master? I had never experienced such a thing in eight years. Joy filled me, as if his absence allowed a sweet breeze to blow through the household.

Even better, I could set my plans in motion without his watchful eye.

Mark would not fail me. My master would not be here to stop me. We would succeed.

It was a lovely day. Without the specter of Mr. Pratt's disapproval, everyone laughed more, talked more, and smiled more. Even supper and washing seemed easier, somehow. With no requirement to trail me on my walk, Jedidiah settled happily to his lessons.

I awaited Mark impatiently at twilight. He arrived soon after me, hopped among the boulders with the ease of frequent practice, and jumped through the falls. He waved a sheath of documents.

"I found another housemaid job."

Even had I not been in good spirits, his enthusiasm would have been infectious. "Tell me quickly."

"Here's the advertisement from the Hillsborough paper." He read from the top sheet, unable to suppress a glow of pride. "'The household of Jonathan Palmer has an opening to apprentice a young woman, fourteen to eighteen, of strong constitution and pleasing manner, to accept such duties as might be given in the house.'"

His words doused me like a cold shower. Did he not know my sister's age? "Phoebe is twelve."

"Does she have a strong constitution and a pleasing manner?"

"Indeed." Enthusiasm lurched to disappointment. The leading families of the state could choose the best staff. They wouldn't settle for a girl when they specifically asked for someone older.

"So, she has two out of three. We'll change their minds about her age."

I ached for it to be true. My sister would be safe in the home of a fine statesman. But why take her where she wasn't wanted? "It will be difficult."

"I'm still giving it a shot. We're running out of time." He folded the paper and stuffed it into a back pocket. "How about Friday?"

Three days away. I would travel to my mother's farm on the day before, thereby giving her less opportunity to share the secret with Mr. Shaw.

"They will be ready by mid-morning."

Thursday proved to be light for chores. After dinner, I left the Pratts's property and followed the main road toward Raleigh.

It was a miserable day to walk. The air was moist and thick. Brittle weeds lined the sides of the road, their razor-sharp leaves slicing my heels. I moved to the forest's edge, where it was cooler and fragrant with pine, but it slowed my pace. Twenty minutes later, I turned onto a beaten-down track leading to my mother's farm.

When I reached the track's end, I paused in the shade and surveyed the property with a critical eye. The house brooded on a yard of hard-baked red clay. A scraggly garden lay blistering in the sun. Behind the house, a horse nibbled grass at the edge of the field, its dark tail flicking lazily.

Mr. Shaw had quite a job ahead of him.

Phoebe erupted from the cornfield, holding a pail. "Susie?" She rushed over and caught me about the waist. "I'm glad to see you."

"I'm glad to see you, as well." I hugged her close to me, memorizing the feel of her thin body. Phoebe was so slight. Would it not be obvious to all how young she was? Indeed, she seemed even younger than her age. Doubts chipped away at my confidence.

"Why are you here?"

I dropped a kiss on her brow. "I have come to speak with Mama for a time. But I have a request for you."

"Yes?"

"I have a special journey planned for us tomorrow. Can you be ready after breakfast?"

Her brow creased. "Where?"

"It's a secret. Will you keep it?"

Her eyes shone. "I shall."

"Very well. The trip is to Raleigh." I laughed at her eager smile. "It will be exciting. Do you have any embroidery you can bring?"

"Perhaps the handkerchief with the bees and vines?"

"Indeed. It will do nicely."

"What shall we do there? Might we eat in a real tavern, or must we pack food? I should like to eat in a real tavern."

I laughed. "So many questions. We must discuss them all with Mama."

Our mother chose that moment to appear in the door. "Susanna?"

"Don't forget, it's a secret," I whispered to Phoebe.

"I shall not."

I hurried across the yard, crossed the sagging porch, and followed my mother into the great room. It had a just-cleaned look. A new rag rug lay in the center of the freshly swept floor. The windows had been scrubbed of a decade's worth of grime. A basket of quilt pieces crouched next to a rocking chair. It was inviting and cheerful, reflecting the efforts of an industrious housewife—a title my mother could hardly claim. Perhaps Mr. Shaw was fooled.

"Why have you come?" She didn't smile.

"You are to marry."

"I don't like to live alone."

"You don't live alone now."

Her lips compressed. "Living with a child isn't the same as living with a husband."

"I expect not." I gave her an unblinking stare.

She flushed and looked away. "Don't judge me. I'm good at being a wife. I don't want to run a farm by myself."

"I didn't want to be an indentured servant, but your Mr. Crawford forced me there anyway." I shifted until I was in her view again. "Mr. Shaw will force Phoebe into an indenture, as well."

Mama shook her head. "You are mistaken. He said she can stay with me if she is useful."

"Did he promise? Is her progress with spinning enough?"

Mama sighed. "Mr. Shaw says that Drusilla Pratt is quite discouraged by Phoebe's progress."

"Discouraged?" Words of protest clogged my throat, but I swallowed them back. "Where did he hear this news?"

"Jethro Pratt." My mother shook her head. "I am greatly surprised. I expected Phoebe to excel."

Phoebe's skill was extraordinary. Her efforts would one day sell for a fine price. My master had deceived Mr. Shaw, and there could be only one reason—so Mr. Pratt could bind her to himself. His despicable behavior worked in my favor. I would leave the deception unchallenged.

I touched her lightly on the shoulder. Beneath my hand, I could feel her bones clearly.

"Until Phoebe turns eighteen, you will wonder every day whether Mr. Shaw will bind her out. Is that what you want for yourself or Phoebe?"

She clasped her arms against her waist and hunched over, her body still. But her eyes were restless. They darted here and there, as if seeking answers.

"No," she whispered, "he won't take her from me."

"He will." My mother was wavering. It was time to press her relentlessly. "He cannot bind her out if you have resolved her future before you marry."

"Mr. Shaw will be angry if I decide without him."

"Until July tenth, he has no claim on her. It is an unworthy man who would fault a mother for taking care of her child."

"I don't know what to do."

"There's no need for you to worry any longer." My mother's dithering tried my patience. I had to get her to agree to my plan. "I have found a job for Phoebe."

"Where?"

God forgive me for the lie I was about to tell. "I have secured a position for her in Nathaniel Eton's household."

Her lips parted in awe. "Mr. Eton, the war hero?"

"Yes. Would it not be an honor to have your daughter working there?"

"Indeed. They are a fine family. But don't they live in Raleigh?"

"They do. But it's close enough that you could travel to see her. Mr. Shaw will have business in Raleigh on occasion. You could ride along. And in October, I shall be living there, too."

She paced the room, muttering to herself. "Can I do this?"

When at last she passed by her rocking chair, she collapsed into it, hands wringing in her lap. "We cannot accept. I should miss her too fiercely if she were to leave."

Her statement cut like a knife. Had she ever thought such things about me? Had she protested when her second husband sent me away? It was barely a mile to the Pratts's farm. Yet, once the papers were signed, she acted as if she had no interest in me. Why, after all this time, did this knowledge have the power to hurt? I had to force these long-buried thoughts away.

"Where else could she go, if not to Raleigh?"

She twisted her hands in the folds of her apron. "Perhaps housewifery at the Pratts's wouldn't be so terrible. Mr. Shaw says they have been good to you."

I gaped in disbelief. "Are you mad?" I asked in a grating voice, forgetting my need for calm at the sheer lack of notice my mother paid me. She had spent little time near me since I left her household. But shouldn't that make my treatment more visible? Had she not seen the scars and bruises accumulate?

Without thinking, I peeled up my bandage and forced my wound before her shocked gaze. "Mr. Pratt burned me. He kicked a hot skillet against my arm."

She studied the wound, eyes blinking rapidly. "Why would he do such a thing?"

Tears stung my eyes. Could there be any acceptable reason for burning someone?

"For reading a book."

She shook her head over and over. Her mouth hung open but no sounds emerged.

"He beats me, Mama." I faced away from her and lifted my petticoat. "Do you see the scars covering my legs? The newest ones are for oversleeping. He struck me five times for serving his breakfast fifteen minutes late."

"No," she said with a sob.

I dropped my petticoat and spun around. "That is the life you chose for me when you handed my fate to your husband. Is that what you wish for Phoebe?"

"I am sorry, Susanna. I didn't know."

Anguish, eight years in the making, loosened my tongue. "You would have known if you ever looked at me." I knelt before her, hands gripping the arms of her chair. "Mama, you must do what's right for Phoebe. Don't let a stranger decide her future."

She raised trembling fingers to her lips. It was quiet in the room, but sounds drifted in from the outside. Birds calling. Chickens clucking. Phoebe singing.

She nodded slowly, then with more conviction. "When?"

"Tomorrow."

She gasped. "So soon?"

"The position won't remain open long. It's greatly coveted." If my sister secured any position in Raleigh, we would leave her behind. I couldn't risk bringing her back and having Mr. Shaw interfere. My mother didn't have to know the details of the transaction. "Mr. Eton needs a willing worker in his home. They entertain often and require many beautiful clothes. Phoebe's skill with the needle will surely be used. Is this solution not a superior one?"

"I agree. Yes." She shivered. "They will be good to her?"

"Undoubtedly." Finally, success. I should have been guilt-ridden by the ease with which I had deceived my own mother. I was not. "I shall see you early tomorrow. Please wear your Sunday best."

Her eyes widened. "Must I go?"

"You may have to sign papers."

She rose and crossed to the window. There she watched her youngest child collecting vegetables in the garden. "I suppose I must keep this decision a secret from Mr. Shaw?"

"Indeed. Your discussion with him will be easier after the deed is done." I looked past her to my beloved sister. Tomorrow, Phoebe would move to Raleigh. It wasn't so very far, but I would miss her greatly.

The end of my indenture would not only bring freedom. It would also bring reunion.

I was anxious to leave for my mother's farm, but Mrs. Pratt and the children dawdled over breakfast.

The morning chores didn't go smoothly, either. Nerves had made me clumsy. The dishes refused to dry. The vegetables refused to lie still while I hacked at them.

From my vantage point at the worktable, I watched Dorcas exit the main house, holding hands with Delilah and

Dinah. Instead of entering the kitchen, she circled around the side. I threw the vegetables into the stew kettle, covered a platter of sliced bread with a cloth, and changed aprons.

Dorcas spoke from the rear door. " Will you give me a lesson in writing? I should like to practice my z's."

"Not today."

"Are you going somewhere?"

For the first time, I found her inquisitive nature to be irritating. "My mother's house."

She eyed me skeptically. "You went there yesterday. Why do you return?"

"I thought I might check for peaches."

She glanced at the dishes waiting on the worktable. "Will you be here for dinner?"

"Naturally." I set the jar of spicy apple butter next to the platter of bread. "Dinner will be ready on time."

Her mouth pinched in a warning. "Mama expects Papa back today."

"She'll be glad to see him," I said with a falsely casual shrug. Since I didn't know precisely where Mr. George Pratt lived, I couldn't know how long it would take for my master to drive home. Perhaps, if we were fortunate, it would be as late as supper time. I would welcome the new supplies he would bring, if not his return.

I shooed the girls with my hands. "Now, young ladies, off with you. Find some shade and play school."

Dorcas swung around, dragging two little sisters after her. "I shall be the teacher, and you may be my pupils."

Once they had settled into mock spelling lessons under an oak, I darted to the trail in the woods. Within minutes, I arrived at the falls, certain I had gone unnoticed. Mark rose from the tall grasses as I approached.

"Hey," he said with a big smile. "Ready?"

"Indeed." I drank in the sight of him. It was lovely to be with him in the middle of the day, speaking as friends, not hidden in the shadows of a cave. "You have found a waistcoat."

He patted the striped fabric covering his chest. "My mother's. Great, huh?"

"Adequate is the word I would have chosen." I gestured toward the trail. "Let us hurry. I don't wish to be gone long."

"Fine with me." He took off, his black shoes kicking up dust.

As I trotted along beside him, I pondered how this day would proceed. There were, of course, problems that might arise, but I had thought through them all. If my mother and sister expressed concern about traveling with a stranger, I would reassure them. Mark could be both their guide and protector. If Mama balked at leaving Phoebe with a family besides the Etons, Mark could say we took too long to claim it, and they had filled the position with someone else.

If any other problems came up, Mark or I would solve them, because we must. Phoebe couldn't remain in Worthville.

"Mark, there are some things you should know about today."

"I don't like the sound of that."

It would be best to get this over with quickly and avoid any lengthy discussions.

"I didn't tell my family about you."

"Why not?"

"I was afraid they might refuse to go."

He stopped walking. I did not.

"Susanna?"

I strained to hear his footsteps but heard no movement. He had ceased to follow. I spun to face him. "What is it?"

"Were you planning to introduce us and wave goodbye?"

"Yes. It is the only way."

"They have to come willingly."

"They will be excited. They will take the trip." I continued down the path.

He caught up. "What if you're wrong?"

"I shall be persuasive, and you'll be charming."

"Let's hope you're right." He sidestepped a snake that slithered with whip-like speed into a tiny hole. "What else do I need to know?"

"I told Mama that Phoebe has a position with the Etons."

"What?" He halted again, this time catching my elbow and pulling me to a stop. "Why did you lie about something so major? It'll be obvious when we get to Raleigh and the last name is Palmer, instead."

I tugged my arm from his grasp. "If I must deceive them to get them there, it cannot be helped."

"Great. You'll be here while I'm the one dealing with two pissed-off women."

"I am sure you will handle the situation with competence." I resumed my walk.

It didn't take much longer to arrive at the farmhouse. Phoebe waited on the porch. She started to run toward me but slowed when her gaze fell on Mark.

"Don't speak unless you must," I said to him, too quietly for my sister to hear.

"You don't need to worry about that. I want you to do the talking."

I went ahead of him and held out a hand to my sister. "I am glad to see you're ready."

She slipped her hand in mine, her gaze trained on my companion. "Who is this man, Susie?"

"He's a friend of mine."

"Why is he here?"

"He's from Raleigh. He'll be the guide for today's trip."

I studied her with a critical eye. My sister was growing into a remarkable beauty. While we shared the same wide, dark eyes as our father, there the resemblance ended. Her hair was a shimmering gold, her body slight. Wearing a bodice she'd embroidered with birds and ivy, Phoebe looked quite grown-up. Perhaps no one would ask her age. I certainly couldn't afford to have Mr. Pratt see her looking this lovely and mature.

"Mark knows where your new master and mistress live."

"Mama told me you found a job." She scowled. "It is too soon. I am still learning to spin."

"It's the best time. There are many families in Raleigh who need your skills now."

"They would like it if I could spin, too."

I stared at Phoebe in surprise. She had never challenged me before. Did this bode ill for the rest of the morning?

My mother came out onto the porch. She wore a new green jacket over her best gown, and a straw bonnet trimmed with blue ribbons. The pink of excitement glowed in her cheeks. She took a few steps forward but stopped as she caught sight of Mark.

"Susanna?"

I forced a calm smile to my lips. "Mr. Lewis, this is my mother, Mrs. Anne Crawford. Mama, Mr. Lewis. He'll accompany you and Phoebe."

"Why?"

"Mr. Lewis is a friend of mine." I smiled confidently. "He's familiar with Raleigh. I think it's wise to have a man for protection on the journey."

Mark coughed.

"I suppose you are right." My mother nodded curtly. "Are we taking the wagon?"

"Certainly. It would be too miserable to walk."

"Will he drive or will you?"

"He will."

"No, I won't," Mark said from beside me. "I've never driven a wagon."

Unease whispered down my spine. They used bikes and horseless wagons in his century. It was a foolish oversight on my part not to have considered this information earlier. I nibbled my knuckle, pondering what to do.

My mother dismissed the problem with a wave of her hand. "You may drive, then."

I took a deep breath and braced for the argument that was about to ensue.

"Naturally, I cannot come. I have chores to return to."

Phoebe's chin thrust forward stubbornly. "I shall not go without you. Mr. Lewis might be your friend, but he is a stranger to me."

"I agree with Phoebe. You must come," my mother said, her voice uncharacteristically firm.

I pressed my lips together, biting back words of anger. It wouldn't be wise to lose my patience with them.

"I cannot leave Worthville without the Pratts's permission."

"Very well," Mama said, "we shall seek permission. We can stop at their house first. I shall make it right with Drusilla Pratt."

I directed a despairing glance at Mark. It was a perfectly logical suggestion and one which I must avoid no matter what. The trip would be abandoned if Mrs. Pratt knew, and my only chance to save Phoebe would be lost forever.

Fear lodged like a hard knot in my chest. I would accompany them, and the consequences would be grave.

"If we are gone a brief time, perhaps it will be acceptable."

"Are you sure...?" my mother began.

"Indeed, Mama." I gave her a determined nod. "We are wasting the daylight. I shall hitch the horse."

Mark fell into step beside me as I walked to the barn. "What will happen to you?"

"I don't know." My fears could be dealt with later. For the next few hours, it was my sister's future that concerned me most.

The wagon ride did nothing to improve my spirits.

I was weary of staring at a horse's rump. The hard ruts of the Raleigh Road rocked our small wagon from side to side, rattling my teeth until they ached. In the back, Phoebe talked to Mark. I couldn't make out their words, annoying me greatly. Whatever reluctance Phoebe had experienced before the trip, she had certainly lost her concerns quickly.

My mother slept, her head bumping against my shoulder.

Agitation ruined my pleasure in the journey. Here I was, in a lovely forest under a clear sky, traveling with my mother, sister, and dearest friend, as if on a summer outing. My first trip to Raleigh should have been a treat, yet foreboding wrapped around me like a stifling woolen cloak. My mistress would be outraged when I didn't return for dinner. If I didn't reappear by the time my master arrived, the Pratts might sound the alarm. I had no reasonable explanation for my long absence.

The road crested a hill. Raleigh spread out below us.

I halted the horse. "Mama, wake up."

Phoebe stood in the wagon's back, her hands gripping my shoulder as she cooed with delight. "I've never seen a town so big."

"Nor have I," my mother said.

I couldn't speak, overcome with awe.

With a flick of the reins, we rumbled down the Raleigh side of the ridge and joined the people and wagons streaming along wide streets, heading toward the center of the city. Everywhere there were houses and stores under construction. The noise was fearsome: hammers pounding, carts creaking, horses snorting. Sawdust floated in the air. Shopkeepers bargained with ladies carrying baskets. Meat roasted on an open hearth.

Raleigh was busy and loud, and I loved it at first sight.

CHAPTER THIRTY

BUSY INTERSECTION

Eighteenth-century Raleigh looked about the same today as it had when I was there five days ago—except it had more people, more noise, and more stink.

I pointed toward the end of the street. "That patch of dirt is Union Square. Let's stop there."

Susanna pulled the wagon to a stop under a large oak near the meetinghouse. While she was securing the horse, I jumped off the back and turned to Phoebe. "May I help you down?"

"Yes, thank you, Mr. Lewis." She smiled brightly while I lifted her from the wagon. "Where are we?"

"We're in the center of Raleigh." I gestured around us. "Most of the shops and houses circle around this square for several blocks."

"Where do you live?"

I gestured vaguely toward the west. "My home is outside of town."

"Where do the Etons live?"

Great. She seemed like a sweet kid, and I'd have to lie to her, too. I had no idea where the Etons lived—as if it mattered. "Not too far. We'll show you in a little while."

She nodded happily, her eyes flicking to the people passing by.

Their mother climbed down, fanning herself. "I shall stay with the horse," she said. "You make the arrangements." She walked to Phoebe and gently kissed her on the cheek. "You are about to do a very grown-up thing. A job is an important part of life. I am proud of you."

"Thank you, Mama," the girl whispered.

After settling the horse in Mrs. Crawford's care, the three of us took off, heading south from the square, pausing at a busy intersection. We stood on a boulevard, long and straight, lined on each side by buildings like jagged teeth. In 2016, Fayetteville Street had hotels, banks, and a performing arts complex. But today we were looking at the newly built homes of some of Raleigh's best families.

Phoebe gasped at each new thing she saw. "Oh, Susie, do you see all of the beautiful carriages? Are they not grand?"

"Indeed, they are."

I pointed straight in front of us and muttered into Susanna's ear, "There's the house we want. It belongs to Jonathan Palmer."

The home was the largest on the block. In the back, there were several small wooden buildings and an outhouse. Susanna headed for a side entrance. We found ourselves in a yard with brick pathways crisscrossing it. There was no grass, just tilled up dirt and a small vegetable garden.

Susanna stopped before the largest of the buildings in the backyard and turned to me. "I shall talk. Please don't say anything."

"Sure."

Susanna climbed the few steps and entered the central hallway. Phoebe waited outside uncertainly, clutching a bulging cloth bag.

I followed Susanna, who had halted outside a small front room. An older woman sat at a delicate desk, writing in a journal.

"Hello," Susanna said and waited.

The older woman continued to write.

After a minute passed with the woman ignoring us, I lost my patience. There was no reason to be so rude. "Are you Mrs. Palmer?"

The woman looked at me with arched eyebrows. Susanna glared at *me*.

"No, I am Mrs. Tinsley," she said. "I'm the housekeeper. How may I help you?"

Susanna elbowed me aside. "We heard there might be an opening for a maid."

Her eyes lit with interest. "Indeed, there is." She lay down her quill, stood, and stepped from the little room. Craning her neck, she studied Susanna from head to toe. "Are you here for the position?"

"No, it's not for me. We're here for my sister, Phoebe."

Her sister stepped into view and curtsied. "Please, ma'am."

Mrs. Hensley's smile froze. "How old are you, Phoebe?"

"Twelve."

The housekeeper shook her head. "We take maids no younger than fourteen." Her gaze latched onto Susanna. "I suggest you take her home and let her play with her dolls a few years longer."

Phoebe's chin lifted. "I don't play with dolls. I am an excellent needlewoman."

Susanna's face had flushed bright red. She grabbed her sister's hand and hurried down the brick path and out the gate.

That had not gone well. I chased after them. "Where next?"

"We should visit Mr. Haywood's home. I prefer to find a housemaid position."

Phoebe halted on the side of the street. "Was that Mrs. Eton's housekeeper? Why did she treat us so?"

"Wrong house, Phoebe," I said. "We'll try another."

Fortunately, I'd copied an old map, complete with names of prominent families and addresses. We doubled back toward Union Square. All around us, the sounds of pounding hammers made it clear that there was a building boom in the new state capital. Taverns obviously had come first, because they were everywhere.

I halted under a tree. "That's the Haywood House."

We crossed the street and repeated the scene from the Palmers. The housekeeper here was even nastier than the last one. Yes, the position was in the house. And no, Phoebe was too young.

Not good. It was weird to be wishing someone would put a twelve-year-old to work, but I was. Better that than marry an abusive pervert in four years.

"Susie, who are the Haywoods? Why did we come to their house?"

Susanna looked at me with pleading eyes.

"Sorry about that. It's my fault. I'm a little lost. The Etons live nearby." I leaned closer to Susanna and spoke directly in her ear. "The tavernkeeper had two more suggestions. One for kitchen maid and one for laundry maid. She wasn't too sure about the laundry maid's family."

"Let me decide." Anxiety seemed to radiate off of her like a fever.

"What if we can't find—?"

"Stop." She shook her head. "I shall not take her back to Worthville."

"You can't leave her here on the street."

"Hush." Her voice was rough.

That must be the 1796 version of *shut up*.

We continued down the block and paused at the corner. Opposite us sat a big—by 1796 standards—house. It was surrounded by a white picket fence. A carriage rolled to a stop before the front gate and a middle-aged woman got out, followed by two teens.

Susanna tapped me. "Is this the home of the Etons?"

I gave the map a quick look and nodded. "Yeah, I think so." I watched the woman curiously. She was smaller than Susanna and wore clothes that looked nice for around here. "She could be your mistress one day."

"Indeed." Susanna stared at the older woman intently. The road cleared, and we could've gone on, but she didn't move.

"Susie, is that lady Mrs. Eton?"

"Yes, I believe she is."

"Then why are we standing here?"

"Hush, please. I'm pondering an idea."

"Let's not wait." Phoebe took off.

Susanna and I exchanged glances, then chased after her.

"Please, ma'am?" Phoebe called. "Are you Mrs. Eton?"

The woman turned and smiled. "I am. How may I help you?"

Susanna stepped in front of her sister. "We are here about a job."

The lady's bright blue eyes had narrowed in confusion. "We have no open positions at present."

"But you will, surely, in the coming months."

"We anticipate needing a kitchen maid this fall." The woman's gaze sharpened. "Have you served in a kitchen?"

"I am asking for my sister. Her talent with a needle is exceptional. Phoebe is a sweet girl. Eager to do your bidding. You won't be disappointed."

"How old is she? Twelve? Thirteen?" At Susanna's nod, the lady's expression shifted into polite but firm refusal. "I am sorry. I don't hire servants so young." She went up the brick steps to her front door.

Susanna stared after her, so stricken it hurt to see.

I leaned closer. "We can go to the Whitakers."

"Phoebe would be better off here. I would have spent many years working for the Etons; this tells me they must be a good family."

"Okay, if that's what you want." The woman had nearly disappeared into the shadows of the home. "Mrs. Eton," I said, "if we could have one more moment."

"Yes?" The woman glanced over her shoulder, her face stern with annoyance.

"Please," Susanna said, her voice squeaking with panic, "if you don't take her, my master will."

Mrs. Eton gazed at Susanna thoughtfully for a long moment, then dismissed her children with a nod. Once the front door had closed behind her, she came back down the stairs and stopped before Susanna.

"Is your master cruel?"

"Yes, ma'am." Susanna's breathing quickened, her chest rising and falling so hard I was afraid she might hyperventilate.

The lady clasped Susanna's hands and nodded slowly. "I sense your master injured you grievously," Mrs. Eton said. "A wound on your arm. Am I correct?"

"You are." Susanna gulped a sob.

"Let me see." The lady eased the sleeve up and pushed the bandage away. The silence lengthened. Finally, she shook her head and met Susanna's gaze. "Your master gave you this burn with intention."

Susanna nodded.

Mrs. Eton's gaze traveled from her face to her neck to her hands. "You have more scars, do you not? Some that I cannot see?"

"Yes, ma'am." The response was so soft, it was almost inaudible.

The lady looked at all three of us in turn, taking her own sweet time. Wagons rattled past. When her gaze reached me, it felt odd, but not in a bad way. It was intensely nice and sympathetic.

The front door creaked open. A tall man in a somber suit cleared his throat. "Mrs. Eton?"

"I shall be there shortly, Fisk," she said, and gestured for Phoebe to approach. "Come here, little one. Tell me, what is your finest skill?"

"I embroider quite well." Phoebe bobbed her head, a shy smile lighting her face. "I am frightfully good at stitching bees. Would you like to see?"

"Indeed, I would."

Phoebe reached into her cloth bag and pulled something out. Mrs. Eton took the square of white cloth, bordered with hundreds of tiny bees, and smiled widely. "It is truly remarkable work. I am attending the Independence Day ball on Monday. I should very much like to carry a handkerchief embroidered with such skill."

"You may have this one."

"How very kind." Mrs. Eton transferred her gaze first to me, then Susanna. "What is the hurry?"

"My mother remarries this month."

"Her husband will bind your sister to your master?"

"He will."

"Then we must act quickly," she said, her voice brisk. "There *is* a new housemaid, but I believe the girl would suit as well in the kitchen. Therefore, I shall take Phoebe in and provide for her education, room and board. She will accept a position in the house, embroider linens or garments when asked, and perform any other duties as required until her eighteenth year."

Beside me, Susanna swayed and clutched at me for support. I slid an arm around her waist to steady her.

"May we leave her now?" she whispered.

Mrs. Eton nodded. "It would be best to have a contract. Are you prepared to sign the papers?"

"Our mother waits at Union Square."

"I shall ask Fisk to fetch your mother and my husband. They can complete the indenture here." Mrs. Eton mounted the steps. "Phoebe, you may come with me. We shall find the housekeeper. She'll show you to your cot."

The sisters stared at each other with big, round, wet eyes.

"Now, Susie?" Phoebe's voice shook. "This very moment?"

"Indeed." Susanna pasted on a decent imitation of a smile. "I can only let you go because you will be so happy here."

"I believe you are right, but I shall miss you and Mama."

"We shall come to see you sometimes."

"Will you write me? I would love to read your letters."

"I promise."

They hugged tightly, as if they never wanted to let go. Susanna kissed her little sister on the cheek and said, "When you say your prayers at night, remember me."

"Oh, I shall." Tears flowed down her cheeks. Phoebe dashed them away with the heels of her hands. "Mr. Lewis, I enjoyed our conversation today."

I smiled. "Me, too."

She hugged her older sister again. "This will be a good place for me, Susie. Truly. Thank you for finding it."

Susanna bit her lip and nodded.

Phoebe followed Mrs. Eton into the house. The door clicked firmly behind them.

Susanna turned away from the house and bowed her head, shoulders shaking, both hands clamped over her mouth. Sadness hummed around her body like a dark fog. I didn't know how to get through it. I wanted to pull her into a hug or do something to help her feel better, but it would probably cause a scandal and make her feel worse. So I stood beside her and waited until her shaking stopped.

After a couple of minutes, I began to worry if I was wrong to do nothing. "Hey, are you okay?"

"I am not."

"Do you want me to hold you?"

"No."

My best idea had been shot down. How much longer should I wait to try something else? I hated to see her so upset. "Is there anything I can do?"

She shook her head, sniffing.

Maybe I should get her talking. "This turned out well. Your lie became the truth."

"Yes."

Better. It was only one syllable, but it had been clear. Maybe we had a trend going.

"I hope your mother gets to meet Mrs. Eton. She'll be glad to know such a nice lady will be Phoebe's mistress."

Susanna nodded emphatically, staring down the street toward Union Square, as if she could see her mother now. "I suspect they will speak as the papers are signed."

Good. She was forming complete sentences again. I had something I was curious about that demanded an answer longer than yes or no. "Mrs. Eton is switching the other housemaid to a kitchen job. Is it possible that would've been your job with the Etons?"

"Perhaps." She blinked her eyes rapidly but didn't wipe them. Tears dripped onto the street, making tiny craters in the dust. "Don't ask any more questions, Mark. Indeed, don't mention this day's events to me ever again. I cannot bear to relive the anguish."

CHAPTER THIRTY-ONE

MY NEXT PRAYER

My mother left the Etons's home an hour later and climbed onto the wagon seat beside me, but spoke not one word. I guided the horse onto the Worthville road.

It was a long, dreary ride—broken by the call of birds and the sobs of my mother. Mark, curled up in the back, appeared to be asleep.

Though I had forbidden Mark to speak about the day's events, my own heart pelted me with troublesome questions. Had I done the right thing? Might Phoebe be miserable with the Etons? Would they regret taking her in? How soon could I see my sister again?

And there was the matter of my future job. Although I had brushed the concern aside when Mark mentioned it, there would likely be no position for me with the Etons this fall. I should have to find something else. The possibility of my working in a tavern loomed larger.

Since Phoebe had taken nine lessons from Mrs. Pratt, I would have to work them off. But I should still be able to leave in October.

Much as I wanted to avoid thoughts of my punishments, they crowded in. Mr. Pratt would be home by now. If his visit with his brother had gone well, might his good feelings soften his response to my absence?

I liked this idea enough to think no more on that topic.

My mother had still not spoken by the time we reached the drive to the farm. After I handed her the reins, Mark and I walked the rest of the way.

It was late afternoon when we reached the falls. The pain of saying goodbye to my sister had saturated me with grief. I had no room left for anxiety.

Mark hesitated at the edge of the cliff, but instead of climbing down, he touched my arm. "What's going to happen to you?"

"I do not know." I would learn within minutes. I would not speculate. "It is time for me to go."

"Wait." His hands dropped lightly on my shoulders. "No matter what happens next, remember, we won. Phoebe's safe."

"She is. That is worth quite a lot."

"It's worth everything. We won." He smiled at me. "Say it."

He looked so eager that I repeated it. "We won."

"We won. Believe it. Your sister will be fine."

"She will." Truly, he was correct. My sister lived in a lovely home with a gracious woman for a mistress. Phoebe would use her talents and not be forced to ruin her skillful hands in drudgery. Most importantly, she was far from my master's reach. It was a victory for which we all owed Mark. Gratitude flared within me. "You saved her."

"No, I pitched in. Phoebe owes everything to you." He gathered me up into his embrace so that my feet no longer touched the ground and then swung me in a circle, laughing. "We won."

I laughed, too, ready to celebrate with him. "We won." My cap flew off, and my hair fell about me like a curtain, yet I didn't care. We were being silly to spin and laugh and enjoy this moment. But it felt good. Whatever the evening brought, my sister was safe.

Mark slowed the spin to a stop, the laughter dying, the foolish grin fading. "Susanna?" His arm remained steady at my waist as he lowered me to the ground. "You are beautiful. So amazingly beautiful."

Me—beautiful?

Alexis was the beautiful one, with her fine, golden hair and silky clothes that exposed so much soft, golden skin. I had abundant scars, sun-darkened skin, and labor-hardened limbs. My garments had been patched together from my mistress's discarded petticoats. I had hair too thick and straight for any style but a heavy braid.

Mark must have lost his mind, yet my heart thumped wildly at his words, wanting to believe.

He cupped my cheek and waited for the space of a breath. Did he want to kiss me? I hoped so.

His head lowered slowly.

What should I do? Remain still? Rise on my toes to meet him?

He had done this before. He knew what to do. I closed my eyes and waited.

His mouth clung to mine. Once...

Twice...

We kissed so many times I lost count. Long, heated kisses. Brief, playful kisses. All achingly sweet. I thrilled at the feel of him, following wherever he led, hoping to give as much pleasure as I received.

He broke away first, his mouth trailing along my jaw, my neck. When his lips reached the edges of my shift, he groaned.

"We have to stop."

"What?" I murmured, eyes shut, drowning in want.

"If we go any further, you'll be missed another hour."

The words feathered along my fevered skin with the cold of dread. The evening stretched ahead of me—my punishment unknown but certain. And if anyone caught me with Mark, here in the open, his mouth on me…

"Merciful heavens." I shuddered and dropped my head to his shoulder.

"Susanna?" His hands caressed my back restlessly. "Don't return to your master. Come with me."

My eyelids fluttered open, as if from a dream. A bold dream. An improbable one. "You're mad," I said, leaning back to savor his handsome face.

He smiled, glowing with eagerness. "No, I'm not. Move to my century."

Move? For a fleeting second, I considered his offer. Freedom awaited me on the other side of the falls. *Freedom.*

I had often tried to imagine what a perfectly free day would be like, and always my mind thought of autumn. Freedom would be like an autumn morning—warm, but not too warm. There would be trees of gold and red. The scent of wood fires and baking apples. Freshly washed clothes, drying in the sun. I would sleep until I was rested. Eat until I was sated. Do only the chores that pleased me. Laugh a little. Smile often.

Is that what I would find in Mark's world?

No, indeed. His world had too much. There were noises everywhere. Banging, barking, wailing. Hot, acrid odors. Rules that made no sense. Movement, fast and purposeful. Danger for the newly arrived. Bare skin.

The only thing I yearned for in his century was Mark. Could he be enough for me? Would my simple love be enough for him? In a world where machines performed magic and girls were the equal of boys, how soon would he grow weary of me?

And what of the life I would be leaving behind? I had people I loved and skills I could sell. No matter how bad it could be, this was a world I understood.

"I cannot move."

"Why not?"

"My contract doesn't end until the middle of October."

He shrugged away my statement as if it didn't matter. "Why do you care?"

"I have given my word. It wouldn't be honorable."

"Your master isn't honorable. Screw him."

I wished Mark hadn't asked. For all that I must turn him down—and I must—it did raise longings within me. The longing for security. The longing to have the misery end.

But running away wasn't the answer. Once my contract ended, I should have no need for Mark's suggestion. I could live wherever I wanted, the past left behind in Worthville.

"I like my century quite well."

"You'd like mine better."

He was so earnest. It was charming and misguided.

"I can't see how that's possible." I stepped away from him.

He held on to one of my hands and leaned toward me. Our lips clung. The kiss was delicious—speaking without words.

He dropped my hands and backed up. "Will I see you tomorrow?"

"Perhaps not tomorrow, but soon."

"Soon, then." He scrambled down the cliff and leapt through the falls. They flashed.

Mark was gone.

"Susanna!"

I spun around, horrified. Jedidiah, the incompetent spy, stood at the edge of the woods, lips curved in triumph, his gaze fixed on me like a cat stalking a mouse.

After shoving me into the kitchen, Jedidiah ran to the mill to notify his father of my return. I restored my appearance to order, tied on an apron, and bent over the hearth. My mistress had put a chicken on to stew. I tasted a sliver and winced in dismay. It demanded flavor. It gave me something to do rather than think about what was to come.

I checked the pantry, relieved to see the trip to George Pratt's home meant we would eat well again. We had new portions of bacon, oats, sugar, and spices. There were bags of apples, yams, onions, potatoes, and a new barrel of smoked ham.

I selected seasonings for the chicken and repaired the dish. It was only then I heard the hiccupping snuffles. I hurried to the rear door. Dorcas sat on the stump, her eyes red-rimmed and watery.

"Have you been crying, little one?"

She nodded, lower lip trembling. "I had to wait here until you came. Now I must find Papa. He is very angry." She slid off the stump and buried her head in my petticoat. "Where have you been?"

"At my mother's," I said, the half-truth coming easily.

"Jedidiah went there. He said no one was at home."

I sighed. On the walk back from the farm, I had made up stories that would sound reasonable, but it didn't matter anymore. No story would be believed after what Jedidiah had witnessed.

I knelt before her and gave her a hug. "I have no explanation for my absence, but I am here now."

"Deborah said you ran away. She said Papa hurt you so badly this week that you didn't want to live here anymore."

"Your sister is wrong. I didn't run away. I wouldn't go without saying good-bye." With the corner of my apron, I dabbed the tears from her cheeks.

"Did Papa hurt you too much this week?"

I wrapped my arms around her and filled my senses with the touch and smell and sight of her. One day, I would leave Dorcas behind, and it would be like abandoning my own child. The pain of it was sharp.

"Yes, he hurt me too much. I shall leave as soon as I am able, but you will always be on my mind." I pressed a kiss to her temple and nudged her away. "Jedidiah has gone to tell your father of my return. You're free to go."

"Is Papa coming now?"

"I suspect so."

"Do you want me to stay with you?" Her voice shook with dread.

I smiled at the brave offer, knowing I would never accept. Whatever happened, I was confident I wouldn't want her to witness. "No, dearest. Run along."

She ran a few steps, then turned and came back. "Uncle George gave us two slaves and a new horse."

"Merciful heavens." I gazed toward the barn but could detect no activity there. "Where are the slaves?"

"Frederick is young. He went to the mill with Papa. And Theophilus," she said, stumbling over his name, "will tend to the horses. He has tall, white hair." She fled toward the garden, disappearing among the cornstalks.

Once she was gone, the silence felt ominous. Even the birds seemed hushed.

I went to the pantry and reviewed the supplies with fresh eyes. How long would they last with two slaves to feed?

With a shake of the head, I forced my thoughts to the evening meal. Boiled potatoes would be nice with chicken.

As I peeled, I reflected on my first kiss, shared with Mark. It had been lovely. I would be quite willing to try again...

Shoes thudded on the floorboards behind me. Resisting the urge to turn and face my master, I picked up another potato.

"Susanna?" His voice was soft. Mild.

"Yes, sir?" I added another potato to the pile.

"Put down your knife and come to me."

With reluctance, I obeyed, staying as close as I dared to the worktable, my breaths quick and shallow.

His hands gripped my wrists and tugged me closer. "My wife says you've been gone all day."

To anyone observing us, it would've looked as if we embraced. I trained my eyes on the buttons of his waistcoat, repulsed by his touch, longing to pull away.

"I have been away a few hours."

"Was the boy with you the whole time?"

I could truthfully say Mama had chaperoned us, but I didn't wish for Mr. Pratt to learn of Phoebe's rescue so soon. "Yes."

My master laughed softly. "Oh, my lovely Susanna, you are determined to lengthen your stay at my house. I must say I am pleased."

"I don't know what you mean."

"You break the terms of the contract if you are caught fornicating."

My shocked gaze rose to his. "I have not done such a thing."

"Jedidiah saw you kiss."

"A kiss isn't the same as…" I stopped, unable to repeat the word aloud in my master's hearing. "It was only a kiss. Nothing more."

"Jedidiah did not describe it so." He forced my wrists behind my back and held them in the iron grip of one hand. "If Mr. Lewis ever trespasses on my property again, I'll have him flogged."

I shrank away from him, hoping to put some space between us, but his hold was too tight. "Mr. Pratt, please let me go."

"When I'm ready." He lifted his free hand to my bodice and snapped a thorn that was pinning the edges together. "Perhaps I should see if your young man left any marks."

Heat flooded my face. "He did not. You may take my word."

"I place no value on your word." He smiled. Snap, snap, snap. The edges of my bodice slid apart.

Before I could think of what to do next, he pressed me hard against the worktable, its rough edge cutting into my back. His fingers groped along my waist. The laces of my stays loosened.

Terror gave me strength. I kicked wildly, connecting with his shin. With a grunt, he moved, trapping my legs between his.

He yanked my shift and stays forward.

Humiliation filled my limbs with a sick weakness. I closed my eyes and prayed to be released from this waking nightmare.

He was silent as he inspected the exposed flesh, the heat of his breath brushing the tops of my breasts. My next prayer was to endure without begging.

"You have the plump tits of a cheap whore."

I could hardly believe this was happening. For years, my master had played a game of wills with me. The rules were simple. If he beat my limbs until they bled, I suppressed my cries. If he whispered vile insults, I ignored their poison. If he offered praise, I neither acknowledged nor smiled. It was all part of the game.

But my body was private—the one line he did not breach. Until today.

He chuckled. "I see no marks on your flesh. Perhaps you've told the truth. Either he didn't caress you, or he's remarkably skilled for his age."

I mustered my strength and kicked a heel hard into his ankle. He hissed in surprise, his hold on me relaxing. I broke away and raced to the other side of the worktable, my shaking hands clutching the edges of my bodice and the torn neckline of my shift.

He smoothed his waistcoat, then leaned against the kitchen wall, arms crossed over his chest. My gaze darted to the rear door.

"No need to flee, Susanna. Your body wouldn't tempt a man of breeding."

"That is hardly comforting, since there are no men of breeding in this room."

His air of calm shattered. With a snarl, he lunged for me. I charged toward the door, stopping short when his fingers caught my hair. In the space of a gasp, his mouth covered mine, his teeth grinding against my own.

"God help me," he muttered against my lips.

I trembled so violently, I could hardly control my limbs.

Dinah and Delilah shrieked in the yard, their calls coming closer to the kitchen.

He shoved me against the wall and stalked a few paces away.

I held onto the door frame, teeth chattering too hard to speak, as small feet stomped up the wooden steps.

"Papa, Papa," two little girls shouted, giggling as they burst into the kitchen.

"Yes, my pets," he said, stepping between me and them, reaching down to tousle their heads. "Let us go to the house." He gestured them out the door again and then glanced over his shoulder. "I hope you enjoyed your hours away, for they will be the last time you leave my property until your indenture ends."

My head ached fiercely. I stared at him, trying to make sense of his statement. "I don't understand."

"For this day's crimes, you will forfeit all freedoms."

CHAPTER THIRTY-TWO

AN INVISIBLE FORCE

I didn't regret spending a day with Susanna in Old Raleigh, but it had cost me training time. So I made up for it with an extra-long ride in Umstead Park and Crabtree. But it soon became clear that it wasn't going to be a particularly good training ride because I couldn't concentrate. I kept thinking about Susanna and our first kiss.

Not singular. Our first kisses.

While I was dating Alexis, I'd spent a lot of time wondering what she thought about making out and how well I was doing. It wasn't that way with Susanna. There was no sense that we were actors in a performance. Kissing her had been a natural next step. Part promise, part celebration.

The enormity of yesterday's events washed over me. What we'd done was huge. *Huge.*

Normal life seemed trivial by comparison. When my senior year started in August, the biggest problem I'd face was which teachers showed up on my class schedule.

It all seemed so stupid now. Yesterday had been real. Yesterday, we'd made a difference. A life-or-death difference. And I'd done it with Susanna.

Ba-bump.

I caught a root wrong and went down—the cost of not paying attention. The extra-long training ride probably shouldn't be extra-long, after all.

As I circled around toward home, I cut through the woods on a barely visible trail. It came out beside Rocky Creek, heading in the direction of my neighborhood. I'd never ridden along this section before. What made me notice it today?

Based on my approximate position and the terrain, I probably wasn't too far from Whisper Falls. The lady from the Raleigh Historical Society had said there were ruins from Worthville in the park. Was I near them?

I secured my bike and went exploring, following the creek to the north. When I reached a break in the woods, I found a narrow, railroad-tie bridge over the creek. I crossed it, heading west. A few hundred meters away, a clearing opened—ten or more acres of grassy meadow with spotty trees. A bike track split it down the middle. This had to be the location of Worthville.

I tried to orient myself. Where exactly was I in the town? I relaxed my mind, taking it back to where I'd been the week before, the creek at my back, hidden behind a rise…

The meetinghouse should be dead ahead of me. I started out, walking slowly through the thick grass. I crossed the bike track and kept going until I practically stumbled into a row of stacked rocks. A second row joined it to form a sharp corner, looking more like crumbling walls than the meetinghouse foundation it had to be. A little distance away rested a dozen gravestones—the town cemetery. If I'd wanted to badly enough, I could've found the mill ruins nearby.

It was eerie. I'd been to this place when it was a thriving town. I'd seen some of the people who had lived here. And now it was a sad pile of rubble.

I'd come back another time when I wasn't on a training ride.

After returning home, I cleaned up and went downstairs to the kitchen. My folks were getting ready to eat. Grilled

Atlantic salmon with roasted root vegetables. Yes, my father's healthy food fetish had taken over.

Mom waited until I was halfway through my first helping to launch her inquisition. "Did you see Susanna today?"

"No." I took a sip of water and leaned back in my chair. From the look on both of their faces, I gathered this might take a while. "But we spent the whole day together yesterday."

"Doing what?"

"Hanging out downtown." So far, sticking to the truth was working for me.

Dad put down his fork and gave me a puzzled look. "I thought she was locked up on some compound most of the time."

Wow. My mother did a pretty good job of keeping him updated on me. I couldn't decide if that was cool or disturbing.

"She is, so yesterday might end up being a problem for her. I won't find out for a few days. She's not likely to risk slipping away anytime soon."

Dad frowned. "Where is this commune?"

Crap. Here came the balancing act. I had to give enough information to shut them up, but not so much that I forgot what I said if they ever asked again.

"It's near Umstead Park. I can get there by bike, but they don't like outsiders showing up. I tried once, and it was awkward."

"Do the authorities know about it?"

I nodded and took another bite of salmon. Chewing was a good excuse not to speak.

Mom broke in before Dad could say anything else. "When can you bring her by to meet your father? I'd also like to take another look at that burn."

"I'm not sure. We'll see."

"She seems like a very sweet girl, which isn't something we can say about other girls you've dated."

"I've only dated Alexis."

"I know." She gave me a pained smile. "Susanna is welcome here anytime."

"Thanks, Mom." I downed the rest of my water and pushed my chair back. "I think I'll go for a walk. See you later."

I headed to the falls—not that I expected Susanna to show. It just felt right to be there.

Sunday wasn't much better. There was nothing to do. My parents went to church and brunch without me. I stayed at home and tried to dream up things to do.

I didn't bother with TV. It was stupid. No need to get on the computer, either. My invoices were caught up, and Carlton wasn't an option. I was bored.

Bored, bored, bored.

Cross-training might be good. I put on my running shoes and headed out on the greenway. I made a swing by the waterfall. Just in case.

She didn't show up all day. I knew because I checked at noon, at two, at six, and at eight.

Fourth of July dawned. It started out like a regular Monday for me. Ride, shower, breakfast. But there it diverged. Mom had plans for her guys that involved shovels, potting soil, and her English garden in the backyard. I didn't mind, though. It gave me something to do.

But it didn't stop me from wondering how Susanna was doing. Independence Day was something she had looked forward to for months. She might be bouncing around in a country dance right now, which didn't make me too jealous since there wasn't a whole lot of touching involved.

It was a gorgeous day in our century. We had a cloudless, Carolina-blue sky and enough of a breeze to blow around the neighbors's cookout smoke. My folks and I drove over to the lake house in the afternoon. Dad grilled steaks and Gran made peach ice cream. Once it got dark, we climbed in Granddad's boat and went out to the center of the lake to watch the fireworks.

We arrived home late, but probably Susanna wouldn't have come to the falls, anyway.

The next morning I was back in the lawn business. With the temperature hovering near one hundred, I'd have to play catch up with my Monday yards another day. Finishing my Tuesday yards would be brutal enough.

Afterwards, I drove the truck down to the State Archives. I needed to make sure that history had really changed.

The same research assistant waited on me.

"Hi," she said. "Back so soon?"

"Yeah. Same box as before."

She eyed me speculatively. "Okay."

I was a pro now. Flipping open the indentures file, I scanned the folders, vaguely tense about what I might find.

Deep breath in. *Happy* breath out. The Marsh folder held Phoebe's indenture with the Etons. Stepdad-to-be hadn't overruled anything.

I returned that box and made out a call slip for the marriage licenses.

When I opened the Pratt folder, Phoebe's name was no longer on the marriage license with Jethro—which was good—but another name jumped out at me. Hinton. Mr. Pratt had married a girl named Joan Hinton in October 1798.

Another call slip to see the indentures box again.

Something tickled at the corner of my brain. *Lydia* Hinton was the indentured girl from his 1800 will. Was Joan her sister?

The indentures file held a folder marked Hinton. Joan had been bound over by her aunt to Jethro Pratt on September 1, 1796.

September *first?* A month or more *before* Susanna planned to leave?

I wrote out a third call slip for Jethro's will and took it to the front.

"You're still interested in this same guy?"

"Yeah." I couldn't shake the feeling that something was wrong. Why had Jethro signed a new indenture before Susanna left?

The research assistant made out a fresh copy of the will, a puzzled frown on her face. "It says his wife's name is Joan."

"Yeah." I took the document from her and paid.

"Didn't it say 'Phoebe' before?"

It was best, in my opinion, to play ignorant. "It says Joan."

"But it said…" Her eyes narrowed. "Did you tamper with any of these documents?"

I shook my head, although I could make a case for saying I had. Indirectly.

"If you did, that's a serious offense."

"The security's too tight in here for tampering."

"Wait here a sec."

She laid the original document on the counter, pulled out a tool that vaguely resembled a magnifying glass, and scrutinized the document. Flipping it over, she scrutinized the back. With a scowl, she snapped on a pair of gloves and lightly held the edge up to her eye. She looked at me suspiciously. "It doesn't seem like it's been altered."

"I didn't expect anything different." I nodded politely. "Thanks."

When I got home, I spread the documents out on the kitchen table. The will had changed from wife Phoebe to wife Joan. That change in history was fine.

But the indenture dates bugged me. Susanna and Joan would've overlapped for six weeks.

Could Susanna be wrong? Maybe the family wasn't in bad shape, after all. Maybe her master had more money than she realized.

Were two house servants a possibility? One to clean, one to cook. Or something like that. Maybe business had picked up.

Yet Susanna had been certain it wouldn't happen. I had to trust her opinion. I needed to think this through as if there was only one servant.

Once we messed with history and moved Phoebe out of the picture, Joan showed up September first. Had the Pratts released Susanna one month early? What happened in August that caused the change?

It didn't make sense.

I couldn't waste my entire day staring at these documents. It was time to do some chores that my parents would consider valuable. I went outside to get the mail. All junk. I checked the potted plants on the front veranda. All watered.

But the problem of the extra indentured girl wouldn't leave me alone. It was like a bad headache, clinging to me, annoying me.

I returned to the kitchen table and stared at copies of old, faded documents.

Maybe they had Susanna training Joan.

But for one whole month? Joan had been fourteen in 1796. She wouldn't need that much training. She would've been doing housework for years in her family's home.

History said Joan was there in September, which meant Susanna must've left in August. Where had Susanna gone?

The pieces of the puzzle shifted in my brain and fell into place. The result was horrible.

I sucked air into my lungs and felt the fear spread. Susanna had left Worthville in August 1796, and I could think of only a couple of reasons why.

I grabbed my helmet, hopped on my bike, and took off for Umstead. It was time for me to visit the Worthville ruins again and take a closer look at the gravestones.

Susanna didn't come Tuesday night. Worry had me so tense I had to find other ways to channel my energy.

Wednesday, I doubled training time on the bike, completed my regular set of lawns, and did catch-up from Monday. Then I washed my mother's car and cleaned my room.

Okay, I *somewhat* cleaned my room, but I did it without being asked.

Susanna didn't come Wednesday night, either. I waited until long after dark, then went home and managed a decent stir-fry. That rated me more concerned looks from my parents.

When she didn't show Thursday, I couldn't stand it any longer. I had to take action. Since she wouldn't come to me, I would go to her.

Friday morning, I woke up early, dressed in the costume, waited for my parents to clear out of the house, and slipped out the back door.

The falls put the first bump in my plans. The drought had thinned the creek. The water was trickling along. I hadn't counted on that. Was there enough to pass through?

I tried but knew instantly I was still in 2016. The passage through time had a tingly feel to it, and this was just wet—and not very, at that.

Freaking out wouldn't help the situation. The waterfall wanted me to connect with Susanna. Why else had it brought us together? So it had to open the portal for me right now and let me get to her.

I stepped back to my boulder and watched the water carefully. There was a pattern. Trickle, trickle, trickle, splat. I gauged the flow, watched the pattern, waited for the splat, and jumped.

That time, two hundred years tingled by.

I scrambled up the cliff and looked around. There was no one here at this time of morning. With luck, I'd make it to the house unnoticed. I crept under the cover of the woods, paralleling the dirt track, hiding in the bushes when possible.

Had Susanna told them who accompanied her to Raleigh? Did they even know yet about her sister? Was she getting punished for all of it?

Was I too late?

I reached the edge of the forest, crouched behind an old oak, and studied the Pratts's property. There was a wilting garden and a barn. The kitchen had to be the building with a thin wisp of smoke curling from its chimney. The main house and the other buildings looked abandoned. No one was around, although I did hear a baby crying.

On the way here, I'd created a loose plan—based more on hope than fact—of darting from building to building until I reached the kitchen where, statistically speaking, Susanna had to be. Seeing the actual farm shot the plan. There was a hundred feet or more of open space to cross.

I didn't know their routines. Had they eaten breakfast? Would the kids be out soon to play? Had Jethro left for work?

A door opened at the rear of the house. Susanna came out, carrying a tray loaded with dishes. A young girl skipped beside her. They entered the kitchen.

I couldn't risk going there while she had a visitor. But after a few minutes, the young girl skipped out again and returned to the main house.

Should I give it a shot?

While I stood there considering my options, the bushes thrashed beside me.

"Hello," said a soft voice. A girl appeared and smirked at me with the confidence of someone who thought she was pretty. I recognized her. The Pratts's oldest daughter.

I waffled between "oh, crap" and "cool." For the moment, I'd go with "cool," since it suited my purpose.

"Hey." I smiled like I was happy to see her. She could be my ticket to seeing Susanna.

"Why are you here?" She fluttered her eyelashes.

That question had an obvious answer. Either she was delusional or messing with me. Probably best to go with a full frontal attack.

"I want to talk with Susanna."

She engaged in a bit of eye-rolling. "Papa has forbidden her to leave the yard, and he's promised to flog you if you come around."

"I am not interested in being flogged," I muttered, looking past her to make sure a pissed-off Mr. Pratt wasn't lurking nearby.

"Don't worry. Papa will be at the mill until suppertime." She blushed. "We have a new horse. She is quite beautiful. Would you like to see her?"

The way a girl stares when she considers a guy cute obviously hadn't changed much over time, because this one acted like she had a crush on me. How had that happened so fast? I'd only been around here a couple of times.

Really, I should view her crush as a gift and use it to my advantage.

"I'd like to see the horse, but could I talk to Susanna first?" I gave her my best imitation of a smoldering smile.

"Perhaps." She fluttered her eyelashes some more and sauntered toward the kitchen.

Susanna emerged a minute later and ran to the woods, glancing over her shoulder often. She stopped at the edge, scanning the underbrush.

"Mark?"

"Over here," I said from my spot several feet off the trail.

She remained still as a statue until her gaze found mine. "You shouldn't be here."

"You didn't come to the falls, so I came to you."

"I cannot leave, not until my indenture ends."

"I'm here to change all that." I held out my arms. "Why aren't we touching?"

She met me halfway. I hugged her tightly, savoring the closeness. The worry of the last few days faded. She was alive and well, and I was going to keep her that way.

"Mark? I can't breathe." Her laugh came out on a gasp.

"Oh. Sorry." I loosened my grip. "I'm just glad you're okay. Has Pratt been acting odd?"

"Terrifying." Her face retreated into a haunted look. "If he finds us together..." Her voice trailed away.

"I'm fine with my chances."

She glanced nervously over her shoulder, her voice roughening. "Please, you must go. My master will beat you if he finds you here."

"I'd like to see him try." Her warning snapped me out of my fog, though. I had to refocus on the mission to get her out of here. "You're in danger, Susanna."

"How?"

I needed to ease her into this. "Mr. Pratt is about to hurt you badly. I want you to move to my world."

"You asked me once before and I refused. My mind hasn't changed." She twisted to squint at the yard. Three little girls had burst onto the lawn, dancing and giggling. "Now leave, before Deborah alerts my master."

"He's replacing you."

"What?"

"In seven weeks, your master will sign a contract for a new servant."

She went completely still. "That can't be true."

"It is true." I pulled a copy of Joan's indenture from my pocket.

She snatched the sheet from me, eyes narrowed. "He's binding her for housewifery?"

"Yes, Joan is taking your place on September first."

Her head made jerky motions side to side. Denial crackled from her body like an invisible force. "No, there must be a mistake. Mr. Pratt has only just returned from begging from his brother. He brought two adult slaves with him. We can't feed another person properly. There is no room left for a second household servant."

"You're right. Joan will be the only one."

"Where will I be?"

"Gone."

"I wouldn't run away, not this close to the end of my contract."

"You won't be running away." I handed her a photo I'd taken at the cemetery. "We have a special kind of painting, called photography, in my century. Here is a photograph of a gravestone."

"Why are you showing this to me?"

"Look at the name and the date."

Her lips moved as she read, the words faint. *Susanna Marsh, August 3rd, 1796.*

She stared up at me, her face pale, disbelieving. "This can't be true. He'll be careful with me now. He won't lose control again."

"What do you mean? When did he lose control with you?"

"He…" She shook her head. "It's behind me. He won't go so far again."

One day, I would get to the bottom of her comments. But for now, I had to get her out of here—even if it meant shocking her senseless.

"Susanna, the photo doesn't lie. Jethro Pratt is going to kill you."

CHAPTER THIRTY-THREE

GREAT HEAVY THINGS

I despised my master. He'd been cruel from the day I arrived. His humiliating treatment of me last week showed a greater capacity for depravity than I would ever be able to forgive. Yet I couldn't believe he would hasten my death.

"He can be brutal, but he isn't a murderer."

"Maybe it's an accident. Maybe he hits you too hard. But why do you care? It has the same result."

Could Mark be right? Mr. Pratt's demeanor had indeed sharpened toward me. He skulked around the property, watching me like a bird of prey.

We all lived in fear of his unpredictable temper. Since Theophilus had arrived, the chores at the homestead had lightened, but the addition of Frederick hadn't increased the business at the mill. Even with millstones for wheat and corn, there were too many people taking their grains to Ward's Crossroads. Mr. Pratt left each morning hopeful and returned each evening seething.

My master was quite capable of flying into an uncontrollable rage and hurting me. I could imagine such a circumstance only too well. He might knock me against the hearth or shove me down the stairs hard enough to cause harm that couldn't be undone.

Mr. Pratt is going to kill me.

It was an indescribable thing, to contemplate one's imminent death. Was this how a criminal felt when sentenced to hang? He might not be sure of the day or the time, only that the end was near. How did he respond? With resignation? Disbelief? Fear?

If I stayed, I died. If I moved to Mark's world...

My gaze swept the yard. The little ones played in their favorite spot under the oak. Three beautiful, golden-haired girls. I had reared them all from infancy. They belonged to me as much as their parents. And my dear Phoebe. She, too, would be lost to me.

"If I go now, I shall never come back." Sorrow squeezed my heart. "How can I bear to be separated from my loved ones forever?"

"You'll be leaving them forever, anyway, on August third. I hate to be harsh, but here's your chance to pick whether you leave by choice or in a box."

His words grated against my ears. Should I put my faith in the history he'd uncovered? If Mark's special painting had the story wrong, I would be abandoning my life here for a place where I didn't belong.

Oh, why was I wasting so much time in thought? I had no wish to die. "Let's go."

Mark ran hard through the woods ahead of me. Terror nipped at my heels like little dogs, spurring me forward.

Deborah had been crossing the yard toward us when Mark and I ran. She knew of our disappearance by now. It would take her but a few minutes to alert her father.

Would they know where to look?

Jedidiah might. He had seen me from the bluff with Mark. How long before they followed? Ten minutes? Fifteen?

Surely, ten minutes was enough. We would be through the falls before they could find us.

I had to stop thinking.

I had to concentrate on running.

My feet pounded on the uneven track. I had hurried along it one thousand times before, but never so fast. Never with such carelessness about where I put my feet. Briars tore at my limbs. I ignored the sting and followed Mark.

He reached the cliff first and leapt down in two mighty bounds. I picked my way along the granite rungs. When I caught up with him, he stood on my rock, blocking my view.

"Go," I said.

"Can't." His voice was tight. Unnatural.

I peered around him.

The water trickled.

No, trickled was too strong a word. The water dripped.

My legs quaked. This was disastrous.

Neither of us would pass through the waterfall this day. Until it rained again—a long, fierce storm—there would be no Whisper Falls.

"They will capture us both."

"Let me try." He hopped to his boulder and then back again. Over and over, each hop more frantic than the last. Water droplets glistened on his cheeks. He never left my century.

I stared at the drips and dribbles, hands clenching and unclenching, my anger rising. How could Mark overlook a detail so crucial as the state of the falls? Had we placed in my master's hands the very nudge he needed to rage out of control?

"God, Susanna. I'm sorry. It's not this bad in my century. I didn't check from your side."

I gazed into his frightened face and knew instant shame. How could I be thinking like this? Mark had risked much to rescue me. I had agreed, an eager accomplice to the deed. Logic cooled my head as quickly as it had heated.

We wasted precious moments staring at water that did not flow. Townsfolk might be searching already. I cleared my mind of everything except the situation before me. The problem must be solved. They would not capture Mark.

I looked up. Above me, water seeped over the rocky edge. "We must return you to the future."

"I'm not leaving you here by yourself."

"Don't be foolish. You must." We had to have more water, a spurt for a second or two at most. How could I make the creek produce more water?

"Leaving would be a seriously dick move on my part. I came to rescue you, and I will." His voice sounded muffled and afraid.

"Rescue isn't possible today." I had to give him a reason to go. The truth was reason enough.

"You are the proof that I'm running away," I said, placing my fingers over his lips as he tried to protest. "If they find me alone, they have no evidence. You'll be safe, and I cannot be judged."

His face creased with indecision. I pressed my argument. "Aiding a runaway is a terrible crime. You will be fortunate to be jailed and flogged."

"Flogging is the best case?"

"Indeed. If you are caught, there will be no one to rescue either of us. Go to your world, and save me when it rains."

"Susanna, please…"

I had no time to debate him. I had to act. The creek had to produce more water. I ran for the cliff and climbed.

"Where are you going?"

"Stay there and wait."

I raced to the upper creek bed, to the sad pools of water that had once been a proudly flowing stream. There was hardly enough to drink.

I pushed rocks, mud, and sticks along the top of the falls, creating a dam while listening for sounds of discovery. The water increased, but not enough. I traveled many feet back along the creek, clearing debris, stones, and mud, dredging a little channel. Water trickled to the dam. A pool formed.

What a peculiar state to be in. For so long, I had feared Rocky Creek, and today I would dearly love to restore its swift current.

"What are you doing?" he called from below.

"Stay on my rock. When I tell you, the water will flow briefly."

There were shouts in the distance. *"To the creek."*

It was the first sign that I was being hunted.

I frowned at the water. It wasn't enough. Not yet. I trembled so much I could barely stand. Terror such as I had never known gripped me. My master had beaten me, burned me, pawed at my body and called me foul names. Never had he had an excuse to haul me before the magistrate.

An hour ago, my life had been tolerable. For the next seven weeks it would be unbearable, as I waited for Joan and my fate.

Mark's arms encircled me from behind. "Susanna," he said.

I turned and pushed blindly at his chest. "Don't be foolish. Go back."

"You're crazy if you think I'll leave you here."

"You have no choice. There won't be enough water for two. Go."

He didn't move, a look of determination on his face, his hands firmly at my waist.

"Are you mad?" When I shoved him with all my strength, he took a surprised step back. Finally. Perhaps now he would listen to me. "Return to the cave floor. We don't have much time."

"I got you into this. I'll get you out."

"Your good intentions are worth nothing if the town leaders capture you." Frustrated tears stung my eyes, and I blinked them away furiously. "I have found a solution that will work for us, but your stubbornness puts it in jeopardy. Go now or we'll suffer for your inaction."

"What will happen to you?"

"I cannot be sure. But I do know that the punishment for disobeying my master is far lighter than for running away. I shall fare better without you."

"I don't know..."

"Mark, travel to the future. It's the only way you can return later and help me escape."

I wanted to say more. So much more. *I shall miss you. I shall be forever in your debt. I love you.* Yet the words would remain unsaid, for I would not utter them in a voice that shook with fear.

Shouts echoed from the trail behind us.

"Fine." Mark hurried to the edge of the cliff. "I'll save you when it rains."

I met his gaze. He believed it. I did not.

He scrambled down the cliff and stood on my rock, waiting. He was so beautiful. I studied him carefully, memorizing each detail. His tall, lean body. His intense, amber eyes.

The townsfolk erupted from the woods.

The water trickled and swirled. It wasn't enough.

"There she is!"

They were close. So close.

The water I had collected would have to do. "Mark, prepare. You'll only have one chance."

"I'll come back for you."

I kicked aside the dam.

Once they had abandoned the search for Mark, the townsfolk argued over how to deal with me. Eventually, they insisted I spend the night in jail. Mr. Pratt declared that he wanted to handle me by himself. I sided with the townsfolk.

One night stretched to two.

The jail cell was most unpleasant. The town leaders hadn't designed the space for comfort. There was unrelenting heat blowing through chinks between the wooden slats. I cursed how small it was. It wasn't as wide as I was tall, and I couldn't stand up straight. As I leaned against the wall, hugging my knees to my chest, I felt great sympathy for the men who had stayed here before me.

The stink of dank straw offended my nostrils. Thin ribbons of bright sunlight slanted across the dirt floor, irritating my eyes. The daily meal shoved under the door would have been unfit for hogs.

Perhaps the worst part was the privy. It was a fair distance away. The jailer only came once each day to escort me there. If I needed to relieve myself more often, I had to squat in the corner of my cell, which only made the stench worse.

I learned to focus my mind away from the miseries. The solitude and absence of demands were not without merit.

There was time to recite my favorite Bible stories or revisit the characters in *Persuasion*.

I could relive the glory of kisses—not the vile punishment from Mr. Pratt, but the luscious delight I had shared with Mark.

I filled the remaining hours by pondering questions of great importance.

Would I die in this place?

Might my imprisonment change history?

From the future, did Mark know my fate?

There was a tap at the wall behind my head. I straightened. "Who's there?"

"I have brought you some food," a girl's voice whispered.

I peered through the boards. Outside my cell, a sprigged muslin skirt floated above small feet. Had she gone mad?

"Dorcas, you will be in trouble if you're found near me."

"Take the food. Then I shall leave quickly without being caught."

A slice of bread was pushed roughly through the slats, followed by a hunk of pork, much mangled and riddled with splinters. I devoured the bread and ached for more.

"Are you all right, Susanna?"

"I am well."

"Deborah said that Mr. Lewis came to see you on Friday."

"Did she?"

"Yes, but no one else saw him. Even the dogs couldn't track him."

I allowed myself a smile of triumph. "Perhaps she was mistaken." I picked splinters from my meat.

"I think she has told the truth. I think he was here to help you. Much as I would miss you, I am sorry he failed. He is very brave." She slid her small hand through the gap at the base of the wall. "You may keep it a secret, if you wish."

I touched her fingers lightly with mine. "You are very dear to me, Dorcas."

"Yes. We are dear to each other. If you go, how soon shall I see you again?"

"I do not know. Your father will not be inclined to let us visit." I hesitated over what I was about to share, choosing the words carefully as the revelation might prove dangerous for me.

"Dorcas, there is a special place near the falls, a place I visit when I need to be at peace. If you go there, you will feel how sacred it is, and you will be reminded of me."

"Where is this place?"

"I shall not say, but you will find it. I am confident of that."

"Then I shall not rest until I discover your special place."
She sighed. "Would you like me to bring Delilah or Dinah
next time I come? They miss you fiercely."

"And I miss them, but do not bring them here. Although
you are old enough to understand my circumstances, they
are not. I should not wish to scare them."

"Very well." Her hand disappeared, and her skirts rustled
as she stood. "Mama cooks while you are in jail. We are
none of us pleased."

A smile twitched the corners of my mouth at the change
to a more practical subject. "I doubt it will last much longer."

"Papa told Mama you will have a hearing before
the magistrate tomorrow. Mr. Worth will decide your
punishment. Papa says you will stay with us longer than you
had planned. Do you think he's right?"

"Perhaps." Her comments reminded me that my
contract no longer mattered. I wouldn't be in Worthville
much longer. What I didn't know was how I would depart.

"Dorcas, it's time for you to go. I shall see you soon
enough."

"I hope so." She slapped the folds of her gown, the dust
drifting through the slats in the cell. "I know that you'll
leave one day, and you'll go where Papa cannot hurt you.
But you promised to say goodbye. Will you remember?"

"I shall remember."

It was barely past dawn when raised voices awakened
me. I sat up, struggling to rouse my dazed mind.

"Open up the cell now, Joshua Baxter. She won't escape."
It was my mother's voice.

"I don't know, Mrs. Crawford. Mr. Worth said—"

"If she flees, you can jail me instead. Let her out."

The door opened and my mother swooped in to gather me with her arms. The jailer flinched away in disgust. I didn't blame him. My clothes were soaked with sweat and urine. My hair hung about my face in sticky hanks. Ants had bitten one of my feet into a raw, swollen mass.

"Come," Mama said, "it's time to clean up." She half-carried me to the privy and from there to the banks of Rocky Creek.

After I undressed to my shift, she set to work scrubbing my outer garments. I stepped gingerly into a shallow pool and sighed with relief as my stinging feet slid into the cool, velvety silt. When I had finished bathing, Mama washed my hair. She wrung it free of water and combed it with her fingers, working carefully through each knot.

I stood as docilely as a child, eyes shut, allowing myself to enjoy the sounds of the world around me and the long-forgotten feel of my mother dressing my hair.

"Mr. Shaw was most angry to learn we had bound Phoebe out," Mama said.

Some of the pleasure in this moment faded. "I do hope he recovers soon."

"He had already promised her to the Pratts." Betrayal colored her tone.

Despicable man. "She wasn't his to promise."

"Indeed. Phoebe was to work in their kitchen, and Mr. Shaw would receive his grain milled without cost for the next year." There was a catch in her voice. "He deceived me."

It was time to tell my mother the whole tale. I felt relief at the chance to confess. "It is unlikely that Phoebe would have worked in the kitchen. She would have spun thread or made cloth for the Pratts to sell."

Mama's hands stilled. "That cannot be correct. Phoebe has no such talent."

"The opposite is true. My sister showed extraordinary promise. The Pratts planned to use her skills for their own profit. My master lied to Mr. Shaw."

Mama gasped. "Jethro Pratt is a beastly man."

Her fingers completed the combing of my hair, then quickly switched to plaiting it, her movements quick. She was soon done.

I spun to face her. "I deceived you, too."

"You knew this all along?"

"I knew of Phoebe's talent, but I kept it from you, fearing you wouldn't let her move to Raleigh. I did not trust Mr. Shaw." I lifted my chin defiantly. "I shall not apologize. I would do the same thing a thousand times over for my sister."

My mother regarded me for a long moment, her lips pinched. A breeze whipped a tendril of her hair across her face, and she brushed it away, her gaze faltering. "I should thank you. I *did* trust him, and it wasn't deserved."

"Hullo," Mr. Baxter's shout rang across the clearing. "Mrs. Crawford, are you there? It's time."

"Yes," she called. "We shall be there shortly."

"He called you Mrs. Crawford," I said. "Wasn't your wedding this weekend?"

"Mr. Shaw has postponed it until your situation is resolved."

My mother and I looked at each other. Her eyes skittered away. Unexpectedly, I felt sorry for her. All four of my mother's children lived apart from her—both daughters through her own bad decisions. The realization must cause her great distress.

I would not add to it now. It was time to leave.

"What shall I wear?" I asked, frowning dubiously at my clothes steaming on a nearby rock.

She pointed to a shady spot high on the bank. "I brought fresh things. They wait for you behind those bushes." Her hand clasped my elbow and drew me up. But she didn't release me immediately, her gaze fixed on my undergarment. "Your shift is badly mended."

I froze.

"How did it tear?"

I pulled away from her silently, unwilling to say, the humiliation still an aching knot in my belly.

"Did your master have anything to do with this?"

I gave a jerky nod.

She swallowed hard. "Did he ruin you?"

My eyes stung. "He didn't..." I shuddered to a stop. The experience had been horribly, painfully humiliating, and yet it could have been worse. "He didn't go that far."

She put a shaking hand over her mouth and turned her back on me. "Dear Lord, forgive me for what I have done to her." The words whispered past me, so soft I might have imagined them.

Slipping behind the bushes, I found the stack of fresh clothes my mother had brought. After dressing, I emerged to find her with a plate of bread, ham, and cheese.

I devoured the meal in greedy bites. "Thank you."

She nodded, her face grave. "I shall accompany you to your hearing."

A crowd had gathered outside the meetinghouse. Mama and I marched solemnly into the building as if they weren't there.

"Mrs. Crawford." Mr. Shaw detached from the crowd and hurried toward us. "Where are you going?"

"Inside with my daughter."

"I don't think that's wise."

"Nonetheless, I shall go."

The front pew was nearly full. The audience for my hearing would include my mother, the town leaders, Mrs. Pratt, and Deborah.

I was shown to a narrow, high-backed chair on the dais. My master and his uncle waited, side by side, at a table.

Mr. Worth cleared his throat. "Miss Marsh, do you know why you are here?"

"I do."

"So you're aware that you're accused of running away?"

I nodded.

"Answer out loud, please."

"I'm aware of the charge."

Mr. Pratt pounded his fist on the table. "This is the second time she has attempted to run away."

Mr. Worth frowned at his nephew. "When was the other time?"

"On July first."

"I see." The magistrate scratched a note in his journal.

My mother stood. "Pardon me, Mr. Worth?"

"Yes, Mrs. Crawford?"

"Susanna was in my company on July first. She drove me to Raleigh and back again."

"Indeed. Did you know that she had no permission to leave Worthville?"

"She had permission to visit her mother. That is what she did."

I looked at my mother, outwardly calm but inwardly smiling. What had come over her? Today she had done more for me than in all the years since I had left home.

"Very well, Mrs. Crawford. I accept your story. Miss Marsh?" The magistrate's gaze bore into mine. "Did you attempt to run away three days ago?"

"I was discovered standing on the banks of Rocky Creek near my master's property. I should be a very poor runaway to make the mistake of not running."

Mr. Worth looked toward the front row. "Can any of you confirm Miss Marsh's statement?"

The town leaders nodded. Every one of them.

Mr. Worth's lips thinned, and his gaze swung back to me. "So, you left your master's property despite his express commands otherwise?"

"Yes."

As each moment passed in this interview, my anxiety eased. With no proof and the town leaders listening, Mr. Pratt and his uncle would have to treat me justly.

"You know this to be deliberate disobedience?"

"I do."

"Why did you go to the creek?"

"To check the water level. It was low."

Some of the townsfolk snickered.

My master's jaw hardened. "Susanna wasn't alone in her flight from home. She had assistance from Mr. Lewis of Raleigh."

Mr. Worth's eyebrows arched with censure. "You were aided by a gentleman?"

It was shocking how comfortable I had grown with deception. "I did not flee. Therefore, I was not aided."

"Are you saying that Mr. Lewis didn't help you escape?"

"Mr. Lewis didn't help me escape."

"Mr. Pratt, did you see Mr. Lewis with Miss Marsh?"

My master's lips barely moved. "No, I did not."

Mr. Worth looked again to the town leaders. "Did any of you see him?"

A muttered chorus of "no" rang out.

"I see." Mr. Worth scowled.

My master's fingers tapped impatiently. "Deborah saw him. She came to tell me the news before I left for the mill, and I instantly started the search. But the boy was nowhere to be found." When my master nodded at his eldest daughter, she stood.

"They were together," she said, her voice high and strained. "Mr. Lewis and Susanna talked at the edge of the woods and then ran down the path."

Mr. Worth tugged at his beard, then jotted a few words in his journal. "You are certain it was Mr. Lewis?"

"Yes, Uncle Worth, I am certain."

"How? Did you speak to him yourself?"

I watched Deborah curiously. Of course, she had had a conversation with Mark. She had fetched me to his side. Mr. Pratt's fury would be fearsome if he knew.

She looked at me with pleading eyes.

"Mr. Worth," I interrupted—although she and I had never been friendly, there was no use in both of us suffering—"Deborah was never close enough to speak with Mr. Lewis. He found me in the kitchen. I walked with him as far as Rocky Creek."

The magistrate swiveled his gray head to peer at me. "You admit that he was there?"

Tension built inside, but I forced it down. As much as I might wish not to implicate Mark, Deborah's testimony required otherwise.

"Yes, he was there, but he did not help me escape."

"Where is he now?"

"Back in Raleigh, I presume."

The magistrate dropped his quill, folded his hands before him, and allowed his expression to set grimly. "Is Mr. Lewis your suitor?"

The unexpected question surprised a bark of laughter from me. "No, indeed. I have no interest in marrying at present."

"A truth you made completely clear to my son." Mr. Worth spoke in a lazy voice, but remembered anger glittered in his eyes.

Mr. Pratt sneered. "Solomon deserves better than her."

"Indeed." The magistrate rapped the table. "I've heard enough. Without any evidence that Miss Marsh was running away…"

My master glared at me, lips pinched.

"…her only crime was to disobey her master's order to stay on his property. I lengthen her indenture by ten days."

I looked at him with calm disdain. It was unusually harsh for disobedience, but this sentence didn't concern me, for a far worse punishment awaited me before September first.

"Miss Marsh, have you nothing to say?"

Was this my moment? Dare I take the opportunity?

I would, indeed—and God protect me from what might happen later. "Throughout the eight years of my indenture, Mr. Worth, you have seen my bruises, burns, and cuts." I rolled back my left sleeve, exposing the red, puckered scar. The townsfolk in the pews gasped. "There has been clear and constant evidence of cruelty. If my scars have not spoken loudly enough already, then no, sir—I have nothing further to say."

Mr. Worth's gaze dropped to his journal. His quill scratched across the page.

My master glared at me, retribution in his eyes. "Uncle, what about my damages? Shouldn't she compensate me for the trouble she's caused?"

"No more," the magistrate said. "Ten days is enough."

"What of the boy?"

"I find Mr. Lewis guilty of trespassing. If he's captured, he'll pay a five-pound fine or spend three days in jail."

Their words flitted about my head like so many bees. My arms and legs quivered from fear released. I would leave the meetinghouse and return to my job. I would watch the horizon for storms, and I would count the days until August third.

But I wouldn't be flogged or returned to the jail. The sentence was tolerable. I looked at my mother and nodded. Her lips curved slightly. Thanks had been offered and received.

Mr. Pratt thumped the table with his fist. Everyone jumped.

"Uncle, I wish to put Susanna in shackles."

"*No.*" The denial rushed hoarsely through my teeth. *Dear Lord, please, not shackles.*

They were great, heavy things. I had seen them only once before on a slave, cutting into his ankles, humbling his walk and rendering pain with every step. "Please, no."

Mr. Worth didn't look up from the scratchings in his journal. "Explain your purpose."

"If she has willfully left my property twice, she'll do it again. The shackles will prevent her disobedience."

The magistrate sniffed. "Shackles are fair."

CHAPTER THIRTY-FOUR

THE RIGHT TOOLS

It had been a week since I'd seen Susanna, and it was going to be a lot longer. There hadn't been a drop of rain, and the forecast didn't give me any hope.

Not knowing how she was doing drove me crazy. I could barely eat or sleep. I couldn't concentrate. Other than cycling and lawns, I was worthless.

Had they flogged or jailed her? Had she been punished in other ways? Was she still…healthy?

I wanted answers.

"Mark?" Mom shouted up the stairs. "Dinner's ready."

"Okay." I stared blindly at the computer screen, propped up by pillows against the headboard of my bed.

"Are you coming?"

"No."

Her footsteps charged up the stairs and stopped at my bedroom door. "Mark, you need to eat."

"I'm not hungry."

There was a long pause. "Have you heard anything from Susanna?"

"No."

She came in and sat at the end of the bed. "So, what can you do to find out what's happened to her?"

"Nothing. It's impossible at the moment." I snapped the lid down on my laptop and slumped deeper into the pillows. If I was lucky, Mom would take the hint and go.

"Have you checked with the police?"

"Can't."

"Is her sister somewhere safe? Can you talk to her? Maybe—"

"Mom. Please."

"Leaving now." She squeezed my bare feet—which was as weird as it was comforting—and walked out.

But I wasn't any happier after she'd left. Being grumpy with my mother was better than worrying about Susanna.

There had been one thing to try, but I'd already tried it. On Tuesday, I'd ridden down to the Archives, ignored the suspicious glares from the research assistant, and asked to see Jethro's will and Joan's indenture. The documents had looked exactly the same. Susanna's failed escape hadn't changed history.

How would it happen—illness or injury?

The tombstone hadn't changed dates—but what did that mean? Did the actual event take place on August third? Had an injury already happened and she now lingered on, unable to recover?

God, I couldn't stand thoughts like that.

It was times like these that I wished Carlton and I were still friends. I wouldn't have been able to tell him the details, but it would've been good to hang out with someone I trusted.

Maybe I should talk to Marissa. That might help as long as she didn't go all Mini-Mom on me.

Where was the rain?

The WeatherNOW site predicted no precipitation for the next ten days, and their models seemed to be really consistent on this point. I knew because I checked the forecast every other hour.

Whisper Falls had slowed from an occasional half-hearted dribble to nothing. Water puddled here and there. I could spit better. I knew because I checked every day.

I even tried rigging up some ropes and buckets of water to simulate a waterfall. But all I got from the experiment was wet clothes. Apparently, Whisper Falls was particular about where its water came from.

I punched my pillows and rolled to my side. Time for my nightly review of The Plan, an elegant series of steps to rescue Susanna. I'd been working on The Plan for a week. From memory, I'd drawn a scale map of the area between the falls and the Pratt property. I'd visited the approximate location in my century and timed various scenarios. I'd brooded and tweaked.

The objectives were simple enough. Grab Susanna and run like hell for 2016.

The only thing missing was a decent-sized storm.

After three weeks of not seeing Susanna, I totally got how people felt when a loved one went missing. I'd become an empty shell of a person, going through the motions, held together by a sickening mix of desperation, terror, and hope.

That would all change tomorrow. Hope had to win.

The meteorologists were getting excited. Tonight, there would be rain, massive amounts of it. A tropical system was blowing in off the Atlantic, and North Carolina was in its path. Even though Raleigh was one hundred miles inland, we were sure to get soaked. There would be lots of rain crammed into a narrow window of time. Flood watches were in effect.

The rain was no longer an *if*. It was a *when*.

It was July twenty-eighth. Two days until the Carolina Challenge. Six days until August third. Earlier this morning, I'd dropped my parents off at the airport for their trip to Mackinac Island. They got out well ahead of the storm.

I rode to Umstead Park and tried to get in a last training run on dry trails before the rain hit. It was such a good idea that lots of other bikers and runners had it, too. The trails were already crowded. I gave up early, too agitated to think clearly.

I checked the WeatherNOW website every hour. The storm moved closer but wouldn't arrive until past midnight. I ate supper with my grandparents, watched The Weather Channel, and waited for bedtime.

My mother called after she arrived at their bed and breakfast. "How are things going?"

"Great so far."

"Have you washed your stinky clothes?"

"Yes." But not the towels. I'd do that the minute I got home.

"Any worries about the storm?"

Nothing besides I wished it had come three weeks ago. "I'll be glad when it gets here."

There was a long pause. "Is something wrong?"

"Yeah."

Her voice grew husky with concern. "Is it Susanna?"

"Yeah."

My mother hesitated. "Be careful, Mark."

"I will. 'Night, Mom."

A few minutes after nine, I slipped from the lake house, hopped in my truck, and drove home. But I couldn't just sit in the dark, waiting for bad weather. So I got busy. I rechecked my biking gear. I washed stinky towels. I emptied the trash cans.

It was around midnight when I heard the sound of drumming on the roof. I raced to the nearest window.

Rain. Lots and lots of rain. Weather radar showed a wide band of storms racing east to west—a solid band of green/ yellow/red, fifty miles wide. Within hours, Rocky Creek would be a torrent.

I was up before the crack of dawn and into the costume. Next came breakfast and the *I'm OK* text to Granddad.

The sun had just risen as I approached the creek. The falls gushed, no longer landing conveniently between my launching rock and hers. Instead, it shot forward like a fire hose. A six-foot-wide fire hose. I waded into Rocky Creek, braced myself against a boulder, and dove through the falls.

Whisper Falls clawed, flashed, and tingled. I emerged in the eighteenth century, up to my waist in water, dragged down by my wet clothes and soggy athletic shoes. There was no time to do anything about them. It was hot enough that they would dry soon.

Dragging myself onto the lip of a rock at the mouth of the cave, I studied the falls. It wasn't nearly as intense in this century, but it was flowing steadily. That was real convenient, because I hadn't made a Plan B for a drought on this side.

I walked parallel to the muddy trail leading to the Pratts's farm, creeping through the woods, careful but not concerned because it wasn't light yet. Once I reached the edge of their yard, I found a spot behind the outhouse and hid in the underbrush.

It was quiet. My location had decent visibility, but there wasn't much to monitor yet. I could wait. I was resolved and calm, my mind blank of all thoughts except The Plan.

The sun crept up the horizon.

An elderly African-American man trudged from the barn, carrying a pail. He climbed the rear steps to the kitchen, disappeared inside, and re-emerged almost instantly, chomping on a hunk of bread. He headed back to the barn.

The main house remained still. An occasional door slammed, but no one came outside. Didn't these people ever piss?

If something didn't happen soon, I'd make it happen. Maybe I'd figure out which kid was Dorcas and ask her to find Susanna.

A few moments later, two girls exited the house— Deborah and a younger one. They entered the kitchen and exited a couple of minutes later carrying trays.

Half an hour passed. They brought the trays back.

Susanna hadn't served today.

Why not?

I had to stay focused. It didn't matter why she hadn't served today. I wasn't going anywhere.

Pratt and his son left together, walking in the direction of the village. Good. I wouldn't have let them stop me— but it was just as well that they were out of the way.

Deborah sauntered from the kitchen and disappeared into the house. The younger girl ran toward the shade of a big oak. Other than her humming, the farm remained quiet. Smoke curled from the kitchen chimney.

No sign of Susanna.

What if I was too late?

Okay, stop. Not going to think that way.

Please, Susanna. Please come.

A strange, metallic clanking broke the silence. The humming girl halted her impromptu twirl to look toward the kitchen.

Susanna appeared in the open doorway.

I closed my eyes and slumped onto all fours, panting through my mouth, shudders racking my body.

"Do you need anything, Susanna?" a clear, young voice asked.

"No, thank you, Dorcas."

The hoarse rasp of her voice refocused me. Shaking off one last shudder, I snapped into a crouch. I was ready and disciplined.

Susanna was coming this way. The change in her shocked me.

She'd lost weight, her clothes hanging off her like she was made of sticks. There were dark circles under her eyes, deep hollows in her cheeks, and her hair lay in greasy clumps about her face.

But the worst were her feet. They shuffled forward in chains. Grimy iron cuffs had scraped sores onto her ankles. With each step, her breath came out in a puff.

I had to clap both hands over my mouth to keep from roaring with rage. If that jerk Mr. Pratt had put in an appearance, I'd have gladly beaten him to a pulp.

She didn't see me as she approached the outhouse. I waited until she would be able to hear my whispers.

"Susanna."

She halted. Our gazes locked. I was aware of the sounds. Birds called. Insects hummed. But nothing from her, even though her lips moved.

"I came back for you," I said.

A tear rolled down each cheek. She tried to say something, coughed, then rubbed a knuckle against her lips.

"Mark. Take me away."

I felt like a warrior of old. The sight of her filled me with strength and invincibility. I didn't care what it took. I was setting her free.

"You won't be living here another day."

Her knees buckled and she fell to the ground. I made a move toward her but she waved me away.

"Mark, watch the yard."

"Okay."

She struggled to her feet. "Can you see Dorcas?"

"Yeah. She's watching you. She's beginning to walk this way."

"Stay where you are." She struggled to rise and slipped into the outhouse.

The little girl returned to her tree.

"Dorcas isn't looking anymore," I said as loudly as I dared.

A few seconds later, Susanna came out again and shuffled behind the building. I drew her into my arms, cradling her like she was a baby. She was so light, so fragile. The last time I'd seen her, she'd been fiercely pushing me around with her arms and opinions. Today, she lay against me weakly, trembling with exhaustion.

I felt the sting of tears in my eyes and fought it back. Now, more than ever, she needed me to be logical, strong, and prepared. There was no place for emotion.

"I'm ready to go." Her voice was muffled against my chest. "Please."

"I'm sorry, Susanna, but not yet." I gently pushed her upright and took a step back. I hated to do this to her, but the shackles were a risk I couldn't take. "He put those on you to keep you from escaping. It was a brilliant move on his part, because we'll be caught if you're in chains. They have to come off."

"Do it, then."

"I can't. I don't have the right tools."

She bent her head and sobbed.

Her cries tore at my heart. "I have bolt cutters at home. It won't take long, Susanna. I'll be back."

She scrubbed at her cheeks and eyes with grubby fists. "What should I do until then?"

"Pack."

CHAPTER THIRTY-FIVE

A SLOW ETERNITY

This next hour would surely be the longest of my life.

I shuffled across the yard, pausing to watch Dorcas singing and twirling. I smiled, drinking in the sight of her. She waved and laughed. I waved back, my smile dying. I had promised to say good-bye, but now that the time had arrived, I couldn't do it. The risk was too great. Indeed, I couldn't speak to her or any of my precious babies. My voice would give me away.

I entered the kitchen and sat on the bench. Perhaps it would be better to think of things I wouldn't miss. I looked about me with fresh eyes, viewing the space as someone who knew she would never return. It was a hot, humorless room. Four walls. Two doors. One table. Over the ash-strewn hearth dangled toasting forks, spoons, and knives, the blackened tools of my trade. The smells of stewed meat and wood smoke pervaded each rough-hewn board of the floor.

No, I would leave this all behind happily.

There were so many people in my life that I would be glad to forget. But the ones I would miss? Oh, how they echoed in my heart. How could I bear to leave my adorable John? Sweet Dinah and Delilah? My beloved Phoebe?

And Dorcas? Irrepressible Dorcas. Child of my soul, if not of my body. Lost to me forever.

The threat of tears ached behind my eyes, but I fought them back. I had to conserve my strength for the dash to freedom.

I must find something to do. Mark had said to pack, but there was no need. I couldn't take my other bodice and petticoat, or my master could say I had stolen from him.

How sad that I had nothing to call my own.

Merciful heavens, I'd forgotten my two books—the legacy from Papa. They were hidden in the attic. If I fetched them, the effort would draw everyone's notice. Chains dragging on the stairs would be heard throughout the house.

But this could not be helped. Papa's books were my treasure. I could not leave them behind.

With a groan, I rose. The walk to the main house was slow and labored. Mrs. Pratt and Deborah sat in the parlor, engrossed in the spinning lesson. The three littlest ones sat quietly in the corner, playing with blocks. All looked up as I passed by.

"Susanna, what are you doing here?"

I paused, regarding my mistress gravely. "Fetching some garments to mend."

She sniffed and returned her attention to her spinning. Her children watched me quietly as I continued to the stairs.

I clanked my way carefully up to the attic and knelt on my pallet in the corner. After prying away a board, I reached deep into a crevice for the two books. The smaller one came out easily and slipped into my pocket, nicely masked by the folds of my petticoat. The larger one would be a problem. I lay on my side and stretched until my fingertips touched the binding. The book relinquished its hiding place reluctantly.

Brushing the dust and the cobwebs from the cover, I considered what to do. It was too big to fit in a pocket. And if I carried it openly to the kitchen, someone would remark.

I had to hide this volume, perhaps in the mending basket. It was in the dining room, on my route to the outside.

I made it down the stairs without seeing anyone. If I could walk past the parlor without being stopped, I would have my problem solved.

"Susanna?" Mrs. Pratt called.

I froze, framed by the parlor door, the book clutched to my side. I angled my body away from her. "Yes, ma'am?"

"If you have enough free time to work on mending, perhaps you can take the little ones with you."

"The little ones?" I glanced their way. Dinah and Delilah dropped their blocks to smile at me. John immediately pounced and added their blocks to his pile.

My heart yearned to hug them and kiss them one more time. If only there was some other way. With children underfoot in the kitchen, I couldn't escape this morning. Until Deborah or Mrs. Pratt reclaimed them, I would have to oversee their safety.

Would Mark's plan work on another day?

I gazed at Deborah with pleading eyes, hoping and praying she would intervene.

"Mama," she said, "the little ones are happy. Leave them be. Susanna has enough to do with mending and cooking."

"Very well." Mrs. Pratt bent over her thread.

I nodded in gratitude at Deborah. She nodded in return. A debt repaid.

In the dining room, I slid the book under a tangled pile of torn aprons, hoisted the basket, and trudged outside.

"Susanna," Dorcas said, falling into step beside me, "do you want me to cook dinner?"

"No, it's nearly ready." I must treat this moment as ordinary. I must not cry.

"Have you packed pails for Papa and Jedidiah?"

"No, but soon." It was good she had reminded me. Delivering the meals would take Deborah away from the house for a while.

Dorcas followed me into the kitchen and fetched the pails while I stowed the mending basket in the corner. With great attention, she set clean napkins in each pail.

I added buttered bread and wedges of cheese to each. They wouldn't be pleased by this paltry meal. I wouldn't be here to care. It was a welcome thought.

Dorcas frowned. "Is that all you will pack for them?"

"Would you like to add fruit?"

"I would." She disappeared into the pantry, returned with two apples, and dropped them into the pails.

"If you cover them each with a cloth, we are done." I kissed the top of her head and smoothed her curls. "It's kind of you to assist me. I am tired of late."

Her head drooped against my chest. "I hate your chains. I hate Papa for putting them on you."

The words chilled me. If she were to repeat them to anyone else, I feared for the response.

"Shh, don't say such things."

"It's true, Susanna."

"That sort of talk will land you in trouble."

"Perhaps it will." She picked up the pails and headed to the door. "I'll take these to Deborah."

I removed the lid on a kettle of ham and vegetables. It was ready. With deliberate care, I lifted the pot onto the worktable, my movements clumsy from fatigue. I ate a buttered slice of bread as I poured mugs of cider.

There. I had finished my last chore.

Excitement gave me a burst of vigor. I retrieved my other book from the basket, left through the rear door of the kitchen, and limped toward the privy. As I shuffled along, the chain clinked in the dust of the yard, bumping between my feet. I stopped at intervals to catch my breath, weary from straining the muscles of my legs with each step.

Mark hadn't returned.

I entered the shade of the forest and jerked to a stop, my chain catching on a root. I shook it free, wincing from pain as an iron cuff dug into my raw ankle.

I looked back at the yard. Had anyone seen me bypass the privy? Would they come to investigate?

Mark and I needed fifteen minutes to reach the falls and freedom. Had I come too soon?

Why was he delayed? Would he come at all?

I shouldn't think this way. He would be here. He had promised. I edged along the path, deeper into woods. Before I had gone far, I heard the crunch of footsteps. Mark separated from the trees and slipped a green cloth sack from his back.

"Where's your stuff?"

I held up my two books.

"Anything else?"

"This is everything I need."

He took them from me. "I'll seal them in this special bag to keep them from getting wet." He wrapped my books and placed them in his sack, then pulled out a peculiar tool, his face grim.

"Let's get the other part over with."

Assailed with nerves, I peered back toward the house. Nothing moved save the breeze in the treetops. Could it truly be so easy? I could simply disappear into the woods, never to return?

With an ungainly thump, I plopped onto a log and pulled up my skirts while he knelt before me. He grunted with the effort of cutting the chains. A link severed in the center.

"Your legs are free. Let me see if I can cut off the cuffs."

As the tool clamped down, the iron cut into my raw ankles. Pain pounded like a hammer. I slapped my hands to my face, pressing the moans back in.

He glanced up, then stopped. "You look like you're going to pass out." He disengaged the tool and slipped it into a pocket. "I'm not hurting you anymore. Let's hope the chains don't give us any more trouble."

"I won't be able to walk fast."

"I'll carry you, if I have to." He stood and drew me up with him.

I clung to his arm and allowed myself to hope. I would be free. Before the hour was out, I would be free.

"Susanna?" a girl's voice said.

We turned around.

"Dorcas?" I leaned on Mark for support. "What are you doing here?"

"Susanna? Why are you here with him?" Her lower lip trembled. "What are you doing?"

The heat of shame skittered along my limbs. I had planned to leave without saying good-bye. I couldn't be sorry she had forced a different choice.

I gestured her closer and caught her hand in mine. I had to give her the truth. "I'm leaving with him."

"Right now?"

"Yes."

"Today?" Tears streaked down rosy cheeks. "You are running away?"

Of all the things I had ever had to do, abandoning Dorcas would be the hardest.

"Indeed. Mark is taking me to somewhere safe."

She rubbed at her eyes with the back of her hand. "Shall I see you again?"

"My new home is far away. I don't think I shall be able to return."

She sobbed in loud, choking gasps and wrapped her arms about my waist. "Now that the time has come, I cannot bear it."

"Oh, my sweet Dorcas," I said, pressing her shaking form to mine. "Leaving you behind is my greatest regret. I shall miss you desperately."

"Susanna?" Mark said with urgency.

Dorcas stared up at him, eyes big and wet.

"We must go now, dear one," I said.

She nodded and reached up with her apron to dab the tears from my cheeks.

Mark crouched, his eyes on the same level as hers. "You can't tell anyone you've seen us."

I considered his request and knew immediately that I had to correct him. Were Mr. Pratt to ever learn she knew of our disappearance and had kept the information from him, it wouldn't bode well for her. I couldn't leave with such a possibility on my conscience.

"No, Mark. She must tell what she knows."

He tensed. "Why?"

"Her father will be most angry if she does not."

"But…"

I shook my head. He backed down, his eyes darting anxiously toward the yard.

"Dorcas, I have something important for you to do. May I trust you?" At her solemn nod, I said, "You must seek your father and tell him I ran away."

A hiccup. "No, Susanna. I shall not."

"You must. Perhaps you should visit Mr. Foster's store first."

"Papa wouldn't be there…" Her voice trailed away, her brow furrowed as she thought. Then she nodded slowly. "Indeed, I shall seek him at the store. And perhaps next at the meetinghouse."

"Wise choices." I straightened and gave her hand a squeeze. "He cannot be angry at your diligence."

"No, he cannot." Two fat tears rolled down her cheeks. She gave me one final hug and ran back to the yard.

"Susanna, let's get out of here."

He took off. I hurried as best I could, but was unable to keep up. He stopped, linked his arm through mine, and pulled me up the incline. The chains clanked and twisted into my sores. I hissed and stopped.

"Your chains are catching on roots." He freed them.

Several yards later, the chains caught again. Mark sighed, his face creased with dread. "We have to take off the cuffs. I'm sorry."

The idea of pain watered my eyes. "Can you carry me?"

"Not for the entire ten minutes. I'd have to stop often. It would be cutting it close."

As if to punctuate his words, there was a shriek in the distance. "*Mama!*"

"That's Deborah. She must've ambushed Dorcas on the path to town." My teeth chattered. Time had evaporated. Deborah would run swiftly. How long would it take for Mr. Pratt to gather a search party? "All right. Be quick."

I sank to the base of a nearby tree and pressed my back against its trunk.

"I'm so sorry," he said. The bolt cutters gripped a cuff.

Agony gripped my leg like a vise. I thought I was prepared, but I was not. A moan escaped my lips.

"I'm sorry."

"Don't waste your breath apologizing." I gasped between each word.

The cuff popped open and fell to the ground. He picked it up and threw it with a vicious grunt into the woods.

"Okay. Brace yourself."

The second one proved more difficult. It slipped away from his grasp, its edges digging into my wound each time. I bent over to retch.

"Done. Come on."

Our progress was slow and painful. Even with the shackles gone, my legs remained stiff and sore, afraid to bend. I forced my mind to ignore the throbbing of my ankles and concentrated only on the path ahead. We had been hobbling along the trail only a few minutes when the first baying of the hounds sounded.

He groaned, his body shuddering. "Climb on my back. We need more speed."

A slow eternity passed before we reached the clearing. The dogs grew louder with each step.

"Damn. Do they know where we're going?"

"They found me here before. They're astute enough to connect this spot to where Dorcas saw me entering the woods."

With efficient movements, he placed me on the cliff's edge. "Can you climb down by yourself?"

Never before had the cave floor seemed so far. My legs wobbled and my head spun.

"Susanna?" he prompted in a strained voice.

"I don't think I can."

Chapter Thirty-Six

Shades of Red

Those freaking dogs howled, breaking free of the woods. The humans couldn't be far behind. I'd never been this scared in my life.

"I'll climb down first, then catch you."

I leapt to the cave floor and reached up. "Now, Susanna."

She squirmed closer to the edge.

"There she is," a voice shouted. "By the falls."

"Time's up, Susanna," I yelled. "Jump."

She slid off the ledge, banged against an outcropping of rock, and screamed in surprised pain. I scooped her into my arms, then steadied her on her feet.

"Go to the falls."

She stared at the water, roaring from the bluff to the creek. "No, Mark."

"Shut up and move," I ordered. "I'm right behind you."

In a bad dream, this type of scene would happen in slow motion. Well, damnit, we were living a bad dream. It was as if I could see each muscle contract and joint bend in her legs. I looped an arm around her back, urging her forward. It wasn't fast enough.

I would stay between her and the search party since I trusted my chances with them better than hers. I was *not* leaving Worthville again without Susanna. And we *were* leaving.

She reached the edge of the creek and wavered, mesmerized by the force of the waterfall.

"Go. It'll be all right. See, I'll throw my backpack through." When I tossed my green backpack full of tools and books, the falls encased it in a glittery cocoon and then spat it onto a rock on the other side.

"Stop," a voice bellowed.

We both whipped around. Mr. Pratt stood above us on the cliff.

"Stop," he repeated. "The water will carry you away, like your father."

She froze.

"Ignore him. You won't die like your father. Whisper Falls is on our side," I said with urgency. "Jump."

Mr. Pratt laughed. "Susanna, you mustn't do this mad thing. Stop now and all will be forgiven."

"I can't step into that water." She stared at me with big eyes. "Save yourself."

"Not a chance. Go on." I cupped her elbow and urged her forward. "You first."

Behind me, rocks clattered.

"Come on, Susanna. We're going to win. But you have to move."

She took a deep breath and then launched herself into the creek, moaning as the water boiled and foamed around her thighs.

"Don't think about the water. The falls *like* you. Trust them."

There was a roar of rage behind us. It echoed off the cave walls. Mr. Pratt had climbed down. "Susanna, my dear, don't leave me."

"I am nothing to you," she yelled as she took another step. Her body disappeared under the surface.

I ran to the boulder's edge. "Susanna?"

She reappeared, still on this side. "Mark, he's right behind you."

"Don't worry about me. Keep moving."

A heavy hand clamped on my shoulder and jerked me back.

I went totally psycho. The air seemed to glow in shades of red, the heat of its fury making me itch to leave a mark. I spun around, fists flying, hoping to inflict whatever damage it took to bring this bastard to his knees. The punch glanced off his arm.

Mr. Pratt laughed, head thrown back.

It was like being in middle school again, trapped in the bathroom, surrounded by bullies who jeered and punched. Well, I was five years older, five years stronger, and—after seeing what he'd done to Susanna—*centuries* angrier. I threw a hook, my fist connecting with his nose.

Crunch.

My turn to laugh. "Yeah, real funny, asshole."

He staggered backwards, clutching his face. Blood dripped from his chin. I smiled with grim determination and landed another punch. His gasps changed to snarls and his arm flew through the air, the blow glancing off my jaw. It should've hurt, but it didn't. It just made me madder.

This guy was bigger and smarter than most middle school bullies, but I would win this fight, too. I rebalanced and came out swinging.

He doubled over, hands braced on his knees, then surged forward, head-butting my chest.

I went down, smacking my head, lying spread-eagled and dazed.

A shadow blotted the sky. I blinked, trying to bring the world back into focus. There was a laugh, like some kind of villain's cackle from a bad cartoon show. Mr. Pratt loomed over me, his jacket flapping like the wings of a vulture.

"No!" Susanna screamed.

He hesitated long enough to glance over his shoulder, staring through the curtain of water, his face scrunched in confusion. "Susanna?"

He couldn't see her.

She'd made it to the other side. She was safe.

The knowledge gave me a second wind. I pushed up on my arms. As if my movement caught his attention, he swung around and reared back, his boot aiming a vicious kick at my crotch. When I twisted away, his foot went sailing into empty air. He wobbled and fell.

I rolled into the creek.

The water was colder and deeper than I expected. I hit bottom and jack-knifed around, disoriented by the gray-green, bubbling foam, not sure which way was up. Another quarter turn and there it was, a glimpse of a Carolina-blue sky.

I shot to the surface, gasping for breath.

"This way," Susanna shouted. "Mark, come this way."

I turned in the direction of her voice.

"Yes, that's good, Mark. The falls are straight ahead."

I sloshed forward, desperately mopping hair and water from my eyes.

From behind me, Mr. Pratt moaned and spat.

"Send the dogs," he shouted. "They're escaping."

I'd forgotten about the damn dogs.

Someone gave a piercing whistle. The entire pack bounded into the creek.

With tired legs pumping, I sloshed harder toward the waterfall. Why was it so far away?

The dogs charged me, snarling and snapping.

I leapt for Whisper Falls.

CHAPTER THIRTY-SEVEN

CURLING AND SWAYING

Mark smashed through the torrent, the water scattering about him in glittering shards. He plunged into the creek in front of me, submerged, and then raised himself again.

Thank you, I said to the waterfall. Mark had been right; the falls had been on our side. He was safe and I was free.

I braced myself against a boulder, my legs no longer capable of support. "Mark, please tell me how you are."

He sputtered. "Okay." And sputtered some more. "Where are we?" he asked between gasps.

"We are in your world." I didn't say more, fascinated by the scene unfolding on the other side.

Whisper Falls poured in a wide arch, its water translucent, revealing the men of Worthville as dark, motionless, human-sized smudges high on the bluff. The hounds whimpered and cowered at the base of the falls, then turned tail and raced for the trail to the cliff, a long, gray shadow moving as one.

Mr. Pratt fumbled to his feet, a hulking menace, and faced the falls squarely.

"Come on, you idiots," he shouted, "we have them within our grasp." He crouched and sprang.

The falls encased my master in a crystal skin and suspended him in mid-air, a huge, hapless trout flapping on a watery fishing line. He flailed and shrieked until the falls released him, dumping him unceremoniously into the creek below.

Whenever he floundered to his feet, the water slapped him under.

"Papa." Jedidiah clambered down the cliff, falling the last few feet. Wincing, he lurched across the rocks to the creek's edge. "Let me help you."

"Get away from me, you fool." Mr. Pratt knocked away his son's hand.

My heart broke at the humiliation replacing adoration on Jedidiah's face. How could Mr. Pratt treat him this way *before witnesses?*

The townsfolk shifted restlessly, muttering among themselves. When someone whistled, the dogs swarmed over the top of the cliff, panting and milling about. As a group, the men turned and stalked down the trail toward Worthville. A flushed Jedidiah limped along the bank and disappeared behind the bluff.

"Come back here," Mr. Pratt shouted as he crawled onto a boulder. "It's not too late."

Silence greeted his calls. The tall grasses waved in the breeze.

"Come back here!"

Jethro Pratt stood alone, a pompous, cruel, despicable man.

"Hey," Mark said from behind me, his hands light on my shoulders, "what just happened?"

"Justice." Satisfaction coursed through my veins. Mr. Pratt was about to reap what he had sown.

"Good. Let's go home." Mark lifted me onto the bank, then joined me. "How do you feel?"

"Weary. Fine." I touched my lips lightly to his. "You saved me."

He cupped my cheek with a gentle hand. "I told you I'd come back for you."

"You did." I smiled and left unsaid what we both knew. It could've ended badly. He'd been both foolish and wonderful.

We kissed again, sweetly, briefly, but full of promise.

"Time to get you home and into some dry clothes." He glanced at my ankles, but made no comment. I dared not follow his gaze. They hurt so fiercely that it couldn't be a pleasant sight.

"What about your sack?"

"Oh, right." He hauled it from the boulder and then secured it behind a fallen log. "It'll be hidden there until I come back to get it later."

Indeed, it was best to concentrate fully on the journey to his home. I leaned on him and focused on the path before me. We climbed onto the trail and tramped up the hill. When we reached the top, I watched people passing on the greenway. They stared, open-mouthed, no doubt shocked at the sight of the two of us, wet and bedraggled. I dropped my gaze to the ground, unwilling to see if their shock turned to censure.

"Can you walk the rest of the way?"

I shook my head, as my body refused to move another inch. Shakes took over. Teeth clicked. Muscles cramped. And my ankles. Merciful heavens, they screamed for attention, robbing me of breath from the pain. Because I dared not look at them, I looked at him, instead. Blood seeped from a cut on his jaw.

"You're hurt."

"It's nothing."

"It's everything." I swayed and clutched at his shirt to keep from falling.

"Are you sure you're okay?"

I shook my head, too worn out to speak, and slid slowly, carefully down to the ground.

"Here." He sat beside me and pulled me into his embrace. "Are you cold?"

"No."

"Then why are you shivering?"

I felt the sting of tears. "Relief."

I slumped into him, closing my eyelids against the sunlight, the passersby, and the fate I had barely escaped. All I wanted was the feel of his strength and the little reassuring sounds he murmured.

Minutes passed, long enough for a lone beam of sunlight to slide by us and reappear overhead. Perhaps I even dozed, but, at last, I stirred.

He shifted. "How are you now?"

"Ready to go."

"It's not far."

The path curved up a slight incline. At its bend, I glanced over my shoulder at the rutted trail. My throat tightened as I lost sight of the falls.

I faced forward again, the past behind me. We reached his property without delay. He opened his gate and urged me ahead of him, one hand securely clasping mine, the other a solid presence at my waist.

My footsteps faltered, but from surprise rather than pain. The immensity of his house still intimidated me. Larger than the Etons's, this house had no dependencies besides a tiny barn, and it had only one chimney. How did they stay warm in the winter? How many people lived here? How many servants did they require?

Would his servants treat me like a guest or like one of them?

Should I act like a guest or a servant?

"Are your parents at home?"

"Not right now."

I cleared my throat. "Do most people in your century have houses like this?"

"No."

Three stories made of brick. And windows everywhere.

"It seems quite extravagant."

"I wouldn't say that, but it's not small."

I looked up at him in wonder. He stared straight ahead, avoiding my gaze.

"Is your family rich?"

"They do pretty well." He crossed to a dark red door and tapped some black buttons on a little white square. "It feels weird to be discussing this."

"All right. We won't."

He stepped back so I could precede him inside.

The first thing I noticed was how pleasantly cool it was. And for a building so full of windows, the first room we entered was rather dim.

We turned a corner and emerged into a huge space— nearly as big as the entire ground floor of the Pratts's home. It echoed with an odd hum and had air blowing from holes at our feet.

He helped me to a chair and then crouched beside me. "Wait here a second. I'm going to get you some medicine for pain, and then something to drink." He disappeared through a doorway.

I crossed my arms on the table and gave in to the desire to close my eyes.

"Susanna?" Mark's voice had softened with concern. "Can you sit up?"

My head and arms seemed reluctant to cooperate, but I did straighten. He dropped two pills in my hand and offered a glass.

The liquid inside was cool and sweet. "What is this?" I asked after drinking it all.

"Orange juice. It's good for you." There was a smile in his voice. He slid a warm wrap around my shoulders and perched on the seat next to me. "How do you feel?"

"Better." I felt as if I had awakened prematurely from an oddly happy nap.

"Do you think you can walk?"

"Soon."

"Okay. Sit as long as it takes. Will you be okay alone for a few minutes? I want to go back to the creek and get the backpack and your books."

I gave a nod and laid my head on my arms. A soft chirp, like a bird, sounded as the door closed behind him.

Sleep claimed me instantly. I didn't stir until I felt a touch on my shoulder.

"Susanna, are you awake?"

I yawned and struggled to sit straight. "Perhaps."

"Stay seated another couple of minutes and then we'll give walking a shot."

"My books?"

"As good as when you handed them to me." He clasped my hand snugly. "By the way, we're in the kitchen."

"Your kitchen is inside the house?"

"Yeah."

A kitchen attached to the house? Strange, but useful. "You don't worry about fires?"

"Not really."

I opened my eyes wide to survey the room, looking for the familiar. There was no fireplace or baking oven. Perhaps the silver boxes scattered about the walls had that purpose. Opposite us waited two sinks. A worktable rested in the center, covered with a large, exceptionally smooth rock. Square stones, of a golden hue, covered the floor. There were ten or more windows.

Where were their pots and pans? I saw no spoons, ladles, or knives. Indeed, the only item I recognized was a tea kettle.

The odors were missing, too. No roasted meat, wood smoke, or baking bread. There was, however, the faintest scent of sweet spices lingering in the air.

This room made my head buzz with awe. "Where is your cook?"

"We don't have a cook. Everyone in my family can fix food, but mostly my mom makes our meals." He watched me carefully. "We don't have *any* servants, Susanna."

I blinked. "None?"

He shook his head.

I didn't know what to make of that. Without servants, the family would have no choice but to do their own chores. I couldn't imagine how that could be true.

"How do you prepare food without a hearth?"

"All those silver boxes. We call them appliances." His lips curved slightly. "The thing with the window is the oven, which is where we bake. The tall one is the refrigerator. It keeps things cold."

The explanation was too much. My aches had taken over again, consuming my thoughts. There was no room for anything else. Learning about my new reality could wait. My head lolled on my neck.

"Hey, I am boring you?"

"Never." I yawned.

"All right." He stood and then drew me up with him, his arm securely around my waist. "It's time to get cleaned up."

I stiffened. "Must we?"

"Yeah, I'm sorry. Your ankles are oozing blood."

He was right, of course. We had to.

A sob swirled in my gut, fighting to break free. A sob of anticipation. I feared the pain. I feared how I would react to the pain, and how he would react to me.

"I'll find you some clean clothes and run you a bath."

"A bath?" I asked in shock. Unbidden, the image of previous baths in the Pratts's kitchen came to me. A metal tub full of cold, dirty water. "Did not Rocky Creek wash me sufficiently?"

"Not at all. I don't trust what's in the creek." He wrapped me in a hug. "I need to put medicine and bandages on your ankles, and I can't do that until you're clean. You might as well get used to it. We bathe every day in this century. Only with this bath, your legs will feel horrible."

I didn't want to get used to it, and I didn't want to sit in cold water. But most of all, I didn't want Mark to help me with a bath in a tub in this house.

He assisted me up the stairs. It was a chore to lift my legs up each step. My feet left grubby tracks on the thick, silvery rug that stretched from wall to wall.

"Mark, the floor."

"I don't care about the carpet." He pressed a kiss to my temple. "You're important. *It* is not."

His arms kept their light yet vigilant hold on me as we completed the laborious climb.

Everything in this part of the house was bigger and more colorful than in the Pratts's house. In Mark's home, the stairs were wide and curved. The walls were painted a pleasing blue. Gilt frames hung at regular intervals, with paintings so lifelike they looked real. Could they be more of those things he called photographs? I paused before one that showed Mark smiling beside a young lady.

"That's my sister, Marissa."

"She's quite pretty."

He snorted. "Yeah? Wait 'til you meet her."

We continued down a hallway and entered a long, wide room full of mirrors and slabs of stone.

"This is the bathroom. We take showers or baths in here. We also use it for..." He paused. "It's like an outhouse, too."

I clung to the threshold. It was the whitest room I had ever seen. It had white sinks and a white floor. The white tub was large and deep, with short, clawed legs holding it up. The tub had been pushed under a window made of odd glass that had no other covering.

I could hardly take in this room dedicated to bathing. Indeed, the tub was larger than the space I had once used for sleep.

My muscles began to quiver, yet I stayed where I was, afraid to move or touch anything. I had already soiled the rug. What if I ruined anything else?

"Where are your parents?"

"On a trip. They're at a wedding in another state. You've never heard of it, though."

I shouldn't have asked. I closed my eyes against this world and breathed deeply. I was here now. I had to accept this place. I had known it would be different and hard to understand. But couldn't I go a bit longer without participating? Wouldn't it be easier to bear in small bits— and when I didn't hurt so badly?

Yes, that was the answer. I would be ready to learn later when I felt more myself.

"Let's get some warm water going."

A *warm* bath? I focused again. Truly? I would be warm?

He knelt beside the tub and twisted something that looked like a doorknocker. Water gushed in.

"You'll need to take off your clothes."

The request embarrassed me. I was uncertain precisely what he meant.

"Explain, please."

"Don't worry, I didn't mean while I was here. You'll bathe by yourself. I'll head to my sister's room to see if she has anything you can change into." He reached into a cabinet, pulled out a stack of white cloths, and set them near the end of the tub. "Those are your towels."

"Thank you."

He squeezed past me in the doorway. "If you need anything, call."

I gave him a tentative smile, relieved that he didn't expect me to undress before him. "What type of clothing does your sister have?"

"I'll pick the most modest thing I can find." He gestured at me. "Susanna, go on."

I shuffled into the room and gasped at the coldness of the floor. A droplet of blood stained a spot near my foot. Had I left such drops on the lovely carpet? I sagged against the counter, fighting an urge to check. And what good would it do? I did not know how to clean silver rugs.

It would be best to do as Mark asked and ponder the other questions later. I unpinned my bodice and untied my stays and petticoat. My cap was gone, a victim of the flight to safety. When I had removed all but my shift, I perched on the wide edge of the tub and ran my fingers through the water. It caressed my hand, deliciously warm. In one corner waited a basket of bottles in various hues. I lifted a bottle and sniffed. Roses. A nice scent. In my old life, perfume was a luxury only the rich could afford.

Mark's family was rich.

I should add that to my list of questions for later. Did poor people get to smell sweet?

There was a light tap at the door. "Are you in the tub?"

I grabbed a towel and held it before me. "Not yet."

"May I come in?"

"Yes."

The door opened slowly. His head poked in. He had changed into fresh clothes.

"Hey," he said. His hands held a pair of shoes, a long, colorful skirt, and a blue shirt like a man's, with wide, full sleeves and many buttons. "Will this stuff work?"

I nodded.

"Great." He piled them between the sinks. "If you want, I'll wash your old clothes."

A young man washing clothes? I nodded again, subdued by both the request and the thought of him caring for me. Yet I would need my clothes laundered, would I not? I would have to give his sister's clothing back.

He scooped my old things into his arms. "Anything else you need?"

"Where is the soap?"

"In those bottles, like the one you're holding. All different kinds."

"This is soap?" Not perfume. How lovely. Perhaps this bath would be enjoyable. But first, I must address another need. "Where is the privy?"

He blushed. "It's over there. We call it a toilet." He pointed at a big, white bowl. "You sit on it and pee into the water. When you're done, push the silver button and it'll take the pee away."

After he left, I tried the toilet. It was noisy but worked as he said. A privy in the house that looked and smelled clean? It was another thing I liked here. How lovely that, with so many new things to learn, there were inventions that I would like.

With burgeoning anticipation, I returned to the tub and picked up the bottle of soap. I should like to smell of roses. Mark would like that also, no doubt. I poured some into the water. The soap slid out, curling and swaying like little pink ribbons.

All was ready. I swung my legs over the side and sank into the tub.

CHAPTER THIRTY-EIGHT

THE AFTERWARDS

I'd offered to wash Susanna's clothes, but I really wanted to burn them. Even in a world where people could get away with just about anything, Susanna's stuff was going to look bad.

Damn, there was a lot for her to learn—things as big as technology and as small as how anal we were about being clean. It was as if she had moved from a primitive culture in a third world country, arriving with no clue about her new life. Once Susanna had recovered from the pain, she was going to be slammed by new stuff everywhere.

And what about us? What would I tell my folks? Mom had said Susanna was welcome, but for how long? Susanna had no one else to turn to. She didn't exist legally. What were we going to do about that?

Okay, I had to stop. The deed was done. She was here. We would deal with it. There was enough stuff to handle today without worrying about more.

Time to focus on problems I could solve, like washing clothes.

I'd thumped my way to the bottom of the stairs when I was stopped in my tracks by a scream, like a wild animal in pain. It broke off in mid-shriek, followed by great, gulping sobs. I dropped the load of clothes on the foyer floor and raced back up to the bathroom.

Susanna huddled in the tub, the shift puffed about her chest like a dirty, gauzy balloon. She stared blindly, tears rolling down her cheeks. Reddened water swirled about her legs.

"Shit. I forgot about your ankles."

She looked at me through half-glazed eyes. Her mouth opened to speak, but all that came out was another choked sob.

It killed me to see her like this. "I'm sorry." I knelt by the tub, feeling stupid and inadequate. What should I do?

I didn't want to take her out of the water. It was keeping her warm. And there was no point in putting bandages on until her bath was over.

Okay, think. What had to be done, and in what order?

"I hate to do this to you, but I'd better take care of your ankles."

She nodded vaguely, not meeting my gaze. Her teeth chattered in between sobs.

I wasn't sure what should come first. Those wounds were awful. They probably needed medical care, which I couldn't seek for her yet. There were too many questions they'd ask, and we hadn't dreamed up answers.

If only my mom was here to help. What had she told me once about taking care of patients? *Talk in soothing tones. Let them know what you're about to do. Never surprise a patient.*

"Susanna, I'm going to drain the water, put on temporary bandages, and then fill the tub again." I released the stopper, grabbed a big towel, and dropped it around her shoulders like a blanket.

She laid her head against the edge of the tub and closed her eyes. As gently as I could, I lifted her leg and propped it on a rolled-up towel.

"I know this will hurt. I'm sorry."

"You are only trying to help me," she said in a whisper. "Please do so quickly."

I touched a washcloth to her ankle. She hissed wetly.

It had to be done. I dabbed away the dirt and the dead skin. Fresh blood welled up wherever I touched. In my untrained opinion, she had an infection. Better to think about that later.

The left ankle was finally clean. Reaching into the nearest cabinet, I grabbed a first aid kit. Thank God for Mom's paranoid nurse act, since it meant we had kits in every bathroom.

I applied antibiotic ointment, added a gauze bandage, then tape. At last, I was done. Time to dress the second wound. I glanced at my patient's face to check how she was doing.

Susanna had one hand clamped over her mouth, as if to dam the cries threatening to spill out.

"I'm sorry. Do you want me to stop?"

She shook her head.

"Okay. Right leg." I repeated everything for the other ankle. At last, it was over. I released her second leg, looked up to smile with encouragement, and froze.

Damn.

The shift had turned into a second skin. A totally hot second skin. And she had seriously nice breasts. Which I really shouldn't have been thinking about at the moment, but I just couldn't help myself.

Focus on the girl in pain. I became busy with cleaning up the mess I'd made.

"Do you need my help with your bath?"

"I shall manage."

"Okay. I'll get you some fresh water." I turned on the faucets, keeping the water to a gentle flow. "Use as many towels as you need to dry off, and then just leave all of the wet stuff on the floor."

"Thank you."

I nodded, not looking at her anymore, feeling a little helpless. "Maybe I should—"

"Truly, Mark, I am fine. I shall see you when I'm done."

"Right. I'll be in the kitchen."

Once I had her clothes washing, I set another first aid kit on the kitchen table and then prepared a snack. Cheese, crackers, and apple slices. I wished I could make something better, but there wasn't much food here. Mom had left the cupboard pretty bare since she was expecting me to eat with my grandparents.

A sense of panic—of being overwhelmed by the total responsibility for another person—paralyzed me. I slumped into a chair, my brain trying to slog through the actions I'd taken. Had they been enough? Had I left out any important steps? I wanted my parents. I wanted to know if I'd done all the right things to take care of Susanna. And since my folks weren't here, my grandparents were a good second choice.

I found my cell and called the lake house.

"What?" my grandfather barked into the phone.

"Is Gran home?"

"Yeah."

There was a long pause.

Okay, I could play the game, although for once it wasn't funny.

"May I speak with her?"

"What about?"

"Granddad, please."

The phone clattered as he set it down.

A brief moment later, she picked up. "Hi, Mark, you left early this morning. Did you eat breakfast? When are you coming back over?" She sounded grandmotherly and in charge, two qualities I needed right now.

I felt oddly nervous. I was about to introduce Susanna to the twenty-first century world and twenty-first century people. How would I explain? How would I keep them from thinking she and I were crazy? In planning for this day, I'd been so caught up in rescuing Susanna that I'd never thought much about the afterwards.

For now, I would explain as little as possible and do some serious thinking tonight. "Gran, did Mom ever tell you about my friend, Susanna?"

"The girl in the cult?"

Cult? Perfect. I could work with that. "Yeah, Mom treated a burn on her once."

Gran's voice was grave. "I've heard about your young lady. Why?"

"Susanna escaped today."

Just saying the words brought waves of emotion washing over me. I dropped my head, sucking in a breath. The events of the morning flashed by in still images. So much had happened. Too many things could've gone wrong, and there was a lot left to be done. But she was alive, and free.

Gran gasped. "Is she okay?"

"She's weak and exhausted, but she'll be fine. Eventually."

"Were you with her when she escaped?"

"Yes, and I'm fine, too."

"Did those people try to stop you?"

"They did." My body ached in delayed reaction. "Gran, I need your help. I'd like to bring Susanna to the lake house for the rest of the weekend. Can she stay in the other guest room?"

"Of course. You don't even have to ask." Her voice grew brisk and businesslike. "Pack her up and bring her over now. I'll get the room ready. Have you eaten?"

I smiled. Food—the southern grandmother's cure for all problems.

"We're about to eat something light. I'm sure we'll have room for dinner."

"Okay, sweetie. And Mark?"

"Yes, ma'am?"

345

"Well done." Click.

Smiling, I set the phone down on the table and glanced up. Susanna stood in the doorway, looking small and adorable in Marissa's clothes and slippers. She gave me a tentative smile.

"Hey." I pushed out of my chair and crossed to her. "How did it go?"

"Well."

When I opened my arms, she walked into them and leaned against me. She smelled like roses. I ran my hand through her hair, down its entire length from head to waist. It was soft, damp, and wonderful.

She sighed. "I have noticed that ladies on the greenway often have their hair cut short. I think I should miss the weight of it on my head."

"Yeah, people in this century can wear their hair any length they want. I think most of them cut it short because it's easier to take care of." I combed my fingers through the dark strands. "You are the only person I know with hair this long. It's awesome."

"I'm glad you like it." She nodded against my chest. "Did I hear you speaking to someone?"

"My grandmother."

"Were you using a phone?"

"I was." I leaned back to gaze at her. "We'll spend the night at my grandparents's house."

Susanna stiffened, then wiggled free of my arms and walked to the windows.

"What will they think of me?"

I came to stand next to her, anxious to smooth away the tension from her expression. "They'll think you're beautiful and wise. It won't matter to them where you're from."

"But how will you explain how different I am?"

"I don't think I'll have to. We have these things in this century called cults. They're often run by people with unusual views on religion, and they sometimes kidnap children and treat them badly. My grandparents think that's what happened to you. They'll blame the cult for anything you do that they don't understand." It would get more complicated later, but Gran and Granddad would be manageable for the next few days.

"Are your grandparents rich like you?"

"They do fine. They have a house on a lake in Chatham County. It's deep in the woods. They can't even see the houses of their neighbors. It might be more comfortable for you."

She gulped. "Do they know Alexis?"

"Yes." I linked my fingers through hers and was glad to feel her grip my hand tightly. "Don't worry about Alexis. No one in my family liked her."

She was breathing hard, not looking the least bit reassured. "This sucks."

I choked down a laugh; she was already picking up some of our words—correctly, too. "Why does it suck?"

"I stopped going to school when I was ten. I have so many scars. I know nothing about how your world works. And I—"

"Stop, Susanna, please," I interrupted. "You sacrificed your future for your sister. You loved a bunch of little kids whose father beat you viciously. And you never gave in. You're the best person I've ever known. My family will adore you."

She scrunched her face as if in pain and looked away from me. "When will we leave?"

"In a few minutes, after I change your bandages again— and after you've had something to eat."

"How will we get there, and how long will it take?" Her voice shook.

"We'll go in my truck, which is like a fancy carriage, only it's a lot bigger. And enclosed. And it doesn't have horses, but it does go fast. We'll be there in less than an hour."

She nodded but didn't say anything.

"We'll do this at your pace, however you like. You're going to be fine. I promise."

She met my gaze, pale and calm. "I'm ready."

CHAPTER THIRTY-NINE

RELENTLESS REMINDERS

Mark's truck had nothing in common with a carriage except that they both moved people. On the outside, this machine was big, black, and noisy. After Mark lifted me inside, he strapped me to a slippery seat with a belt that nearly choked the breath from my body.

Worst of all, his truck moved at a frightening speed. I made an attempt to watch at the beginning of the trip. But as other vehicles moved past us at even greater speeds, I found it best to keep my eyes shut for the remainder of the trip. I pressed a hand to my roiling stomach and prayed that I would not be sick in his fine, horseless carriage.

"We're here," he said.

I shook off the apprehension of the last hour and looked around me. We sat in a small clearing in the woods. A house made of logs rested between us and the glimmer of a lake. A garden with tall cornstalks and vines heavy with vegetables flourished to one side, while flowers crowded into any spot around the yard where a beam of sunshine might stray.

This place didn't feel nearly so foreign.

He left the vehicle and walked around to lift me down. I couldn't hide a wince as my aching legs took my weight. My whole body felt battered and bruised.

A door slammed nearby. An elderly man and woman waited on a wooden porch with no roof.

"Are you okay?" Mark asked, his hands warm at my waist.

"Yes." I sucked in a relieved breath, glad that the rushing ride had ended.

"Don't worry about how to say or do things. You'll be fine, and I'll be right beside you."

"Okay." I tried to smile at him. I wasn't sure if I succeeded.

He linked his fingers with mine and led me to his grandparents. When I sought to tug my hand away, he wouldn't release me. Were such signs of affection no longer private?

"Hello, Susanna," the elderly woman said. She had the same amber eyes as Mark and a sweet, welcoming smile. "I'm Norah, and this is my husband, Charlie."

The elderly man bobbed his head once.

"Hello." I would have to use their Christian names for now, since they'd given me no last name to use. How very familiar. "It is nice to meet you."

"We're glad to meet you, too. Come inside, dear."

The front room took up half of the house and had no ceiling, but extended straight to the beams of the roof. I marveled at this room that soared two stories high— unusual and majestic.

There was a stone fireplace, and a wooden floor waxed to a lustrous shine. Rugs in bright colors lay scattered about. They had two large sofas and several chairs in pleasant shades of brown. The furniture looked more comfortable than elegant, a choice that I applauded.

"Mark," his grandmother said, "can you tell me about Susanna's ankles?"

I looked around to find the other three staring at my feet. How odd that I had forgotten them. The pain had not left me. It had merely lessened. Yet there was so much to see in this new place that my mind had been occupied otherwise.

Mark sighed. "You need to take a look at them, Gran, to check for…stuff."

"What happened?" Norah asked, her gaze shifting from her grandson to me.

How much of the truth should I share? When I looked to Mark for guidance, he gave me an encouraging nod.

"My master shackled me three weeks ago. He was afraid that I would escape." I couldn't stop a tiny smile of satisfaction that his fear had come true.

Her eyes widened, but she did not comment further. Instead, she gestured for me to follow her. "All right, dear, let me show you the most important part of the house. The bathroom."

I trailed after Norah down a short hall. She stopped halfway to push open a door.

"Would you like to have a moment of privacy, dear?"

"Yes, please."

There were things in this room that needed explanation, things that Mark had not explained at his house and I had been too dazed to ask about. At one end stood an empty closet with a glass door and no shelves. Beside the toilet sat a fat spool of white paper. Lined up on the counter were two bottles with spigots on top. Would it be better to discuss these things with Norah or Mark?

Probably Mark. The answers might be embarrassing to discuss with a man, but there might be some things even a "cult girl" should know.

When I finished relieving myself, I opened the door to find Norah in the hallway waiting for me. Behind her on the wall was another lifelike painting. A photograph. It held two little girls, the older with short blonde curls, the younger with long hair of a rich, dark red. They both had amber eyes. I paused in admiration.

"May I ask who they are?"

Norah nodded. "My daughters." She pointed to the blonde one. "That's Sherri, Mark's mother. And the other is my other daughter, Pamela." She turned to me, a sad curve to her lips. "She died five years ago."

"Does this reminder not pain you?"

"Forgetting her would pain me more." She inclined her head. "Did you leave a lot of loved ones behind?"

"Yes, ma'am." The kindness in her voice nearly undid me. "My mother and sister are still there. And several children I tended."

"Do you worry for their safety?"

I shook my head. "They live in better circumstances than I did."

"Maybe you'll see them again someday."

The ache of unsaid good-byes rippled through me. "I do not think it likely."

"Oh, honey," she said, pulling me into her embrace, "you've done a courageous thing today. Let yourself grieve. Don't be surprised if you're sad and confused for a very long time."

I rested against her, weary, without tears. Could the sadness ever completely fade? Perhaps not. But it was so lovely to have her understanding.

"Well, now. Are you ready to return to the living room? I want to see what Mark did to take care of your ankles."

Mark and his grandfather were talking, sitting across from one another on sofas. They stopped when we arrived. I perched beside Mark and waited, unsure what to do, while Norah knelt at my feet.

He whispered into my ear, "It's fine to relax. She loves fussing over people."

While his grandmother exclaimed over my wounds, I reclined into the sofa, my body sinking into the soft cushions.

Charlie stared at me from beneath beetled brows. "Mark's been telling me about your ordeal, Susanna. I'm sorry I couldn't have beaten up the bastard alongside him."

Norah looked over her shoulder. "Charlie, really."

I turned toward him, fighting the urge to smile—and yawn. "I am grateful for the sentiment."

He grunted. "This is a beautiful place we have here on the lake. Stay as long as you need."

"Thank you, sir."

Charlie stood. "Mark, I could use you down at the dock." He gestured toward the door.

Moments later, I saw them walk past the windows on the side of the house and disappear in the direction of the lake.

"Susanna, I'll re-dress your ankles, but I'm going to give you something to ease the pain a little." She patted me on the knee and then disappeared from view. I didn't move, the desire to drowse too strong.

I dutifully took the pill she offered and then observed, through half-closed eyelids, Norah carefully removing the bandages and applying fresh medicine. Eventually, I allowed my attention to drift.

It was all so peculiar. When I had awakened this morning, I had been bound by chains. My thoughts had been fixed on this day, the children I loved, the sister I missed, and the numerous chores that stood between me and returning to my straw pallet. I had refused to think of the future and the unfathomable event that would require Joan Hinton to replace me. Only a few hours later, I had lost both the chains and my loved ones.

A new future stretched before me, yet I could not compel my mind to think on it. There was too much to learn, too much to see, too much to feel. The enormity of what lay ahead pressed against me, making it hard to breathe. I wanted to weep and hide.

Closing my eyes, I yielded to Norah's ministrations. She was gentle.

So very gentle.

And I was so very tired...

The cushion beside me shifted.

"Hey, sleepy head," Mark said. "I hate to disturb you, but you'd better get up now."

My eyelids fluttered open. Had I fallen asleep?

"Your grandmother must think I am terribly rude."

"No, she thinks you're exhausted." He smiled at me. "She and Granddad went to the store to get more bandages and stuff."

"They left us alone?" I tried to smile but yawned instead. "This is another difference in our centuries. It is not proper for us to be without a chaperone."

"They trust us to make the right decisions."

"Do you deserve that trust?"

"Unfortunately, yes."

His face wore such a sorrowful expression that I had to chuckle. "It would be tempting to see how true that is."

"Oh?" His eyes lit with anticipation. "Go for it."

I lifted my face for his kiss. It was sweet and brief and lacked the fascinating heat of our earlier kisses. Yet I liked this kind, too.

"You saved me." I tucked my head against his shoulder.

"We've saved each other—in more ways than I can count." He pressed a kiss to my brow. "I couldn't let you die, Susanna. I would've come back every day until you were safe."

"I owe you so much."

He laid light fingertips against my lips. "You don't owe me a thing. You're alive. That's the only thanks I need."

I nodded in acknowledgement of his statement, but knew this wasn't the last time we would speak of it. My gratitude would never end.

He brushed his mouth against mine. "Now, is there something you would like to do?"

"Indeed, there is." I sighed happily. There was much to learn. I was ready to start. "I want to understand some items in the bathroom."

We ate our dinner at a table by the kitchen. The food was simple: chicken, potatoes, and green beans. They drank tea, sweetened with sugar and poured over chunks of ice. It was strange, but I drank it, nonetheless.

"Have you had enough, Susanna?" Norah asked, eyeing the food still on my plate.

"Yes, ma'am," I said with an apologetic smile. "It is delicious. I am…"

"It's okay. I'm done, too." She pushed back and stood. "You and I will sit outside on the deck and watch the sun set. Mark and Charlie can handle the dishes."

So they called the uncovered porch a "deck." The list of words I must remember grew longer with each sentence.

And the gentlemen doing chores? Mark and his grandfather would clean up while Norah and I sat and talked. It might take me a while to adjust to such a truth—but I would, no doubt, grow to love it.

As Norah and I crossed to the front door, she said, "You have beautiful hair. So thick. And such a gorgeous shade of brown. Did you wear it down where you used to live?"

"No, I had to wear it up on my head under a cap as I worked."

"That's a shame. But no more. You can wear it any way you like now." Norah's eyes took on a shiny glow. "Would you let me brush and braid it while we visit?"

No one had asked this question with such eager anticipation since I was a little girl.

"I should like that very much."

For the next hour, we sat on the deck while she brushed my hair with soothing strokes and talked to me of gardens. While we were still engrossed, Mark and Charlie came out, watched us for a moment, and then wandered together into the darkness of the yard. They didn't stray far, for I heard voices among the trees and the snap of branches.

"Susanna, you've been trying to hide your yawns. I think we should get you to bed."

"Do not be offended, please. I am deeply grateful for all you have done." I watched her reaction earnestly.

"No, hon, I'm the one who should apologize. You've had a traumatic day. You need to rest." She stood. "Come on."

She led me into the house and up a narrow staircase against the far wall. At the top was a simple space overlooking the front wall of the house with its huge fireplace. This tiny, open room held a chair, a table, and a low, backless couch.

She pointed to a door at one side. "The guest bedroom is in there. You'll have peace and quiet."

I nodded.

"Mark?" she called over the railing.

He appeared below and looked up. "Yes, Gran?"

"I'll help Susanna get ready for bed. Sleep in the loft tonight, so you can hear her if she needs you."

It didn't take long. Norah handed me a garment she called a "granny gown." It was beautiful—pale, silky, and trimmed with lace. Once I had it on, I was under the covers in no time. As she exited the room, her fingers tapped a white square, shutting off the lights. I flinched at the abrupt darkness and wondered if I would ever stop preferring the soft glow of candles.

Mark appeared in the open doorway a minute later, his body a silhouette against the light from the ground floor.

"Tired?"

"Indeed." I lay stiffly in Norah's nightgown, quilts pulled up to my chin, head cradled in the thickest pillow I had ever seen on a bed.

"How has your day been?"

I smiled as best I could. "Your grandparents have been gracious. I am most grateful."

He shook his head. "I didn't ask about them. I asked about you."

"I should have liked to spend the whole evening holding your hand." I blushed at the boldness of my statement. This new world had already begun a stealthy reshaping of me.

"Me, too." He stepped into the room and stood by the bed, leaning over to press his lips to mine. "I'll be right outside your door all night long. If you need anything, just call."

"I shall."

"Anything at all." He straightened and then returned to the doorway. "I mean it, Susanna. Just say you need me, and I'll be here."

"I shall remember."

I slept fitfully at first. When the tossing and turning awakened me again, I lay in bed, staring at the ceiling, listening for sounds of movement, but the house remained still. I glanced at the clock, with its numbers glowing red in the dim room. When had clocks lost their hands? They had become easy to read in this century and could be found everywhere—relentless reminders of the passage of time. Their precision alarmed me. I didn't wish to measure minutes so carefully.

It was after midnight.

Mark's grandparents slept on the ground floor in a large chamber with its own bathroom. Directly above them were my room, the loft, and another small room with a narrow bed. There were four people in this house and four bedchambers. So much space for so few people.

I rolled over. The bed was big enough for three, yet I had it all to myself. It was thickly cushioned and smelled like a flower garden. I hugged the edge and smoothed my hand along the sheets. They felt like silk.

I had never been so uncomfortable in my life.

The lake house was cold. I lay under a blanket. A warm blanket in a cold house in the middle of summer.

The house hummed. I couldn't hear insects chirping or coyotes howling or the clicking of tree branches in the wind. Only the hum of a cold house.

What had I done? Why had I come here?

My mind revisited the events of the day. How could it be that barely twelve hours ago I had lived in a different place and a different century?

Why hadn't the townspeople tried to follow me across the creek? They wouldn't have found me there, but they couldn't have known that.

Might they believe I had been swept away by the current like my father?

Had the Pratts punished Dorcas?

When would Phoebe learn that I had disappeared? If only I could have left her a letter.

The sheet grew wet beneath my cheek. I was afraid to be here, yet I did wish to live. Why had I been faced with such a choice?

I crammed my fist into my mouth. I did not wish to be alone.

CHAPTER FORTY

AWESTRUCK REVERENCE

A muffled cry awakened me, a sad whimper lingering in the stillness of the loft. I sprang from the sofa bed. Had I really fallen asleep in my clothes?

I crossed to the guest room door and listened.

There it was again.

"Susanna?"

Her words cut through the darkness. "I need you."

Damn. Of course she did. I crawled onto the bed behind her and cradled her in my arms. She turned to face me. She had wet eyes, and she was shaking.

"Please, hold me."

"I'll be here as long as you want."

"Thank you, Mark." She nodded, her eyes studying me in the faint light. "Were you asleep?"

"Yeah, but I'm glad you woke me up."

Shivers rippled through her, wave after wave. She inhaled and exhaled through her mouth. I tucked the covers around her, slid my hand from her shoulder to her back, and rested my head near hers on the pillow.

Was this too much? Too little? I didn't know for sure and hoped that she would be brave enough to correct me if I was wrong.

Her breaths slowed from puffs to normal. The shivers faded to nothing. Maybe I hadn't totally screwed this up.

"Better now?" I asked.

"I am." She touched her fingers to my cheek. "In my world, when a couple lies on a bed like this together, we call it bundling. It's acceptable as long as a blanket separates us."

"You're in the twenty-first century. We can sleep together any time, any way, any reason—and no one cares."

"Except, perhaps, for your grandmother." She smiled. A slow, beautiful smile.

"True." I smiled, too. "Go to sleep. I won't leave."

She kissed me once, then rolled over, facing away.

I pulled the covers to her shoulders, wiggled closer, and draped an arm across her waist.

Her breathing settled into a rhythmic pattern minutes later.

I lay beside her, staring out a window high in the wall. I could see stars, a faint glow of the moon, the occasional sway of a pine tree. I felt weighed down by feelings. Exhaustion from three weeks of waiting. Aches from my first—and hopefully last—fistfight. Pride and gratitude at the way my grandparents had taken Susanna in. Fear of the huge responsibility I had accepted by bringing her here.

But weaving all those feelings together was love. I loved her. Susanna made everything else worthwhile.

It took me a lot longer to fall asleep than it took her.

The smell of cinnamon tried to tease me awake, but I didn't give in, not ready to relinquish my hold on a really great dream. I stretched out a hand and hit nothing but blanket.

My eyes blinked open. I was in the guest room, in the middle of the bed, alone. It was early in the morning. No sunlight spilled through the high, round window, but the sky did have the faintly gray glow of pre-dawn.

I sat up, rubbed my eyes, and strained to hear something. Anything. From the kitchen came the sounds of pans and muffled voices. I slid off the bed and took the stairs two at a time.

Susanna and Gran stood in the kitchen, wearing aprons, huddled over a bowl. While Susanna watched through narrowed eyes, Gran lifted a lump of dough and dumped it on a sheet of waxed paper.

"Be gentle with the dough," Susanna said with authority, "but do not fear it. Trust its texture to your hands."

"Hey," I said, pulling a tall stool out from the bar and dropping onto it. "What's going on?"

They looked at each other and smiled. Gran nodded and returned her attention to the dough.

"We're baking," Susanna said. "Norah taught me how to make biscuits." She put one on a plate and pushed it over.

"Susanna is teaching me how to make a pie crust from scratch." My grandmother smashed the dough flat with her fingers.

"Great," I said before biting into the cinnamon biscuit. I chewed and then stopped in awestruck reverence. The biscuit was masterful.

"What kind of pie?" I mumbled around a stuffed mouth.

"Apple and peach," they said together, and laughed.

"I'd be willing to sample a slice of each."

Susanna's gaze met mine, her eyes shining. "No doubt you will receive the chance."

Footsteps thudded down the hallway from the back of the house. Seconds later, my grandfather appeared, already dressed in jeans, a golf shirt, and sneakers.

"Why are you up so early, Granddad?" I asked.

"The race," he said with a scowl.

The reminder punched me in the gut. I pretended to misunderstand. "What race?"

"The Carolina Cross-Country Challenge." Granddad's eyebrow shot up. "The race you've trained for and talked about for the past four months. The race that starts in two hours. We need to leave soon if we're going to make it."

"I'm not going." It hurt to say those words.

Susanna frowned at me, fists on hips, arms covered with flour to her elbows. "Why not?"

"I have other plans."

"Other plans?" Granddad's voice boomed in the small space. "Sherri made me promise to be your cheerleader. I assure you, young man, I didn't get up this early for my health."

Wow. That was cool. Really, really cool.

"Thanks, but I've changed my mind."

Susanna leaned on the counter and lowered her voice. "You must go. I insist."

She had to be nuts. Did she really think I'd abandon her today? Even if I *had* been training for this race for months?

"You need me."

"Please go."

Was I still dreaming? "You want me to do this?"

"Indeed. It makes no sense for you to miss the race because of me." She reached across the counter and clasped my hand. "I am baking with Norah, and you want to race. We can do this at the same time."

"But it's your first day."

"Yesterday was the first. Today is the second." Her smile held pure joy. "Please ride in your race. It's important to me."

Okay, so it was important to me, too but, oddly enough, not as important today as it had been a month ago. Mountain biking had given me strength and endurance. It had given me what I needed to save Susanna. Everything else was a bonus.

"It isn't necessary. Not anymore."

"Then do it because I have asked you."

It was hard to wrap my brain around what she was saying. Alexis broke up with me because I wanted to race. Susanna was pushing me to race when I was willing *not* to go.

"I got pretty banged up yesterday."

"Enough to fail?"

"No." I was too sore to put in my best time, but not sore enough to completely fail. "It's too late to go. I haven't got my gear with me."

Granddad snorted. "Then stop mooning over the girl, and let's leave. We have two hours before the race starts and ninety minutes before you have to report at the race meeting. There's plenty of time to drop by your house if you'll shut up and leave."

I'd made the decision last night not to race. But everything was ready to go at home. The bike and my gear had been organized for weeks. Granddad was right. There was enough time. I felt a jolt of adrenaline.

"Are you sure, Susanna?"

"I am sure."

Damn. How could she be so perfect? I rocketed off the stool, flew around the counter, and yanked her into my arms.

"You are amazing." My voice sounded rough even to my own ears.

She blushed.

"You're beautiful and wonderful and brave and..." I ran out of words, so I spoke with action. I kissed her, my hands pressing against her back, soaking up her warmth through the thin shirt. It was a good thing her stays were part of the past, although she would definitely need a modern replacement, because she had seriously nice...

Granddad cleared his throat. "Excuse me, but your grandparents are here. Not that we don't remember the days—"

"Charlie!" Gran growled.

My hands dropped away from Susanna. "Sorry about that." I nodded at my grandfather. "Okay, let's go."

He exhaled loudly. As he drew even with Susanna, he tugged her braid. She reached for his hand and gave it a pat.

I stared in awe. Granddad used to do that all the time to my Aunt Pamela. Had he even realized he repeated the gesture with Susanna? I glanced at Gran. She was dabbing at her eyes.

"Gran, take care of her," I said.

"You have nothing to worry about, Mark. We'll be fine."

"Okay. See you soon."

CHAPTER FORTY-ONE

ABUNDANT AND VARIED

The chirping of a bird quite close by awakened me. The sound cut off abruptly as Norah spoke in a murmur.

"Hello, Sherri."

I lay in a warm, soft cocoon and listened to the soothing rise and fall of Norah's voice without listening to the words. The house was filled with the smell of apple pie and baking bread. I did not wish to open my eyes, lest it chase away this lovely sense of peace.

"Yes, Susanna is sleeping. When did Mark call you?"

I allowed my eyelids to open halfway. Norah sat curled in the chair next to the sofa, a phone pressed to her ear.

"The ankles worry me. I'm not sure what to do... A walk-in clinic? Yeah, there's a free clinic in Pittsboro on Saturdays... " She bit her lip, sighed heavily, and looked at me suddenly over the top of her spectacles. "Just a moment, Sherri," she said and lowered the phone. "How do you feel?"

I allowed my eyes to blink open fully. "Rested."

"Good." She nodded. "I'm talking to Mark's mother. I'm almost done."

I pushed myself into a sitting position, still wrapped in the blanket, and looked about the room. The clock over the fireplace had hands. It was just past noon.

Norah set the phone on a small table and wiggled forward to the edge of her chair. "Are you hungry?"

"No, ma'am." Food here was abundant and varied. There were too many opportunities to eat. I did not know what to make of it. "A drink would be welcome."

"I've made a pot of tea. Would you like some?"

"Yes, please." I tried to stand and hesitated, waiting for my head to cease spinning.

"Don't get up. I'll fetch it."

I must have been suffering from the sin of sloth, for I did not reject her offer. Reclining into the sofa, I waited until she returned with a cup. I sipped with pleasure. She had added a bit of honey.

"Susanna, the boys will be back soon."

"The race is over, then?"

"It is."

"Did he win?"

"I'll let him tell you." Norah blew on her own mug of tea and smiled. "Our opportunity for a private conversation will be gone once they get here. Do you have any questions about life outside your...community?"

Questions? Indeed, yes. My mind buzzed with them.

Would Mark's parents approve of me?

How would I operate all of the appliances?

Why did they take baths every day, and what would happen if I did not?

Would I ever feel comfortable in this place?

"Norah," I said and shook my head, bewildered, "I wonder about everything. I have so many questions that I do not know where to start."

"Why don't you let me pick a topic? I'll talk, and if you don't understand, then stop me and ask."

"Yes. I would like that." I placed my cup on the table at the sofa's end, burrowed into the blanket, and listened expectantly.

"First, let's talk about lady things."

I felt the heat of a blush sting my cheeks. "Lady things?"

She nodded. Her face was calm. "I'll tell you how we take care of our bodies. What do you call what happens each month to women?"

The blush eased at the mildness of her tone. "Monthlies."

"That works. People around here would understand that term, although the word we use more often is *periods*…"

I took another sip of my tea, enjoying the sweetness of honey and ginger. Norah continued to speak of many things. Baths, teeth, shaving, hair. She used words I knew, like brush and razor. She used words I did not know— words that I would ask to hear again.

Yet always she spoke in that same calm, mild voice. She paused between subjects and watched me kindly. And I grew ever more confident that I could learn anything with a lady such as she in my life.

CHAPTER FORTY-TWO

LIMITS AND POSSIBILITIES

When I pulled the truck into the driveway of the lake house, I saw Gran sitting on the deck, drinking iced tea and reading a book. She put it down as Granddad and I got out.

"Susanna's inside, resting," Gran said before I even had the chance to ask.

I bent down to kiss her soft, soft cheek. "Thanks for taking care of her today."

"My pleasure." She caressed my hand. "You make me proud, Mark."

I nodded but didn't speak.

Granddad lowered himself into another deck chair and groaned. "I'm glad that's behind me. It was too damned hot out there."

"Oh, stop grumbling. You loved it and you know it," Gran laughed.

I shut the front door on the two of them, my eyes hastily scanning the room. But I didn't have to look far. Susanna was sitting sideways on the couch, eyes closed, lips parted. She looked small, pale, and helpless. I felt this enormous surge of love—really, more like a tidal wave.

Easing onto the couch beside her, I reached for her hand where it lay on a cushion.

Instantly, her eyes popped open. A dreamy smile curved her lips.

"Hello," she said in a low, husky, almost-normal voice.

"How do you feel?"

"Lovely."

"Good." I hesitated. "Did Gran mention taking you to see a doctor? I'll be with you."

"Yes." Susanna stretched and then shifted closer to me. "Did you win?"

"No, but I didn't embarrass myself, either."

The course hadn't been all that difficult, but there were too many good racers and my body had been too banged up for me to do any better than top twenty in my age division. Keefe came in first, of course, and went out of his way to rub it in, except his victory dance hadn't bothered me the way he intended. Top twenty was great—amazing, even—after what I'd been through. My amusement pissed him off, and he'd stalked off, mumbling.

Susanna searched my face. "I am sorry to hear this. Are you upset?"

I answered with a kiss—a good, hard, hungry kiss. "Not a bit," I said against her lips.

She smiled and drew back, her gaze darting to the door. "Mark, truly, Norah and Charlie might come in."

"All right, it's time you had a lesson in twenty-first century relationships." I scooped her into my arms and hauled her onto my lap, settling her in a way that was comfortable for us both, at least for now.

"First fact: I can get away with much more questionable stuff around my grandparents than I can around my parents."

She laughed. "Is it proper for me to sit on your lap?"

"It's fine. Holding hands, hugging, some low-intensity kissing—all good."

"And your parents?"

"I think, with them, we'll have to draw the line at holding hands. Especially with my mom."

"Mark," she said, then stopped. Her brow creased, like she was thinking hard. She studied our clasped hands, resting on her knee. "I am not accustomed to such open displays of affection. I do not know how comfortable I shall be."

"Hey, don't ever worry about that. We're a team. It has to be right for both of us."

She relaxed against my chest. "I don't want you to be disappointed in how long it takes me to adjust."

"Never." I pressed my lips to her hair. It still smelled like roses. "How about this? I'll be in charge of possibilities, and you'll be in charge of limits."

"Limits and possibilities. A fair division of labor." She smiled against my shirt. "Mark, I am so grateful—"

"Don't." I wrapped her small body more tightly into my arms. Holy shit. When we were together, I felt strong and invincible, like we could do anything. "I love you, Susanna. You're here and you're safe and the rest of it is behind us. Okay?"

"Okay." She sighed happily. "I love you."

Outside, chairs squeaked. I could see the shadows of my grandparents shift as they stood. It was time to leave for the free clinic. But for one moment longer, it was enough to be alone—just the two of us.

"I am sorry about your race." She nuzzled her cheek against me. "I wish you had won."

"I did," I said with a smile, "and it's the best win ever."

AUTHOR'S NOTES

I started researching *Whisper Falls* six years before I wrote a single word.

North Carolina is an amazing place to live for someone who loves history as much as I do. There are dozens of historic sites to visit within easy range of my home—as well as some of the nation's best state museums. I've tramped through reconstructed gardens and musty cellars, climbed through colonial and federal-period houses, and watched re-enactors fire muskets and mill corn. At the NC Museum of History, I've tried on period clothing, practiced a country dance, and observed the proper preparation of tea.

After making so many visits, it was only natural that I'd want to learn more. I located a copy of *Women's Life and Work in the Southern Colonies* by Julia Cherry Spruill and immersed myself in the hard, distinctive lives of 18th century Southern women. Through Spruill's meticulous research and painstaking footnotes, I explored what Southern women faced in their education, jobs, religion, marriage, children, homes, culture, and legal realities.

It was while reading a section on crimes and punishments that I first encountered the harsh treatment of indentured females. From those pages, Susanna Marsh was born.

Although Susanna grows up in the fictional village of Worthville, NC, the places in Mark Lewis's world— Umstead State Park, the Raleigh greenway system, the state government complex—are real. And just like Mark, I've traveled to the State Archives and pored over the same two-centuries-old primary sources: wills, court records, newspapers, marriage licenses, and indentures.

Among the old documents, however, few were written by the indentured servants themselves; it would've been rare for them to write well enough to leave behind journals.

But their stories still speak from historical sources, such as in newspaper accounts of runaways, in the inadequate laws that sought to protect them from their masters, and in the letters and journals of the upper classes whom they served. From these sources, I created the life that Susanna might reasonably have lived in the sort of small town that existed outside Raleigh at that time.

For more information on how indentured servants like Susanna Marsh might have lived and worked, please visit the Extras page on my website, http://www.ElizabethLangston.net.

ACKNOWLEDGEMENTS

I owe deep and heartfelt gratitude to: historians, docents, and re-enactors for their patient and thorough answers; my wonderful family and fabulous friends for their support, encouragement, and curiosity; HCRW, the Rubies, my retreat friends, and the ever-generous writing community; Mike Mazzella, for showing me how to break noses; Tom and Christina, for their candor and faith; Laura Ownbey, whose gently-posed questions polished this story to a shine; the team at Spencer Hill Press, especially Jessica Porteous and Richard Storrs, who create magic with their craft; my amazing agent, Kevan Lyon, who never gave up; the best and brightest daughters a mother could adore; but most of all, thank you to my husband, who believed in my "highest aspirations" and let them be so.

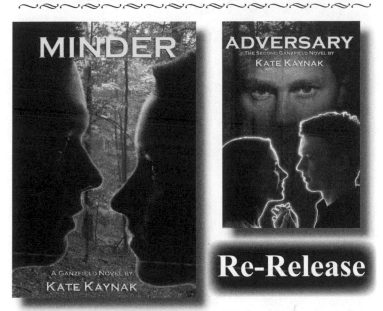

Middle Grade Books

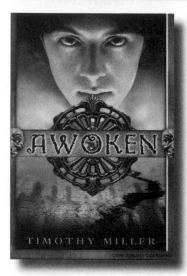

Fourteen-year-old Michael Stevens has never been ordinary; no orphan who hears music coming from rocks considers himself a typical teenager. When two-foot-tall, albino, doll-like men sneak into his room one night, transforming the harmless music into a frightening ability he cannot control. Michael finds himself in the middle of a war that could forever change the world he knows - reconstructing the very definition of humanity.

AUGUST 2013

Finn (not bleedin' Finnegan) MacCullen is eager to begin his apprenticeship. He soon discovers the ups and downs of hunting monsters in a suburban neighborhood. Armed with a bronze dagger, some ancient Celtic magic, and a hair-trigger temper, Finn is about to show his enemies the true meaning of "fighting Irish."

MARCH 2013

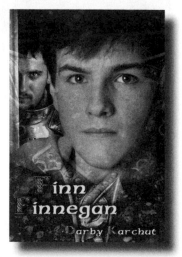

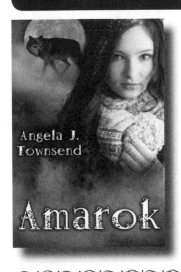

ABOUT THE AUTHOR

Photo by Liza Lucas

Elizabeth lives in North Carolina (mid-way between the beaches and the mountains) with two daughters, one husband, and too many computers. When she's not writing software or stories, Elizabeth loves to travel, watch dance reality shows, and argue with her family over which restaurant to visit next. *Whisper Falls* is her debut novel.